RUNNING WILD NOVELLA ANTHOLOGY, VOLUME 4, BOOK 2

EDITED BY BARBARA LOCKWOOD

CONTENTS

DOES' RUN

BY ARON WOLDESLASSIE

I hate the way this sounds, but there aren't enough missing kids. Lost kids are my bread and butter. You know what, actually they're my bread. The butter comes from cheating husbands, lost dogs, Craigslist clients, looking for lost bikes, stuff like that. But now, kids have, for the moment anyway, stopped going missing in the small part of Saint Paul I call home. Without the reward money from finding wayward tykes I haven't been able to do anything that requires money. Restaurants, dates, comic books they're all off the table — too expensive.

It's wild to think how much life changes when you're sans cash. I'm thinking about becoming a barista, but to be honest, it doesn't seem like a great way to make money. Sounds like a good way to steal muffins. Bus trips, like the one I'm on now, always make me one part contemplative two parts hungry: not great for problem-solving.

I'm headed to the South Saint Paul Police Station. There I might find a new missing persons poster which would really make my day. I need something to work on. If nothing comes up, then my afternoon will consist of a meeting with a client. Not sure who they are, but they responded to my ad. The listing garners attention on the Skilled Trade section of Craigslist where it explains I'm an official unofficial gumshoe. A totally legal way to announce I'm a decent, unlicensed detective. Although 200 dollars for a freelance detective lets them know I'm not the cream of the crop; but like I said, stuff like this isn't my bread, it's my butter.

Out of the bus, the December wind gives a ten-degree hello. I rush past the cold and into the station. The humming fluorescents are the first introduction to the tapioca colored interior. Bolted down chairs split the room in half making it easier to identify reluctant criminals from anxious parents and

3

victims. The tight corner of the precinct's front lobby disappoints. The little area dedicated to missing persons is populated with stale coffee stink and posters of people from across the state. Everywhere but Saint Paul has missing kids. Just my luck.

Beneath the posters sits a disappointing end table with a poorly placed acrylic pamphlet stand. I'm reading the front of a pamphlet on drug abuse, contemplating if there was ever a time when I would "Just say no" to drug use. Officer Tillerson interrupts the thought with a shout.

"Neil! What're you doing out here? You know there aren't any missing kids cases up for grabs!" Officer Annita Tillerson, she's the kind of person who does things right, so she can point out everything you do wrong.

"Thanks," I hesitate for effect; Chandler Bing was my first television father. "I *hadn't* noticed."

"Well, I did." She's ignoring my sarcasm. "How about you get going then? It's 11 AM. Shouldn't you be at work?" God, I hate Annita. Like this isn't work for me: waking up, thinking of jobs to apply for, taking the bus, taking another bus, looking at posters. Appearing like I've nothing to do is a major component of my process.

"This is my job, Annita. I find missing kids. I'm the Pied Piper. It's what I do." About a year ago, the Pioneer Press ran a story on how I found six missing kids in a year and a half. It was a huge deal. People were stopping me in the street. I was told in confidence Cecil's deli would name a sandwich after me if an even dozen could be found. Cecil's deli! Not to be confused with Baldwin's deli, that gentile hole in the wall.

"You haven't been the Pied Piper in months. How about you try searching for some missing adults for once?"

"Yeah? Maybe I should start with your husband!"

"Nigga, fuck you!"

"Nigga me? Fuck you!"

"I'm a Goddamn officer of the law, mother-fucker! Don't make me come over there!"

"Oh, you're an officer of the law, are you? Is that why you're calling me a 'Nigga' and threatening me? They teach that at the academy?"

"I can say Nigga as long as I want. My black ass has earned it. You and your dumbass afro need to move on out of here."

"Well pardon me, Annita! Some of us can't spend our money willy-nilly at the barber for a haircut!"

"Can the two of you please stop yelling the N-word?" Officer Ringenberg desperately yells into the lobby. Being the only white man between us, our trio becomes an Oreo of circumstance. "Neil, good heavens, what are you doing here?"

Nothing smart comes to mind in the awkward moment. Instead, the empty wall usually littered with missing persons draws my attention which in turn grabs Ringenberg's. The officer throws his hands on his hips, demonstrating a pose I call the "Disappointed Wonder Woman". Officer John Ringenberg, the six feet two inches of Norwegian/Irish descent, makes for a disappointing idea of law enforcement. He's the best thing the city of Eagan could produce, and unfortunately, the cake eater's just enough for policing Saint Paul.

"You know you can check the internet for that, right?" That's true but hope and fear of becoming a barista had created the idea the precinct might have jobs, aka bread, the internet didn't.

"Yes, well I just thought this would be easier" The little half-truth hurts to make. No one likes admitting something that kills hope. "How aren't there any missing kids in the entire city of Saint Paul?" The officers shake their heads in disappointment.

"Well, there are plenty of missing persons in Bloomington, Neil. Lots of families looking for help over there." The idea of taking the bus to Bloomington makes me gag. All those conversations referenced by the Mall of America. I've got standards.

"I don't work outside Saint Paul. I know all the bus routes here. I know all the hangouts here. I've got the names of all the bartenders here. Don't you have anything I can work on? I've done too much for you guys to scrimp on me now." Annita gives a scrunched frown; probably the same frown her husband saw before leaving. Officer Ringenberg, on the other hand, clicks his teeth in frustration. He motions me forward into the bullpen of the police station.

Polished tile and fluorescent lights create a glare my eyes can't avoid. Beyond the little door in front, the lobby holds the crime-fighting power responsible for maintaining order within 20 miles. Cops who have never fired their service weapons outside of the range converse among themselves. Truant kids sit in sullen silence waiting for their parents. A box of un-ironic doughnuts grows stale next to a coffee maker. Slow day in the office. Cautiously, Ringenberg directs me to a small interrogation room. The shine dies down and my eyes focus revealing a black-brick room with a single table and a standing bulletin board beside the door.

"Have you heard of anything happening near Frogtown or West Saint Paul?" he whispers. I'm not a snitch, but even if I were, I wouldn't have anything to say that isn't known. Frogtown and the Westside tend to be a tad hectic. Shoulders jump up and down in a quick shrug, a quizzical stare follows. Officer Ringenberg points to the bulletin board. It holds seven pictures of men and women. All share the off-putting expression dead folks make when lying in a morgue. "These men and women, a few children, are dead. Killed."

The officer can't seem to find the right words. Either he's

confused or emotionally sabotaged, hard to tell.

"Jim?"

"Right, they're dead and we don't know the who or why." The way he ends this implies the conversation is over. Even though there needs to be so much more. A strange gap of silence follows the anticipation for a timeline, extenuating circumstances, a pattern of clues one might use to build a search. Nothing happens.

"Jim, do we know when they were killed? Are they related to one another? Are there any kind of similarities between the victims?" I speak plainly to needle Jim into the detective mindset without his knowing. He hears the tone and breaks his candor.

"I know how this sounds, Neil."

"Do you? Because for the record, I find people who are alive. And you've shown me a lot of the opposite of that."

"Nip it, Neil. These people aren't your joke. I showed them to you because we don't know anything about them." Well, that is surprising. "No IDs, no missing persons reports matching their descriptions, and every one of them died in a different location with different time intervals between them. We don't have a damn clue to what's going on." Jim appears right about that. The photos give nothing in terms of a possible pattern.

"The only noticeable thing here is that the men, women, and children are all Asian. Which could either mean a lot or nothing at all." The officer gives the small nod of a man unsure if he is allowed to comment on race like this. "Frogtown has a large Hmong community, so if there were a killer there, they would be killing Asian people. But you gotta go through Downtown to reach West Saint Paul from Frogtown. Which means you ignore a lot of other ethnicities to coincidentally kill more Asian people."

"Why don't these people have IDs?"

"The bigger issue is no one is looking for seven dead people. It's hard to believe all of these don't have someone that cares about them. Hell, a few of them are kids, why aren't any parents looking for them?" The last question hurts a little, no doubt that's why he said it.

"What are you telling me this for, Jim? These people don't need a guy who can search a few arcades and bus depots. They need a big search with crazy resources. This should be federal."

Jim deflates at this. "We can't tell people that specifically Asian and Pacific Islanders are getting killed without first proving this is going on. Aside from their race, these people don't seem to have anything in common. And my C.O. doesn't want to antagonize the public. If we're wrong, then we'll seem more ignorant than cautious."

"You'll seem ignorant if you ignore the murders of a bunch of Asian people! What the hell is the matter with you? Who cares about appearances? People need to know about this!" Officer Ringenberg points his finger like a dagger, forcing me to stow any more questions.

"I know this is wrong. I agree with you. But I can't break orders. So, I need you to find me something, anything, I can use to connect these murders."

"If you couldn't do it why could I?"

"You find missing people all the time, and usually you do it without any clues, Neil. This is the same concept but in reverse."

"No, it's not. I find kids. For money." At the clarification, Jim claps and returns his pointer finger.

"I can get you money. It'll be exactly like any other gig for you. Missing people, you go out, you find them, you call us, and you collect your reward." The rudely candid description leaves out a lot of intricacies and passion, but that is remarkably close to what I do. Except there's one thing the officer failed to mention.

"How the hell is there a reward if these folks are named Jane or John Doe?"

He snorts in bashful delight. "Well, as it happens, the department is a bit more in the black then we planned. Last Wednesday, we caught a guy with around $40,000 in cash and $20,000 worth of meth headed to Madison. We forfeited both, and as of last night, he's signed a plea deal. Now nobody is looking at all that money."

"You're going to give me 40K for this?"

"Are you kidding? I can't give the 40 away without anyone noticing." The sudden realization that we're breaking the law silences all thoughts of the dead Does. We were always committing a crime. It's why we're in this dark room, why Jim won't speak louder than a whisper, and why he won't allow me to yell otherwise. "I'll give you five grand for something substantial."

"They wouldn't notice five thousand dollars missing?"

"I'll just say it was for a car or something."

"You shouldn't be a police officer." Like a lot of young people, yelling at the cops comes easy to me. But unlike most others, my relationship with Ringenberg means he won't take the complaint with malice, which is unfortunate because this man really shouldn't be a cop.

"Come on."

"That's not just the NWA talking. You might be a bad person." He smiles at the reference. Somehow NWA sneaked past the suburban fortress he grew up in. He's enjoying this part of the conversation; the creep.

"I know you don't like admitting it, because you think being a detective is very cool."

"It is cool, sometimes I wear a panama," I retort.

"But I know you started doing this to help a few panicked mothers. The money came as a surprise, and you've been helping people ever since." Jim's forgetting the name/sandwich recognition that comes with this, but he's largely right. "Help me help these people. What do you say, we have a deal?" There's dead air for a second. The likelihood of saying something funny diminishes with every second.

"Yeah, I guess," I concede. "Is there a time limit on this or-"

"Let's just say the faster you do this the more likely you are to get the money. We might be building an addition to the station, Cyber Crimes wants a few new monitors, and some of the guys want to get the K-9 unit a few new officers." Can't tell if he means dogs or people with that last one. Unlike these Does, the joke's not worth the trouble.

"Well then, I better hustle." Taking my exit, Officer Ringenberg shakes my hand and opens the door. Annita waves sarcastically as she watches me start the case; she thinks she got the last laugh. Jokes on her because I'm fairly sure I'll be back before the day ends.

While West Saint Paul isn't exactly my home turf, Frogtown is a stone's throw from an associate's stomping ground: Midway. Thanks to the nearest bus, I'm a 35-minute ride away from finding my first clue; more than enough time to get over the cringe that comes when thinking of my destination. Midway is kind of an odd place. Depending on who you ask, you'll either hear about a bad part of town with its abandoned businesses and crime or a Gotham soon-to-be with its never-ending construction and multiple transportation hubs. The hood can't seem to make up its mind, and because of that, strange things happen there. Like a Target appearing across the street from a strip club, or two pawn shops sandwiching a haberdashery. Midway makes for a mix of extremes: Upper-middle vs lower-middle-class, 2010 vs 1990, history vs hope. People don't know if they should fight for the community or save it with a new one.

Officer Ringenberg texts me the pictures of the dead. Examining the faces on my phone, I realize I should be texting my contact: Lamar Wallace. The two of us exchanged information regarding missing kids a few times before and he usually does me right. Hopefully, he knows something about this, seeing as he happens to run a small "business" spanning from Midway to Downtown Saint Paul. With that much territory, he knows most of the crews on our side of the Mississippi. When an ethnic minority dominates the city morgue, gang violence tends to be involved.

Thirty-four minutes later I reach my bus stop. Snow's coming down just a tad, everything around is dusted with a small layer of white. No matter what people say about the weather here they always forget about the magic. The swirling pieces of winter can make everything from a bus stop to a two-story brownstone look like it came from a fairy tale. The view of Lamar's looks incredible. There's a story here, but the cold warns of frostbite, getting buzzed indoors becomes an escalating necessity.

"Man, what do you want?" Spike of Cowboy Bebop hides from canon fire on the flat screen.

"Which one is this?" I say, pointing at the TV with the left hand and throwing my jacket off with the right.

He rolls his baggy eyes. "I'm not sure. It's been on a loop. Don't get comfortable, man. I'm trying to get some sleep. Are you here for the Indica? Cause I got less than you think." Lamar has been sober for over a year. "But I just got some mushrooms if you do that shit." It was a personal decision initiated for monetary reasons.

"No, I'm good. I'm actually broke, but that's why I'm here." Unfortunately, sobriety came with a surprising problem: insomnia.

"I'm not looking to buy or employ." After six years of successful drug use, it was clear Lamar had forgotten how to fall asleep organically. Making him permanently lethargic.

"No, I'm here for info. Do you know anything going on between any Asian gangs or whatever? Are there even Asian gangs in Saint Paul?" The funny thing is, Lamar seems higher when he's exhausted than when he's baked.

The TV distracts the poor insomniac for a moment. Spike is playing it smooth with a gun and some girl. "I mean not really. Some Hmong guys were trying to run around under something, but that just fell apart. These things rise and fall, but I haven't heard about anything going down." With a rag in hand, he moves past the living room towards his kitchenette. He procrastinates by cleaning. It's clear he's been doing it for a while.

Lamar's apartment features a shockingly white carpet that has been vacuumed multiple times today. A single brown coffee table shiny from too many cleanings sits next to a leather couch and loveseat. I try to spot a single dust bunny, cinder, or smudge of dirt, but the place is spotless. The guy's dying.

"Although, there's this new restaurant on West 7th that's weird." He bobs a tea bag into a mug full of hot water.

"Weird how?"

"They've got Escalades and BMWs rolling in and out of the place. But it's never open. A lot of people thought it was a front, but nothing's coming out of there. And no one I know has noticed a change in the streets or their business." The last part is a bit odd. Lamar hasn't noticed a single change? Business or otherwise, if multiple people end up dead there should be some kind of notice. People don't just die, they're missed, lost, or mourned. And if Lamar hasn't heard anything about it, I doubt that's by accident.

"What's the place called?" This restaurant warrants a look. God willing, it'll hold something useful to the case, if not, at least a new place to eat is always exciting.

"The Seventh Sun. It's flowery and has a sign with a little sun on it." Lamar's info isn't great, but at least I finally have something to go on. Heading to the restaurant should be my next move, but I wait for another episode of Cowboy Bebop to start. The theme song kills me.

Outside the snow makes a crunch rather than slosh. The city's getting cold. Way colder than any investigation should be. If this case continues after dark, my priority will shift from the Does to someplace warm. The nice thing about winter here, it tends to pick up the pace in everything. People don't dawdle.

A beeping notification distracts from the crunch of my quick pace. My Craigslist meeting is in a half-hour in the opposite direction of the restaurant. Part of me wants to blow it off, but clients pay at least half up-front, and this case might require more resources than the bus pass and $20 I've got in my back pocket.

I bite the bullet and head for a bus stop on the other side of the street.

Tiled white walls and intentionally large windows make the spacious shop glow in an annoying light like an Instagram filter just waiting for an idiot's snapshot. Tiny wooden tables hold men and women with computers. A single homeless man with a cup of coffee gets warm near the door. I'm in Cathedral Hill. A simple jaunt from Downtown, this part of town holds decent money but is far enough from the city both the homeless man and I are outliers in the coffeeshop. Aside from the Ethiopia blend coffee, I'm pretty sure I'm the only dark thing in the room.

I order the familial blend and hide the impulse to ask for a job application. Coffee in hand, professional etiquette dictates re-reading the client's email. What if this client is looking for a missing horse? Or a bike's been stolen in Macalester? Or some creep ex-boyfriend wants me to tail his former lover in Dinkytown (which is a problem because I hate Minneapolis)? These things need to get sorted out before the meeting. The digital envelope jumps from my inbox. It reads:

Hello, I saw on your ad that you have experience finding things. I would very much like to employ you. Thanks.

Not much to go off of. Maybe a lost pet or a husband who skipped town? For a moment I think this might be Annita and frown. What cruel God would give Annita a husband? What a sad man.

"Neil? Neil Edlow?" Above my screen, I find her. Standing at five feet five this woman appears stuck in between adolescence and maturity. She could be 20 or 14 years old, there's no way to tell. Bundled in layers of beige and light pink, her jacket, cardigan, and blouse speaks to a comfortable level of wealth. Meanwhile, my brown leather jacket, white shirt, and orange tie speaks to an appreciation for Goodwill. With a cup of coffee in her right hand, she motions to shake with her left. Neither of us enjoys using our southpaws for this. My right-hand wants to jump and shake her coffee cup, but I suppress the urge. Awkward introductions are common with Craigslist jobs.

"It's a pleasure to meet you..." I leave the dead air for her to fill in her name, but she misses the cue taking her seat. "Miss...?"

"My name is Amelia, Mr. Edlow. I'm sorry. I've been up

much later than I should have." There's a curl to her voice. Most people couldn't spot the bend in the words, but in the dips of her speech certain syllables linger longer than they ought: her accent has been trained away, but her mother tongue still nags. "How are you, Mr. Edlow?"

"I'm fine, if not a bit busy. Your email didn't say what you needed me for, Amelia." She's a bit flustered. Something about my candor no doubt. She acclimates to my pace of conversation.

"Yes. I did not say." Her posture shifts. "I would like you to find my brother." That's a surprise. Craigslist jobs are usually small time. Find a bike or locate a lost cat. A missing brother is bread territory.

"If your brother is missing you need to call the police. You should call them as soon as possible, even now."

Her head cocks at police. "My brother isn't missing. I know he's in town, I just don't know where. I would like you to find out where he is and tell me; nothing more."

"Why not call him?"

"I can't."

"Email, Facebook, anything could work better than this. Is he avoiding you?"

She tries to find the words. "Yes, for some time," her shaking hands and pursed lips make it clear she hates admitting this. "But he shouldn't be. When you find him please make sure he doesn't become aware that I hired you."

"How would he become aware of that? Have you done this before?"

"Does it matter?" The formality of the meeting breaks apart. No doubt she's looking to leave before my manners offend her even more. Just gotta hold on to her for a few more details.

"I'm going to need his picture and name."

"I can do that along with his phone number."

"Also, the $100." She pulls her phone out and swipes a series of actions. My phone buzzes with the notification telling me I've received a $100 transfer and a text containing an attachment. Amelia places her hand in mine, shakes it, and begins her exit.

"How long do you think this will take you?"

"I've got his name and number, shouldn't take me more than a day or two." She forces a smile and glides out of the café like she's never spoken to a gumshoe in her life. Swear to God, sometimes I think women take a class on how to be insouciant. A pleasant ding comes from depositing the money. The good feeling doesn't last when the attachment of Amelia's brother bounces on my home screen.

"Fuck."

We've never met, but I know this kid is dead. I tick my screen and the headshots of the John Does, Officer Ringenberg sent me, spin about my photo gallery. After three rotations I find the right picture. The kid's face is hard to place without any life behind it but he's there. The candid photo Amelia sent me shows a teenager running out the door of an apartment. He's not happy, but he isn't angry at the photographer. The two photos side by side show a tragic before and after like you wouldn't believe. What the hell happened to this guy? Suddenly, I realize Amelia is a good lead.

She's already on the other side of the street waiting for the crosswalk to let her through. Traffic stops me from getting to her, it's a little embarrassing but I've only one option left.

"Amelia!" My mother's told me I have a good voice for yelling. Amelia turns around quizzically. Ordinarily, a slew of other questions would be more appropriate but with Amelia's literal and figurative distance from the search, this seems like the only thing that can connect the Does. "What are you?" I can't hear her across the street, but I assume from her posture she's said, "What?". "I mean, what's your ethnicity?" The few people I'm disrupting make faces at the question. If it were up to Cathedral Hill, crude talk like this would be a crime "What's your ethnicity?"

She screams a reply, but it gets muddled in traffic.

"What?" I scream past a zooming Prius. She says it again, clearly agitated with the entire exchange and leaves. She's too far to chase but her answer confuses the hell out of me. "Who is Caren?"

What is Caren ethnicity?

Did you mean: What is ***Karen*** ethnicity**?**

Google has it right, I do mean Karen apparently. A quick look on Wikipedia tells me they're a small minority from parts of Burma. Their story takes some time to read through, although the short of it is they're currently in war, and with every war comes refugees. A people without their land, starting over, tragic if not painfully familiar.

Unlike its owner, my phone works fast and finds the picture again, this time with the text accompanying it. Kid's name is Mickey. The name doesn't fit which leads me to believe "Mickey" is an American name; a second title immigrants use to simplify the day to day tasks that require having something an American can pronounce. The idea doesn't agree with me. Not because changing your name for others makes my eyes roll so far back they almost break, but because Amelia is probably the American name of my client; meaning I don't know a thing about her. The case snowballed faster than expected.

Over half a dozen John/Jane Does are found dead with no

one looking for them, nothing links the Does besides an inkling of their ethnicity, a client who might be using a fake name is looking for her brother who also might be using a fake name, a brother who is dead and is/was avoiding her, and this afore-mentioned brother is one of the John Does. God help me this is hectic.

My phone beeps. Fuck me.

Only 15% battery left. It's around three, and in the Minnesota winter, means I'll be fighting for daylight soon. Short on time, but rich in leads: not a great position to be in. What's worse, the barista eyeballs me before pouring another piece of latte art. I've been here too long; we both know it. Time to go.

The street's cold surprises again. Two steps outside and a gale of wind cuts right through me. My coat's decent, but a pair of jeans can't do much when you're nearing single-digit weather. A conveniently passing bus becomes a refuge; an old technique a homeless friend taught me: If you're ever cold, take a high-frequency bus and ride it in both directions. You'll manage to escape the cold and give yourself a spot to get a wink of sleep in.

I'm not too familiar with this route but know the direction well enough. We're headed down to the Mississippi. A little out of the way, but close enough to where I wanna be. A few cats sit on the bus trying to get warm same as me. Other's decom-pressing the way people do when getting off of work. Some of these strangers make much more than the rest of us, but it's funny, we're headed in the same direction. That's the best thing about the bus, besides not needing to buy a car, it equalizes us. Points out the human necessity to keep moving.

Like right now, I have exactly what Ringenberg wants. With everything I've found he and the rest of the police could mount a full investigation and pull some people in. They might muck it up with their good ol' boy police work, but I'll get my money. Or I could keep moving, avoid the mistakes I'm sure the police made, and catch whoever's responsible for killing these people. One choice is much easier than the other but seeing as my face matches the stoic looks on the bus, I figure I'm going to keep moving forward.

The Does don't have anyone, besides me, looking for them. They also don't have any ID so they're clearly not from here. At least not originally. With the Karen lead, someone who works with refugees comes to mind. The only downside is she might not take my call.

It rings.

"Hello?" She hasn't saved my number, otherwise, I'm sure she wouldn't pick-up. Sister Pamela Dunfield, or Sister Pam, is a shining child of the North Star and head of the Catholic Charities Center. Born in Duluth, she gained recognition as a powerful Right-Wing for the U of M's Duluth hockey team. Everyone was shocked to find after graduation Sister Pam wouldn't join the women's Olympic team. She was more interested in the Lord. Now the religious bear spends her days praying, working, and occasionally coaching St. Thomas's men and women's hockey teams.

"Sister, I need your help."

"It's a homeless shelter, you dolt!" She remembers my voice. "Everyone needs my help! Everyone, but the hackneyed, halfwit, delusional, amateur piece of filth P.I. obsessed with taking children away from the loving embrace of the lord!" A few passengers react to the screaming voice coming through my phone.

"Hackneyed? Pam, I wear a tie now," I joke.

"You don't get to play with me, Mr. Edlow! Not after what you did!"

"He was 14, Pam. He didn't belong there; his parents were looking for him."

"A convent full of nuns make better parents than a pair of drug addicts, you profiteering degenerate!"

"Jesus, Pam, Tyler was my first case as the Pied Piper. Keeping a reputation like that requires consistent results."

"I'm sick of your selfish excuses!" She can't see it, but my fist flies into the air. Silent punches and kicks are all that's stopping me from yelling into the phone.

"I wasn't being selfish. Come on, his mother and father were looking for him."

"They were also looking for heroin and skag!" She doesn't know what skag means. Hearing her say it makes my skin crawl. "You ought to be ashamed! Turning a child away from love and comfort!"

Any Catholic will tell you when a nun is screaming at you the responsible thing to do is to let them know you're wrong and they're right. Indulging the sister seems like the best thing to do, but I can't afford to lose out on the information. Hockey was never for me, but I've seen enough of it to know a Defenseman should check hard when facing a strong right-wing. So that's what I do.

"Yeah? What about the bible? Isn't one of your favorite commandments honoring the mother and father? Shouldn't we be doing that?"

"Don't you dare chastise me with scripture! Those people stopped being parents when they put him in harm's way. And because of you, he's in danger again." She's rocky, her anger is shifting to sadness.

"You know I'm right, Pam. I didn't send him back, the police did. He's probably in foster care now. Safe and sound. He didn't belong with you."

"It's Sister Pam. And foster care isn't the church. That boy came to us by following the ancient tradition of the lost, that any may call on us for refuge. And you ripped him away, shattering his faith." It's just barely audible: the little gasp of a sob being held back. The big gal is a secret softy. Nothing more than to guide her to help.

"I'm sorry, Sister Pam. I wasn't following the 'tradition of the lost', but the letter of the law. But I'm calling now to help the church. Someone out there is hurting those you refuge, specifically the Karen. If you care about them, you'll help me." The good sister goes silent for a bit. No doubt she's asking God what to do.

She sighs. "You're a terrible person, a terrible Catholic, you know that?"

"I'm fine as long as I'm not a Lutheran, right?" The haughty chuckle of someone happy to be beaten is her only reply. With the little joke, she's mine.

"Alright, how can I help?"

"I know you work to settle refugees and hoped to learn more about one in particular, a young Karen man. I think he's connected to a case I'm working." With the gravitas of a 20-something, I text her Mickey's photo while staying on the line. Even on my end, the pling her phone makes is heard. Pam makes a few muffled "umms" and "ugghs" as she tries to carry the conversation and open the text at the same time. I wait for the pleasant "oooh" of her finding the photo Amelia shared with me. It would be heartless to send her the face of the dead boy Ringenberg gave. Besides, this case needs to run clean. If the sister learns about the Does, then every nun in town would know about them. Nuns love to gossip, comes with the vow of celibacy.

"I know the face well, I used to see it a lot a few months ago." Thank God.

"Mickey love to pray?"

"He's kind, but that's not what I mean. He and his brother are twins. Took me a few weeks to figure them apart. Ler was more outspoken than his brother, but Shaw Thaw was always willing to help anyone in need."

"Which one is Mickey? Who's in the photo?"

"Couldn't tell you from the picture, they're twins. But I'm pretty certain Ler goes by Mickey. One of the sisters had the bright idea to call him Mickey on account it was easier than his real name. Had to give her a long talk for that." Fuck me again. Pam's closed a door and opened a window. Twins complicate and simplify things a bit. Presumably one of them is dead, I can't tell which, and if I'm lucky, the other is out there. But if he is, where the hell is he? If my brother went missing, I'd be looking for him, and I'd probably start with the police, why hasn't Shaw Thaw?

"What about their parents?"

"No idea."

"Are you kidding me, Pam?"

"We only have 90 days to get refugees out the door. That's 90 days to meet them at the airport, find them a home, a job, schools for their kids, get them ID's, government assistance, and if they're lucky, new friends. The Karen- every refugee- have to hit the ground running. There are so many people to help after we settle them, we just start over with someone new. There's no follow-up, just more people to help. I only remember them because they're twins. Heck, it's a wonder I remember them at all." Strange to think there isn't any follow up for a group of kids. But it wouldn't be the first time the system failed; hell, this isn't even the system. Sister Pam does this out of the goodness of her own heart. Even she can't pray for every single person looking for help, and she's a professional. Makes me feel a little better about what happened to Tyler.

Gravity lurches forward as the bus slows. "Thanks then. I think I've got an idea of where to go next." I'm a bit too curt, but daylight is a rare commodity. New downtrodden faces come aboard as I exit, there's a look shared between all of us; we don't know each other but because of the ride we know where we're headed, how we're getting there, and where we've come from. Information like that has been nearly impossible to get on the Does, but for these people, I only needed $2.50 for some bus fare. Makes me think the case is fighting me.

"No problem, Neil." Another sharp crunch greets me outside. "Those boys are alright, aren't they? You said they were just connected to this case you're working." The cold doesn't allow much for anything more than what you desperately need. It takes a moment longer to muster a lie.

"Yeah. I saw one of them this morning. I'm about to see the other now." Somehow, she knows. Hears the little discomfort in my voice no doubt.

"Be safe, Neil. Goodbye, and God bless." A pang of guilt comes with knowing mine will probably be added to the list of names for evening prayer - although every little bit helps.

Collecting myself, my breath plumes in white balls of vapor before me. The clouds of hot air dissolve revealing the 7th Ave Apartment Complexes. Amelia's photo made me curious about Mickey's identity, but it also gave me a clue in the form of its background: the candid photo of him was taken at one of these apartments. Should have figured, America takes place in these complexes. Transitional housing some call it, but for others, the first place you call home in a foreign country might not be seen as transitional, it might seem like an oasis.

The photo's background shows the colored brick of a building near the edge of the block. A few other features, the cracks in the sidewalk and the cream-colored intercom tell me this is the right place. Craning upward I count the windows: Five stories, presumably with a basement level. From the size, I'm going to guess four standard or five modest apartments a level. So, one in thirty places holds my guy. Those aren't terrible odds for this.

An intercom with dirty little buttons waits beside the entrance to the building. With little candor, I slide my hand down the buttons calling every resident. It doesn't matter who answers, just as long as they buzz me past the front door.

Nothing happens. A second attempt is had. Nada two times. Great. Finding another way in becomes my number one priority when a large man comes out of the door. "Hold that!" The smile and cocked eyebrow tell me he considers me an adorable trespasser; because I am. "Thanks a lot. Nice tie." Regardless of the favor, I mean that: it really is a nice tie.

Thanks to luck and little work, Mickey's apartment is identified as number 22. The intercom didn't hold names, but the mailboxes in the lobby do. There sticking out among the Yangs, Xiongs, and Yaos is freaking Mickey. Karma's paying me back for the tie compliment, or saving some kid, impossible to say. The idea jumps around my head, with each step up the staircase I'm fairly sure it's the tie thing. Saving kids has been happening for a good while and things aren't necessarily better for me. Although, it's worth arguing that with every child rescued the deed's reward is the attempt at saving another. Kind of implies that saving someone is just as valuable as a steady paying job. Which it is, but teach a man to fish, Karma, come on.

Rolling my eyes at the spiritual principle is the last thing I do before arriving at the door marked 22. I knock gingerly.

"Who is it?" Asks a voice inside.

"Hi, I'm looking for Mickey, also goes by Ler." Should have said that the other way around, but what are ya going to do?

"Yeah, hold on." Lovely, he's here. The Karmic debate ends at the scent of this magnificent hallway. The cooking of a dozen different hometowns fills the air. None more so than whatever's bubbling behind the apartment marked 24. Etiquette frowns on knocking on one of these doors and just offering money for any of the foods responsible for the smell. Why does being a person have to be so hard? I settle for deep inhales in front of 24's home. Praying that no one walks in on me performing olfactory voyeurism.

Bang!

I snap to the gunshot. Just two steps from where I'm standing a bullet blew out of 22's door. Presumably for me. Like a vaudeville sketch, the door opens with perfect timing. A chubby man holds a gun out as he enters the hallway. Darting to the left and right he finds me standing in shock.

Astonished, my limp hand gestures at the gun, then to me in confusion. He nods. My completely non-threatening frame shrugs before I point to myself in self-deprecation. He flaunts the weapon, points at me, then angrily points at himself. I'm offended, "If I were here to kill you, why would I knock?" I explain.

Unconvinced, he points the gun at me. Death, a finger twitch away, and fantastic smells are the only cover I have. But we both forget something: apartment 21. The screeching pain of his neighbor pulls my captor's attention. Directly across 22's door, a weeping teenage girl screams as she bursts into the hallway. Strong aromas emerge as she exits her home, it's clear she enjoys onions, and not getting shot. It's something we have in common. Holding her bloody shoulder with her left hand, the young girl looks for the source of the bullet that wounded her. My attempted murderer is holding a gun, he is clearly responsible.

22 tries to calm her down, but you can't shush randomly

being shot at four o'clock. It's more than gauche: it's attempted murder. Maybe Karma is paying me back with the crying girl, regardless, her entrance is my cue to leave. Walking, power walking, then running I getaway.

"Hey!" he shouts. Can't look back, gotta bounce. We're running the way murderers and their victims run: with life-altering purpose. He won't shoot or risk another bystander, but once we leave the building, he'll gun me down like the chorus of a country song. His poor neighbors, the ones he didn't shoot, probably suffer from the collective clomping we make sprinting through the stairwell. The scene of an elderly man waking up after working two shifts at the old man factory plays through my mind after a particularly large leap down some steps creates a ruckus like no other. That poor man. Somehow empathizing with him is easier than with the girl from 21. Does that make me a bad person? Am I a bad feminist? Is this how I die?

Together we sprint down the lobby towards the basement up the stairs and down again. The big loop would be pointless if not for one thing: the weight of my pursuer. Sooner than later the big lug is going to tire out. Not to body shame, but 22 is a big guy, and big guys simply can't catch me.

Pushing myself down the third floor, there's a loud yelp followed by a thump. He's fallen in exhaustion. His short black hair matted with sweat against his red face, his little nose now pressed against the carpet. I'd feel bad if he weren't trying to kill me. With gusto, I ignore the visage of the old man in my mind, leap down flights of stairs, run through the lobby, and outside where the winter winds greet my sweaty body in congratulation.

The 54 bus, A reliable line for me, is as warm as any shelter.

Out of breath, a tad frantic, the case and I have this in common. All-day I've been playing defense: too many interviews not enough investigating. And for what? So I can get shot at? Lead around town? I'm painting a picture, but motive and opportunity are still unknown. All of the leads and the obvious told me to look for this kid. Anything related to Mickey is obviously dangerous. If I'm going to do something dangerous, I'm doing it head-on. Should have done what I wanted to do in the first place.

Thanks to the 54, The Seventh Sun is a few minutes away. If this place is full of gangsters I ought to play it safe and have something smart to say. A few different ideas come to mind: a joke to do with Swedish meatballs and horse might get laughs, but the larf doesn't measure up to the con I land on. Bit by bit the lie takes form as my stop approaches.

The loudest color scheme on the block, vibrant reds and yellows of the massive sun scream against the black and white text which boldly proclaims, "The Seventh Sun" followed by a series of Asian characters in equally bold type. Considering how much attention the building catches, Lamar might be wrong about this being a front, but with the three BMW's, two Teslas, and a Ferrari I've seen the team of valets park, I seriously doubt it.

The entrance of the lobby doesn't leave much to be desired. The big red foyer holds a wide curving desk with an ornate door to the right of it. Situated behind the desk a man and woman work behind little monitors. They perk at the click of my heels, the man's eyes dart from me to his monitor to me again before landing on his counterpart for reassurance. My mystery doesn't affect the woman a bit. With a few swaggering steps the con has begun, and they don't even know it.

Reaching the desk, the little woman recites her greeting,

"Welcome to The Seventh Sun, home of gourmet Chinese cuisine. Do you have-"

"Yeah, I'm here for a pick-up!" I belligerently interrupt. This tactic aptly called the pick-up, works on a variety of people: waiters, managers, bodyguards, anyone that can't confidently say they're good at their job. Learned it from a friend during my last trip to Duluth. The friend explained asking someone for something they don't have but ought to have makes them insecure, and insecurity makes people amiable (a word I did not know before I met him).

"What?" The little man's wobbling voice tells me the con's working. "We were never told of a pick-up."

"What is it you're picking up?" The woman asks. With her short hair, short stature, short attitude, and red lipstick I feel like Sam Spade talking to a sassy dame.

"Sweetheart," I'm having fun with the idea, "I think you know what I'm here to pick-up." I let it hang for a bit, darting a knowing, but not really knowing, look at the two of them. The man, a squirrely bucket of anxiety, doesn't belong here; he should be off at some boarding school. His perfectly pressed cream shirt with onyx collar says so much about where he's come from: money, and lots of it. The woman's persona has the same effect, yet unlike her partner whose identity redeems itself with money, hers complements aristocratic traits. She's inhaled more Chanel no 5 than air, while he's hired others to converse for him. The question is: why the hell do they need jobs as hosts then?

She exhales long enough to roll her eyes, "Do you have a name or an appointment for this 'pick-up'?" Wish the man would have responded. The con falls apart when someone confident responds.

"Yes," I lie, "I do. The name is..." Often, but not too often, serendipity tends to be a deciding factor in how my cases develop. Where others would stop to examine life's impromptu gifts, I receive them with little hesitation. A cracked crate full of beer helped me find a runaway boy hoping to become a drummer. The pang from a pigeon flying into a window alerted me upwards where I spotted a 15-year-old drug dealer who'd gone missing two years prior. And a misdialed phone call once led me to the voice of a very chatty 3rd grader who needed help finding his mother. Lingering on why life spontaneously forces reactions is unimportant. What's important is acting and getting rewarded. Which is what I assume will happen when I say, "The name is Mickey, sometimes goes by the name Ler."

Her confidence shatters in front of me, behind the pompous smirk sits a frantic animal who's fallen for the pick-up. She slaps the man's shoulder and gives him a command in a language I don't know. His little loafers slip and slide dashing through the door. For a spell, nothing is said in the odd little moment I've initiated. Best to use the time I've got before things get rolling. Alone with the woman, I test her with a happy smile. She reciprocates, her little cheeks nearly touch her forehead. Not sure what changed, but the pick-up requires interrogating anyone unsure of themselves. The scripted spiel they opened with said this was a Chinese restaurant. Wondering if she is, too.

"You Chinese?" Perfectly trimmed eyebrows jolt up at the question and stay up for a quick beat before she realizes her answer.

"No. Karen." Like I fucking believe that. "You?" Most people don't ask black people their ethnicity because the explanation is generally tragic. Either this woman wants me to plunge the icy depths of my diaspora or she isn't from here. The latter seems more likely as even I have no interest in my identity before the conception of Jazz. Her workmate returns, with a handsome young stranger behind him. Like the wealthy two, this man has money to burn. With a navy blazer, gingham button-up, designer jeans, and mahogany oxfords, one can imagine him explaining he'll definitely attend the regatta as he owns most of the boats.

"Hello," he places his hand before me, "I'm told you're here to pick me up?" I shake his hand and interpret the luck life has presented me. For the face of the dead man and identical twin look nothing like the one belonging to the stranger standing before me. Who the hell is this then?

"Yeah," The con shouldn't last this long. With a possible resolution, the whole thing falls apart. Leaving is the safest thing to do now. But before I do I try one last thing: the number Amelia gave me. "Stay right there." The stranger claiming to be Mickey cocks his head with a smile. To him, a stranger claiming to pick him up has just given him an odd order. With a sense of confidence only found in affluence, he laughs at the command. He sees this as a comically bizarre moment, whereas everybody else in the room is afraid and insecure. Two rings roll out.

"Hello?" a voice from my phone answers.

I'm staring right at this Mickey and he doesn't know what's going on. No doubt the Mickey on the other side of this phone call feels the same way.

"Is this Mickey?" I ask aloud.

"Yeah?" the phone replies.

"Yes?" Mickey replies.

"Hey!" Amelia screams. Having just arrived, she doesn't understand why I'm here, she's just bothered by it. Angry, my client screams something in a language I don't know.

I take the cue for what it is and quickly ask, "Are you Chinese?" and run.

· · ·

Booking it down West 7th gives me a perspective on the street I've never experienced. The little houses, the old Schmidt's factory, the wide, almost abandoned road that leads downtown, and, most notably, the lack of any law enforcement when I need it. The large man chasing me never introduced himself, but in my mind, I've been calling him Tom. He sprung out of the same door "Mickey" emerged from. The behemoth moved on me at Amelia's call, and we've been running ever since. And while it doesn't help the situation, it's important to note, he is the same man with a tie who passed me at the 7th Ave Apartment Complex.

We've run six blocks at least. What's worse, while I'm a bit faster, Tom has the body of a movie villain. Over six feet tall and at least 250 pounds, my imagination runs wild at the thought of what the beast might do if he were to catch me. In the cartoons, Jerry always made getting chased look easy, but it turns out an adorable brown mouse is much more agile than an adorable brown man. Every fence I hop, any zig I zag Tom is right behind me doing the same. Sliding into a bus might be safe but being shot on the 54 isn't unheard of. Escaping seems almost impossible when suddenly a white hill comes into view. I formulate a way to end this.

I dash up the incline; the cold cuts into each stride. The other side of the slope holds an obvious trap, but I'm betting Tom doesn't know the complexities of ice. Living in what is essentially the final ring of hell for twenty-seven years, you learn a thing or two about winter. The snow is sharp and tough, but one layer beneath it happens to be ice. Taking advantage of the hill, I leap down its summit. Tom does the same. But while I simply land with a crunch, the man-shaped pachyderm flops onto the ice and slides down the hill at an alarming pace. Attempting to stop, Tom tries to reach for the only thing available: more snow. The sheer white gives little traction.

Flub after flub, he fails to stand on the angled ice before reaching the bottom. He's probably swearing and slapping his knee and other things bad guys do when they fail, there's no way to know for sure because I manage to glide down the other side of the hill with such grace you might as well call me rosebud. Tom's long gone, stuck wherever losing antagonists go during the commercial break.

My lungs ache, my shoes are damp, the sun's making for the horizon; this day's ending with more questions than when it started. How are there more people involved now than when I left the precinct this morning? People have shot at me and chased me in the street. This whole thing is spinning out of control. In the chaotic mess of it all, there still isn't a concrete reason why.

Amelia didn't tell me why she had Tom chase me down, but I imagine she was hiding something. The same can be said for 22. The rub of it is, neither Amelia nor 22 are suspects in the Does' case. 22 may know something, but if you can't kill a single man in front of your home it isn't likely you'll kill half a dozen strangers across the city. Maybe being a barista wouldn't be so bad. They probably see fewer shoot outs than a P.I.

I pull my phone out to Google the mortality rates of the average barista; the battery icon shows only 9% remains. Doesn't matter, don't need much power for what comes next. Calling Ringenberg makes more sense now than ever. The ethnic minority of one of the Does, the twin angle, what went down at the 7th Ave. apartment complex, and The Seventh Sun, that's more than enough to warrant the reward he promised. I should have called him after getting shot at, but the edge of it made me feel bold. Sometimes I forget, the Pied Piper doesn't have any back-up, authority, even health insurance.

My little phone rumbles. The number isn't saved to a contact, but I know it. 9% can hold for two calls.

"Hello?" I ask.

"Who is this?"

"You called me, Ler." The voice on the other end exhales an angry stream of air into the receiver.

"You called me first."

"Right, yeah. Sorry for doing that." I walk west. Watching the milky orange in the sky fight the drab white and gray on Earth. "I keep running into you when you're not you."

"I'm sorry. My English is still new."

"Never apologize for --"

"What do you mean, you keep running into me?" There isn't any noise besides me and the phone. The road's been plowed, the sidewalks shoveled. Despite everything that's happened today normalcy takes over. I'm preoccupied with the question. My guard drops.

"Ler, who are you?" The question spills out of my mouth and his speaker creating an echo. I'm not fast enough to realize what that means. He punches me with the same hand holding his cell. 22 got the drop on me, I don't know how. This close he can do real damage, and before I can think of anything smart or evasive, he throws me to the ground. Back to the concrete, I'm beneath him now. My hooked fingers claw up for the mouth, the eyes, anything to discombobulate. This won't run like a fight; it'll either be a murder or a scurry.

Placing his hands over my mouth and nose he presses down. Mortality seeps through his arms into me. The heels of my converse slip on the paved sidewalk hoping to find enough purchase to wriggle free. Nothings working. The little bit of feeling that isn't fear is cold and wet. Panic grows like a cancer smothering any ounce of hope that this will get better. His dark-brown eyes, bloodshot from determination, stifle every attempt at logical thought. Death feels so real when looking in the eyes of a killer. The crisp in my vision starts to wane.

Somewhere in the distance, a car door slams shut. 22 reacts to the sound, a witness of his soon to be his act of murder has just arrived. He jumps off of me and darts away but doesn't get far. A long body flies over me tackling 22 into a snowbank. Tom, my latest predator of the evening, saves me. For what reason, I do not know. Ignoring the mystery of my rescue comes easy as another problem presents itself in the fast-paced madness of this moment: my phone won't work right. The touch screen, uninterested in my wet fingers, won't let me dial past 9-1. Despite being freed panic is still in control, the flight portion of fight-or-flight instincts kick-in and I'm running without thought. Four steps out, and another suit and tie is waiting for me. Not as big as Tom, but who could blame him.

He cocks his arm and swings. The world blinks to black.

All things considered, life has been worse. Sitting alone in a dark basement somewhere, with a tiny beam of light above me, huddled next to a large Asian man for warmth because it's so cold my breath appears in prominent white clouds, should seem bad, but I consider it a six on the Richter scale of terrible life moments. Although I probably have a minor concussion, meaning I can't fully consider most things.

A gurgling snort shoots out of 22's nose. I'm guessing some sort of sleep apnea, hard to know for sure. Just another uncertainty about my attempted murderer; like why he's upset with me. When he shot at me, I didn't stop to consider why. The error on my part was falsely presuming things about the man who tried to kill me. The error on his part was not making his motives clear.

Amelia, Tom, and the man who claimed to be Mickey sort of had a reason to come after me. Lies of omission don't bring out the best in people. However, the overreaction to my lie implies they hid much more from me and inadvertently gave something very important away in the process. 22's snorting abruptly stops as he begins to stir awake. Finding himself in some unknown location tied up next to a man he tried to kill, 22 does the only reasonable thing one can do in this situation: weep. His shoulders jump up and down in syncopated sobs of defeat.

"There, there, big guy." Like him, my hands have been tied behind my back and my feet have been bound together. Back and forth I wiggle to get closer to my now pitiful attempted murderer. "I was just thinking about how things could be worse."

22, red-faced, snaps, "How could they be worse?"

"They could have remembered to take my phone." The tiny square force pressing on my thigh tells me my phone is inside my pocket. I'm not sure how I'll get to it, but I will. In the meantime, "Since we're alone, how about you tell-" Our heads pop up at the sound of moaning floorboards. Above us, unknown bodies move around. We hear some voices go back and forth, nothing in English. "Do you understand any of that?"

"No!" 22 yells. "I don't speak Chinese! I'm not Chinese!"

"Will you calm down? They're going to hear us."

"You racist Americans, this is all your fault. I'm not Chinese, I don't speak Chinese, I'm nothing to do with the Chinese! But you're so stupid, I'm going to die!" 22 doesn't make things better by yelling. Follow-up questions start to formulate although they won't get asked as our situation jumps from a six to a nine. Across the room, through the dark, a door opens. A wide sheath of light emerges from it, and in its center stands Tom.

He doesn't look at me much, instead, he slowly approaches 22. Kneeling he gives him a searching stare. Behind Tom, a printer sits newly illuminated from the light of the doorway. It appears to be the center of a whole print station, equipped with Exacto-knives, glue, square edges, pens, possibly a few rulers.

The details ping a few thoughts in my brain. Pieces of the case come together when Tom starts to laugh. The chuckle comes in deep rows of happiness. Pulling a passport from his pocket he holds it up to read its information. Comparing 22 to the picture in the ID seems to be some great joke. Tom tussles 22's hair and makes an insulting oink. After nearly falling to the ground from laughter, he happily leaves. He exits through the light and yells something I don't understand. A slew of voices laugh from the other room. The condescending concert ends as he closes the door leaving us in silence.

I don't know what that was. I want to ask 22 but know better. Defeated, the guy sits with little sobs bursting out of him; as hard as he tries, he can't hold them back. Ignoring the sad moment, I consider what just happened. Tom doesn't seem like the type to waste time with a fat joke. What was with the passport? How was it funny?

Pieces of the case try to come together to form a theory when something in the back of my mind hits me. Racist Americans he called us. Jingoism is a really specific form of prejudice. Makes me wonder why he doesn't consider himself American. Then I wonder why he knows his captors are Chinese? Or, why the hell, they wanted him to begin with?

A mental lap of this insane day highlights some key clues. The replay puts things into a new context, especially the oink. It pulls me to an anxiety-riddled possibility. The idea of it being true is terrifying, but if I'm right then it would explain a lot. Testing the bizarre notion, I ask 22, "Oh my God, Ler?" With the weight, he's nearly unrecognizable, but imagining his features atop a sharper chin and shallow cheeks and the face before me matches the one seen in both photos.

The man formerly known as 22 responds, "Ler is dead. I'm Shaw Thaw!" Holy mother and marry, I figured it out. All of it, minus one last detail. The last bit doesn't matter now, but with the rest of the case solved the Does can be accounted for and their murderers caught. Holy crap! With a few of those Does and Shaw Thaw found that makes over a dozen. The only thing keeping a promotional sandwich from being named after me is a basement door and a few large men.

Rolling into the dark, I head over to the station once previously unknown. Nothing's visible in the cold black, so I swing my body around waiting for the thunk of my wrist smacking the table's legs, prop it up at an angle, and wait for the clatter of its contents hitting the ground. It isn't safe to look for an Exacto-knife in the dark, but time isn't on my side. A tiny cut to my thumb is all it costs to find the blade. Grabbing at the tool I work on the ropes binding my hands. Twisting my wrist up and down, the cutting motion takes time, but halfway through and even I can rip the rope apart. The bonds holding my legs don't last long and soon I'm standing.

This isn't my first rodeo; I know how to escape a cold basement. This is bread territory, which is why I know saving Shaw Thaw comes after I call the police. There's an impulse to explain everything to the kid, but I need to move. Calling 911 makes sense, but my phone's useless. The little slab of metal makes no light, no sound, dead. Rolling your eyes in the dark means nothing, yet I do it anyway.

"Shaw Thaw," I whisper. A small growl comes from his direction. He's still upset, which is fair. "I'm going to get help. I'd let you loose, but you're safer here." He begins to object but I cut him off with the hard thunk and soft clink from the door. I angled the kick carefully to break the knob off, I need it for what comes next. Piercing through the blackness, I find the metal orb that was once the doorknob. Holding it in hand I knock on the door; shave and a haircut; two bits, Chandler would be proud.

Three guys pool-in while I hide in the dark. As one flicks the light, I've already snuck around and closed the door behind me. The big bolt makes an excellent lock, but without the knob on their end, the three stooges won't be getting out soon. A lit-up stairwell going up waits before me. While escaping as fast as I can, I rehearse the story for Ringenberg.

Across Saint Paul dead people are randomly found. With no IDs they're considered John and Jane Does. The only thing we know for sure is their nationality. With nothing to go on, I searched the city for gang or drug violence: nothing came up.

The staircase leads to a door. Past it, a large man sits on an ottoman while playing with his phone. He jumps at the sight of me. While not as large as Tom, the man is still a problem.

Sizing him up I ask, "English?"

"We all speak perfect English," he balks. I'm a little embarrassed. I wanted to make sure he understood my snappy repartees but acted racist in order to check. My assailant doesn't let me apologize; he lunges too quickly. The gap between us leaves me space to fling the doorknob at him. The orb bounces off his cheek and eye, he grasps his face and I take that as my cue to run. Zipping past him, my next exit is another staircase leading up.

The biggest clues in the case were the missing IDs and the lack of missing persons reports. The Does weren't just dead, they were technically missing, but no one seemed to be looking for them. The oddity implied anyone who cared about them didn't know they were dead when in reality everyone that cared about them was just gone; scattered in refugee camps, other countries, and busy volunteer centers. The Karen are new here, people didn't know to look for them. But there was one more reason, a big one.

The stairs lead to a dining hall. Red chairs surrounding nine wooden tables of various sizes wait for a lunch-rush that'll never come. My ragged breath and steps echo in the empty room. The crash of the door being kicked open echoes too. Caution asks me to turn around right before a chair flies in my direction. Instinctively I pivot, the chair snags my shoulder and I fall into a table. It doesn't make up for the English thing, but I'm really hurt. Tom emerges from God knows where eager to end the night violently. The two goons nod to each other and stalk forward. Toppling chairs and tables as I go, I make for the only exit left.

Ler and Shaw Thaw were just kids. They didn't have much, but they had each other and a form of citizenship that would help them start anew. For 90 days they had Sister Pam and others watching them, helping them become indoctrinated to the ways of this country. They were safe then. But soon enough, Shaw Thaw was introduced to an American tradition few recognize in time: overeating. The realization, known throughout the nation, surprised a kid who learned eating what you have and what you need can be vastly different. In quick time, Shaw Thaw physically became a different person, someone who didn't resemble some rich kid in China, which meant his twin would die in his place.

The exit leads me to another floor. A hallway full of doors greets me. Out of breath, I open several doors before ducking in a room. My hideout holds cases of red wine, bags of rice, cans of beans, cases of thyme, pepper, salt, and ground garlic. A small window faces West 7th Avenue, snow spins past the glass in the dead of night. I'm in The Seventh Sun.

Ler's killers took the only thing he, and the Does had: identity. Replacing the dead boy, the Mickey I met hours earlier slipped into Ler's life not knowing he had a twin. Inexplicably, they learned their error but didn't know who was who. Unable to find anyone that resembled Ler they came to me, the Pied Piper.

I hear Tom and his lackey reach my floor. From the sound of things, they split up to search the rooms. There's nowhere to go. My shoulder aches, I'm tired, I'm cold; even with the frantic running, I'm still cold. The little bit of ice inside me reaches out. I'm a son of Saint Paul. A child of the North Star. Winter, the season of death and judgment, knows everything about survival, if you're quiet it'll teach you how to move; even now it tells me how to flee.

A can of garbanzo beans finds my hand when Tom steps into my doorway. He knows I'm at the end of the line. My arm raised ready to throw gets Tom to smile. He's not even defensive, the idea of me hurting him won't register to the giant man. My ego might take a hit if I were planning on attacking. Like a pitcher on the mound, I twist my body perfectly, and the can flies. To his err, the beans go in the opposite direction of Tom toward the window. Rebounding off the glass it bounces back at me as I run after it. The pitch can't break through the window, but it can crack it, which is all I need. With two steps for momentum, I dive. Tom's dashing strides make him close behind, but it's too late. My arms cover my face bracing for impact. Success comes with a gale of gushing wind. The glass shatters, and for a moment I'm another piece of snow.

In the chilled dark, a million flecks of white surround me. The spinning magnificence of winter, tinged from the red and orange of the neon sign, distracts from the approaching pavement. What a world to fly in. The dream ends with an abrupt landing. My ankles sing the same ache as my shoulder. Limping away is all I can muster for my escape.

Shaw Thaw is right, we're stupid Americans. These people, whoever they are, have been killing Karen men and women, stealing their lives, and have been getting away with it exclusively because they happen to be Chinese, and no one in this country cares to learn enough about their neighbors.

I limp again and again. Blocks come and go with no cars to save me. The cold makes everything from my ears to my toes numb. Not exactly the smartest escape, but as long as I find someone to call the police, it'll be a success.

"Neil?" Hearing my name inspires hope. Eager to respond to anyone makes me slow.

"Wai-" Bang! Amelia shoots me dead. I'm no longer cold.

I hadn't known it, but the police were looking for me. The woman from apartment 21 ended up in the emergency room. Hospitals in the city have protocols that require the police be called whenever someone comes in with a gunshot wound. 21 explained her neighbor and a man with a "massive afro" were responsible. Thanks to the obvious description, the cops got a warrant for my phone and traced its last whereabouts. My cell may have died before I did, but it pinged its location to the nearest cell tower. With that, a few cruisers were in the area, eager to respond to a gunshot in the middle of the night. Amelia didn't stand a chance.

They got SWAT to go inside The Seventh Sun. Tom fought harder than Amelia, but it didn't matter much. There they found everything, including a still-living Shaw Thaw. It was the largest bust in Saint Paul history. Human trafficking, but in reverse.

The Pioneer Press ran the whole story. A group of rich Chinese expats attempted to flee their home by replacing the bodies of refugees with their kids. They planned for everything from forging fake passports to laundering money through a fake restaurant. The case shed a light on over forty replaced men and women, including the Does the police already had. They called me a hero.

Cecil's even named a sandwich after me. They didn't know what I liked so they made it basic. The Edlow isn't even a meal, more of an appetizer or a side dish. Doesn't matter though, because anytime you show up and say my name, they'll give you a big plate with bread and butter.

GREAT EXPECTATIONS

BY SARA HOSEY

PART I
NICE LIFE

Cinnamon Lou stood on the front porch, trembling and sweating, her breath making white puffs in the cold air. Not seeing a doorbell, she used the side of her fist to knock, hard and urgently, before taking a step back to look around, as though expecting Jason to tear up the driveway behind her. In the dim light of the late afternoon, she saw what she'd missed in her dash from her car to the porch: the front yard was littered with beer bottles, Dorito bags, cigarette butts.

* * *

Inside the house, Amanda Carey, expecting someone else, took her rifle from where it rested beside the fireplace, tucked it into her shoulder, and flung open the door with her free hand.

"Holy shit," Cinnamon cried as she covered her head with her arms and stumbled backwards. "Don't shoot!"

Amanda Carey lowered the gun. "Who the fuck are you?"

* * *

Had Cinnamon come to the right place? She was in Miserable. She'd seen the sign welcoming her to town. She remembered the house, but this was not the reception she expected.

* * *

In 2013, some of the residents of Miserable, Wisconsin mounted a campaign to rename the town Elliston, after John Paul Ellis, a civil war hero and early town mayor. Naturally, a committed block of old-timers opposed the change, but it came as a surprise to the reformers that many young people apparently found the town's name "hilarious" and also voted against the referendum. Miserable remained Miserable.

Amanda Carey Birchbaum (née Schmidt), was herself perhaps the most miserable resident of Miserable, and if anyone had ever said so to her face, she would have narrowed her eyes and said something rude in return. Most people, though, didn't say anything to her face, because she'd become a bit of a shut-in: she lived alone in the old wooden farmhouse that was no longer attached to a farm but now abutted a Super Walmart, its gas station, and its enormous parking field. Amanda Cary was so mean and miserable, it seemed to some folks she really must be kidding; no one could possibly conform so closely to the stereotype of the cranky old cat lady. She wasn't even that old—only in her sixties—but she'd let her hair go gray and she scowled and cursed and never smiled. And she had numerous cats!

One of those cats weaved between Amanda Carey's ankles as she regarded the stranger on her porch: a young woman, skinny and tan and shivering in the biting wind. The woman lifted her shaking hands in the air as though this was a stick up.

Amanda Carey lowered the gun.

"I'm Cinnamon," the woman said. "Cinnamon Lou Schmidt. I think you're my aunt? I think I'm your niece?"

Amanda Carey frowned. Another cat, Marshmallow, took the opportunity to dash in through the open door. "You're Carl's daughter?" Amanda Carey asked, suspicious.

"Yeah," she said. "I'm Cinnamon. Cinnamon Lou." She lowered her hands.

Amanda Carey squinted, looked down the driveway into the darkening afternoon. "Hmm. Come on in, I guess." She stepped aside and waved for Cinnamon Lou to enter.

* * *

If Cinnamon hadn't been desperate to pee, and so tired, shaky and sick from her time on the road that she didn't think it safe to get behind the wheel again any time soon, if it hadn't taken her last bit of everything to get to the farmhouse front door, she would have turned right around and used her last two hundred dollars to stay at the Knight's Inn she passed an hour earlier. Because this was a shitshow.

* * *

The more charitable residents of Miserable maintained that Amanda Cary's meanness was the result of a hard life; the kind of suffering Amanda Cary endured would sour anyone. Although she'd had a run-of-the-mill miserable childhood (her father drank too much and beat up his wife on Friday nights and when the Packers lost, demonstrating that a loyalty to stereotypes maybe ran in the family), capital-T Things seemed to have turned around for Amanda Carey in early adulthood, after she'd gotten her degree at the Mid-State Tech and after she'd met and married the unimpeachable Phil Birchbaum, and after her father had died and she and Phil had bought out her brothers' shares of the farmhouse.

Back then, Amanda Carey and Phil believed this was just the beginning and there were many more Good Things in store. They believed they too had a right to dinner parties and beach vacations and Sears family portraits they'd take too seriously during the sitting and laugh so hard about later.

They were mistaken.

Because when people whispered that Amanda Cary had a hard life, they weren't talking about Phil's too-early demise (at 50 from a melanoma); they were talking about Amanda Cary's five (known) miscarriages. In addition to the five (known) miscarriages, Amanda Cary had also delivered two babies who died shortly after birth.

People who knew Amanda Cary and Phil said whenever they saw her in those early years, she was pregnant. At first, everyone stayed hopeful. They'd pat her gently, squeeze her arm. But as the years passed, with Amanda Cary pregnant then not-pregnant and still no baby, never a baby, everyone became a little reticent, a little less likely to acknowledge any changes at all. Amanda Cary's pregnant belly became like the Swastika face tattoo Paul Weinbrot got when he was in prison: an announcement of shameful stupidity and rashness, a public display of unimaginable personal suffering, a damn foolish sin. Didn't she know it wasn't to be? Hadn't she gotten the message? Why didn't they just adopt some poor, suffering orphan who needed parents as much as they, apparently, felt they needed a child?

There was speculation it had been the two babies—born years apart but each living a short while—that had encouraged Amanda Cary and Phil, made them feel it was possible, kept them thinking they should give a it go *this one last time*.

Those poor folks. All those almost-babies ought to have added up to something eventually. Couldn't all those almost-babies been put together to make them *just one* complete little baby?

* * *

Cinnamon could not stop panting and shivering as she followed her aunt inside and closed the door behind them. The old lady placed the gun against the fireplace. .

Amanda Carey gestured for her to sit in the opposite-facing love seat currently occupied by a massive orange cat. "You're a long way from home, aren't you?"

"Yeah," Cinnamon tried to get her face under control. "Do you mind if I use your bathroom first? I've been in the car for a long time."

Amanda Carey nodded. "Through the kitchen," she said, waving her hand. "Do you remember?"

"Um, sorta." She walked on unsteady legs toward the back of the house.

In the kitchen, Cinnamon imagined her father growing up in this cold, ugly place. It was hard, because her memories of her father were all based on photos of him in Hawaiian shirts, hamming it up next to palm trees. He looked so happy in the photos; probably so happy to be in Florida, so happy to be away from Miserable.

Cinnamon's father, the unintentionally-ridiculously named Carl Louis, had taken the money Amanda Carey and Phil paid him for his share of the house in Miserable and moved first to Cleveland, Ohio and then to Plantation, Florida, where he met Marisa, his very own cinnamon-colored dream girl, and had a daughter with her, before dying in a multi-car accident on I-95 when he was 47 and Cinnamon was only 7.

Up until then, Cinnamon Lou had had a really nice life and she too believed the future held more pool parties and visits to Disney and Christmas surprises, like a box under the tree with a puppy in it. The puppy had peed in the box, sure, but she was wearing a bow.

Cinnamon was also mistaken.

* * *

Amanda Carey stood very still, her heart pounding in her chest. She didn't quite know why, but the arrival of her niece was more surprising and more upsetting than any of the juvenile pranks she'd anticipated—or even the manslaughter she'd been considering committing.

And the cats too (with the exception of the incurious Baby Snooks, who remained on the love seat), were all riled up, some hiding and others dashing about. Perhaps they could sense Amanda Carey's alarm, perhaps the cats were acting out in the ways she herself could not.

There was no doubt the girl was telling the truth; she looked like Carl in a wig, and Amanda Carey recognized the child's face in the grown woman's. When was it they'd come up from Florida? Twenty years ago? No, must be longer ago than that. It was the same year she and Phil had sold the land. It was the summer the trucks and scrapers and chainsaws came in, when they'd started chopping down all the trees and digging up all fields.

But now what the hell was Carl's daughter doing in Wisconsin?

And what the hell would Carl's daughter make of Amanda Carey's behavior?

It was only recently that she'd begun answering the door shotgun-first.

What had happened was, on Halloween, some teenagers egged Amanda Carey's front door and lit a brown paper bag of (presumably) dog shit on fire on her front step. Amanda Carey watched stonily from the front window—she did not rush out to step on the bag as the boys had hoped. She recognized the kids —despite their lurid masks—and called their mothers to complain.

The boys arrived the next day to clean up. Amanda Carey listened to their apologies then nodded, expressionless. But as she closed the front door behind her, one of the boys whispered, "dumb bitch" and another snickered. Amanda Carey turned to look at them and they gazed boldly back with wide eyes and mouths sealed against laughter. She heard them laughing as she went into the house and they were still laughing when she opened the door and stepped back out carrying Phil's hunting rifle.

"Listen, you little shits," she said, aiming the unloaded rifle at them. "You clean up my goddamn porch and then you get the hell out of here and if you ever step foot on my property again, I'll blow you to kingdom come."

Frozen and pale, no one was snickering now.

"Do you understand me?" she asked.

"Yes," one of the boys stammered. "Yes...ma'am?"

"Get to fucking work," she hissed.

Of course, the little shits told their parents and one of the fathers called the police. Officer Jerry Beck, who'd made it clear he dearly wished he had something better to do, mounted the front steps to try to talk to her.

"They were trespassing on my property," Amanda Carey declared before he opened his mouth.

"You did ask them to come over, Mrs. Birchbaum," Jerry said.

"Are you going to arrest me, Jerry?"

"No, Mrs. Birchbaum," Jerry said.

"You tell those goddam kids not to fuck with me again," Amanda Carey told Jerry. "Or you might have to."

Amanda Carey felt so pleased with herself for what she had done, she went to bed smiling that night. But the next day, Jerry returned to Amanda Carey's house to, in fact, arrest her and to confiscate the rifle. One of the parents—a stepfather, it emerged—insisted on pressing charges.

Amanda Carey did not argue. She solemnly handed over the rifle, shaking her head "no" when asked if she had any other firearms in the house. (This was a lie). Despite her outward calm, however, inside she had been panicking, thinking of the cats, wondering how long she would be away, ruing her self-isolation not because it hurt her to be alone but because it might inconvenience her goddam cats.

She wasn't held long, simply charged and released on her own recognizance, and ordered to stay away from the boys. She was tempted, as she walked home with great dignity through the misty afternoon, to follow her own recognizance and get the shotgun and further escalate her already ridiculous feud with the local children—what did she have to lose?—but she didn't do it, mostly because she was hungry and looked forward to getting home and eating the fried eggs and toast she often had in the early evening.

But perhaps emboldened by her arrest, the kids began a campaign of harassment. It started off with litter thrown from cars. Because Amanda Carey refused to clean it up herself, the front of her property now looked like the grassy shoulders of the busy highways near Milwaukee, strewn with Big Gulp cups and cigarette butts, plastic bags, and beer bottles.

Next, the kids started tossing firecrackers and stink bombs in the middle of the night—again thrown from cars, but sounding as though they were right there in the room, and she'd wake with a gasp, sure she'd been fired upon.

"Jerry, I might just fucking kill someone if you don't get this under control," Amanda Carey warned, one hand holding the phone, the other soothing a skittish cat that Amanda Carey hadn't seen in months, but who'd been flushed out the night before by the racket. On the muted television, the Green Bay Packers were losing.

"Please, Mrs. Birchbaum, that language makes me really uncomfortable," Jerry said.

"I don't give a fuck," she said. "Are you listening to what I'm saying?"

"You bet I am, ma'am."

And that was when the doorbell had chimed. The cat dug its nails into Amanda Carey's thighs before springing away.

"There's one now," Amanda Carey growled. "Goddamn it, Jerry. I warned you."

"Please don't shoot anyone, Amanda Carey. Just sit tight and I'll be right over..."

But Amanda Carey had hung up. She stood and took the shotgun from where it rested against the fireplace.

And then there was Cinnamon Lou, shivering on the front porch.

* * *

Cinnamon, who had acne well into her twenties, could feel her pores clogging, her skin breaking out just from being in the filthy house. Every surface was covered with a fine dust and she knew, even though she didn't want to know it, that it wasn't just the regular dust made by an old person; it was kitty litter dust. It was cat shit dust.

Even the bar of Ivory soap looked ancient, brown in the

cracks. Cinnamon used it anyway, scrubbing her hands hard, like she was a surgeon, before wiping them dry on her leggings.

Cinnamon had fond memories of the farmhouse, which she'd visited exactly once, when she was five, the year of the construction of the Super Walmart. She didn't remember much about the trip, except for the farmhouse's cool dark staircase and the biting flies that tormented her when she went outside to watch the snarling construction vehicles tearing at the land. She remembered, too, her aunt's swollen belly and when she'd asked if Aunt Amanda Carey was going to have a baby, her father had shushed her and said, "We'll have to wait and see."

When she was a child, the house was full of dark wood but also windows and sunlight. She had fun, sliding in her socks on the polished floors. She been enchanted by the steep staircase— their houses in Florida were always one-story—and came up with countless games involving the steps: she lined up her Barbies and stuffies stadium-seating style to play school, she threw superballs from the gumball machine outside the Wegman's against them, she lay herself flat and let gravity take her, her rubber-band body sliding off each step.

Now, this house did not conform to her memories or expectations: it was filthy and cramped and full of felines, whose yellow eyes followed her as she walked through the kitchen, peeking out at her from behind the legs of chairs and perched on high cabinets.

Cinnamon thought of a book she read in Mrs. Costello's class in high school, about an old lady who lived alone in a house with a rotting wedding cake. Cinnamon Lou couldn't remember the name of the book. That's what she was trying to think of when the doorbell rang.

"That's just Jerry Beck," her aunt called. "I'll send him away."

Cinnamon, about to reenter the living room, stepped back

into the kitchen doorway. It would have been impossible for Jason to have found her so quickly, she knew. It would have been impossible, except that it wasn't. She wondered, not for the first time, if he'd put a GPS on her mother's car. She hadn't thought he would, but it wasn't unimaginable. It also wasn't unimaginable that he'd follow her all the way here, to see where she was going first, before he caught up with and killed her.

She was having a hard time breathing, made worse by the thickness of the dirty air, the dander floating around her and the smell of cats and cat shit and cat piss. It was as though her nose and throat and lungs were rejecting the environment, refusing to allow it in, the way a body might reject an organ transplant, except, she thought foggily, she was the transplant.

She was drowning. She couldn't get a breath, couldn't fill her lungs and she leaned against the doorframe. She felt herself slipping down. She felt herself dying; it wasn't so bad, really.

* * *

When Amanda Carey turned to follow Jerry's gaze, she saw the girl's eyelids flutter as she leaned against the doorframe. Although it immediately occurred to Amanda Carey that Cinnamon had probably gone into the bathroom and overdosed on drugs, she was hesitant, for some reason, to say this to Jerry Beck. Her indecision was irrelevant; before she could turn back to him he'd already dashed, with surprising swiftness, and caught Cinnamon, placing his hand along the small of her back and easing her into a sitting position against the doorframe.

"What's happening?" Amanda Carey shouted.

Jerry didn't answer right away. "What's happening?" Amanda Carey yelled more loudly.

The cop half-glanced over his shoulder. "She passed out," Jerry answered, taking the girl's pulse. "She's all right."

* * *

Cinnamon's body shivered, but it didn't feel bad. Just strange.

She opened her good eye and saw a police officer crouched beside her.

"You passed out, ma'am. You passed out, but we got you and you didn't hit your head. Don't hurry to get up. You relax there yet."

She took his advice and shut her eye.

"I can't stop shaking," she panted.

"You're in shock," he said. "It'll go away soon." She noticed he had a funny accent.

At some point the tremors ceased. Cinnamon opened her eye again. The police officer peered into it.

"How are you feeling now?" he asked.

"I'm okay," she said, so grateful, so grateful to be there, that it was a police officer and not Jason, that she was alive. But who had called the cops? Had Jason been there? How long had she been out?

"I feel a lot better," she added.

"I'd like to call an ambulance and have them check you out over at the hospital," the cop said.

"No," she shook her head. "I'm all right. I just had a long drive. Too much coffee. No sleep."

"She's dehydrated," she heard her aunt call from across the room. "I'll get her some water."

Cinnamon nodded at the cop, both eyes open (although the bad one was still swollen a bit and felt as though a curtain had fallen over the top periphery; Cinnamon wondered if this was, perhaps, a new permanent condition). "I'm dehydrated," she affirmed.

"What happened here?" the cop asked Cinnamon, touching, very gently, the swollen area around her right eye.

"Oh, that's nothing," Cinnamon said. "A few days ago...car accident." This was truth-adjacent. It had happened in a car. And Jason had claimed it was an accident.

The cop seemed doubtful, but Amanda Carey said, "She said she's fine, Jerry. Now get

the fuck out."

The officer, who, Cinnamon realized, had been holding her wrist in one of his hands, looked at his watch. He pursed his lips in concentration. Then he laid her hand on her thigh and then, to Cinnamon's surprise, lightly patted it, as though he were comforting a sweet and fragile old person.

The cop rose and turned his face to mumble something—it sounded like numbers—into the walkie-talkie on his shoulder. He turned back to Cinnamon. "All right," he said. He put his hand out. "But if you feel dizzy again, or feel strange or sick, you call 9-1-1 and have them send an ambulance." Cinnamon took his hand and rose, slowly.

The cop looked over his shoulder at Amanda Carey. "You'll keep an eye on her, Mrs. Birchbaum?"

Cinnamon's aunt made a noise that could have meant any number of things. She walked forcefully on bowed legs to the door, flung it open, and waited for the officer to leave.

The cop held Cinnamon's elbow as he guided her to the small, now feline-free, sofa.

He looked back once and nodded at Cinnamon before leaving. Her aunt locked the door behind him.

"Hmm," she said, looking at her niece.

* * *

Amanda Carey watched as Cinnamon drank two glasses of water. Amanda Carey made her eat an Oreo cookie, which the girl chewed as though it were made of sand. Then, Amanda

Carey insisted Cinnamon lay down on the love seat while she fried up some eggs.

Though the fall had confirmed for Amanda Carey that the girl was on drugs, Jerry Beck hadn't seemed to think there was a serious problem. Nevertheless, Amanda Carey found Cinnamon Lou's appearance profoundly upsetting: Cinnamon looked like one of the girls on the shows that were all over the television these days, girls so like each other they had to splash their names beneath them every time they appeared on screen so you could tell them apart: *Kandace* or *Versace* or *Jaydana*. Skinny girls with big breasts and impossibly long hair, girls with painfully white teeth and eyelashes like Halloween-spider decorations pasted on their faces. Her niece looked like one of them, but she also looked tired and beat up and a little greasy.

Amanda Carey wondered if the girl had come to steal from her. Or worse, to try and manipulate her, a long-game con that ended with Amanda Carey changing her will and leaving everything to Cinnamon Lou. Ha. She'd have another think coming.

Amanda Carey was planning on living forever.

* * *

Cinnamon had actually fallen asleep, surprisingly comfortable on the strange little couch, when Amanda Carey called her from the kitchen.

"Eggs are ready," her aunt said.

Standing up, still slightly dizzy, she made her way slowly to the kitchen. Her aunt had made a stack of toast and a pot of coffee and the aforementioned eggs. She also put out a tall glass of orange juice.

"Drink the juice," Amanda Carey barked as Cinnamon sat down. "You need the sugar."

Cinnamon did as instructed.

Amanda Carey watched her out of narrow, frowning eyes.

"I heard you were a drug addict."

Cinnamon shook her head. The toast was delicious. She couldn't remember the last time she'd had white bread. She thought, wryly, that she might just pass out again.

"I was," Cinnamon said. "But I've been clean for almost five years."

"Hmmm," her aunt said, as though she had her doubts. "You're not on drugs now?"

"I'm not," Cinnamon confirmed, although there was a part of her—had it always been

there or only embedded itself in her twenties?—that remained skeptical even when she told the truth, that believed she was always still a little guilty. She wasn't on drugs, of course. She didn't do that anymore. But that didn't mean she was clean.

"Well, why did you pass out then?" Amanda Carey asked.

Cinnamon shrugged. "I think...the doorbell scared me. I couldn't breathe. I'm just real tired from the drive, I guess."

Amanda Carey watched her, scowling. After a moment, she snapped, "What the hell are you doing here anyway?"

Had Cinnamon imagined her entry into her aunt's life would be easier? She had, at the very least, assumed her mother would have called to give her aunt a heads-up. Oh, Marisa.

The last time she'd tried to leave Jason, she'd gone straight to her mother's house and stayed there. And Marisa would have let her stay there again, but Cinnamon wouldn't do that to her mother. She couldn't do it, because after she'd returned to Jason, he waited a week before he sat her down to tell something. Very serious, he said she caused him profound pain when she left. He couldn't even begin to explain his suffering to her. And his pain was compounded by the shame he'd experienced. He asked why Cinnamon had felt compelled to include her mother in their private business. He wanted to know, what exactly had she told her mother? Did Marisa hate him now? Had Cinnamon explained Cinnamon's own role in the argument?

Cinnamon did her best to soothe him, to assure him that Marisa still loved him although, naturally, she was concerned. Cinnamon conceded, yes, she'd told Marisa about what she herself had done, but that he had, well, he had choked her, hadn't he?

Jason had listened. And then he told Cinnamon if she ever embarrassed him like that again, if she ever ran away to Marisa's house and told her mother their private business, he would kill her and her mother. Because that was how insane and crazy Cinnamon made him feel. So, she should just be aware. She should know there would be consequences for her actions.

As a result, when Cinnamon left this time, she didn't go to Marisa's house. Instead, she walked to the Starbucks down the road and borrowed a stranger's phone. She called her mother to say, *please, mommy, I need money. I have to get out of town.*

And Marisa, who received this call with an implacable calm her daughter had never before observed her to possess, had filled up the gas tank and then driven over to the Starbucks, her eyes like those of an ancient watchman taking in the immediate and the horizon simultaneously. Marisa, who had not been a bad mother, who loved her Cinnamon Lou and loved little Ambria too, but who simply had her own problems, said,

"You just go ahead and take my car. I'll get Sammy to pick me up. You take my car and you take this money and you go on up to Miserable. Your aunt'll take you in."

And what, exactly, had Cinnamon expected to find in Miserable, really?

During the first five or six hours of the drive, Cinnamon didn't think too much past getting out of the state, getting north, watching the gas gauge. She used an actual map, a task confusing, frustrating, and scary enough to keep her mind occupied for a long time, and then on the long stretches, thirty, fifty, two hundred miles on the same highway, she thought about Jason. Those many miles afforded her the opportunity to cycle through various emotions.

She remembered last Christmas, when he gave her a Rolex. They'd gone to Colorado and, standing in three feet of snow, she worn only the watch, snow boots, and a white bikini for a photo shoot. Those pictures came out great.

She imagined the coming Christmas. They'd already bought their flights to Puerto Rico. She thought about how generous and gentle he could be and how his love for her became the motivation for everything she did. She had become this version of herself she'd never even imagined was possible before she met him, *she'd run three marathons* because of him and because of his love. They talked about getting a puppy after they came back from Puerto Rico; about how a whole puppy thing would not only be fun and wonderful, almost like having a baby together, but would be perfect for their story. People love puppies. And they could write off the dog and all the accessories as a business expense.

Or Jason could, at least. Because on paper, none of it belonged to Cinnamon. Except for the motherfucking house. This was something else Cinnamon considered during her drive. The house they lived in was in her name and was supposed to be this huge empowering thing for her except it wasn't, because the house was in foreclosure. Cinnamon couldn't even get a fucking credit card anymore because of the fucking house. As she drove, she went over it again and again, how she wouldn't be able to do anything, have any sort of life without working that shit out with him first. She knew it wasn't on purpose and it wasn't his fault, but the house had become this huge thing in her life, so huge and such a problem for her that she wondered just a little if it had been on purpose and if it was, in fact, his fault.

Occupied with these thoughts during the drive, she only vaguely imagined her reception at her aunt's house. She knew, of course, her quiet, sweet uncle had died, but she half-expected him to be there too. She expected the house to be warm, like it had been when they'd been there in the summer and for her aunt to be tall and maybe a little distant, but so happy to see her, so grateful she'd come.

She hadn't expected to find herself staring down the barrel of a shotgun, or a house filled with cat shit and dander or this old lady sitting across from her scowling, insisting she eat this food which was at first so enticing but which her stomach wasn't used to and which was rapidly making her ill.

Cinnamon put down her fork and clutched her hands in her lap.

* * *

When Amanda Carey asked—reasonably enough, she thought —why the hell she'd come to Miserable, the girl startled as though she hadn't expected this question and dropped her fork and then immediately crumpled in upon herself, expanding and collapsing like an overfull balloon. She looked so strange, hunched over like that, and Amanda Carey wondered for a moment if she was having a seizure or some other health emergency again. But no, she saw that the girl was crying silently into her chest.

"Well," Amanda Carey said, unsure. She had never before had to walk back her tone, at least not in recent years.

Amanda Carey cleared her throat, but before she could say anything, the girl spoke in a high-pitched, apologetic voice. "I didn't have anywhere else to go."

"All right," Amanda Carey said, as gently as possible, which wasn't really all that gentle. She made a little humming sound and cleared her throat again. After a while she said, "No one is kicking you out. You're Carl's daughter. You can stay here."

The girl continued to cry and Amanda Carey, at a loss, continued to watch her. Patches leapt into Amanda Carey's lap and she petted the cat absently. The crying went on for much longer than Amanda Carey thought possible, and then, feeling slightly disgusted by the way the girl unselfconsciously wiped her nose not only on the back of her hand, but up her wrist and forearm, finally rose and returned with a roll of toilet paper.

She handed it to the girl and said, "I'll put out a clean towel. The shower is upstairs." Cinnamon would sleep in her room (there weren't any other rooms made up and besides, Amanda Carey sometimes preferred the couch), but she didn't want the girl going in there and rubbing her snotty face and greasy hair all over her pillows, so she'd have to find some other linens to put on.

Amanda Carey dispatched the girl to the shower and then, with minimal conversation, established her in the bedroom. It was only 7:30, but the girl looked grateful to be left alone.

Amanda Carey went back downstairs and let some cats in and other cats out, refreshed their food and water and scooped their boxes, and then settled down with her Oreos in front of the television. The Packers had won after all—Amanda Carey was sorry to have missed it—and now it was time for the British mysteries they aired on Sunday evenings on Channel 4, *Rosemary and Thyme* and *Father Brown* and *Wallander,* comforting shows about older people politely solving the murders of other older people. She lay on her side, buffeted by cats: fat Baby

Snooks rested inside the curve of her knees and Patches perched on the back of the couch and Frieda sat on her hip and sweet Peter snuggled up to be spooned.

She tried to focus on the shows, but her thoughts returned again and again to the girl.

It seemed at once impossible and absolutely true that Cinnamon Lou had nowhere else to go but Miserable. She had a mother, of course, but Amanda Carey didn't fault the girl for avoiding her: Marisa wouldn't be the first person Amanda Carey called in a pinch either.

If Amanda Carey had to guess, she'd say Cinnamon was running from a boyfriend. That's what had scared her so much about the doorbell ringing. Scared her almost to death, Amanda Carey thought. He must've done a number on her.

Amanda Carey—who did not often bother to wonder what other people thought of her—couldn't help but see herself as the girl must see her. She supposed having a surprise visitor would do that to a person. Amanda Carey found herself wanting to protest, to explain she hadn't set out to become a shut-in; that wasn't at all the future she'd once envisioned. She'd never imagined herself alone in the farmhouse, talking to cats, and resolving to get out more, to go to the Bingo fundraiser or the pancake breakfast at the church. And yet here she was. Because being around other people was like October sunlight; always angled in a way that irritated, made you want to get back inside and away from this supposedly blessed thing.

When she did get herself out, dressed nicely but not too nicely because she didn't want anyone to think she'd gone to any trouble, people made such a fuss, as though the reason she'd emerged was to be reassured she looked wonderful, that she wasn't aging at all, that they missed her. Amanda Cary had no stomach for it. She'd turn her back, take another sleeve of Royal Dansk cookies from the blue tin—she liked the ones shaped like pretzels with little sugar crystals on top—and mumble her apologies before leaving. Or not.

When she'd get back home, she'd ruminate. She knew it didn't matter one damn to them whether or not they ever saw her again. They didn't think of her except when she was right in front of them. They might honk if she was outside gardening when they drove by and some of their goddamn kids might spray shaving cream on her trees at Halloween and some of them still sent her Christmas cards. But she wasn't vital to the life of the town or it's people. She wasn't vital to anyone. Except the cats, of course.

Amanda Carey dozed. She woke later on her back, in the blue light of the television, Peter asleep on her chest. He felt like a small baby, like an infant, like her little Philip Jr., Pip, the baby they'd laid on her in the hospital bed.

Pip came too early. He spent most of his three days alive dying in an incubator, but on the third day they'd taken him out and placed him, wires and tubes and all, on Amanda Carey's chest. She had craned her neck down to him and wept, feeling his tiny weight, smelling his fuzzy head. It had been everything.

Now she pretended that Peter was Pip, that Pip had come back to her, that he was asleep right there on her chest. Her sweet little baby.

It had never gone away. She'd gotten older and Phil had died but it had never gone away. She thought about it less, of course, which is to say she didn't think about it all the time like she used to. Back then it was always on her mind. She was always thinking, well, maybe this time next year things will be different. Maybe this time next year we won't be able to take that trip or we will have our hands full or we'll be needing that room.

She never had any trouble getting pregnant. No, her trouble was staying pregnant. Nobody knew why. One of the last doctors they saw, Dr. Marshall, had said "Why?" as he lifted his hands, palms facing up, looking like the priest asking for a blessing. But Dr. Marshall wasn't asking for anything; he asked "why?" and shook his head sadly to tell them not to expect an answer. There was no answer coming. It was a mystery.

For too long, Amanda Carey refused to believe this. There was always something to try: more vitamins, less vitamins. More exercise, less exercise. No fish, but maybe fish oil. Was it because of the fumes at the auto dealership? Or the crop-dusting planes her father used to brag about running behind, sucking in the pesticides, and look at him, he'd turned out fine. Was it the fever she had one June or the slip on the icy porch steps one March? Was it the stress of the Super Walmart or some disease spread by the biting flies?

It was a mystery to the last; at least she didn't think so much about it anymore. Although sometimes when she wasn't alert, her mind drifted down that familiar path, and she'd be jolted back: driving behind a smoke-spewing tractor, she might find herself thinking, *this isn't good for the baby, breathing that air might hurt the baby* and she'd hold her breath even before she knew what she was doing, before she remembered she was alone in her body, there was no one else there who could be hurt, that she was an old lady whose husband had been dead for almost twenty years.

The old ache and then the outrage.

She moved Peter to the side and rolled over.

PART II
YOU ONLY LIVE ONCE

The next morning, when Cinnamon came down to the kitchen, her aunt sat at a table crowded with boxes of cereal, her eyes flat and impassive as a cat's. Amanda Carey said, "good morning," then gestured at the coffee machine. Cinnamon helped herself.

"You sleep all right?"

"Yeah. I did. Thanks," Cinnamon lied.

"You're real skinny," her aunt observed as Cinnamon poured herself a bowl of Honey Nut Cheerios. "You're sure you're not on drugs?

"I just exercise a lot."

"Who did that to your eye?"

"My boyfriend." Cinnamon's hand went to her cheek. It was puffy and still sore. "I left him."

"Hmmm," her aunt said. A cat leapt to the table and Amanda Carey, without taking her eyes off Cinnamon, used a well-practiced forearm block to knock it swiftly away.

Cinnamon, conscious of being watched, poured the milk, and ate the Cheerios. They were even better than she expected.

"What's that there?" Amanda Carey flicked her hand in the direction of Cinnamon's neck.

"Oh." Cinnamon chewed and put down her spoon. She touched her neck and waved her hand. "A dumb tattoo.'"

"I can see that much," Amanda Carey said. "What's it say?"

Cinnamon pulled the hair up and back and twisted her head so her aunt could see. "YOLO." Her aunt registered no recognition. Cinnamon added, "It's an abbreviation for 'You only live once'."

Amanda Carey narrowed her eyes.

"I know it's stupid," Cinnamon said. "I got it when I was on drugs."

The first time Jason saw Cinnamon's tattoo, he remarked, "You only live once. And not for much longer if you don't make some fucking changes." He meant her drug use. She thought his remark very profound, but after a year together, those words took on another meaning; he saved her from one kind of danger but he himself presented another.

"I suppose it's true enough," her aunt said, sighing. "Personally, I don't know that I'd want that on my neck for the rest of my life. My life that I will only live once."

Cinnamon smiled at her, but Amanda Carey didn't smile back.

"As long as you're not doing drugs, you can stay here." The cat pounced on the table again and was again dispatched. "If you can stand the cats."

* * *

Amanda Carey thought the girl was too skinny, but Cinnamon claimed she wasn't addicted to drugs anymore. Now she was addicted to exercise. Cinnamon explained that she was "kinda famous" on the Internet. She made a living posting pictures and videos of herself exercising and drinking shakes and showing off her rangy muscles to inspire other people to do the same.

"They know you used to be a drug addict?" Amanda Carey asked bluntly.

"They do," Cinnamon took a sip of coffee. "It's actually part of the appeal. Like, part of the brand. It's aspirational. If I could do it, you can too. That sort of thing. Before and after posts are actually some of our most popular."

"You make money off this?"

"Yeah," she answered. "I mean, not a ton, but there's a lot of potential for expanding the business. Right now, we run ads on the site, but we make most of our money on sponsored posts. Basically advertising. Buy this and you can look like me." Cinnamon Lou smiled, sheepishly.

Why anyone would want to look like her niece, Amanda Carey didn't know, but she supposed that showed how old she was getting. She supposed her niece was the pink of perfection to people her own age.

* * *

They talked a little more and Cinnamon discovered even Amanda Carey wasn't sure how many cats there were in the house, that one, in particular, hadn't been seen in several years but Amanda Carey believed he was still around, just hiding. At first, she just had Frieda, but then another showed up under the porch one day—Marshmallow—and wouldn't you know it, she was pregnant. Amanda Carey meant to give the kittens away and even got rid of two of them, but there were still three left that nobody wanted (Baby Snooks, Peter, and Snickers). When she took them to get fixed, the vet persuaded her to take Snowball, a stray, promising free medical treatment. It went on like that: once people knew she was a sucker, they kept unloading their cats on her. When her sister-in-law, Cinnamon's aunt Dawn, moved to an apartment in Chicago, she left Patches and Midnight with Amanda Carey. Then a woman from church up and "rescued" a handful of cats from a kill-shelter but found she was allergic and couldn't get rid of them, so she dropped off Princess, Freddie, and Smurfette. Amanda Carey resolved to take no more cats, but both women knew that if, pressed, Amanda Carey would take more cats.

Once her house was paid off, Amanda Carey stopped working at the auto dealership in Disco. She never "darkened the doorway" of the Super Walmart, and, in fact, she didn't leave the house at all if she could help it.

Cinnamon asked if her aunt had a phone. Amanda Carey pointed at the telephone hanging next to the stove as though Cinnamon were a moron.

Cinnamon clarified. "I mean, like a cell phone?"

Amanda Carey snorted with disdain.

Hearing all of this, Cinnamon wondered again if her aunt's house in Miserable was such a great place to catch her breath after all, and not simply because her aunt leaned into the cat-lady thing a little too hard. Cinnamon was cold and couldn't imagine ever feeling not-cold again. She found it hard to breathe in the dusty house. And her aunt seemed mean and liable to kick her out at any minute. And finally, Cinnamon desperately wanted to get online and check Instagram, Although, she realized, maybe being unplugged for a bit wouldn't be the absolute worst thing.

Cinnamon washed her dishes and looked longingly at the Walmart through the little window above the kitchen sink.

"I'm sorry for just showing up, I didn't mean to...surprise you."

"Surprise me?" her aunt barked. "Nothing surprises me anymore."

Cinnamon didn't know how to respond. "Well." She looked at the Walmart.

Her aunt cleared her throat and followed Cinnamon's gaze.

"What do you need?" Amanda Carey asked. "You keep looking at that Walmart. What do you need?"

"I'd like to get some clothes," Cinnamon said. Draped in one of Amanda Carey's sweat suits, a deep purple with a light pink stripe running down each arm and leg, Cinnamon thought she looked like a Spice Girl, the athletic one, and not in a good way. "I guess I'll just go over and maybe get some warmer clothes. I know you don't go there," she added, turning to face her aunt.

"I don't go there," Amanda Carey said anyway.

"Yeah," Cinnamon said. "Well, can I pick you up anything?"

Amanda Carey shook her head again, no, and poured herself a cup of coffee. "Do you have money?"

"I have a little."

"I can give you some."

Cinnamon nodded. A little sob caught in her throat, although she didn't know why. "Thanks," she said. "I can pay you back. I just don't have it right now."

"It's all right," Amanda Carey said, waving a hand.

Cats swarmed around them, mewling, but Amanda Carey didn't seem to notice. She frowned as she looked past Cinnamon, out the window to the Walmart.

"All right," she said, as though she'd had enough of Cinnamon's haranguing. "Fine. I'll go with you. I suppose I could use a few things."

* * *

"Well," Amanda Carey said, as they walked briskly through the parking lot to the Walmart entrance. "Here we are."

"I remember when they were building this place. We were here that summer."

"You remember that?" Amanda Carey asked sharply.

"Yeah".

"What else do you remember?"

"Not much. I remember the house. I remember those biting flies."

"The flies are terrible in the summertime. They were especially bad that year. Because of the construction." Amanda Carey remembered those flies, too. They pursued a person. Just when you thought you'd lost one, it would be back again, tormenting you. And even when they weren't landing on you and biting at you, you thought you felt them, you hallucinated them. Those goddam flies. Amanda Carey had been particularly worried that summer, convinced they were carrying disease, worried they'd make her sick, that it would hurt the baby. And maybe they had. Although it mightn't have been the flies. It could've been lot of things. Anything, really.

It could have been the construction itself. It had broken Amanda Cary's heart to see those trees chopped down. She hadn't known that would happen. She hadn't known she would feel that way.

When they started chopping down those trees, she looked out the kitchen window and she could hear the trees scream. The stumps were still alive, their severed wounds open to the stinging air, and their roots clung to their loved ones under the earth, their mothers and fathers and sisters and brothers and children, who screamed too as they were cut down in turn.

Amanda Cary kept what she heard to herself. Phil would have told her to lie down, would have worried she was over-wrought. Maybe she was. The next week, after Carl and his family left, that very next week, she had another miscarriage. The last one and the worst one, too; she lost a lot of blood that time. They told her she had to stop after that one. They said that one almost killed her.

The Walmart's automatic doors burst open and they were struck with a blast of warm air. "Well, this will be fun," Cinnamon said.

And it was. Almost. Though fun might not be the word Amanda Carey would have chosen. It felt more like surrender, or maybe even relief. Amanda Carey surprised herself, giving up so easily after all these years. It hurt less than she thought it would to just say, "Fine," to drive down the driveway and make a left and then another left and arrive there, at the superstore. It was like every other store, just bigger and cheaper and so close, so conveniently located it was absurd she'd avoided it all these years.

And it turned out that you could get a haircut at Walmart. You could get your eyes checked. You could get a hot dog, a pop, and a bag of chips for $1.29. You could buy all the feathered cat toys and jumbo-size Snickers and plastic plates shaped like turkeys your heart desired and that Amanda Carey, to her surprise, found her heart desiring. She had to restrain herself. She wanted it all.

And so there she stood, on land that had once been hers but was now a warehouse for plastic shit made by exploited children in China, with a niece she barely knew but who looked like her once-best brother, if her brother had starred in porno-graphic movies, a heavy cart full of kitty litter and plastic crap and a lightness in her head and chest she hadn't felt before, or at least not in a long time.

"If you'll buy me some cleaning supplies, I'll clean your house for you," Cinnamon offered.

"My house is clean," Amanda Carey snapped.

"Oh," Cinnamon said, casting her eyes down, embarrassed. "I just meant."

"I keep it clean," Amanda Carey muttered. She shook her head. "I keep it fucking clean." She put a new mop in the cart. "I suppose it could use a good going over, though." She gestured for Cinnamon to take what she wanted.

They split up so Cinnamon could try on clothing. They reunited by the dairy case and Cinnamon put a pile of outdoor athletic gear in the cart. Amanda Carey noticed a bright-pink nylon jacket with a sticker that boasted "Freeze Defense Technology." There was not a real coat, though. Amanda Carey told the girl to go back and get one. "With that thin Florida blood," she said, almost smiling. "You're going to need a big one."

* * *

Cinnamon went out running right away.

Still weak and weird-feeling, she almost immediately found herself out-of-breath, but pushed herself forward in the cold, heavy air.

To exercise was to not-do-drugs. Jason taught her this. Jason, who rescued her, who supported her.

Before Jason, Cinnamon had been adrift. She'd been, they agreed, a loser. It wasn't entirely her fault, Jason sometimes assured her. Her circumstances hadn't been the best.

After Carl Louis died, Cinnamon's life was difficult in unfortunately predictable ways: Marisa was a wreck, money was tight, and a series of boyfriends, stepfathers, stepbrothers and even one step-grandfather attempted to, as Marisa primly phrased it, "interfere" with Cinnamon. Marisa successfully prevented the most egregious interferences; however, Cinnamon's adolescent and teenage years were a master course in studied indifference to suggestive and lewd remarks, as well as narrow escapes.

And while the schools Cinnamon attended were not what anyone would have called high-quality, things took a turn for the worse after Cinnamon's sophomore year of high school. She let her boyfriend take pictures of her naked and doing some other, sexual, stuff. It wouldn't have been a big deal if she hadn't broken up with him, and he hadn't spread the pictures far and wide. But he did and, although Cinnamon thought it was bullshit, she wound up being the one who got in trouble and was sent to an "alternative" high school, two busses away, that made little pretense of not being exactly what it was: an internment center for autistic, sociopathic, and/or profoundly impoverished teenagers, as well as, apparently, sluts.

In those days, Mrs. Costello was a bright spot in Cinnamon's otherwise depressing existence, as English teachers often are. Mrs. Costello gave Cinnamon her cell phone number, answered when Cinnamon called or texted, listened to Cinnamon's musings and complaints, and let Cinnamon sit and look at her phone while she ate lunch, every day, in Mrs. Costello's classroom, and thus prevented Cinnamon from leaving school without a diploma. At Mrs. C's urging, Cinnamon enrolled at Palm Beach State College, where she did surprisingly well, until she met a really nice guy who ate Alprazolam by the fistful and invited her to do the same. She didn't return to college the next semester.

The next several years were punctuated only briefly by short stints of sobriety. At 24, Cinnamon discovered she was pregnant. Although she didn't want to be pregnant (primarily because her then-boyfriend Charles was, by any measure, also a loser), Cinnamon was secretly relieved to know, despite all the poison she'd put into her body, it still basically worked. She was an optimist at heart. Although she pretended to consider abortion, she regarded pregnancy and motherhood as an opportunity to make the changes she really wanted to make. She knew others who'd gotten sober for their children. She wasn't still in touch with them, for obvious reasons, but she knew it was possible.

And for a little while, it looked like Cinnamon would do it, could do it. But not long after Ambria's birth, Cinnamon began to eat pills again, dipping a toe into muscle relaxers and moving rapidly back into Xanax's warm embrace and, as it became necessary, hating herself and smoking heroine.

Things went from bad to worse when, again, Cinnamon was undone by a cell phone camera: this time, some asshole took a video of her nodding off in the front seat of a car while Ambria slept in an infant carrier beside her. Because this was Florida, the video was quickly and widely distributed and Ambria was "removed."

To remove something, Cinnamon thought, was to take away an obstacle, a problem. You remove warts and garbage and illegally parked cars. But she discovered children, too, could be removed.

Ambria went to live with Charles' mother in Lake Worth. Cinnamon hadn't seen her in years.

* * *

Amanda Carey held Peter and watched out the front window as Cinnamon made her way down the driveway to go jogging. Wearing her new mittens and thick leggings and the Freeze

Defense jacket, she ran on the shoulder of the road through the dark November afternoon.

Amanda Carey had a headache. It was going to snow that night.

She worried about the girl the whole time she was gone.

* * *

On the fourth night, Cinnamon got into bed prepared to lie awake, freezing. She was tired and bloated, sluggish from all the processed foods Amanda Carey kept shoving in front of her —the Ronzoni pasta and Oscar Meyer cold cuts and Oreos— but even under several blankets, in her long underwear and socks, she couldn't get warm enough to sleep.

She considered closing the window. She'd opened it because even after having vacuumed and mopped, washed the bedding and the curtains, she could still smell cat stink, not just the shit and piss, but the smell of cat fur and breath and saliva. It was an impossible trade-off: her body longed for warmth, but her lungs needed the clean cold air. She covered herself with blankets, only her nose poking out, and imagined she was camping.

The only time she felt not-cold was in a hot shower or, absurdly, outside running in the freezing air, sweating underneath her Freeze Defense jacket. She had a hat that pulled over her chin, leaving only her nose and eyes exposed, although she would pull the cloth away from her mouth so she could breathe better, and because she often wept as she ran, her tears freezing on her eyelashes.

She'd get warm out on a run, but the minute she stopped moving, she'd be chilled again. The house was drafty, and Amanda Carey kept the thermostat on 65—65!—turning it down to 55 at night.

Cinnamon didn't see how a person could live here. She didn't see how she could.

But, she figured, better fat and cold in Wisconsin than hot and dead in Florida.

* * *

Awake in her bed, Amanda Carey resolved to return to the Walmart. She wanted those turkey-shaped plates after all.

The plates were the sectioned kind. You could put your meat in the body of the turkey, and then a side dish in one of each of the feathers: a feather for mashed potatoes and a feather for sweet potatoes and a feather for string beans and the smallest tail feather for cranberry. You could put your stuffing right there in the circle of the turkey's head.

The plates were durable too—a heavy plastic you could use year after year.

Amanda Carey thought about the cooking equipment in the basement she hadn't seen in years: a roasting pan, a meat thermometer. She thought about the food she needed to buy. A small turkey would be fine, and they could have the leftovers the next day and then maybe even make a bone stew, which Amanda Carey, just at that moment, remembered she loved.

* * *

Cinnamon's desperate longing to do drugs was worst at night.

At first, it had come as a bit of a surprise to her. Although she'd thought about drugs pretty regularly in the past years, she hadn't experienced a desire so acute in a long time. She wished she could eat a couple of Xanax to ward off the longing, to calm her nerves. With Xanax, you remained aware of your worries, but they were like distant clouds, nothing serious, charming, even. She used to like to take a few Xanax and drink beers and have some snacks, potato chips or chocolate-covered pretzels, and chain smoke before drifting into a delicious, happy sleep.

She thought of her aunt's cats snoozing in a patch of sun next to the radiator. If disturbed, they'd stretch and almost smile before falling back into their doze. Xanax sleep felt like that—a doze in the weak but warm November sun.

Remembering the sensation soothed her, but this wanting was exactly what Jason had warned her about. Giving into one temptation would lead to another and another. It's why he was strict about what she consumed, how much, and how often. He knew her better than she knew herself.

He'd lose his mind if he saw what she ate now. It almost made her laugh to think about it.

* * *

A booming explosion jolted Amanda Carey awake. The cats jumped off the bed and skittered across the wooden floor. Amanda Carey heard screaming from the bedroom. She moved swiftly and automatically, out of bed and down the hall.

Amanda Carey turned on the light in her niece's room. She found her sitting up in bed, pale and shaking. "He's here," the girl whimpered. "I'm so sorry."

"Who's here?" Amanda Carey asked. "No one's here. Calm down. That's just the stupid kids. The goddam little shits setting off firecrackers." As she said it, there was another crackle and boom, and a laugh, a fake laugh issued for their benefit, before the sound of flying gravel as the boys tore out of the driveway.

The girl cried out and covered her head. Amanda Carey got in the bed next to her and patted her roughly. "It's not anything," Amanda Carey told her again, slapping her back. "Just some stupid kids. They're gone now."

"I'm so sorry," Cinnamon said into her hands.

"There's nothing to be sorry for. It's just those damn kids. They won't be back again tonight. You don't need to worry." Amanda Carey felt impatient and angry. She wasn't angry at her niece, although it might have seemed so. She was angry with those goddammed motherfucking kids. It was a good thing she didn't have that shotgun in her hands, she thought to herself. A damn good thing.

The girl continued to shiver. Amanda Carey noticed the open window, a practice which she generally approved of, but which was ridiculous in this circumstance; the girl hadn't any body fat.

"You're shivering," she said. She rose and shut the window and then sat down beside her on the bed again.

Cinnamon continued to shake. She tugged the blankets up around her. "I'm okay," she said.

Amanda Carey resumed her awkward patting, hitting at the girl as though she were an old rug that needed cleaning. "Your boyfriend did a number on you."

Cinnamon nodded.

"My father used to beat my mother up," Amanda Carey said. "Only when he drank, though."

Cinnamon Lou didn't respond. She was wide-eyed and staring and still shaking, although maybe a little less.

"You're afraid of him yet," Amanda Carey said.

Cinnamon nodded. "But I don't think he knows where I am. I don't think he could find me here."

"Hmm," her aunt said. "Well, let him find you. This house is locked up tight. You're safe. I've got that shotgun," she said. "I know how to use it, too." Amanda Carey was quiet for a minute, thinking that Cinnamon was afraid of the wrong things. She'd be just fine in the farmhouse; it was running out on the shoulder of the road that was dangerous. She was just asking some drunk to run her over. Amanda Carey, however, did not say this out loud.

Instead, when Cinnamon didn't respond, Amanda Carey asked, "Carl never did anything like that, did he? Beat up your mother?"

Cinnamon shook her head, no.

"He was a good father?"

Cinnamon nodded. "Yes," she said. "He was."

"He never drank because he saw what it did to our father," Amanda Carey said. She ceased patting and put her hands in her lap. "Yep. Carl was my best brother"

Cinnamon looked at her aunt.

"Well, at least you're shut of him now. The bad boyfriend. What's his name?"

"Jason."

"Well, at least you don't have to worry about him anymore."

"Uh huh," Cinnamon pretended to agree. She squeezed her eyes shut.

* * *

Cinnamon, light-headed, couldn't stop her heart racing.

Time felt strange. She remembered when she was thirteen and she and Marisa were in a car accident. Some kid blew a stop sign on a side street and side-swiped them. In the smack and crunch and spinning, Cinnamon felt herself dislodged, knocked out of time. She felt at leisure to consider the situation. She thought of her father, of course, who had died in a car wreck six years before. She wondered, in those long seconds of spinning, if she would die too. She'd concluded that she and her mother would be okay because she felt the car stop spinning even while it was still in motion; she saw the past and the future and the present all at once. Some people said that time was a circle and Cinnamon could understand that, but in those moments she could also see that it was a line, the way the horizon is a line when you are living on the Earth and is only a circle when you are in outer space.

Those were thirteen-year old Cinnamon thoughts as she and her mother skidded and spun to a stop on someone's front lawn.

Shivering in a bed in Miserable, Wisconsin, Cinnamon again experienced a slowing of time. The cold air was painfully sharp in her nose, and her breathing seemed too loud. A cat, Peter, leapt up onto the bed and tried to settle on the front ridge of her leg, like a fat lady in the circus trying to walk a balance beam.

"What kind of person does that?" Cinnamon gasped. "Sets off firecrackers in the middle of the night to scare an old lady?"

"What kind of person?" Amanda Carey said. "A piece of shit person, that's what kind."

* * *

Amanda Carey congratulated herself. She had broached a difficult topic, addressed it head on, made some sort of sympathetic connection by sharing her own experiences, and issued words of comfort. It hadn't even been that hard. She could be a goddam therapist.

But it didn't feel right to leave her niece there, all alone, pale, and big-eyed and shaking. "Can I get you something?" Amanda Carey asked, her voice low and gravelly with sleep. She cleared her throat and tried to sound soothing. "A glass of water? Or do you want to watch TV?"

The girl shook her head, no. "I'm okay," she said. "I'm sorry. I just freaked out."

Amanda Carey nodded to let her know it was all right. "I'll call Jerry Beck tomorrow. I'll tell him to make those little shits cut it out." She scooted toward the edge of the bed, preparing to leave.

The girl looked at her, urgently. "Do you think you could stay here? Or maybe I could stay with you? Would you mind that?"

Amanda Carey pursed her lips. Then she shook her head. She wouldn't mind.

"Shove over," she told the girl.

* * *

With Amanda Carey in the room, the cats began to filter in and up onto the bed, some with more grace than others. Cinnamon would start to doze and a cat would walk across her or start kneading the quilt on her legs. Eventually they all settled down into warm lumps around her, several of them snoring, like the biggest warm lump beside her, Amanda Carey.

Even when the cats ceased their settling routines, Cinnamon remained awake and still, afraid any movement would stir them up again.

She thought about what Amanda Carey had said and what she had asked. She thought about describing what Jason did as "beating her up." That was accurate enough. He did that, yes. He beat her up.

She could tell her elderly aunt, "Yes, he beats me up." She could even say, "He slammed my head into the dashboard of his car." But she probably couldn't say, "He locked me in a closet once, for two days," or, "I think that sometimes he raped me."

She didn't think she could say those things out loud, but

then a part of her wondered if maybe her aunt actually meant that too. Maybe that's what Amanda Carey was talking about when she asked if Jason beat her up. Maybe she already knew.

* * *

Before she fell asleep, Amanda Carey wondered if this was one of those monkey's-paw scenarios, one of those dirty tricks the universe played. Back when she used to pray, she'd prayed—for years she had prayed—for a child. And now here was this girl.

Pip was the one she had held; Pip was her touchstone. But in her imagination, it had been daughters. Little bald infants wearing pink bows and little blonde girls in Mary Janes, arms full of baby dolls. Little girls who ripped their stockings at the church picnic. Puberty-stricken girls in braces, chubby again after years of skin-and-bones, terrible and sensitive but still sweet, still eager to go to the state fair with their parents, to go fishing with their father and to let their mother teach them about bodies and boys, washing yourself and putting on makeup.

The girl beside her was a mystery to Amanda Carey—and she wasn't a girl at all. She was one extremely screwed-up youngish-woman. Traumatized. That boyfriend had sure done a number on her. More than that, life had done a number on her.

And yet here she was. Amanda Carey wasn't sure she even liked her. But here she was.

* * *

Cinnamon woke in the dark to find a small cat asleep in the crook of her arm, settled the way Ambria used to when she was a little baby. Cinnamon had been told several times by nurses and social workers that you weren't supposed to let babies sleep in the bed with you, but she'd done it anyway; it was the only time Ambria really slept, for hours at a time, without stirring. It was the most natural thing in the world, Cinnamon thought. Of course a sleeping baby wants to be held. Doesn't everybody?

She could hear Amanda Carey breathing beside her.

PART III

ASSISTED LIVING

Amanda Carey didn't have to call Jerry Beck, because they ran into him at the Walmart the next day.

Amanda Carey saw him in the grocery section pushing a cart full of frozen meats. Cinnamon was looking at produce and Amanda Carey pulled Jerry aside.

"It's nice to see you out and about," Jerry said amiably.

"Those goddam kids are setting off firecrackers in my yard, Jerry. You better tell those little shits to cut it out," Amanda Carey hissed.

Jerry frowned and nodded. "I've had a car parked by your place most nights this week."

"Well, you musn't've been there last night because the fuckers woke us up and almost gave her," she nodded accusatorily in the direction of Cinnamon Lou, "a heart attack."

Jerry followed her gaze over to Cinnamon. "She feeling better?"

Amanda Carey scowled back at him.

Jerry asked, "Is she going to stick around for a while?"

Amanda Carey shrugged, "Hmmm." She watched Jerry Beck watching Cinnamon and it occurred to her that he probably thought her niece was something else. Oh, she was hot stuff, if a bag of bones with hair extensions was your thing.

Amanda Carey imagined a scenario in which Jerry Beck fell in love with her niece, and the two of them got married and moved into the farmhouse. Jerry—who was divorced—already had a son, but the two might have their own children yet, and maybe Cinnamon could get back the other child too. The farmhouse had five bedrooms. Right now, they were mostly occupied by cats.

But Amanda Carey let herself, just for a minute, imagine something else.

* * *

"What about the daughter?" Amanda Carey asked, running the electric opener around a can of Hormel chili. The buzz alerted all cats not already present. Some skittered, some flew, some sauntered into the kitchen.

"What?"

"Your daughter. Where is she?"

Cinnamon picked up the enormous Baby Snooks and held him with his front paws resting on her shoulder.

"Ambria," Cinnamon said at last. "She lives with her father's mother."

Cinnamon watched as Amanda Carey let the name pass without remark.

"It's not for you, you idiots," Amanda Carey barked at the assembled cats. She opened a second can, nudged Frieda out of the way with her foot, and dumped both cans of chili into a pot on the stove. "Do you think you'll get her back?"

Cinnamon chewed her lip. The cat was fussing, and she

tried to put him down gently, but he landed with a thump on the kitchen floor. "I wanted to," she said.

* * *

Amanda Carey watched as her niece sniffled miserably. "I think she's probably better off without me," Cinnamon said. "I know that's what parents always said when they take off and leave their kids with someone else. But look at me. I've messed up my whole life. I don't know if I'll ever be able to..." She stopped talking.

Amanda Carey, who regretted having said anything at all if it was going to result in this kind of scene, washed and dried her hands and then handed Cinnamon a paper towel to wipe her nose with. "You can still get her back. Once you get your life in order."

Cinnamon, who had her daughter's name tattooed on her breast, above her heart, wiped her face recklessly with the paper towel.

When Cinnamon didn't respond, Amanda Carey tsk-ed impatiently. "You'll get back on your feet. Maybe it doesn't seem like it right now, but you'll get back on your feet."

Cinnamon sighed, her shoulders slumped pathetically. "There's a house," she began.

Amanda Carey listened.

It turned out the son-of-a-bitch had Cinnamon sign all the paperwork for some god-forsaken McMansion which he'd immediately stopped payment on. The house was in foreclosure, and this Jason-person had some sort of long-game scheme predicated on the bank saying "chicken" and selling the house back to him for a fraction of its original cost. Amanda Carey wasn't clear on the scheme, in part because Cinnamon wasn't apparently all-that informed about it herself, but the bottom line was that he had Cinnamon over an economic barrel. He controlled the money. He ruined her not-good-to-begin-with credit and saddled her with a half-a-million-dollar mortgage.

Apparently Cinnamon was the face—or rather the body—of this so-called business they ran. The cash cow, it would seem. Amanda Carey wondered if this Jason planned to come up to Wisconsin, to try to get Cinnamon back.

And Amanda Carey could see how it could happen, how sweet, dumb, cow-eyed Cinnamon would take the loser back.

Amanda Carey thought, but didn't say, that maybe she could help Cinnamon out, money-wise. Maybe together, they could talk to the bank, explain the situation, make an arrangement.

Phil had been good with money, with investments and whatnot.

Amanda Carey sometimes allowed herself to wonder how things might have been different if Phil had lived. She thought about that as she and Cinnamon ate their chili dinners in front of the television. She shooed Peter off the coffee table. For starters, Phil wouldn't have tolerated all these goddamn cats.

What would Phil have made of Cinnamon? She cut a sideways glance at the girl, who wore a hat and a scarf and had a blanket over her knees. Seemed a little dramatic, although the girl did have that Florida blood. Amanda Carey nevertheless took the bundling up personally; what did Cinnamon expect? It was goddam Wisconsin, and she had nudged the thermostat up to 70 that day, although it almost caused her physical pain.

If Phil were here, he'd turn the place into a sauna. Cinnamon would have Phil wrapped around her little finger, that was for sure. He'd been so sweet with Cinnamon when Carl had brought his family out to visit that summer. Cinnamon innately knew to ask Phil for a quarter for the gumball machine, to walk her out to the field to watch the construction vehicles, for just one more story before bed. And he obliged. He always obliged.

They only saw her once after that, when they went down to Florida for the funeral.

That poor little girl. After the burial, they all went to an Italian restaurant in a strip mall in Boynton Beach. Cinnamon wore a huge, lurid black velvet bow that matched her black velvet dress and sat at a table with three or four other children, all huddled around a hand-held video game. Amanda Carey wondered: is this what the girl will remember about the day of her father's funeral? Playing Super Mario or whatever the fuck it was? The idea made Amanda Carey so violently sad that she excused herself and fled the restaurant. Outside the air was heavy and warm; she threw up in the garbage can in front of a dollar store.

Cinnamon put her half-eaten bowl of chili on the coffee table.

"Something the matter?" Amanda Carey asked.

"Just not used to this food," Cinnamon said, in a way that Amanda Carey wasn't sure about. "I mean, I'm just used to eating more fruits and veggies and stuff."

Amanda Carey rolled her eyes, offended. She didn't even like chili. She'd bought it because she thought it was, if not health food, maybe healthier, what with the beans and all. She turned, frowning, back to the television.

* * *

It was a relief to tell her aunt about the house.

It was a relief because when she was out running, she went over it in her head and usually arrived at the same place: at the precipice of surrender. It would be so much easier just to go back to him.

He'd be angry but he'd be happy to have her back, and she wouldn't have to deal with the house stuff anymore, or worry because jobs required background checks these days, or wake up with her heart pounding because the dread was the worst feeling, worse than anything else.

Her aunt listened, impassive. She seemed pissed, but that was her default attitude. And she asked for more details, which Cinnamon couldn't provide and then she said, "All right. Well."

Cinnamon watched as her aunt turned the whole thing over in her mind. It made her feel less-alone. Like when a officious IT guy on the phone makes it clear he thinks you're a moron but he'll assume your problem as a personal challenge and he's going to resolve it no matter what.

Not telling her aunt about the house had felt like a lie, as though Cinnamon was pretending she could up and leave whenever she wanted. It was a relief now that Amanda Carey understood how profoundly messed up Cinnamon's life was.

The chili was disgusting. Cinnamon ate it anyway. At least it had beans in it.

* * *

The remark about the food stuck in Amanda Carey's craw. It smacked of ingratitude. Even snobbishness. Where the hell did the girl think she was going to get fresh fruits and vegetables in Wisconsin in November? Did she expect her to pay six dollars for a carton of mealy strawberries at the Walmart?

Although, possibly, the girl had a point. Amanda Carey thought she could stand to eat more apples or maybe a grapefruit now and then. And Cinnamon had had a hard time of it. It wouldn't kill her to try to make the girl comfortable. And she decided to add carrots to the Thanksgiving menu. They'd have both string beans and carrots, see how she liked that. There weren't enough turkey feathers on the plate to accommodate so many sides, but you could mix two vegetables together.

Cinnamon really wasn't much trouble at all. Amanda Carey hardly saw her most days; when the snow or the cold kept the girl from running outdoors for hours on end, she did loud, pounding exercises in her room, or she went to the library and looked herself up on the Internet. When she was home, she cleaned, endlessly. And it was nice to have the company, in the evenings, especially, when they watched *Jeopardy* and *Wheel*. Amanda Carey put on *Law and Order: SVU*, a few times, but stopped when she noticed that, though she tried to hide it, Cinnamon found the show upsetting and embarrassing. All those husbands murdering their wives and girlfriends must have hit too close to home.

Cinnamon Lou remained a bit of a mystery to Amanda Carey. Amanda Carey wasn't sure Cinnamon had a sense of humor; she laughed at serious things and didn't laugh at funny ones. But she was good company, all the same. And she was nice to the goddamn cats.

* * *

In the morning, Cinnamon tried to run out the dream she'd had the night before, a dream in some ways worse than the nightmares because she woke up longing for Jason: he'd come up to Wisconsin to get her and everyone agreed it was time for her to go back to him. And she wanted it so badly too, but she also knew, in the way you know things in dreams, that once they left Amanda Carey's house, he would hurt her, maybe kill her. And yet leaving with him was irresistible.

She ran and thought of the dream and thought about the early days when it had been such a relief to surrender to him.

Jason actually stole Cinnamon away—that's what they always said—from his own cousin, a guy named Xavier who Cinnamon had dated primarily because he liked the same drugs she did.

One night, Xavier and Cinnamon ran into Jason at a street fair in Delray Beach. He was manning a booth for the gym where he was a personal trainer, giving out free glow sticks, personal training coupons, and reusable water bottles made of cheap, probably toxic, plastic. Jason and Xavier embraced in the strobe lights and Xavier introduced Cinnamon.

"When you're done checking out the fair, come back around," Jason said, staring at Cinnamon. He moved in close so she could hear him over the music. "Let's hang out." He turned to his cousin. "Yo, X, I am totally gonna steal your girlfriend."

"Fuck you, man," Xavier said and lamely punched Jason's bulging bicep.

"I'm totally serious." Jason gazed again at Cinnamon. "You're fucking mine," he said to her. And she believed him.

* * *

While Cinnamon was out running, Amanda Carey called her lawyer, Gary, and left a message. Next, she called the Credit Union and got no help from the moron she had the pleasure of speaking to there. She called Trinity Lutheran and talked to Sue, who gave her the number for a women's resource center, but when she called that number, she got a message to contact them through their website.

Amanda Carey grudgingly admitted to herself it would be convenient to have a computer at home. She wasn't one of those doddering old idiots who didn't know how to use one; she had plenty of experience at the auto dealerships. So maybe she'd pick up a tablet or something like that. It would be easy to get one over at the Walmart. Something to think about at least.

* * *

Cinnamon knew that missing Jason was part of the "cycle of abuse." The first time she saw the image—a circle with arrows to indicate the swirling, dizzying, repetitive nature of abusive relationships—it took her breath away. She didn't think she was a genius, but she hadn't known that she was a cliché.

She learned about the circle at a support group she secretly attended once, a year earlier. She told Jason she was helping her mother sort out her closets. She went to Marisa's, left her phone in her car there, and borrowed Marisa's car to drive to a facility that looked like a warehouse in Margate, where she was buzzed through multiple doors and escorted to a conference room where a dozen sad and angry women sat, waiting to tell the moderator how impossible their lives were. They relayed their stories in shorthand and in gasps, often concluding with the inevitability of their own helplessness: "I don't have any money," one spat. "The kids," another sobbed. "A restraining order will just piss him off more," one explained, exhausted.

Cinnamon herself was unable to speak and sat, shaking, throughout the meeting.

She discovered she wasn't alone, but she wasn't in very good company either, and found both comfort and shame in the echoes of her own story in theirs. She felt foolish that she'd believed her relationship with Jason was anything other than common and predictable.

It was a relief to get back home, where Jason, suspecting nothing, was cheerfully steaming broccoli to go with the salmon he was baking. He embraced her, said she looked fan-fucking-tastic in that dress, asked if it was new.

In that moment, she'd needed him to love her so much he would always act like this, always adore her, never hit her again. She didn't want to be like the other women in the group. She would be different because Jason would be different.

She knew she was a cliché, but there were worse things you could be.

* * *

Amanda Carey had forgotten all about dessert. "I should have bought things to make a pie," she said to Cinnamon. "I didn't even think of it."

"That's okay," Cinnamon assured her. "I could run over to the Walmart tomorrow and pick one up."

"I suppose you'll have to." Amanda Carey frowned at the thought of a store-bought pie for Thanksgiving. "If I'd thought of it, I would have made one today."

"We don't need pie. There'll be more than enough food."

"Well, it's nice to have pie on Thanksgiving," Amanda Carey groused.

"Whatever you want to do," Cinnamon said. "You're done with that?" She nodded at her aunt's plate on the coffee table.

"Yes," Amanda Carey said. "Thank you."

On her way to the kitchen, Cinnamon looked out a front window. "Cop car parked out there."

"Good," Amanda Carey said. "That'll be Jerry Beck."

"Sure is cold tonight," Cinnamon said.

Amanda Carey grunted.

"You got a thermos? I'll bring him out some coffee."

* * *

Like many people, Cinnamon was generally uncomfortable around law enforcement. To be fair, Cinnamon had met kind officers, men who looked the other way as Cinnamon, clearly high, stumbled down the street, who told her to get home safe when they woke her up to clear out the bar. A female cop, once, gave Cinnamon her card and told her to call, any time. But there were three cops down in Miami, one night, who hadn't been so nice. And there were countless unsmiling state troopers who issued tickets or put the plastic cuffs on so tight she couldn't feel her fingers, or made remarks to let her know how little they thought of her, how terrible they hoped things would be for her. As though she chose to become a drug addict to annoy and inconvenience them.

Even after getting clean she was nervous around cops because in the end, they were magicians: they could take a little problem and turn into a big one. Or they could take a big one and make it disappear. The outcome wasn't about you, it was usually about whether they were good people or bad or whether they were in a good mood or bad or whether they wanted to get home or wanted the overtime. It wasn't usually about you.

Cinnamon could tell Officer Beck wasn't the bad kind. He emanated a kind of long-suffering good cheer when Amanda Carey swore at him and he smiled impassively at Cinnamon, to communicate he was not unconcerned, but he also wasn't looking to involve himself anywhere he wasn't wanted.

Cinnamon pushed open the front door, tucked her chin, and dove into the cold air. Snow swirled, glittering in the porch light and streetlamps.

Officer Beck saw her coming. The window of the SUV slid silently down.

Cinnamon jogged across the street. "Hi!" She held out the

thermos. "We thought you might like this. It's coffee mixed with hot chocolate."

He raised his eyebrows and took the drink. "You didn't have to do that."

"Thanks for watching the house," Cinnamon said. "It makes us feel a lot better knowing you're keeping an eye on things."

"You bet," Jerry said. He unscrewed the thermos and sniffed. "How's it going in there? You getting along all right with Amanda Carey?"

"Yeah." Cinnamon smiled. "She's real sweet."

Jerry, who had taken a sip from the thermos, gagged. "Sweet?" He laughed. "I'm sorry. Just not the word that springs to mind when I think of your aunt."

Cinnamon smiled. "Well, there's sweetness there,'" She tilted her head in a conciliatory way. "Underneath. Like, I see her nudging up the thermostat when she thinks I'm not looking. Cause she's knows it's cold for me."

"I'm glad to hear it." Jerry nodded. "This sure is delicious," he added, holding up the thermos.

The air from inside the vehicle was warm and smelled of air freshener. Talking to Jerry Beck, Cinnamon felt, was like pressing your palm against something smooth and substantial.

"Well, Happy Thanksgiving," Cinnamon said, moving to leave. "And thanks again for watching the house. It helps. You know," she waved her hugely-mittened hands in the air. "With everything."

"Happy Thanksgiving," Jerry replied. He opened his mouth to say something else, but Cinnamon had already turned to go back to the house. She sprinted across the street and up the small hill of the front yard.

As Cinnamon's sneaker hit the first step, Frieda leapt out from where she'd been concealed under the porch, as though she were a predator and Cinnamon a mouse. Cinnamon startled and almost tripped, but when she registered the cat, now licking a paw as though the attack had never happened, she laughed, scooped her up and brought her indoors.

* * *

Overnight, the weather turned mild. In the morning, the girl went running and Amanda Carey got the turkey going in the oven.

Amanda Carey set the table with the new turkey plates. When Cinnamon Lou saw them, she clapped. "These are perfect!" she exclaimed. "They're adorable."

Amanda Carey smiled and nodded. They were adorable.

* * *

Cinnamon called Marisa to wish her a happy Thanksgiving.

"Do you need me to send more money, baby?" her mother asked.

"I'm okay," Cinnamon said. She ran Marshmallow's ear through her fingers. "Aunt Amanda Carey's been really generous. I don't know. Maybe I'll get a job or something? I mean, I don't know what I can do. But maybe, like, a secretary job? Or waitressing?"

"But when do you think you'll come back?" her mother asked. "Are you ever coming back?"

"I am, but not yet." Cinnamon lowered her voice. "He hasn't come to your house again, has he?" She knew he hadn't, her mother would have led with this information, but she needed to confirm it, needed to know for sure.

"No, baby, he hasn't come back. Do you think maybe he's moved on?"

"Maybe. I hope so."

She did hope so. She'd thought about that on her run, wondered if Jason had found a new girlfriend and wondered if he beat her up too. She didn't want him to, didn't want another girl to suffer or anything like that. But if he didn't—if he got together with someone else and then, like, started therapy or just got it under control or simply didn't feel like hitting or humiliating or choking this new person—maybe it had been Cinnamon's fault after all.

That's what she had thought as she ran that morning, crying, her tears sliding down her cheeks and falling to the wet asphalt where they mixed with dirty snow and rock salt.

* * *

Amanda Carey was pleased with how the turkey came out. The sides also looked good. She wound up making potatoes and sweet potatoes, some biscuits, cranberries, string beans, and the carrots too.

They sat down to eat at the table but left the football game on in the living room, the ambient noise recalling for Amanda Carey, other, earlier days.

With all the food laid out before them and the pie on the buffet, Amanda Carey felt moved to clear her throat and say, "Happy Thanksgiving, niece. I'm glad you're here."

Cinnamon started to cry and, as usual, Amanda Carey honestly had not the slightest idea why. Maybe she'd been moved by Amanda Carey's almost-grace or maybe she just missed her old life. Or maybe Amanda Carey thought, it was a bit of both. She reached across the table and patted the girl's arm. "All right, there," she said.

She wanted to tell Cinnamon that she'd overheard her on

the phone, that the girl should get a job if she wanted one—
Amanda Carey still knew some people over at the dealership—
but she didn't have to. Amanda Carey didn't mind paying for
things. Cinnamon should just rest a little longer, take her time
getting back on her feet.

She wanted to tell the girl she was thinking about getting a
tablet or something, get the Internet and all of that, maybe they
could pick one out together over at the Walmart. Of course, she
didn't want hysterics and you never knew how the girl would
react. Maybe it would be a surprise. Maybe it would be something nice for Christmas.

* * *

There was a thump at the front of the house. At first,
Cinnamon thought it was Frieda, who sometimes flung herself
against the door until let in. But Frieda usually came to the
back.

There was a second thump, and then a third.

"What the hell is that?" Amanda Carey asked from the
kitchen

Cinnamon was closest to the front door, having just come
down the stairs, but couldn't bring herself to open it.

There was another thump and then the slamming of car
doors.

"Well, open it," Amanda Carey commanded, charging into
the front room. She saw Cinnamon standing there, frozen and
pale, and she went and opened the door herself, revealing the
empty porch set against the gray November sky.

"Goddam little shits," Amanda Carey growled when she
registered the yellow ooze sliding down her front door.

"You calm down," Amanda Carey said, turning to Cinnamon. "It's just goddamn eggs."

Although her aunt had literally screamed at her not to clean it up, Cinnamon, still shaken, got a bucket of warm soapy water and a dish rag and cleaned off the front door and porch. It was fine, she told her aunt. Better to do it now when it wasn't too cold out.

Her aunt called the police station, several times, while Cinnamon cleaned the front door, crying silently, crying with relief because it had not been Jason but also crying because this meanness toward her aunt cut her in two. She knew it was just stupid kids, but she couldn't believe some boys hated old Amanda Carey so much they'd egg her house on Thanksgiving. It was so mean. It was just so fucking mean. What was wrong with people?

They watched *Jeopardy*. Amanda Carey knew many answers and murmured them forcefully, so Cinnamon could hear.

Cinnamon was appropriately impressed. "You should be a contestant."

Amanda Carey shook her head, no. "They don't let mean old ladies on television."

Cinnamon didn't disagree. "Well," she said instead. "You're not that old."

"Hmmm," Amanda Carey said. "They don't let gray-hairs on television."

Cinnamon smiled. "You could dye your hair."

"Why would I do a thing like that?" Amanda Carey snapped back.

"All the women in Florida dye their hair," Cinnamon said, unperturbed. She worried a spot on her scalp before plucking out some of her own hair. She laid the long extension on her lap and one of the cats—Snickers—started licking at it.

"Well, this isn't Florida," Amanda Carey huffed.

"That's true," Cinnamon said, in a way that Amanda Carey wasn't sure about.

The show started and they didn't talk again until the next commercial break, at which point Amanda Carey asked, "You think you'll stay on here?" She kept her eyes on the television—an ad for Zantac—so as to not betray her longing.

She saw, in her peripheral vision, that Cinnamon shrugged.

"I guess I'll have to go back eventually," she said. "There's the house. I'll have to deal with that."

Amanda Carey would have liked to have said: "We can figure that out together. I've been talking to my lawyer. Shit, I'll pay off the goddam mortgage. You can stay on with me here. I like having you. Sometimes you make me unaccountably angry, but I like you, Cinnamon. You don't seem to have the best sense and you've made some awful mistakes. But. You've been nice to my goddam cats. And maybe it is blood; maybe there is something in me that recognizes something in you. Because I'd like you to stay. I don't want you to leave."

Amanda Carey was vaguely aware that maybe if her life had been different in a few important ways, she would have been able to say all that. But it hadn't and she couldn't. Besides, there would only be one or two more commercials before "Final Jeopardy" came on.

Instead, Amanda Carey said, "Don't let Snickers eat that. He'll choke." Then she added, "Do you want to have some ice cream?"

"That sounds good," Cinnamon said. "I'll get it. You want the pistachio, right?"

Amanda Carey nodded.

"You know," Cinnamon said, rising, "You could always come back to Florida with me."

Amanda Carey didn't say anything in response. She kept her eyes on the television, which showed another old person commercial: a fit, white-haired couple smiling at each other on a sailboat.

* * *

The next day, Cinnamon went to the library. She used one of the laptops to email Marisa and googled around to see if there were any local job listings. There wasn't much.

She used her dummy account to check Instagram, where she saw, after weeks of silence, Jason had posted a picture they'd taken months ago: Cinnamon doing a handstand at sunrise on Delray Beach. Beneath the picture was a long caption explaining to their fans that Jason needed to be "honest" and that Cinnamon had disappeared. He added that he hated to tell them this, but "Cin relapsed" and he was so worried about her. Interspersed in his rambling and self-pitying tirade were veiled threats, promises to "find Cin" and to "take care of her."

Four hundred replies followed his post: prayer hands and well-wishes (*so worried love u so much*), but also ill-wishes (*i knew it* and *maybe if you gave that anorexic bitch a sammich now and then* and *I hope she kills herself*).

Cinnamon, who even as she did it had the self-deprecating awareness that she couldn't seem to learn a fucking lesson, posted a reply. She used the laptop camera to take a picture of herself. She took a couple, actually, trying to find a flattering angle. She picked the one that looked least like she was using drugs, although she appeared a bit haggard and greasy-haired in all of them. She put a gauzy filter on it, logged into their account and wrote her own message. Her post began,

Community, its a lie i am not using i did not relapse. the truth is that i am running for my life. For years, Jason has been abusing me

and went on in her own rambling tirade, filled with allusions to, although not specifics about, Jason's depravity and sadism, before asking for prayers and support and assuring her followers she loved them, she lived for them, she would return, if not for herself, for them.

She didn't hesitate before posting. It was as natural as exhaling. She only had to wait a few seconds before the first responses began to flicker in, like the first drops of rain before a much-needed storm and soon she was showered with messages of adoration and affirmation. They were rooting for her. They loved her *so much.*

It was a physical relief, the scratching of an itch, the moment the painkiller kicks in, the stepping into a hot bath after a cold run. Cinnamon basked. She basked and smiled at the screen, but then something occurred to her and she sat straight up. Her breath caught in her chest. Her heart beat in her head.

She hadn't thought she was a genius, not even before Jason's punches knocked her down a few IQ points. But that moment confirmed for her that she was, in fact, stupid. She didn't know what was wrong with her. She was just so fucking stupid.

She googled: "Instagram location trace"

She googled, "Can you find someone Instagram post"

She hadn't tagged a location. And regardless of what he said about himself, Jason wasn't that smart. He probably wouldn't be able to figure out how to see where the picture was taken, to trace it to Wisconsin. Even if he saw she was in

Wisconsin, he wouldn't know where her aunt's house was, probably wouldn't remember her telling him she had family in Miserable.

She logged off and left the library, not responding to the friendly librarian who chirped, "Stay warm out there now!" as Cinnamon pulled open the heavy, glass door. It was snowing, something it did every day, something that still delighted Cinnamon, Florida-girl that she was, but she hardly noticed as she walked back to the farmhouse. She even forgot she had driven herself to the library, thinking about how stupid she was; she deserved whatever happened to her. She was so fucking stupid.

PART IV
BITING FLIES

Jason had a lot of time to think during some of his long runs or swims or bike rides and the thing he liked to most to think about was himself: what kind of person he was, what kind of person other people thought he was, how he looked, and what other people thought about how he looked. His conclusions were generally positive: Jason knew he looked great; he knew other people thought he looked great. He thought he was pretty funny and cool and smart, and he was fairly certain other people thought he was funny and cool and smart too.

He was the kind of person who would say things like, "Look, I might not be the smartest guy," before floating out an opinion which he believed clearly demonstrated that he really was the smartest guy after all.

The day Cinnamon resurfaced on Instagram, Jason was feeling pretty fucking smart. It had taken him literally fifteen minutes to find the dumb cunt's location—and he wasn't even all that tech-savvy. *I mean*, he might say to someone if they'd asked, or maybe even if they didn't ask, *don't get me wrong. I know my way around a computer*. He might add that, *The thing most people don't realize, is that computers, phones, all of it, they're tools. And we make tools work for us, not the other way around.*

Tools—that was Jason's thing. Instruments. Making things work for you; that was his idea, his "intervention." It informed all aspects of their business plan. *The body,* he explained endlessly to Cinnamon and to their followers, *is an instrument. It is a tool for you to get what you want. So, now's the time to decide. What do you want?*

The body is a tool. The computers are tools. The gear and supplements are tools. The puppy, if they had wound up getting one after all, would have been a tool.

And people fucking loved it. They loved the instrumental-ization of the body. He was smart enough to know he hadn't, like, invented the idea. People had been talking forever about bodies as "temples" and bodies as "machines." But his followers just ate up the way he presented it and the way Cinnamon embodied it. Some of their most popular videos featured him barking at her like a drill sergeant; there was even one with her crying—not staged—where he got so disgusted he said, "So, give up," and then she pushed and did three more reps. After, she was still crying, but with gratitude and shit.

Some people posted that it looked abusive, but in general, people liked to see a woman bossed around. Punished, even. He took zero shit from Cinnamon. And he got results. All you had to do was look at her to see it.

Cinnamon's body was a tool for her to get what she wanted, but it was also a tool for Jason to get what he wanted. And that was partly why he felt so bad about what had happened, although it really hadn't been that big of a deal. It wasn't like he had kicked her ass or anything. But he shouldn't have slammed her head into the dashboard the way he had. He shouldn't have done that. He honestly hadn't wanted that to happen.

He just got overwhelmed. He was pissed about a letter he got from the bank that morning. So sure, he was driving too fast. When he pulled into the parking lot and slammed on the breaks, the coffee she was holding spilled out through the little hole on top and ran down over her hand and she said, "What the fuck, babe?" so critical-like, and then his hand had shot out and, like swatting a fly, like scratching an itch, wham, her face cracked against the dashboard. He didn't mean to do it as hard as he did. The coffee cup dropped straight down to the floor of the car, splashing coffee everywhere.

He apologized almost immediately. "Oh, shit, babe, I'm sorry," he said. He kind of laughed. He felt almost embarrassed.

She sat up and blinked and her head wobbled on her neck a bit, looking the way old cartoon characters do when they've been swatted and are about to pass out. But she didn't pass out. She looked at the coffee and then looked up at him and then her mouth turned down like she was going to cry. She said, "I hate you" and jumped out of the car and ran into the apartment.

Even then, he was ready to apologize, but she locked herself in the bathroom which, fuck her, whatever. He yelled through the door that he was taking her car and that his car better be fucking straight when he got home.

He had back-to-back clients scheduled that afternoon, so he headed over to the gym, thinking that if Cinnamon's face didn't look too bad, she would probably show up there too, after she cooled down. But she didn't and by seven, after his last client, he started to feel guilty again. She was so fucking annoying, but he really didn't mean for it to be so hard. He meant it to be more life a biff, or a like, a gentle slap upside the head, really.

And if her face looked bad, it would be such a pain in the

ass. They'd scheduled a not-yet-discovered Miami photographer for the coming Wednesday; it was going to be such a pain in the ass to have to reschedule. He wished he'd gotten a better look at the damage before Cinnamon had locked herself in the bathroom.

He took a detour on the way home and stopped by Lululemon. He bought her a five hundred dollar warm-up—he was hopeful about maybe arranging a sponsorship with them—and then he stopped at the gas station and bought her a pack of Twinkies. That was like a joke; it was her favorite treat from when she was a kid. It would be okay to indulge this one time, he'd say. She'd probably puke it up anyway, or at least he might suggest that it wouldn't be a terrible idea to do so. Anyway, it had been super-sweet of him.

But when he arrived home, his car was still there. He looked in the passenger window and saw the coffee cup just lying there on the floor of the car; the cunt hadn't cleaned it up.

And then when he went inside, he saw that she wasn't at home. He accessed "find my phone" and it showed that she was nearby, probably at the Starbucks in the shopping center down the road. He felt a little relieved, because she wouldn't have left the house if her face was really that bad. But it pissed him off that he had gone out of his way for her and she hadn't cleaned up the fucking car. She could forget about the Twinkies.

But then it was nine o'clock and she was still at the fucking Starbucks. He called, but she didn't answer, which meant she was dead-fucking-intent on being a cunt. There was a small part of him that thought, *oh, shit*. Like, what if she went to Starbucks and then passed out from a concussion or something? What if they'd taken her to the hospital and left her phone behind?

He took her car down to the shopping center and his phone showed that she was, in fact, in the Starbucks, but when he walked inside, she wasn't there. He pinged her phone and —nothing.

He was kind of astounded. He had to sit down for a minute.

When he recovered himself, he marched into the bathroom and pinged it again and there it fucking was, on this little shelf above the toilet. Her phone and fucking Apple watch too.

He left the Starbucks and drove by her mother's house. The lights were out and there wasn't a car in the carport, which was kind of suspicious.

He stopped by again the next day and Marisa's car still wasn't there, but her boyfriend's car was.

"Where's your car?" he asked when Marisa opened the door.

"It's in the shop," she said, quick and nervous, her eyes darting around. He pushed his way in. Her weird old-man boyfriend sat on the couch in the next room, watching.

"Where's Cin?"

"I don't know where Cin is," Marisa lied, her eyes wide, her words clipped. "Why? Is she not at home?"

"Don't fucking lie to me, Marisa," Jason had said. "I'm worried about her. I'm

afraid she's relapsed."

Marisa's failure to react with surprise or dismay confirmed for Jason that she knew exactly where her fucking daughter was.

In the past, Jason had always enjoyed the way Marisa cowered and whimpered around him; you could tell he impressed her and scared her too. But that day she tried to act all tough, saying, "It's time for you to leave now, Jason," her voice shaking. Jason looked at the old man, all jowls and owl-eyes, and then back at Marisa.

Jason laughed in her face. "You're mother of the year, aren't you, Marisa?"

Fuck her, he thought. He didn't even need her. Her dumb cunt daughter would turn up.

And turn up she did. He posted about a possible relapse with an absolute certainty that, if she hadn't actually relapsed, it would totally piss her off. He knew it would flush her right out. And he figured if it didn't, it was probably because she was fucking zonked out of her mind somewhere, which might actually be the outcome he preferred.

But there she was, looking like crap and posting self-righteous bullshit slandering him. Called him a fucking abuser. She was so full of shit. He saved her life. Sure, he was hard on her, but she was free to leave if she didn't like it. And he felt bad about the thing in the car, he definitely felt shitty about that, but he had apologized.

She knew he had a temper when she met him. It wasn't like he tricked her into being with him. She'd known what he was like. She knew what she was getting herself into. And now that she had fucked him up, now that she had manipulated him into building his whole fucking life around her, making herself the star he orbited, now she was going to fucking leave him and drag his good name through the mud?

YOLO, her stupid tattoo said. *YOLO.* You only live once, and not for much longer if you keep this shit up, he once told her. He'd tell her that again when he found her.

She was so fucking stupid.

* * *

Those idiot kids egged Amanda Carey's house on Thanksgiving night.

Jerry was disappointed in himself for not having anticipated it; he'd actually allowed himself to believe that even if the hatchet hadn't actually been buried, it'd been set aside, at least for the holidays.

Jerry wished he'd been there Thanksgiving night; maybe if he'd been there for an hour or two it would have discouraged them. He didn't mind parking at the house. He could look at ESPN on his phone just as easily in the car as he could on his couch. But he hadn't been there because he'd been in Chicago at his brother's—he'd driven down with his mother and son—but also because it had begun to feel pathetic, as though he didn't have anything better to do than sit outside Amanda Carey's house every night, as though he wasn't there because of a professional interest in serving and protecting. Especially after Cinnamon had brought him the coffee and hot chocolate. After that, he'd concluded that if he sat out there on Thanksgiving, they might feel like they had to bring him out a plate or invite him in or something. They—she—might start to think he was pathetic.

What did it matter anyway, he wasn't out to impress anyone. And in the end, he would prefer to appear pathetic if it meant he could avoid dealing with Scott Carson again.

Scott wasn't from Miserable, so Jerry hadn't met him until they both had children in the elementary school. Jerry's son Drew was two years older than Scott's son Lloyd. Lloyd wasn't actually Scott's son; he was Scott's stepson.

And Jerry's son Drew was somebody else's stepson—more precisely, he was Dan Libby's stepson and Jerry wouldn't be able to sleep at night if he believed Dan Libby was anything like Scott Carson. Because Scott Carson was a first-class prick, a self-important blowhard, the kind of man who actually and uncritically referred to himself as an "alpha."

Jerry discovered Scott Carson was a prick as a result of some drama at the school years ago, when Drew was in 6th grade. Scott kicked up a fuss about a teacher, saying she didn't assign enough homework, and she picked on Lloyd. Scott felt Lloyd's behavioral problems were Mrs. Dowd's fault and not Lloyd's own. He wanted her fired.

Scott's crusade against Mrs. Dowd annoyed Jerry because she'd been Drew's fourth grade teacher as well. And, more importantly, Mrs. Dowd had adored Drew. She was old and maybe a bit strict, but she'd recognized Jerry's son as the exceptionally exceptional child Jerry believed Drew to be. At their parent-teacher conference, she'd reached across the small desk to take Drew's mother's hand. She told Courtney and Jerry that it had been a "pleasure" to have Drew in the class. She *thanked* them for raising such a special boy. She told a story about how one day, when she'd asked for a volunteer to help her carry some boxes of books their class was giving to the kindergartners, Drew stayed behind to help and, as they made their trips up and down the stairs, he asked her if she was feeling all right. You see, she'd explained, she *had* been upset. It was September 11th and although she knew everyone felt a bit more melancholy than usual on that day, she had a cousin who'd died in the attacks and it always hit her a little hard, thinking of poor Nolan jumping from the towers, and all the people who died and all of the people who lost someone, and all the ways the world had fundamentally changed. But of course, she never shared this with the students, or even her colleagues. It was just something happening inside of her. She'd been amazed at Drew's intuition, his empathy. When he asked her if she was all right, she answered honestly, that September 11th always got her down and he turned to her and patted her arm and said, "It's a hard day."

"He's a good boy," Mrs. Dowd concluded, her eyes, behind her glasses, swimming with tears. "You raised a good boy."

In Jerry Beck's private pantheon of saints and heroes, Mrs.

Dowd had pride of place, right there between his own mother, Ruth, and Aaron Rodgers.

Not so, Scott Carson. Scott actually called the station to claim that the broken nose Lloyd got in a schoolyard fight was a result Mrs. Dowd's negligence.

The whole thing was bullshit. Scott Carson was clearly the problem, and Mrs. Dowd should sue *him* for harassment. And Jerry would have told Mrs. Dowd that he thought so, but Scott's vendetta occurred just as Jerry's domestic life imploded, and Carson v. Chippewa County school district only registered as a vague and nagging worry, like the half-dead tree over the garage Jerry meant to take care of but only remembered when he was too busy to do anything about it.

Mrs. Dowd retired the next year and moved down to Madison to be closer to her grandkids. She'd eschewed a retirement party and slipped away after the last day of school; the "For Sale" sign appeared on her lawn after she was already gone. Jerry meant to send her a card, congratulate her on a fine career and thank her again for taking an interest in his son. He might do it yet.

As anyone could guess, Lloyd's problems didn't cease with Mrs. Dowd's retirement. The kid only got bigger and surlier; Jerry knew this thing with Amanda Carey Birchbaum was just the beginning of years of professional interactions he could look forward to with Lloyd. It was too bad. Lloyd's mother, Linda, seemed nice enough. Jerry wondered what she saw in Scott Carson, but he supposed, some women like a bully.

Jerry Beck would never suggest he was smarter than other people, but he was, in fact, smarter than other people. Smart and intuitive, he didn't miss much. The shotgun, for example, leaning against the fireplace at Amanda Carey's house. He noticed it the day the niece had passed out. Jerry noticed it but didn't confiscate it, because he thought it wouldn't be a bad idea for the women to have something like that around. Jerry knew a woman in trouble when he saw one. And he'd seen enough of them. He'd seen enough of them to know that most of them couldn't help it; that you could cajole and threaten and plead, they'd look at you and you could see the longing in their injured eyes, but there wasn't much you could do, other than throw the guy in the cooler for a couple of days, make him feel like shit and hope you don't push him too far, because the last thing you wanted was to get the call every small-town cop has to answer eventually, if not once every five or six years: the bastard couldn't be satisfied with just offing himself—he had to go ahead and take whole family with him.

No, you wanted to scare him a bit, but not too much. You didn't want him to take it out on her. And you didn't want her to be afraid to come to you either, although somehow, when you'd run into her at the Walmart or the pancake breakfast at the firehouse, you'd walk away feeling as though you were the one who'd done something wrong. It seemed everyone felt embarrassed and ashamed, except of course, the guy who beat her up.

Jerry wondered about the niece, about what exactly had happened to her, and how, and would he come up to Miserable to look for her. And would she take him back?

* * *

Despite Jerry's superior instincts when it came to battered women, he was, like many folks, pretty obtuse when it came to predatory stepfathers.

Scott had been, in Marisa's term, "interfering" with Lloyd since he'd married Lloyd's mother when Lloyd was eight, although Marisa would have used another, stronger word, for what Scott did to Lloyd. Regardless, the abuse stopped when

Lloyd was fourteen; Lloyd didn't know how or why, as he hadn't done anything dramatic to demands its cessation, at least not anything like he dreamed of doing. But Scott stopped coming into his room at night when Linda was at work at the hospital, stopped trying to show Lloyd things on his phone, stopped slipping into the bathroom when Lloyd was in the shower. He stopped and Lloyd never thought about it, not really, although when he did think about it, he wondered if it ever happened at all or if he made it all up in his own sick mind. Then he would remember that it had happened and he would think vaguely this was something else Scott had done to him: Scott fucked with his head so much that now he questioned his own memory, questioned if he himself had somehow made or invited Scott do it. Lloyd wondered if he was gay. He didn't want to fuck guys, but he wondered if Scott saw something gay in him, and now he was so fucked up that he didn't even know if he was gay or not.

Lloyd knew it was fucked up and that he was fucked up, but this was not something he would ever be able to imagine thinking about telling someone. Lloyd was not stupid; he had read books and seen movies and knew some people believed if you talked about something enough you'd feel better about it, but Lloyd hadn't found that to be the case. Once, a year earlier, drunk at a party, he went into a bedroom with Morgan, a girl he was friends with, and they were talking, really talking, and he told her that Scott was hard on him, that Scott fucked with him all the time, and Morgan looked at Lloyd with disgust, as though she realized what he was getting at, and stopped him and said they'd all had hard times, he didn't have to be a faggot about it.

Lloyd had pretended to laugh and said, "fuck you" and left, saying he needed another beer. But he never talked to Morgan like that again, avoided her most of the time, talked about how drunk he'd been that night, and if he could have, he'd go back and erase that night, erase Morgan and everything about her completely.

* * *

Jason took his time driving up. He listened to podcasts about distilling your workday down to three hours and being a fucking baller and how you couldn't just hope for things to happen, you had to *manifest them*.

Everything these people said made sense to Jason and he started to manifest having his own podcast. It would be the natural outgrowth of the work they were already doing. He and Cin would focus on fitness and health but also provide business and relationship advice. They could talk about how they pushed each other to excel, about communication and compromise. It would be inspiring, but also be funny—Cin was so batty and weird—she would be the Lucy to his Desi. The podcast would be called "Synergy with Cin and Jay." Yes. Perfect.

Then he remembered he was going to kill Cinnamon, which made him a little sad, especially because that title was so good, but maybe he could do the podcast with Gloria or even that new girl at the gym, what was her name, Cass.

* * *

Drew lived in Stevens Point with his mother and Dan Libby, but he came up to stay with Jerry every other weekend and alternating holidays.

On Sunday, before the game started, Jerry said he had to step out.

"I'll be back in twenty," he called to his son. He planned to make his way over to Lloyd's, talk to Scott and Linda. It might've made more sense to talk to Mike's father—Mike was older than the other two and Jerry questioned why he hung around with Lloyd and Aaron in the first place—but Jerry did have a secret self-righteous streak. He couldn't say he didn't take a little pleasure in vindicating Mrs. Dowd.

* * *

When Mr. Beck, Officer Beck, whatever, came back a second time to talk to his parents, Lloyd listened from the kitchen. The stupid old bitch had called the cops again. But there wasn't any proof it was him. No way they could prove it.

Scott said, "Are you calling me a liar? Are you calling my son a liar?" and the cop said, "Scott, now, I'm not calling anybody anything. I am telling you what was reported to me. I'd like to speak to Lloyd—"

Scott cut him off. "You're not speaking to my son. This is harassment, Jerry. That old—that *woman*—aimed a gun at my son and now she's having the police show up at my house, my home, with false allegations? I don't want to file a lawsuit against the MPD, Jerry, but I'm not afraid to either."

"Scott," Lloyd heard the cop say. "Please calm down. I am here to ask you to help me out with this."

"Let me give you a tip, Jerry," Scott sneered. "You're harassing the wrong people. Lloyd never pulled a gun on anyone. Why is he the one you're harassing?"

"No one is harassing you," the cop said. "I'm here to ask you to—"

"I know what you're here to do and it's time for you to go. How dare you interrupt our time at home, my time at home with my family, with this bullshit. You can get out of my house, Officer Beck."

The cop said something else, but Lloyd couldn't hear it. He heard the front door slam and he heard Scott bellow, "God dammit!"

Lloyd waited, his heart loud in his ears, at the kitchen table.

Scott crashed into the kitchen, Lloyd's mom trailing him, her hands up, a caricature of an alarmed woman, her mouth and eyes wide. Scott pulled his arm back as though he was going to punch Lloyd in the head, but Linda hung on to his bicep, crying, *Scott, please, Scott.*

Lloyd rose and took a step back. He towered over Scott now; he had a full six inches on his stepfather. Earlier, he had hoped Scott would hit him, but he discovered he didn't really want that to happen. He thought if Scott hit him, he would hit Scott back, maybe, but when they came into the kitchen and Scott cocked his arm, Lloyd thought maybe he had been wrong. He felt sick and like his arms had been hollowed out.

"I swear to God," Lloyd protested, blustering and whining at the same time. "I don't know what he's talking about. The old lady is crazy, like hallucinating this or something. I never did anything! Like, not after that first time or whatever."

Scott lowered his arm. Linda still clung to him with her fingertips.

Scott's upper lip spasmed. *"Like,"* he mimicked in a falsetto. *"Like, really?"* He narrowed his eyes at his stepson. "If you're lying to me," he warned Lloyd.

"I'm not," Lloyd protested, trying to deepen his voice.

"Jerry Beck," Scott said bitterly, shrugging away Linda's grasp. Lloyd, relieved but wary, stayed standing, his back against the fridge. "This goddam town," Scott said.

Linda whimpered something unintelligible. Her eyes darted from Scott to Lloyd and back to Scott again.

"That piece of shit gets off on giving me a hard time," Scott said, and grimaced. "It's not even about you," he spat at Lloyd.

"But you gave him an excuse, you goddam retard." Scott looked at Linda. "A million feet tall and no goddam brain."

"Oh, now." Linda shook her head and looked down, as though she were politely scolding the linoleum.

"Coming into my house," Scott continued. "Coming into my home." He remained on this theme for another twenty minutes, until Linda coaxed him back to the living room. They appreciated him so much, Linda assured Scott. He made so many sacrifices for them, she said, and they were so grateful. The game would be on soon, she told him. Let's go sit down.

Lloyd went to his room and filled his backpack with fireworks. Maybe they'd go to the old lady's house after the game. It would serve her right. Stick a bottle rocket right up her ass.

* * *

Jason drove around for a while, but it didn't take as long to find her as he thought. The stupid cunt left her mother's car with the Florida plates parked right in the fucking driveway. Maybe she was brain damaged after all.

Conveniently, there was a Walmart next door. Jason went there and used the bathroom. He bought himself a hot dog and a coke for $1.29. This wasn't the kind of food he generally ate, but then again, he didn't generally find himself in a Wisconsin Walmart, buying batteries and an electric screwdriver and matches and weapons.

* * *

Drew had recently gotten his driver's license, which meant, when he came up to Miserable, he could stay and watch Sunday football before taking himself back to Stevens Point. This was a nice, new thing; in the past, Jerry, always one to adhere to the letter of the law, would drive Drew home by noon on Sunday. Not that Courtney was a stickler or anything. It was simply that Jerry preferred, if possible, not to negotiate. He preferred not to ask for favors or be in anyone's debt. But now it was Drew's call. Drew could get himself home to Stevens Point by noon, or he could stay and watch the game. It was up to him. And whatever he wanted to do was fine with Jerry.

They ate steaks in front of the television. Jerry had a Miller High Life—another nice thing about not having to drive his son back—and Drew had a Sprite.

"So why were you over at Lloyd Hess' or whatever?" Drew asked, looking at his phone.

Jerry shifted in his recliner. "That kid's a pain in the ass. He and his buddies torment Mrs. Birchbaum, the old lady out by the Walmart. They throw trash in her yard, set off firecrackers, that sort of thing."

"What? Why?" Drew asked. On the television, women and men held Coronas as they partied in a tropical paradise.

Jerry shrugged and sipped his beer. "Just to be bastards, I guess. But then she threatened them. With a hunting rifle. It seemed to make things worse."

"What the fuck?" Drew said, looking up from his phone at his father and then to the television. "Sorry, dad. But, really. This place is crazy."

"Well, I'm sure you have your share of juvenile delinquents in Stevens Point. Miserable isn't so much worse."

"I mean Wisconsin. This whole state is fucked—sorry." Drew looked back to his phone and shook his head, world-weary. Or maybe just Wisconsin-weary. "I can't wait to get out of here."

Jerry felt as though he'd been stabbed. (He had, in fact, been stabbed once—not badly—but he knew how it felt). Imagining himself an expert dissembler, he laughed. "You're going to leave your old man behind in Miserable?"

Drew, Jerry's favorite person, sometimes the only person Jerry really liked, even when Drew was miserable to be around and Jerry didn't like him at all, shrugged. "You could leave too, you know."

"Where is it that you're so anxious to get to?"

"Well," Drew looked up from his phone finally. "I mean, I'll probably just go to UW. But, you know, I would really like to go to college somewhere warm. University of Miami?" he proposed.

"Huh," Jerry said. "Miami, Ohio?"

"Ha," Drew said. "I mean, maybe I'll go somewhere warm for grad school or whatever.

Maybe Madison for undergrad and then Florida or California or North Carolina for grad school. Like Stanford. That's in California? Or is that in Florida?"

"I think it's California."

"Yeah. Stanford."

Jerry, who had gone to community college, suspected Madison was unlikely. A solid-C student, Drew said he liked math. And history. But he didn't like school. Courtney said he was lazy. She said he didn't apply himself. She once even said that Drew had "average" intelligence. Jerry hadn't liked that one bit.

This assessment was, to Jerry, a dizzying reversal from their earlier positions, back in the early days of Drew, when his every action evidenced his superiority. This was yet another one of Courtney's betrayals. She'd changed her mind about everything, and now she'd changed her mind about their son. Drew was exceptional. He had spoken early and had an astounding vocabulary. Courtney and Jerry spent those first years gaping delightedly. Had a child ever been so brilliant?

Jerry secretly believed that Drew was psychic, an idea he once floated to Courtney, but she was skeptical.

"Sometimes I'll be thinking of dinner," Jerry told her. "And then out of nowhere he'll ask, 'What's for dinner?' It's like he reads my mind."

"I'd say it's a safe bet that you're always thinking about dinner," Courtney returned.

"But you're right. He sure is tuned-in. That kid doesn't miss a trick."

And too, Drew had a natural athleticism at a young age, although he never shined again like he had in pee-wee wrestling. Most importantly, he was kind: the sweetest, most thoughtful, most compassionate child you ever met. Just ask Mrs. Dowd. She'd seen it, back in fourth grade.

Jerry was still impressed by his son, but he worried, obsessively, the divorce had somehow thwarted Drew's moral and intellectual growth, that despite the promising start, the heat of those difficult years proved too much, and had warped and ruined his son.

Jerry knew he was overreacting. Drew was still a good boy. He didn't get in trouble, at least not too much. When there had been a scandal at the Stevens Point high school—some stupid kids had dressed up like Nazis for Halloween and their grinning photos somehow got picked up by the national news, another blow for Wisconsin's ever-faltering reputation—Jerry was relieved to learn Drew wasn't involved, although his relief was its own kind of indictment. But Drew rolled his eyes at Jerry, grumbled he barely even knew those kids, and he didn't dress up for Halloween anyway, dad.

He was still a good boy, if not as smart and athletic and thoughtful as he was once. When Jerry suggested as much to Courtney, she sighed in exasperation. "He's just a teenager, Jerry. They're all terrible."

Jerry didn't think he'd been terrible as a teenager. He hadn't dressed up like a Nazi or thrown trash at old ladies or suggested casually to his parents that he hated where they'd chosen to raise him and that he couldn't wait to escape it.

"Want another Sprite?" he asked his son, as he took the plates to the kitchen and grabbed another beer.

Drew didn't look up. "I'm good," his son answered.

* * *

As they watched the game, Lloyd told Mike and Fat Aaron that the cop had come by his house. He tried to be cool about it, but Fat Aaron's eyes widened in alarm.

"Shit," Aaron said. "Do you think he's going to my house next?"

Lloyd shrugged. "How the fuck should I know?

Mike sucked on a vape. "He didn't come here, so, probably not. He just has a hard-on for Lloyd."

"My mother will kill me if the cops come to my house," Fat Aaron said. "Like, kill me."

"Stop being a pussy," Mike said.

"I totally want to go over there tonight," Lloyd said. "I brought my backpack. Smoke bombs, the big shells. Let's do some grand finale shit. Just light it all up. One last time."

"Fuck that," Mike said. "I'm going to Kayla's after the game."

"Come on," Lloyd said. "You can go over to her house after. It would be so hilarious."

"Nah," Mike said, his eyes on the television. "I just want to fuck a bitch." They all winced: Aaron Rodgers was laid low; he wasn't getting up. "Fuck," Mike said.

Lloyd waited and then turned to Fat Aaron. "You have to

come with me. You have to help me get back at her for calling the cops."

"No way, man," Fat Aaron said. "No way."

"Pussies," Lloyd said, relieved that Mike was watching the television so intently, otherwise he might have gotten pissed off about what Lloyd said.

But Lloyd was pissed off. He didn't want to make Fat Aaron come with him because Aaron was annoying and slow, and Lloyd didn't like him anyway. He was pissed Mike wasn't coming. It was fun when the three of them went together. Plus, Mike was the only one old enough to drive.

The Packers lost. Mike dropped Lloyd at the Walmart on his way to Kayla's.

* * *

After his trip to Walmart, Jason sat in a booth at the Come Back Inn. He drank a dark beer slowly. He didn't usually drink, and he definitely didn't want to get drunk. But there was nowhere else to go, to be inside and warm, to kill a few hours before he went back to the house.

The bar was crowded with men in Packers jerseys. The women also wore Packers jerseys, but tiny, shrunken ones, the better to show off their rolls of fat.

The men in the bar didn't pay attention to Jason, other than to note he wasn't watching the Packers, which marked him as strange, an outsider, and possibly homosexual.

It was almost eleven when the game ended and the bar mostly cleared out, miserable people shuffling into the miserable world.

Besides Jason, one other man remained, an affable loser, in Jason's estimation, who nodded at Jason and, when Jason made the mistake of nodding back, sat across from him in his booth.

"Tough night," the man said. He set down his almost-empty glass.

"Yeah," Jason agreed. He regarded his own empty glass.

"You a Packers fan?"

"The Packers are great," said Jason, who knew and cared precisely enough about football to socialize with and, he thought, impress other men. "But I'm a Dolphins fan."

"Oh yeah?" the man said.

Unwilling to continue the conversation or to drink another beer, Jason took out his wallet. "I've got to go," he said to the man. "But you have one on me. Sorry for your loss, and all."

"Thanks, friend," the man said, smiling and nodding. "Not too shabby for a Dolphins fan."

* * *

"Maybe I'll crash here," Drew said when the game ended. "Get up early and drive back in the morning."

Jerry, whose heart was swelling in his chest, replied, "I don't think that's a good idea. Your mother wouldn't like it. You should get on the road."

Although Jerry would have liked him to, Drew didn't insist, and Jerry hugged his son, pulling him hard into his chest. His son smelled good— a little sour but also a little salty—and Jerry felt as though he might cry, which he would not do, clearly, in front of Drew. So, he held on for an extra-long moment, until Drew said, "Okay, dad," pulling back. "I love you too, man."

* * *

Lloyd's contempt for Amanda Carey felt like someone was pressing a burning cigarette against his heart. That stupid crazy old bitch, in her ugly fucking house. Like a witch in a storybook. When she pulled that gun on him, he peed his pants a little. Literally. He didn't think Mike and Fat Aaron knew it, but he knew it. It wasn't like he was scared she'd shoot him. Except that he was. There was something behind her glasses, something mean in her eyes, something that scared the shit—or the piss—out of him.

Lloyd knew another bitch lived with her now. He'd seen her out running on the shoulder of the road. It offended Lloyd, in a murky, obscure way, that another person lived with Amanda Carey. That mean old bitch was supposed to be alone. Now there was someone else there and although he couldn't name it or even think it clearly, the corruption of Amanda Carey's isolation unnerved him, enraged him. He hated her more than ever now that there was someone else with her. Like she was happy or something. Like she thought she could be old and ugly and alone and still have a friend and be happy. It offended him.

He watched the house from a small patch of trees and bushes adjacent to the Walmart parking lot. He watched as lights went on and off. He could imagine them, getting a glass of water, turning down the thermostat, making their way upstairs. He wondered if the other lady was like a lesbian or something. Even though he knew it was a relative he let himself imagine that the other woman was actually Amanda Carey's girlfriend. The thought filled him with disgust, made him hate her even more.

If he could rig something up, like a series of explosions, maybe find a window, jigger it open, throw a stink bomb in. That was it. Throw a stink bomb in her fucking house, close the window again and run away. Or a stink bomb and some of the M-80s. Tie a bunch together and set them on fire and throw them into the house. That would be perfect.

Jason had a more elaborate plan.

He got the idea from a documentary he saw, about an architect whose name he couldn't remember. He didn't remember much about the documentary. It wasn't that interesting, but he forced himself to sit through it because they'd recently been a party at the club he was affiliated with and a real-life architect spoke with weary disparagement of the very housing development where Jason and Cinnamon lived. The architect described their neighborhood as a collection of "ticky tacky houses with paranoid schizophrenia." The architect didn't elaborate, but people laughed, and while Jason did too, he secretly seethed. Though the nuances of the architect's remark escaped him, he knew his over-half-a-million-dollar house was being dismissed as tasteless and trivial. The dismissal would not have stung quite as much if the house hadn't put Jason in the hole, big time, and depreciated in value to a shocking degree. Technically the house was Cinnamon's, which was a hilarious if you thought about it; the bank gave a loan to an ex-junkie who'd had her own child taken away. You had to ask: whose fault was it really?

As a result of being made to feel unsophisticated, small, gauche, and foolish, when Jason saw there was a documentary on the History channel about a famous architect one night, he left it on. Jason hoped the show would reveal to him what he hadn't seen about his own home as he sat in that mostly unfurnished, cool, and quiet house. But the houses in the documentary, hailed as revolutionary and inspired, were, Jason thought, fucking ugly. He'd take his own "ticky-tacky house with paranoid schizophrenia," with its steam shower, great room, state-of the-art surveillance and alarm system, and kidney-shaped pool over one of those ugly fucking houses any day of the week, thank you very much.

But the part of the documentary that stuck out to him was a subplot, a footnote to the bigger story, about a woman—the architect's girlfriend? his sister?—who lived in the Midwest somewhere. A former employee with a grudge against her snuck up to the house one night, during a big dinner party, and nailed all the windows shut except for one and then lit the house on fire. When the people tried to escape the fire, and started streaming out the one window, he was waiting with a machete and chopped them up one by one. That was the part that Jason remembered. It was fucking crazy.

Jason left his car in the Walmart parking lot. He squeezed through a hole in the fence he'd observed earlier and settled down near the house to watch and wait.

* * *

"Hey there, Jerry."

"Hey, Court," Jerry said. He opened another beer and walked into the dining room. "Just calling to let you know that Drew's on the road."

"Thanks," His ex-wife said. "Of course, he forgot to let me know himself. But how are you? That was hard to watch. Poor Aaron."

"Poor Aaron," Jerry agreed. He regarded his dim reflection in the dark dining room windows. He needed a haircut, but overall, he looked pretty good. Too bad Instagram didn't have a "darkened window" filter. "He'll be all right though, I bet."

"You had a nice time with Drew?"

"Oh, yeah."

"Okay, then," Courtney said. "Thanks for calling."

"Courtney?" Jerry said, unwilling to let her go just yet.

"He's a good boy, right?"

"Who, Drew? You know he is, Jerry."

"I do."

"You have a couple beers tonight?" Courtney asked. She sounded indulgent, amused.

"I did," Jerry admitted.

"Come on now. Did he say something to upset you?"

"No, no. He's fine. He just said, you know, he can't wait to get out of Wisconsin, he told me. He wants to go to school in Florida or California. Has he told you this?"

"It's the first I'm hearing about it," Courtney said. "I wouldn't worry about it too much, Jerry. He'd be very lucky to go to Whitewater or Green Bay."

"That's what I think too."

"You know he's got this girlfriend now?"

"Girlfriend?"

"Oh, yeah. I'm surprised he didn't tell you about her."

"He didn't. You tell me, though." Jerry sat down at the dining room table, his back to the
windows.

"Her name is Neve. She's named after the girl who used to be on that show. *Party of Five*. Remember that one? Now does that make you feel old or what?" Courtney continued, not waiting for a response. "She's a cutie. He says it's not so serious, but you should see the way he looks at her. You should probably be talking to him. You know. About all that stuff."

Jerry said. "I guess so. We did, you know, talk about it awhile back."

"He was in fifth grade, Jerry," Courtney pointed out. "I can have Dan do it if you want. He doesn't get embarrassed talking about that kind of thing."

"Oh no," Jerry said hurriedly. "No, no. It should be me."

"Yeah," Courtney agreed. "It really should be you. You

regret calling now or what?"

Jerry forced an audible laugh. "No, no. This is good. Neve, huh? Well."

"Our little boy," Courtney said.

It was nice to talk to her like this, Jerry thought. It was good that things were easier between them now. It was hard to remember how it had been before, but sometimes, sitting in his cruiser or in a deer blind or even in the shower, it would bubble up and take him by surprise: the crushing ache of the late days of their marriage, the searing cold of the early divorce.

"Our little boy," Jerry repeated.

* * *

At first Lloyd thought Mike had come after all. He was about to hiss-whisper, call Mike over to where he was concealed in a small outgrowth of bushes, but he worried Mike would be like, "What the fuck are you hiding in the bushes like a pussy for?" That moment's hesitation allowed Lloyd to see it wasn't Mike after all, it was some other person, a grown man. Even in the shadows, the man walked with a confidence that suggested he belonged there, that he owned the place. Maybe it was Mrs. Birchbaum's, like, son or something or maybe some relative of the relative who was staying with her. But it was weird because the man carried bags, like he had work to do, though it was near midnight and deeply dark. |It didn't make sense. It occurred to Lloyd the man was a burglar.

Lloyd stayed quiet and waited, reconsidering. He could get out of there and come back another time, with Mike and Fat Aaron. He would wait for the man to move far enough away and then he'd creep out of the bushes without being noticed. But the man settled just a few feet from where Lloyd sat and started unpacking his duffel bag.

One of the things he unpacked looked like a shotgun. Another looked like a machete.

* * *

Jason unpacked and assessed his tools and then crouched, looking at the house, trying to take his time. He waited until midnight. He would have liked to wait longer, until two or three, but it was cold, and he was bored and tired.

He crunched through the frost-covered grass and approached the house. He did a quick circuit. There were seven windows on the first floor, a front door, and a back door. He wouldn't worry about the window next to the front door because that's where he planned to stand and whether they used the door or the window, he'd be right there to pick them off either way.

He started at the window farthest from where he'd last seen a light on. The electric screwdriver was relatively quiet. He'd asked the guy at Walmart for the quietest one he had, made up a song and dance about wanting to work in his workshop at night and his wife being supersensitive. The hick in the hardware department had nodded knowingly. "Oh sure," he said, in that retarded Wisconsin accent. "Oh sure, I know just whatcha want."

Of course, Jason felt as though the sound of the tool echoed and careened in the quiet Wisconsin night, but that was the price of business.

* * *

Jerry finished his beer and got in his car to pass by Amanda Carey's place. He didn't think the kids would be back tonight—

not right after a warning—but it wouldn't hurt to swing by. The Packers had lost, and that put everybody on edge.

He thought about the niece more than he cared to admit. Her face was thin and pointy, but she had a nice smile. And he liked her long hair and the brightly-colored clothes she wore. She seemed both worldly and vulnerable, skinny, but strong and unafraid, running on the shoulder of the road. Her rolled her funny name, Cinnamon, around in his mouth.

There existed no chance Jerry would ask her out or even try to talk to her, but he thought about her brown eyes and the way her wrist had felt when he held it to take her pulse, her skin so soft it surprised him.

All was dark at the house when Jerry passed by at midnight. He'd stop in at the Come Back, see if anyone was around, see if anyone wanted to have a beer and commiserate with him over Aaron's injury.

* * *

Lloyd had seen plenty of animals paralyzed with fear; once, he saw a baby bunny at a girl's birthday party literally die of shock after too much rough handling. The birthday girl let loose a keening cry and her mother took away the little bunny corpse, and told the assembled children that it would be fine, that there were other bunnies in the barn and this one had been sickly, as though the promise of torturing another small animal to death was the comforting balm they needed.

Lloyd felt like that bunny now; frozen, terrified, his heart beating so fast he was afraid it would shake itself lose.

The guy got up and moved toward the house. Lloyd arranged his numb legs in a crouch position, ready to bolt to the parking lot and then across the street when the man was out of sight. But just as Lloyd was ready to spring, the man came back around the other side of the house. He didn't look in Lloyd's direction. But still.

The guy drove something into the window frames at the back of the house.

In a flash, Lloyd remembered a lurid story about Frank Lloyd Wright's wife that Mr. Huber had told in history class. A guy had been fired and, for revenge, nailed up all the windows but one at his boss's house. He set the house on fire and waited at the one window with his machete.

"Sick," Fat Aaron had called out in class, making everyone laugh.

Lloyd's heart still raced, but he noticed that he was breathing better. Instead of taking in puffs of air, now he took regular, if a little hiccup-y, breaths.

He knew, suddenly, that this was one of those moments in his life. That regardless of what he did next, that this would become a part of who he was forever and ever amen, that what he did now, or didn't do, would become a part of him.

The man disappeared. Lloyd knew what he was doing. He was closing up the windows on the far side of the house, although he must be using a screwdriver or something, because he wasn't hammering. Lloyd thought that this was his best shot, that with the man on the other side of the house, he should run, get to the parking lot, call the police.

* * *

Something landed with a thump on the inside windowsill. Jason leapt back, dropping the screwdriver. He looked through the glass at the form of a cat before bending to fetch the screwdriver. He was tempted to slap the window, scare it away, but restrained himself. The cat arched its back then dove down as Jason drove the final screw into the frame.

* * *

Jerry settled himself at the bar.

"Oofta," the bartender said. "Rough night."

"You got that right," Jerry said. "Just a Leine's, then."

* * *

Lloyd watched as the man splashed gasoline around the base of house. He tossed the empty red container to the side and opened a second one, and disappeared from Lloyd's sight again as he made his way around the house then back again.

Lloyd watched him toss flaming matches at the ground. With a thumping noise, curtains of flames rose around the house.

The man walked to where his gear waited in a neat pile. He put on a backpack and picked up the gun and the machete. He walked around to the front of the house, where Lloyd couldn't see him.

* * *

Jason waited at the front of the house. He congratulated himself on remembering to cut the phone line. It had been a small, easy thing, and they probably had cell phones anyway, but still. It would have been easy to forget. He wasn't worried in any case; the fire would flush her right out before the fire department or the police or anyone out here in East Bumble-fuck arrived. By the time they got here, the house would be gone, the cunt would be dead and he'd in his Mercedes, headed due South.

There was a movement at one of the upstairs windows—just a flicker. And then again. A cat—maybe the same one—

jumped onto the windowsill, disturbing the blinds, and jumped down again. Then he heard that same window open—it was strange how some noises carried above the sound of the flames, which were getting bigger and louder—and he saw an animal, yes, a cat, being thrown from the window. It landed on the porch roof and made a strangled, yowling sound before jumping to the ground and darting off into the dark.

He heard Cinnamon's voice, and the belated bleating of a smoke detector.

Jason waited.

* * *

Jerry, who was feeling avuncular, generous, old, bought another beer for himself and one for a kid named Jodie, who was not really a kid, but a new father, with baby twins at home who were probably right that minute waking up for the third time since they'd been put to bed, god bless his wife. Jerry wanted to talk to Jodie about stepping it up a bit, about how maybe it wasn't such a hot idea to be out on Sunday night getting drunk at the Come Back Inn and leaving his wife at home with five-week old twins, but this gentle lecture necessitated buying the kid another beer and keeping him talking at the bar, which of course Jerry realized sadly undermined the very argument he was making.

The cold, foamy beers had just been deposited before them when Jodie remarked about this being his lucky night, what with the other guy who had bought him a beer, some sort of bodybuilder, you know the type and Jerry said, "What's that now? Who?" and Jodie said some guy, a Dolphins fan, would you believe it, nice enough but strange, if you asked him, tough luck to be a Dolphins fan, don't you think?

* * *

Lloyd moved at last.

With the flames rising and the man out of sight, Lloyd dashed back through the trees to the hole in the fence. He planned to keep running, but he turned back and, from there, he could see the man, lit up by the fire, standing in front of the house.

He called 9-1-1 and whispered answers to an impatient, unfeeling operator. She wanted to know what the emergency was, and Lloyd didn't know what to tell her. He spluttered, "Fire," but that didn't capture what was happening. When she asked what town, he was nonplussed; of course, it was Miserable. Didn't they know that already? When she asked for the address, he wanted to cry and he said he didn't know, it was the house over by the Walmart. Then he hung up, despairing. He could see the flames from the parking lot. There was no way anyone would get there in time.

They could trace his cell number and they would probably think he set the fire. But he didn't care. His skin was tingling all over his body and he couldn't help but feel it was, in fact, his fault, that he had somehow thought this into happening, that his hating the old lady so much had summoned this other person forth. And this man wasn't playing around, this wasn't fireworks and smoke bombs; the old lady was in there and she was probably going to die.

Lloyd moved back toward the house.

* * *

Jason's stomach was upset, which was something that happened to him when he was nervous, but also probably a reaction to the hot dog and beer. He shouldn't have had anything at all. It would have been better to have stayed empty.

But he was ready. He stood a little further from the house than he had imagined. He wanted to stand right by the door, ready to hack away as soon as she appeared, but hadn't realized how hot it would get, or how quickly the fire would spread. He waited, imagining the way the glow from the flames lit up his face, posing with his machete, feeling like a ninja. He wished someone was there to take pictures.

The front door pulled open and a strange figure seemed to fall out onto the porch. The figure straightened and Jason saw that it was two people: Cinnamon and another woman, both carrying cats, which they flung out before them. The cats landed with thuds on the front steps before darting in several directions away from the house.

Jason held his pose and waited. When Cinnamon saw him, she stumbled backwards, her mouth and eyes wide. She grabbed the woman and pushed her back into the burning house.

Jason smiled. He put down the machete, picked up the gun.

* * *

The thing about the bodybuilder had thrown Jerry and he couldn't help but wonder if this was the niece's husband or boyfriend; it was too much of a coincidence about the Dolphins, wasn't it? He nodded as Jodie held forth again about his wife's unreasonable expectations, turning these thoughts over in his mind.

Jerry put down his beer and shot up in his seat. "Excuse me," he said to Jodie. He nodded at the bartender, let him know to keep the money he'd left on the bar.

"Fuck," he said, starting up the cold police car.

Lloyd knew he was hidden in the darkness, but nevertheless, on spaghetti legs and with shaking hands he lined up the bottle rockets, sticking them into the crust of snow on the ground.

Lloyd looked up to see the guy standing there with the shotgun trained on the front door.

Lloyd tore his eyes away and forced himself to attend to the work in front of him. He was grateful for the Click-n-Flame lighter he kept specifically for fireworks; otherwise there would be no way that he could command his hands to stay still enough to light the rockets. One push of a button, though, and he was ready to go, right on down the row, the flame trembling but steady enough to light each rocket.

Just as the first rocket was about to launch, Lloyd hastily lit and threw three red hots—not at the guy, but just to the side of him—and then, as the first rockets began to whistle and hiss and blow, Lloyd, feeling like Aaron Rodgers on a break, ran to the flank, lit and threw a smoke bomb, then reached into the back-pack he wore on the front of his chest for an M-100.

It was fucking insane.

* * *

Jason screamed. He thought, at first, he was being shot at. He screamed, covered his head, and spun around. The fire burnt into his eyelids, burnt into his eyes, and he couldn't see. By the time he turned back to the house, with the noise and the blasts still popping and bursting around him, it was too late. The women were out of the house again, and this time, Cinnamon's friend had her own shotgun.

PART V
GODDAMMED CATS

Cats can be hard to save. As any cat-lover will tell you, it's a rare feline that knows how to accept help. How many times has the well-meaning human trapped a feral and then wondered what the fuck she thought she was doing; how many times has the cat-stuck-in-the-tree lashed out at the helping hand of the firefighter? Too many to count.

Jason was gone, having run toward the screaming siren as soon as he'd seen Amanda Carey's shotgun. Cinnamon held Amanda Carey and Lloyd held them both, wrapping them in his long arms. The house burned and cracked and spluttered behind them; but there were other noises too: screeching and wailing. Lloyd pulled back and looked at the old lady. "The cats," Amanda Carey gasped.

Lloyd had never felt as amazing and capable and fearless as when he pried her fingers from his coat and dashed forward, his body flying as he leapt on strong legs, cleared the three porch steps in one bound, and ran straight into the burning, smoke-filled house.

Inside it was unbearable, and yet he bore it. He got on his hand and knees and found that even the floor was burning. He was beginning to register the foolishness of running into a house on fire when he saw their eyes flickering in the smoke, two cats, small and grey, crouched in the corner by the fireplace. He held his breath, dove and scooped them up, holding them like footballs one under each arm, and although one slashed at him, powerfully and painfully kicking him with its back legs, he didn't let go until they were outside and he was coughing and gasping, on the ground, the thin crust of snow soothing his throbbing hands and knees.

The old lady climbed on top of him, like he was giving her a piggyback ride. She covered his body with hers and told him he wasn't going back in there; it wasn't worth it for a goddamn cat. She held him in place and cried into the back of his neck.

* * *

The fire at the Birchbaum place was the biggest news Miserable had had in a while, and more news followed fast: Aaron Rodgers, still recovering from his recent injury, visited Amanda Carey, Cinnamon, and Lloyd in the hospital. It was the absolute highlight of several individual's lives, including Jerry Beck's, who speechlessly gazed into Aaron's smiling eyes before he was pulled into a fraternal embrace.

* * *

Running into a burning building to save a cat endeared Lloyd to the residents of Miserable (and beyond) much more than saving a human life ever would have. He was profiled in the *Wisconsin State Journal* as well as by NBC news and Aaron Rodger's visit was filmed for a *60 Minutes* segment. Only the

60 *Minutes* host had the bad manners to ask Lloyd what it was, exactly, he'd been doing at the Birchbaum place that night with a bag full of illegal fireworks, to which he responded with a dopey shrug and said, "Just walking by, I guess."

When they were discharged—none of them were hurt too badly, although Lloyd would carry scars on his palms from where he'd pressed them to the floor—Amanda Carey and her niece Cinnamon Lou stayed at a nearby Knight's Inn motel, in a room generously paid for by Trinity Lutheran. Some of the folks from the church were looking into a rental for Amanda Carey when she announced she didn't need or want any more help; she was moving, although she didn't say where or when. It was Jerry Beck who started telling people that Amanda Carey and her niece were getting shut of Miserable. They already had a house waiting for them, apparently, down near Delray Beach.

When people heard that Amanda Carey was moving to south Florida to live with her niece, that crazy girl with reality-television-person hair who ran along the shoulders of the road in all weather, they couldn't believe it. It seemed a fate unthinkable, that someone as miserable and ugly as Amanda Carey Birchbaum would be granted a means and method, could walk through a fire, and come out the other side with more than she had lost. Although she had lost several cats, Ruth Beck pointed out. And she'd been crazy about those cats.

Most people said that they personally would never want to live in south Florida. Jodie, who'd failed to take Jerry's advice and still haunted the Come Back Inn most nights (the cause and result of continued domestic turmoil), told Jerry Beck that sure, Florida was a nice place to go on vacation, but who would want to live there?

"Well, looks like Amanda Carey does," Jerry replied.

Jerry Beck wouldn't have wanted to live in Florida either.

Not really. He'd only been to Florida once—they took Drew to Disneyworld when he was five—and it hadn't impressed him too much. Jerry liked Miserable; he liked Wisconsin. He couldn't imagine living in a place without snow or deer-hunting or ice-fishing, without cool lakes and deep woods or the Packers.

No, he didn't like Florida. But he sure did like that Cinnamon Lou. He liked her funny Southern accent and the way she looked surprised and a little scared, but then relieved and maybe even happy whenever he walked into her hospital room to visit her. He liked how, when they went out for lunch at the Cracker Barrel (her idea), she looked at him hard and said that she'd made a lot of mistakes and that just when she thought she was done making them, she went and made another and at this point, well, she couldn't promise things would be any different.

Jerry shrugged. "I suppose I'm an optimist," he said. "I don't think it's ever too late to change. To turn things around."

Cinnamon shrugged back. "Maybe," she said. She took a sip of her milkshake and put her loose fists on the table. "Sometimes I think, fuck. Like, this is who I grew up to be." She looked down at her body and shook her head. "So, that's depressing."

"I don't think so," Jerry said. He leaned a little toward her. He put his big hand over her small fist and shook it gently. "No, I don't think that at all." He took his hand away and smiled at her. She looked into her milkshake, smiling too.

He didn't know quite what to make of all her pictures on the Internet, but he knew he couldn't stop looking at them every free minute he had. He'd find himself smiling at them, smiling at pictures of her smiling, or grimacing as she did complicated push-ups, gravity-defying sit-ups. He smiled at those pictures, although not when the ex made an appearance, a voice from off-camera or sometimes a sepia-toned selfie, the two of them on the beach at sunrise. Those pictures made him angry, but also grateful, for all involved, that they were holding the son of a bitch over in Urne and not in Miserable.

* * *

They were lucky. That's what the doctors and the nurses and the cops and the firefighters told them. Things could have been a lot worse for them. They'd been very lucky.

Cinnamon felt lucky. For the first time in her life, really, she felt lucky. It had been lucky that Lloyd had been there and that he'd been able to scare and distract Jason, to buy Cinnamon and Amanda Carey the time they'd needed to get out of the house after they'd discovered that they couldn't get out the back door, that the windows were shut up against them. It had been lucky that Amanda Carey had that gun by the door. It had been lucky that, in advance of the smoke alarms, Frieda had jumped on Amanda Carey's head to wake her and then dashed into Cinnamon's room and jumped on Cinnamon's head and then run back to Amanda Carey. It had been lucky that they'd lived, that they'd not been mortally injured, that Jason was in jail, held without bail and that, according to Jerry, he'd already had some problems there, with the guards and whatnot, and that she wasn't going to have to worry about him bothering her, at least not for a long time.

The social worker at the hospital told Cinnamon that she had and would continue to have PTSD; it was over but that it wasn't over, that some of the work was just beginning. Cinnamon thought the social worker knew better than Cinnamon did about these things and was probably right. She also thought that a fire changes things, it burns some things away and forges some things together, and maybe it would be all right, again, to start wanting and planning, it might not be too late for Cinnamon to make herself a nice life.

* * *

The worst part of being in the hospital for Amanda Carey was not being able to wait at the site of what had once been the house. She imagined the disoriented cats returning, looking for their home, looking for her, and finding only a smoking pile. She enlisted Jerry Beck to go by every day and look for cats, but, as she had long suspected, he was useless. He always reported: no cats.

But a few days after the fire, someone found Baby Snooks in the Walmart parking lot. And Peter turned up on route 108 a few days after that. The whole town of Miserable, it seemed, was on high alert for Amanda Carey's cats and when Lloyd got out of the hospital, he found Midnight—the cat Amanda Carey hadn't seen in years!—in the woods near the house. He might not have even been inside at all during the fire, smart cat.

A little girl found Patches in her garage; the mother called Amanda Carey at the hospital to say the girl had gotten very attached and they were hoping to keep the cat. Amanda Carey's first impulse was to say something not-very-nice, but she swallowed it down and said that would be "fine."

Dr. Hotstetter in Urne agreed to board the other recovered and recovering cats, but he called Amanda Carey at the hospital to tell her they were going to have to put Peter down, that the cat was in a lot of pain, and Amanda Carey couldn't speak to give her consent so she hung the phone up instead. That was one of the worst days.

Amanda Carey went to see Baby Snooks and Midnight as soon as she was discharged. Baby Snooks leapt, mewling, from his kennel, straight into her arms. Midnight, who had always been skittish and remote, seemed happy to see her too, although in a more subdued way.

She couldn't bring them back to the Knight's Inn, though, so eventually she surrendered them to the vet tech who returned them to their cages.

"Goddam cats," she said, rubbing at her eyes and not even pretending she wasn't crying as she let herself out the back door of the clinic.

* * *

Cinnamon Lou hadn't wanted to tell her aunt that they shouldn't bring the cats with them to Florida, but nevertheless, she told her aunt that they shouldn't bring the cats with them to Florida.

"It would be a tough trip for them," Cinnamon tried at first. "It's a really long drive. And cats don't like cars."

"Don't tell me cats don't like cars," Amanda Carey snapped. "I know cats don't like cars. And I don't want to bring the goddamn cats. But I don't know what you expect me to do. I can't just leave them."

Cinnamon thought that they could always get more cats down in Florida. They weren't in short supply or anything. But if she said that, Amanda Carey would get pissed off and tell Cinnamon that first she didn't want just any cats, that those were her cats, and second, she didn't even want any of the goddamned cats to begin with, which Cinnamon knew, of course, was a lie.

Cinnamon thought that maybe once they were settled, she'd get Amanda Carey a kitten as a belated Christmas gift. She thought her aunt might like that, despite herself.

"Goddamn it," Amanda Carey said.

"I'll help you find homes for them," Cinnamon said. "I bet Jerry would take one.'

"Fuck Jerry Beck," her aunt said. "I wouldn't trust that idiot with one of my cats."

Cinnamon laughed. She knew Amanda Carey didn't mean it. At least not really.

"What about Lloyd?" Cinnamon had asked. "Midnight came right to him that day. I bet he'd like to keep Midnight."

Amanda Carey did not have a snappish reply ready for that one. She frowned and nodded. "Maybe."

* * *

That was how Amanda Carey arrived on Lloyd's doorstep, the doorstep of the kid who not so long before had set a bag of dog shit on fire and left it on Amanda Carey's own doorstep. She stood, anchored on each side by a blue plastic cat-carrier. The damn cats, nervous and mewling, refused to stay still, making her crazy and throwing her off balance. She put the carriers down and rang the bell.

The stepfather—the one Amanda Carey had heard menaced poor Lorie Dowd—answered the door. Amanda Carey looked at him, unsmiling. "I'm here to see Lloyd," she said.

"Mrs. Birchbaum," Scott said, cocking his head to one side, also unsmiling. "Glad to see you're feeling well enough to be out and about."

Amanda Carey narrowed her eyes at the man and then gazed over his shoulder. Lloyd shuffled into view.

"Hey," he said.

Scott looked at the plastic cases and turned, retreating to the back of the house.

"What's going on?" Lloyd asked. Amanda Carey pursed

her lips and nodded at the cages; Lloyd picked them up and carried them into the living room.

The boy slouched; Amanda Carey had to stop herself from grabbing his shoulders, telling him to stand up straight. He was tall and he might even be handsome someday, but not if he slouched around for the rest of his life, looking like he'd just committed a shameful crime.

"I'm going to Florida, Lloyd," Amanda Carey began.

* * *

Lloyd found Scott in the kitchen, looking at his phone.

"Um, so Amanda Carey is moving to Florida," Lloyd began.

Scott looked up, waited.

"She asked if I could, you know, like, take care of her cats?"

"Cats?" Scott asked, raising his eyebrows. "As is in more than one cat?"

"Just two cats. She says one hides all the time. We won't even know he's here."

"Uh huh," said Scott.

"So, um, can I?"

"These are the cats the big hero saved?" Scott asked. He put his phone face down on his thigh.

"I don't know actually. I didn't get a good look at them. But, maybe?"

"And you're going to pick their crap out of a box?" Scott asked.

"Yeah, yeah," Lloyd rushed to assure him.

Scott flipped over his phone and looked at it, bored. "I don't give a shit," he said.

Lloyd was breathless and smiling when he reentered the living room. He nodded at Amanda Carey.

"I'll take good care of them," he said, so excited, holding out his hands, his palms still pink and shiny.

Amanda Carey nodded. "You better," she said.

Lloyd crouched down and sprung each cage door. Midnight slunk out and immediately hid under the sofa. Baby Snooks allowed himself to be picked up under his front legs and held.

Amanda Carey stood. "I have some more gear in the car," she said, moving toward the door. "Litter boxes and food and toys."

Lloyd nodded and held Baby Snooks aloft. Baby Snooks leaned in and touched his nose to Lloyd's.

Amanda Carey let herself back in and through the open front door came the cool, sweet smells of diesel, wet leaves and wood fires.

"I'll send you pictures," Lloyd said. He slung Baby Snooks over his shoulder, but the cat had other ideas and he slithered from Lloyd's grasp and walked down the boy's back before jumping loudly to the floor. "Get a phone or whatever and I'll send you pictures and updates all the time."

Amanda Carey nodded. "You know," Amanda Carey began before shutting her mouth up tight, a door blown closed.

Amanda Carey and Lloyd stood side-by-side like two strangers waiting for their bus, watching as Baby Snooks gingerly sniffed the carpet. Amanda Carey shifted from one foot to the other. "All right, Snooks. All right, Midnight," she said.

Lloyd followed her to the door.

"The house, the one in Florida," Amanda Carey said, suddenly brave. "It has four bedrooms. And a goddamn swimming pool." She turned to Lloyd, this person she seemed to see clearly now in a way she hadn't back when he was terrorizing her and leaving dog shit on her porch.

"Cool," Lloyd said.

She took another step toward the boy and grabbed his arm, shaking it, not even trying not to be too rough. "I thought you were a real piece of shit. But you're a good boy, Lloyd," she said, looking at him, hard, harder than he had ever been looked at before. "After all."

He smiled. "I guess you're not so bad either," he said.

Amanda Carey laughed.

A VISIT TO MY FATHER WITH MY SON

BY EDWARD M. COHEN

ONE

A dam and I arrived to find the mailbox frozen shut. Ice coated the road, caressed the rocks, and dripped from the trees, as fragile as lace but treacherous. A steep hill buried in snow, hid the house from view. The only indication a driveway existed was the "No Trespassing" signs which also served to attract the attention of vandals.

"Are you sure Grandpa is here?" Adam wondered.

There were no footsteps in the snow, no tire marks, no cigar bands. Maybe he had given up smoking, but didn't he visit the neighbors to gossip? Didn't he drive into town to shop? What if he were sprawled out dead on the porch, how would anyone know?

"Give me a minute to think."

"He's not here."

"He is so."

"How do you know?"

"He's lived here ever since Grandma died."

I stopped the car at the foot of the hill and could do nothing more than stare blankly ahead. It had been a lousy drive up in

Mimi's Toyota with the heater on the blink and words had to crack through my frozen lips.

"If he had moved, he would have let me know."

"There's no sign of life," Adam announced.

"I'm still his son, for crying out loud."

"A lousy one, if you want my opinion

"I remember when he bought this place."

"Hello!" Adam howled but there wasn't an echo.

I remembered this hill with its twists and turns and trees popping out of every crevice. I had nightmares about crashing off cliffs ever since I finagled myself into this trip.

"Hello! Grandpa? Anybody home?"

"I helped him fix the roof."

The driveway was perilously steep and the view, as you ascended, was dizzying. You could easily take a dive off the narrow, unmarked edge; your back wheels created a flurry of gravel on the unpaved surface, especially if, as my father used to, you raced up and down at manic speed. In the winter, iced and slippery, the going was even rougher and there was no way Mimi's car could have made it.

"It's like landing on the moon," Adam sighed.

She was forever having it repaired and sending me the bills, which I never paid, but still the damned thing took ages to start and threatened to stall and sputtered and spit in response to my touch. Just like Adam.

"My parents used to spend summers here. Then, he moved here permanently."

Adam did not respond. Mimi says she was awarded the car in the divorce because I would have cracked it up anyway. Then she complains that I don't visit the kid, but she can't understand I have to take the subway home, and on Sunday nights too when the trains hardly run. For years, Mimi refused to lend me the car because, the last time she did, it got towed. Which wasn't my fault.

"There isn't a sound," Adam whispered.

I admit I am a lousy driver, mainly because my father taught me up here, barking instructions into my ear so that a rare trip like this always left an ache in my shoulder blades and was preceded by dreams about crashing off cliffs.

"Are you really sure this is the place?"

"Do you really think I would lie to you?"

I was doing it for the kid, and Mimi was getting a Christmas vacation out of it which her analyst said she needed.

"Mom says your lies are a sign of your insecurities."

"I am the most secure dude you ever met."

Not exactly true. What was true was my father had no phone so there was no way to call and he hadn't answered my letter telling him we were coming. It's highly conceivable I'll take Adam back to the city with my tail between my legs because I failed to finagle the money he needs out of my father.

"He left the cemetery, packed a suitcase, moved up here without a word. That was

two years ago."

Adam was waiting for me to outline a plan of action, as I was waiting for him. At thirteen he attacked the world with such bravado he frightened Mimi who called at midnight, crying.

"Didn't mourn for his own wife. Didn't say goodbye to me."

"Maybe he went bananas when Grandma died. Why didn't you help him out?"

"Who?"

"Grandpa."

"Maybe he always was."

"What?"

"Bananas."

"Must you always put him down?"

"You said it. I didn't."

"I said maybe he went, not maybe he always was. If you went bananas in your old age and moved to the top of a hill, so I didn't know if you were dead or alive, I'd pay you a visit and check it out. You'd still be my lousy father!"

I was, in fact, a lousier father than I was a driver. I had no patience. I did not visit. I hated him as much as I loved him but never talked things out like Mimi's analyst said I should. We spent the entire trip up in silence. For a while, I thought he was sleeping but dared not turn to look. I was either too careful a driver, and my father used to say that it was the frightened ones who caused all the crashes, or I allowed my glance to wander at exactly the wrong moment which infuriated Mimi.

"Well, I'm here now," I muttered, not adding that my bladder was full, my head throbbed and there was no way I could tackle my father's hill in Mimi's lemon of a car.

"Two years after Grandma died. To get your hands on some money."

"The money is for you, not me."

"You blame everything on somebody else."

Adam was short for his age, but feisty like me, and I admired the way he hopped from the car and surveyed the scene with authority.

"And did I tell you about the telephone?" I shouted. "He had some question about the bill, refused to pay and threatened to sue; so, the company disconnected. What does that say about him, living up here without a phone?"

"It says he's got the balls to take on the phone company, which is more than I can say about you."

I remained in the car, frozen and confused, while Adam went to check out the hill. What if my father had not received my letter? Would he holler and make us return to the city, humiliating me in front of my son? What if he'd shacked up with some local bimbo? How would Adam react to that?

"We'll never make it in this fucking junk heap," Adam came back to report.

"It's your mother's car, not mine. Don't blame me for the fucking car."

"It's your fucking father."

"It's you who failed French."

"I didn't fail. I got suspended."

"A failure is a failure. It's time you faced it."

If I admired him so much and he went to such lengths to imitate me, why did we attack like clattering machine guns every time we met?

"We could leave the car and walk," I suggested.

"We'd never make it alive!"

"We could forget all about it and head back to the city."

"What about our stuff if we walk?"

"We take what we need and get the rest in the morning."

"I'm not leaving my guitar!"

"I'm not the one who needs tuition."

Adam pursed his lips into a soundless whistle, a habit he knew annoyed me. He sucked on breath instead of blowing it out, defiantly not communicating. He looked just like Mimi when he did it, her mouth pulled tight like a draw string purse.

"I never said a word about tuition."

"Your mother calls me every night, insisting I dig up private school tuition."

"I never said a word about private school. Don't lay that trip on me."

"Her gums have started bleeding again and she has to go back to the periodontist. That will cost me another fortune."

"If she gave up smoking, her gums wouldn't bleed."

"If you're so smart, why can't you pass French?"

"If Mademoiselle Marlowe fails me in French, I am dropping out of school
    all together."

"THAT'S ENOUGH WITH THE IFS!" I lost control but he had made me do it and, he smirked to let me know that he knew.

"If that's cool with you, we can head back to the city."

I breathed deeply to regain my composure. Adam refused to say a word.

"How are we going to get up this hill? That is the trip before us."

"If you go on my trips, I'll go on yours."

"My trip was first!"

I was shouting again but he had forced me into it. Threatening to drop out was an act of war. He pushed his pelvis forward like some street hood and perched against the fender, supporting his legs on the balls of his feet so an electric tension curled up his calves. He could pose like that for hours. His young body absorbed discomfort with ease. Mine ached from standing in line at the market.

We compromised; we left the car at the base of the hill and walked up – hauling Adam's precious possessions. I, at least, could grab for a tree when I felt my feet spinning beneath me, but Adam protected his guitar with both hands.

"What do you mean, dropping out altogether? What the hell are you talking
    about?"

Sound had a hard time registering on our numbed brains and caused enormous pauses between questions and answers and counter-replies; sometimes I had to wait until he was on firmer footing or he had to wait for me to catch my breath.

"You dropped out, didn't you?"

The air was so weightless that talking made me dizzy but

staying silent was worse. If I allowed one single wisecrack to pass, he snarled and issued another.

"And so did Miss Bleeding Gums!"

"We dropped out of college," I answered. "You're dropping out of Junior High."

"This is the age of Instant Gratification. I can't wait as long as you could."

Mimi said my hostile humor brings it out in Adam. I thought the reverse was true. Whoever was at fault, everything grew worse when we had to imagine each other's responses before we actually heard them. It seemed to take forever for sound to leave frozen lips, to float through frozen air, to land on frozen ears.

"What do you know about Instant Gratification? Stop reading New York Magazine while you wait to get your braces tightened."

"True creative artists haven't needed school since the beginning of time."

"And who is the true creative artist in this instance?"

"I am. You were. Don't blame me for being a chip off the old blockhead."

"Well, here's news for you, Chip. True creative artists have to pay the rent and the gas and your mother's miserable dental bills."

"Screw my mother!"

I could have wise-cracked that I obviously had and that was the reason we had dropped out of school, but he took his eyes off the road and was unprepared for a frozen branch which whipped in the wind and scraped across his tender cheek.

"And screw you, too!"

I winced and offered support, but his body recoiled from my touch even as snow turned to ice, and pain brought tears to his eyes.

"We're never going to get up this hill!" he whined. "One wrong step and we'll slide to the bottom!"

"Why don't you stop worrying and let me take care!"

"When was the last time you took care of anything?"

I gasped that the house was around the next bend, but I turned out wrong and grew secretly convinced we would get lost in the dark or freeze to death before we ever reached the top.

"You sure you've got the right place?"

"Sure, I'm sure."

"When was the last time you were here?"

"Your Mom and I spent our honeymoon here. We didn't have enough money to go anyplace else."

"If it was so long ago and the marriage was such a bust, why shouldn't I worry?"

"Trust me for once. I remember."

How could I forget? The minute I started climbing, I remembered Mimi, as exquisite as she had been then. But Adam would never believe she had been, never believe I'd thought so, never believe I still remembered.

Breathless beside him was a wily con man; always putting his mother down, always slipping out of demands, always failing her and him, always blaming somebody else. How could he believe I had really loved her, and she had loved me, and we both had loved him, even before he was born? I would not have believed it myself, except that the memory had been locked in these rocks and, as I kicked them away, I remembered.

"Because in the thirty years my father has owned the place, he has refused to have this hill paved. My parents argued about it constantly and I can still hear their fights in my inner ear. That's how, smart-ass!"

My words exploded in puffs of air, but not my memories of Mimi; her tissue paper eyelids so translucent you could see the blue of the veins beneath; her hair, the color of straw, tumbling into twists and curls just like the path before us.

"Some advertising big shot who had been dumped by his wife built the house; he gave up his job and patched together this lonely retreat to devote himself to his painting." Adam had to lean closer to hear so I was able to steer him along, remembering more with every turn. Me hanging onto branches, Adam hanging onto me, three steps forward- two steps back.

"In the end, he went crazy and his wife took him back. He owed my father

legal fees for the divorce so the old man picked up the pieces for a song."

That was the way Pop had shouted the story to me that first summer he owned the place. He was fixing the roof at the time and I was holding the ladder.

"The crazy artist wanted isolation, Jeffey. Don't you see? That's why he picked this spot, way on top of a huge hill, hammered every nail himself, depended on no one, painted daily."

"I want to be an artist," I had said. "A writer is an artist, too."

"And he purposely left the road bad to give his wife trouble if she came crawling back!"

"I'll move here when I grow up and write my first novel here. I'll make the place famous, Pop."

"Don't do me any favors. Your mother only wants her friends to visit. I like it the way it is."

In his thirties, my father was heavier than I am now, but he carried it well -- his arms stronger than mine, his shoulders broader, his back wider. Repairing the roof in the sun, he moved with a startling grace.

"And what did he give a damn?" I shouted to Adam,

sounding just like my father. "Crazy artist used to ski down for supplies in a snowstorm!"

Adam giggled at last, relishing every detail, and by the time the top came into view, we were hugging and howling, a rare pleasure to share with my son.

I was surprised the trip was over so quickly, but we maneuvered the terrain with ease once memories led the way. I even glanced over the edge from time to time and saw the worst that would've happened if I'd driven off the cliff is plopping into a neighboring cornfield. A lifetime of night-mares over nothing. Still, the final curve took us beneath a frightening arch of posters, nailed to trees and hung from branches.

"No Trespassing! No Hunting! No Loitering! Violators Prosecuted! THIS MEANS YOU."

"Post No Bills!" "Dead End, No U Turns!" "This Land Is Posted. Hikers Keep Out. Proprietor, Emanuel Dash, Attorney-At-Law."

One scrawled message had been placed in the middle of the roadway, on a rock which would have torn the guts out of your car if you failed to stop and read it.

"BEWARE OF DOG!"

Though not as high as I recalled, the top of the hill was still breathtaking. The sky stretched overhead, taut, and transparent like cellophane. The silence was eerie after the chaos of the climb.

Like landing on the moon.

Straight-ahead, my father guarded the way in my mother's fur coat, earmuffs under an army helmet, galoshes on his feet, and sawed-off shorts, that must have been thirty years old, belted by a rope. His naked legs, almost too spindly to support the bulk of his torso, shivered in the cold. I would have laughed except that, in his mittened hands, he held my old BB gun which, he had told me a hundred times, could take an eye out if I wasn't careful.

"Who is it? What the fuck do you want?" His voice was firm. His eyes were fierce. The gun was aimed directly at us. "What's the matter?" he barked. "Cat got your tongue?"

I clasped a hand on Adam's shoulder and felt him trembling also.

"It's me, Pop."

"You were making plenty of noise coming up the hill! Laughing to beat the band. Having a ball, right? Thought the place was deserted. Right? Thought you could break right in, sleep in my bed, piss in my toilet, drink my booze, waste my water, just like you owned the world!"

"It's me, Jeffrey -"

"This is private property, God damn it!"

"Put the gun down, Pop. You can take an eye out if you aren't careful."

"Private property up to and including that hill you just trespassed on! Didn't you see the signs? Don't you speak English?"

"Your son, Jeffrey. Pop..."

"Lousy sons of bitches, who do you think you are? Nelson Rockefeller? Franklin Delano Roosevelt? Richard Fucking Nixon?"

"Put the gun down. Please."

"Listen to him, Grandpa."

Our words tumbled on top of one another, so my father did not understand. Everything I said escalated his madness. I remembered him like this with my mother. Usually, it ended with him storming out of the house and her weeping by the window, worrying until he returned. Once, he threw a vase and it splintered up and down her arm.

"This property is posted. I don't allow no hunting here!"

"Your son, Jeffrey - and your grandson, Adam..."

I figured the only way to get through was to continue to repeat our names calmly. The worst I could do was to scream in return or, God forbid, weep as my mother used to, rubbing her arm where he had hurt her. Then, he would surely shoot.

"Last time I went to Albany, you vandals used the place and don't think I couldn't
tell."

"Jeffrey, Pop...Jeff...Jeffey..."

"Get your ass down the hill or I'm calling the sheriff!"

"Pop, you don't have a phone."

"That doesn't do any good, saying he doesn't have a phone." Adam tugged to get
away from me.

"Don't go near him!"

"Maybe he can't see."

"Can't you see he's crazy? He'll shoot in a minute if you move!"

I wrestled to hold Adam back, but he insisted on approaching my father. Out of the corner of an eye, I could see the old man grow more bewildered. And then, maybe I saw it, maybe I didn't, he took aim and I pushed Adam so hard he sprawled in the snow.

Except for the awful echo of his fall, there was silence.

"Pop, it's me - Jeffey."

"Who?"

"Your son."

As always, he seemed disappointed. But he lowered the gun and I looked at Adam, who fought tears with his mouth clenched shut.

"Jeffey..?

"Didn't you get my letter, Pop?"

"I've got no time for your letters." He turned toward the house as I leaned to help Adam. I wanted to apologize but he hopped up too quickly, brushing snow from his clothes as we followed my father inside.

* * *

My father and Adam trudged down the hill to get our stuff from the car. I was too exhausted to move. I said we would pitch in tomorrow and shovel the hill so we could get the car off the road and into the garage and then I would unpack. After all, we only brought along old clothes, who cared if we got robbed? But my father told a fairy tale about hunters plundering the neighborhood and the kid believed every word. The old man said hunters would break the windshield to get our bags which would cost in the end and why didn't I think of that.

Adam explained that the car was not even mine anymore and I never paid the bills I had agreed to in the divorce which, said my father, made my stupidity even worse.

"In my day and age, couples stayed married, no matter how lousy, so bills for one was bills for both and don't think your grandma didn't suffer when he busted his marriage, no matter how lousy. I think that's the reason she had a heart attack."

Adam added that I had wanted him to leave his guitar, which would have been another tragic loss since he planned to be a musician when he grew up.

"A musician is an artist too, Grandpa. My mom thinks only writers are true creative artists and performers are second class citizens in the hierarchy of art because they interpret instead of creating. That's why he doesn't give a damn if anybody steals my guitar!"

My father said Adam was right. I inserted that all he ever did was strum on the thing. I never heard him play a single song all the way through. He skipped from vamp to vamp until he drove me crazy.

Adam's eyes filled with hatred and my father rippled his hair. He found him dry clothing and new boots and a smiling kid accompanied my father down the same hill he complained about with me.

Alone, faced with the silence, I wished I were back in the city, waking to the sound of garbage trucks and furious drivers honking because they'd been blocked in by double parked cars.

HAARNK-HAARNK-HAARNK.

And noise all day long -- the radio playing and the phone ringing; Mimi complaining or an editor screeching over a deadline. I'd be talking my way out of trouble, or into it, hanging on by a flapping tongue, and when I was too tired to work or no one was calling, I'd go to the market and fight with the girl at the check-out counter.

It may have sounded crazy, but it was saner than living up here like my father fearful of phantom hunters. Silence had pushed him over the brink.

* * *

"I'd be fine if it wasn't for these fucking hunters. Think the place is Central Park even though it's posted. Next time I see one, he gets it smack in the eyeball!"

So said my father when I asked how he liked living here alone. He has always answered my questions with threats, terrifying me as a child.

"A BB gun may be a toy, but you can still take an eye out."

"I know, Pop. You've told me a hundred times."

"Well, maybe if I had done it, you'd have finally paid attention."

Adam's laughter slashed the air. He doubled over in his chair, clutching his stomach, drawing his knees to his chin, clapping his sneakered feet.

"Lucky your Daddy said his name nice and clear or he'd be blind in one eye by now! Pow!" The old man pantomimed a rifle and took another belt of Scotch. "I thought he was one of those hunters and you were also, only a midget, when a little bird whispers into my ear, 'Hey! That's no hunter! That's what's-his-name! Your son! The Writer Who Never Earned A Dime.'"

Adam's laugh flew to falsetto. "Grandpa! Grandpa! You'll make me pee in my pants!"

"Pee outside," my father commanded. "This is not the city where you can flush a hundred times a day. In nature, you have to learn to conserve."

Adam obeyed and my father was lulled by the hissing sound. When Adam returned, the old man had fallen asleep, lips puckered around another "Pow!" and the kid giggled and whispered, "The Writer Who Never Earned A Dime."

I refused to defend myself.

Instead, I scribbled notes on the perpetual pad in my lap. It was such an old habit that Adam paid no notice. Years ago, he asked what I was writing. "A novel," I lied, and he still believed me.

He plucked at his guitar. I plucked at my pages. We have survived many hours this way. The silence woke my father.

"I've got deer!" he roared as if he had never slept. "Plenty of deer. But it was nothing for nothing when I grew up in back of a candy store. The big spenders want deer, wait until I put a ski lift in, a hundred bucks a night, they'll stand in line to get a place! What do you think, I'm a dummy?"

He fell back asleep, snoring contentedly, and Adam strummed his guitar, doodled and plucked until his fingers fell into a melody. My ears perked up. As soon as I felt a glimmer of fatherly pride, he stopped the tune to doodle again. The sound was an echo of what I did on these pages. I couldn't stand to listen.

"Hey Adam," I whispered, hoping the old man would stay asleep.

"What?"

"I'm sorry."

"Sorry for what?"

"For pushing you."

"When?"

"When we first got here."

"Oh."

"He was in such a crazy state."

"That's cool."

"I didn't want everyone talking at once."

"I don't know why you're so scared of him."

"Scared of him? He was holding a gun!"

"A BB gun."

"You can still take an eye out."

"You really believe he would do that?"

"I'm trying to apologize."

"I said it was cool. Didn't I?"

Abruptly, my father woke. None of my plans worked out.

"I don't give a damn if the fucking world blows itself sky high. This is my fucking world and I'm king here. Anybody wants to argue gets his ass blown off!"

There was nothing frail about his arms or his shoulders. His skin was leathery and still tanned and his belly overhung his belt with majestic ease. But his beard and chest hair was snowy white, and he jiggled his false teeth on and off his gums, and when his cheeks collapsed into his mouth, his face was very old.

* * *

Mimi and I met at an audition for a student production of "Who's Afraid of Virginia Woolf?" She read for the shrewish wife and I for the young stud; neither of us got the part. She claimed it didn't matter; she wanted to be a painter, not an actress. Her analyst said only those who originate the work were true creative artists. Performers merely interpret; they're second class citizens in the hierarchy of art. I answered that, if she gave me her number, maybe we could go to the Museum of Modern Art together.

I watched as she doodled her name, "miriam wolfson," all small letters, and leaned over to inquire if capitals were second class citizens also. Her lips puckered in disdain.

"Capitalization of your name is a distortion of reality because you are not the center of the universe. Art is the center of the universe and everything else is a second-class citizen. Matter of fact, performers are third class citizens in that hierarchy. Art first. Painters second. Performers third."

"What class citizens are analysts?"

"You hide behind hostile humor because of your insecurities. It is a sign of narcissism that you feel your name is more important than any other word."

She did not speak, she lectured, giving the impression that she and her analyst had

discussed every philosophical question of the ages and had found the right answer to each. I was confused at the time and needed to believe that somebody had the answers to something.

"Capitalizing your name is just a custom," I gulped. "Like capitalizing God."

"I don't do that. I'm an atheist. All true creative artists are atheists." Her lips curled around a cigarette and she dripped ashes onto the floor with defiance. I proclaimed I wanted to be a writer, not an actor, so it did not matter that I had not been cast, either.

I loved the way she waved her cigarette in yellow fingers, creating perpetual fog, inhaling noisily, exhaling through her nose, sucking the smoke back in with relish.

Her eyelids were like butterfly wings and, every time she blinked, my heart fluttered.

"Writers are true creative artists like painters, not merely interpretive second-class citizens, aren't they Miriam?" Or third-class citizens. Whichever the hell it was.

"You can call me Mimi," she replied, blushing as if she had asked me to touch her secret softest part.

TWO

I t was morning. The fire crackled in the living room. The oven warmed the kitchen. Still, we dressed in sweaters and coats and earmuffs and mittens and long johns because my father kept the thermostat low, cursing the oilman who demanded an extra fee to drive his truck up the hill.

He told Adam about living in the back of the candy store with his mother and sister after his father died. He survived.

"Survival of the fittest, Adam. That's your Grandpa's philosophy."

"Grandpa, that's Darwin."

"Did he drive a cab all day, cover the soda counter on week-ends, graduate law school at night? My family sat on seltzer crates to eat. I won't stop complaining until the bastard is fired."

"Who, Grandpa?"

"The oilman."

"I thought you meant Darwin."

"I have a stack of letters this thick," said my father.

The refrigerator was bare, but the cupboard shelves were stocked. No eggs. No milk. No bread. He apparently survived on canned chili. I made tomato soup and sardines for breakfast and even Adam ate with gusto.

We woke early, and the cold made us hungry and cracked our eyes wide. I remembered summer streams and chirping birds and rustling leaves but in the winter nothing moved.

Everything was new to Adam, who hopped out of bed eager to embrace the cold. My father showed him how to dress without exposing skin to the elements, how to flush without wasting water, how to build a fire to last all day.

They trotted around like a pair of clowns, sweeping ashes and gathering kindling while I prepared our exotic breakfast and, afterward, my father marched us about, seeking out leaks and collapsing beams, pouncing on spots which required immediate attention. From the look of things, he never did more than march and seek.

Then they started shoveling the hill since he claimed the neighboring farmers would steal the tires off the car and he was amazed at my lack of survival instincts. He told Adam what a lousy driving student I was; how I nearly barreled into a tree because I had tried to turn left when he said to turn right. The kid's laughter punctuated the story like static.

"I knew the little bastard couldn't tell left from right, so I made him wear rubber bands on one wrist. Do you think that helped? Not on your life. Up here, on a mountain top, the jackass wouldn't survive a day."

The old guy never missed a punch line. The kid was the perpetual straight man and I was the butt of every gag. A new Three Stooges.

* * *

My father unearthed the typewriter I used in high school, the one I was going to write my novel on. He was wrong when he called me "The Writer Who Never Earned A Dime." I support Mimi and Adam in middle class splendor in Rego Park and my own humble lifestyle on the upper west side of Manhattan. Mimi works but I pay for her massive periodontal bills and the kid's braces and "medical extras" like vitamin pills and summer cabanas and cable TV and magazine subscriptions which Mimi claimed are "educational." And upkeep on that dismal car. Trouble is my father doesn't know how I earn a living. Neither does my son. The taboo was supposed to protect Adam and, according to Mimi's analyst, his ego was still too fragile to bear the burden.

I write sex stories for male magazines. Not Esquire or Playboy or other chic slicks. Grimy rags for flakes. Quickie novels for "underground" publishers. I have several pen names so nobody knows. I was in solid with a couple of editors. It was a formula business and I was an old pro. First, I turned out ten times more outlines than sales needed for survival. Then I hovered over the mailbox, waiting for the bounces. There was some predicting what would sell and what wouldn't, but one house would love what another would hate. The rates are low, so I need to know quickly to keep the mail moving and meet my quota to pay the bills.

Sex on wheels always sold. Cycle stories. Airplanes. Drag races. I'd do an outline with a stationary couple and get a bounce. I'd put them on wheels and resubmit. Bingo! I've got a winner. A good title and an upper-class villain helped. I once did a piece on how big-shots screw stewardesses in those tiny airplane johns. My editor was ecstatic.

Anything tied to the news is good. I read all the papers for inspiration. Youth stories are always fashionable -- how your kids were getting more than you and in what perverted ways. There's constant interest in the super-natural. Getting blown in the dark by a Martian. Spy stories were always successful; how the bitch tried every trick to get the plans but at the last minute our hero sensed danger and held back.

It's a tough racket. There are amateurs galore. The editor turn-over is high. The anxiety level is worse. I deserve credit for sheer survival, but Mimi sneers at every sale. She says my humor is hostile to women and I cannot explain to my son that I get paid by the word, every one chock full of juice, so I have to sell twelve stories and two books a month just to stay afloat.

Still no matter how drained, I plant myself at the keyboard to produce another plum and, now, it appears, instead of relief, I have to up my output to pay for private school.

And that was the reason I was too busy to shovel, banging out hostile humor on a remnant of my youth.

The house had sunk into the ground or, half of it had so it seemed cockeyed and crippled and you could not imagine it new and loved. But beneath the peeling paint, you saw that once it was. A huge window in the living room took advantage of the view. A sweet archway had been carved above the door. A hand-made weathervane sat on the chimney.

My father had added a porch to the kitchen, piecing it together with mismatched lumber, out of proportion to the rest of the structure. He had unearthed a supply of paneling remnants and used them to create a ceiling. He had made repairs sloppily, patches on patches, regardless of shape or color.

Every room was lined with pails to catch the rain, but he had a project in mind. He planned to create a leak-proof roof by nailing tin traffic signs over the weak shingles. "No Parking." "One Way." "Speed Zone Ahead." He had already started to steal signs from the highway and Adam offered to help.

The house leaned like a crumbling wedding cake, weighted by sagging drainpipes and screen doors hanging askew. Whatever was shiny had rusted. Whatever was solid had cracked. When my father bought this house, he was only slightly older than I am and I was only slightly older that Adam, who slept now in my bed, in my room, beneath photos of Norman Mailer I had pasted on the wall. My father slept in the bed he shared with my mother. I had the sofa in the living room, but the pillows were hard with memories.

He bought the house without consulting her, partly as a cockeyed trade with the crazy artist. My father said we would use it for summers and move here when he retired so he could hammer to the skies and no one would stop him.

She said over her dead body – which was exactly how it happened.

"He doesn't give a damn," my mother used to weep. "Not about you. Not about me. What does he care it's a hundred miles from nowhere, up a hill so steep you can't get the mail, not a neighbor in sight, so quiet the crickets will drive us all crazy, so dark we'll be murdered in our beds?"

She had been a tiny woman. He had been, and was, a massive man. But her weeping overwhelmed his hammering and still it haunted the room.

* * *

The old man never asked why we had come to visit because he sensed it would cost him and my tongue was so thick with memories, I could not get the words out.

"I have to wait for the right moment or else he'll turn us down for sure," I explained as Adam walked beside me in the sulky posture I hated. He plunged his clenched fists into the pockets of his coat and drew them together in front of his crotch. He could pace like that for hours.

"There's really no hurry," I simpered. "The new term doesn't start until after New Year's."

His body became a coil of tension. He hunched his back, held his arms rigid, and walked careful and prissy. It was a statement of total withdrawal and it made me want to scream at him to cut the crap and take his hands out of his pockets but he would only stare back and shrug that I was the madman, not he.

"And you're having a good time. Aren't you?"

Mimi claimed he was getting increasingly withdrawn and Mademoiselle Marlowe said there were signs he was turning schizophrenic.

"Say something, for crying out loud!"

"He's such a sweetheart. Why are you so scared of him?"

"Who the hell says I'm scared of him?"

"What do you think, I'm a dummy?"

"No. I think you're a smart-ass kid who doesn't know when to keep his mouth shut. And, maybe if you did, you wouldn't have failed French and we wouldn't be here in the first place."

"Chill out. You're saying things you're going to regret."

"And he's not such a sweetheart, for your information. He never gave me anything and, if he turns me down now, I'll kill him. I'd rather see him dead and buried than give him the satisfaction of groveling."

"You're heading for another psychotic episode," Adam said. "Just like you had with Mademoiselle Marlowe."

"Don't psychoanalyze me. You sound just like your mother."

"Who the hell else should I sound like, shmuck?"

Adam cocked his head and glued his glance to the skies, absorbed in his own tuneless whistle, looking, for all the world, like a schizo. This is the age when it happened, Mimi said.

They overdose on drugs and develop the screaming meemies, anytime, day or night. They lock themselves in their rooms and starve until bones show through their skin.

"He made my mother miserable with this crazy house, but he wouldn't spend a

dime to fix it up and now he's afraid because I'm the one who knows it."

They take fistfuls of pills and go up on the roof and try to fly.

"You got all wound up with Mademoiselle, too, and that's why you cracked up like you did."

"He's just dying to prove that he's the sane one and I'm the loony."

"He probably can hear every word. Sound travels like crazy up here."

"If there is any reason you have to rush back, say the word and I will ask him today. That's how scared I am of him!"

"You don't have to ask for anything on my account."

"Don't be an idiot. What will you do if I don't?"

"Pick up my guitar. Travel around the country."

"You've got time to start a career."

"Things have changed since your day, Dad. If you don't make it young, you don't make it."

"Adam, you're only thirteen."

"One flick of the wrist and I've got busloads of twelve-year-olds hot for my bod."

I turned to him in amazement. The giggling boy had only been trying to tease me out of my fury, but I grew suddenly scared that I would screw up with him – the way I have with everyone else – and could not giggle in return.

* * *

One reason my father loved the house was because of all the storage space. Every time my mother refurnished; he dragged the old junk here. And neighbor's old junk. And junk he picked off the streets. I was seated at a table covered with mismatched oilcloth, one broken radio on top of another, surrounded by chairs, splintered and taped. The kitchen shelves sagged with unnecessary dishware, supermarket giveaways, grimy canisters, plastic flowers coated with mold.

The two of them whittled walking sticks with such concentration that I dared not say a word. The silence allowed buried images to rush my brain. I recalled one afternoon on the very couch Adam now sat upon. Mimi and I made love right there, out of control and unafraid.

I remembered that afternoon. The hours have been hoarded here. I could still smell her body in the cushions. I could not recall what had happened before or after and there have been many bodies since but I saw her beneath me as easily as I saw, out on the lawn, under the snow, a pile of rusted auto parts, broken bikes, empty crates.

My loony father throws nothing away.

Right from the start of the fall semester, Mimi had been getting notes from Mademoiselle Marlowe that Adam had been causing fights and talking back and cutting classes and cheating on tests and worse. I hadn't sold a thing in weeks when Mimi called to say that Adam had hidden in the coat closet and refused to come out. He had torn up his homework rather than have it corrected. He had passed dirty notes around the classroom and drawn obscenities on the blackboard. Mimi said it was all my fault. I was an irresponsible, woman-hating neurotic and Adam had picked up my sexism and was taking it out on Mademoiselle Marlowe.

I had not been out to visit in months. Mimi claimed the least I could do was send the money I owed and if I was a real father, I'd take him to school and talk to Mademoiselle Marlowe. Then she started to cry which has always pushed me into heroics, so I agreed to go.

* * *

The snow fell so regularly, almost without movement, like a polka dot curtain in the window. My father and Adam tackled the hill each morning to get the car up. He insisted they can shovel snow faster than God can replace it. I prepared a hot meal for their return and then listened in silence as Pop crooned how his client, the crazy artist, sold for a song when his wife took him back because he owed so much money for the divorce.

"And this guy was no dummy. He had talent up the wazoo, you hear? Built this house from scratch, hammering every nail, depending on no one. Crazy artist used to ski down for supplies in a snowstorm. Did I ever tell you that, Adam? What did he give a damn?"

"So, what happened, Grandpa?"

"He was in love and, when she snapped her fingers to come back, the shmuck would have turned the place over for a bus ticket if I hadn't taken pity on him. Seventeen thousand for a house and five acres, two and a half hours from Manhattan, and he left all his paintings for me!"

He laughed and we joined him, all of us pretending to enjoy the gag. But he was drunk, and Adam was confused, and my mind was beginning to cloud.

"A winner grabs the world by the tits and never takes his

eye off the ball. That's what your father didn't learn when he was your age."

I had spent hours staring into those abandoned nudes of the crazy artist's wife. My adolescent eyes wandered over her voluptuous hips, breasts nippled by inky buds, thighs soft as the velvet lining of a jewel box. My father has used them to replace broken windowpanes, cover cracks in the ceiling. The entire ramshackle house is a tribute to his triumph over the painter's love for his wife.

"I figured, at least, with seventeen grand in his pocket, he could build another dollhouse when she kicked him out again."

Dollhouse is right. The rooms were tiny, and the ceilings were low. The floors slanted. The doors stuck. Still, Mimi and I discovered that the living room was designed for making love before the fire. When we lay there together, we could see the sky through the window, pinpricks of stars peeking through. It was like sleeping outside on soft leaves, the moon at our heads, the fire at our heels. When we started to move, the floorboards creaked, the windows sighed, the walls breathed with us until the entire room lifted from its moorings, a rocket ship propelled by my pelvis.

"If I was twenty years younger, I'd peddle those paintings myself. Make me another fortune. If he wants them back, he'd have to sue, and I'd win."

When we rested together on our backs, the house resettled into the earth. The roof covered us like a quilt and our nerve endings crackled along with the logs.

"Thirty years ago, I knew how to be a winner – never take your eye off the ball – and that's when I bought this house. Ask your father if that isn't the truth."

The truth was he had plenty of money and he had been

right about soaring real estate values. But in matters of love, Pop, we were both losers. The crazy artist, on the other hand, did not build this house to escape his bitch of a wife. He built it to win her back and it worked.

But me and my father, we both lost our loves and there is no way they will ever come back.

* * *

They finally finished shoveling and my father drove the Toyota up, Adam hanging out the window and singing, "Hooray for the red, white and blue!" They slid it into a spot they had cleared in the garage next to my father's Cadillac, as if the big car had given birth to the little, and they danced around it in triumph, making up songs and victory cheers.

I watched from the porch and laughed until tears froze at once on my cheeks as my father dug into a corner for a tambourine for Adam, a toy trumpet for himself and the dance moved out from the garage, my father leading, my son behind, a Cadillac and a Toyota. They tumbled over each other in the snow and tossed some in the air like confetti and tried to get me to join but I wouldn't.

Only now do I understand why it was important for him to move the car and what the celebration was all about. It was his way of saying he was glad we had come, and he wanted us to stay and I was suddenly sorry I had not responded by rolling around in the snow.

* * *

Every day got easier. My father and Adam emptied closets and the old man loaded the kid with white on white shirts Adam found stylish, a carton of old 78's, a felt fedora which Adam wore constantly. Where in this maze were the bankbooks, I wondered.

When the two of them burned garbage outside, Adam's laughter circled the trees and invaded the house like a bird. And not his strained city laugh either. The sound was reckless and airborne, and the collapse of terrors could be heard in each giggle.

I was getting work done and my rattling typewriter comforted the others. At dinner, we managed a conversation and, afterward, there were long pauses as we drank before the fire. My pen forever scratched at my pad. Nobody mentioned the problems that brought us or how we could solve them and when we should leave. Adam tuned his guitar. My father cracked a joke. Adam giggled but I had missed the punch line because I had been listening to echoes of Mimi: "Mademoiselle Marlowe thinks he needs special attention so you'd better dig up private school tuition or I'll drag you through the courts to pay. If he ends up schizoid, the guilt will be yours, not mine."

My father, of course, heard nothing of this. Now that we could drive down the hill to shop and I was doing the cooking, he had soda with every meal, fruit after lunch, cake for dessert just like he used to when my mother was alive to complain: "What kind of nut buys a place like this, hoarding jigsaw puzzles with missing pieces? For crying out loud, throw out some crap so a person can breathe around here!"

A chorus of sour women hummed in my head. Sometimes I sounded like them and often I thought like them: "Listen here, Schizoid! If I put up with my lousy father and still hung onto sanity, you can do it too! You will not fall apart on me. You will not leave me to pick up the pieces and haunt me with those childish eyes like the crazy artist's wife! If I can walk and talk and pretend to be a man, so the hell can you!"

Sometimes Adam looked at me with such hurt, I thought I

must have actually yelled it. But my father didn't wake so I probably hadn't. I wondered if the poor crazy bastard – my son, that is, not my father – I wondered if he was so angry because he could read my mind.

* * *

I told my mother that I wanted to live like the crazy artist when I grew up, on top of a hill, and she said my father was the crazy one.

"Don't say he's crazy. He isn't crazy."

"Isn't it crazy to buy a fully furnished home without even asking his wife and isn't it crazier still to pick up junk off the street so he has broken lamps on every broken table and stolen ashtrays and matchbooks he can't resist even though he doesn't smoke and I don't smoke and, God forbid, you don't either?"

"Of course, I don't."

"So what smokers are coming to visit with that crazy hill the way it is?

"That doesn't make him crazy."

"And don't forget placemats that he takes from every luncheonette and enough toothpicks to stuff a horse. If that isn't crazy, what is?"

What had he done that had filled her with rage? They fought the same battles over and over, just like Mimi and me, when things went sour and all we ever argued about was who should take out the garbage. But, in the kitchen, the ancient refrigerator was chugging, and I could hear both women weeping in the noise.

THREE

Somehow, sitting in the living room, staring at my pad, I had let an important moment pass. I could only piece together the conversation after the fact, but I gathered that Adam expressed to my father his concerns about being short.

The kid was short. Big deal. Was that the cause of his schizophrenia? He could have mentioned it to me.

"I was short for my age," I would have told him. "All my friends were. You'll shoot up. Matter of fact, for one two-week stretch, I was the tallest kid on the block and got picked for all the basketball games."

I entered the conversation as the old man was describing how short my mother was and he held out his palm as if she could perch right on it.

"That's how tiny your Grandma was, Adam. You take after her."

"Pop, don't be crazy."

"Another county heard from. We thought you were writing your novel."

"He wants to hear that he will shoot up, not that he'll be stunted forever."

"Who said he'd be stunted forever? Did I say that, Adam, or is your daddy making up stories again?"

"You're talking about Mom as if she were some pigmy and telling him he takes after her. How is that supposed to be reassuring?"

"Just keep scribbling, will you?"

He had been drinking since dusk, and I had had a bit too much, myself. It does not matter. An explosion had been brewing since we arrived.

"I was short for my age too, Adam. All my friends were..."

"Who's talking about your cockamamie friends? What makes you think you know the answers to everything?"

"Matter of fact, for one two-week stretch...."

"We were talking about your mother; may she rest in peace."

"You were making her sound like a shrimp."

"Don't start defiling the dead around here."

"She was a perfectly normal sized woman. Maybe five foot two."

"The woman was a bird. Maybe four foot two."

"You're crazy! She always said it and she was right!"

"She never said such a thing in her life."

"Stealing placemats with every cup of coffee and enough toothpicks to stuff a horse! If that isn't crazy, what is?"

He hauled himself out of the chair, face flushed, wrinkles crackling, weaving on his feet. "The woman is dead, Mr. Writer Who Never Finished College! Does it matter what lies you tell?"

I remembered him like this when I was a boy. I remembered him throwing the vase.

"This is so dumb," Adam moaned. "I don't understand why you are fighting."

"Don't get smart with me, Mister Writer Who Never Earned A Dime. I'll smack your face. You think I'm proud of the mess you've made of your life? A son is supposed to give hope to his father but you, you're a one hundred per cent failure in my book!"

His face was so bloated, it looked ready to burst. All the veins in his neck turned purple.

"You'll shoot up, Adam,' I mumbled. "All my friends did."

"The woman was a bird! That's why we're fighting! I could lift her in the palm of my hand and, if anybody says no, I'll crack him in two!"

He raised a fist high in the air and posed before me, trembling.

"All right, Pop. All right."

My mouth went dry with terror. Adam looked away. Tears threatened all our eyes. Finally, Pop dropped his arm and stumbled to the kitchen for ice cubes.

"Why can't you keep your big mouth shut?" the kid sneered.

"All right, Adam. All right."

* * *

She added a pat of butter to soft boiled eggs to make them even creamier. We ate pears and bleu cheese and did the crossword puzzle with such communion that we had to make love when we filled the final space. There was a whole world of sensuous delight that Mimi and I discovered here. Wine with a picnic lunch in the sun and napping, afterward, entwined in each other's limbs.

FOUR

y father and I did not speak for a whole day after the explosion. Adam shot poisonous glances at us both. Three loony birds on top of a hill, flapping our wings as threats.

The old man, of course, talked endlessly to Adam about how he had met my mother, how much he had loved her, rubbing it in that she was tiny. I dared not contradict.

"All my life, I was surrounded by ugly women. My mother was a horse. My baby sister looked just like her. Client's wives and bookies' girlfriends and frightened hookers were always calling in the middle of the night for legal advice or I should come bail somebody out of jail.

"But Dot, when I met her, was silent and small, barely four foot two, with tiny hands and dimples in her cheeks. She had special rings to show off her hands and a special smile for the dimples. She wore a different hat to work every day, some with veils, some with flowers. I had never seen a woman like her.

"I was this up and coming lawyer, always laughing and cracking jokes, and she was this shy typist in the secretarial pool and, if you want the truth, Adam, I was crazy about her from the first minute. But she didn't know I was alive. Or so I thought. Every time I passed her desk, cracking a joke that set the other girlies off, she buried her head and typed fast and how was I supposed to know?

"But I was skinny then, and good looking too. All the girls were after me. The same thing will happen to you, Adam. If you have any doubts, I have pictures to prove it; me, skinny and Dot in a hat."

* * *

Mimi had not aged well. She drank too much, blamed it on me. She had stopped painting years before; the brush had dried up in her hands. Before we split, she used to get depressed and eat whole cheesecakes in a single sitting. She was still trying to get the weight off her hips. I remembered when we comforted each other, calmed each other, urged each other on. Now, it seemed, we passed on terrors like relay racers.

"You're smoking," I greeted her the morning I arrived to pick up Adam. "What's wrong?"

She led me into the living room which, as usual, was a mess. Adam's clothing, books, magazines, a pile of gardening tools. Every picture on the wall hung cockeyed. Every ashtray overflowed.

"Mimi, the periodontist told you a million times how smoking aggravates your gums. Last time I was here, you promised to give it up."

"How many years ago was that?"

"Months, not years."

"How many months?"

"Who remembers?"

"Adam remembers."

"Mimi, what's wrong?"

Even her hair was frantic. Her eyes, shining dark marbles when we were younger, had tightened into suspicious slits.

"What could be wrong? My kid is getting thrown out of school. His father, of

course, is forty minutes late. Mademoiselle Marlowe expected you at nine."

"Well, I'm here now, aren't I? And I'm taking the kid to school, aren't I? And I'm

getting down on my hands and knees before this almighty Mademoiselle so she doesn't have him suspended. And I'm sure to succeed, aren't I?"

"Hallelujah! Norman Mailer is here! Forty minutes late, of course! But I'm still supposed to be grateful!"

"I know I am always late, and I owe you so much money, and I didn't turn out to be the great American writer, either"

"Please keep the details of your disgusting career to yourself. Adam can hear every word."

"Some day he is going to learn the truth, Mimi."

"My analyst feels his anti-social behavior is due to the distortions of his role model."

"Does your analyst do oral surgery, also?"

"Adam!" she shouted. "Your father is here!"

He did not appear, and we were left, smirking at one another because we had gotten under each other's skin so quickly.

"And it's none of your business whether I smoke or not."

"I pay the bills."

"Since when?"

Mimi shut her eyes as if she could make me vanish and Adam, suddenly on the stairway, took up where she had left off.

"Hello, kid. How the hell are you?

"How the hell should I be, Norman?" he sneered.

* * *

The three of us went into town. When I was a kid, there was only one grocery and a gas station. Now, there was a mall with a movie theatre, even a pizza parlor. My father pointed out each new addition as if he had built it himself.

We had been tiptoeing around one another for days so the trip was a relief and I announced that, in all the time we had been there, I had eaten no junk food, three straight meals, lots of fresh air, working and sleeping. I offered to treat to a pizza, and we ordered a whole pie with pepperoni and three large root beers.

We were like children, cheese dribbling down our chins, each talking faster and louder than the others. I told them how well I was working, and Adam said my novel would win the Pulitzer Prize. My father said I had better not put his stories into it. He was thinking of writing a book, himself. Our voices and giggles were so alike, I would think it was me, babbling and laughing, but it was one of them.

* * *

"Then, one day, out of the blue, I plant myself on top of her desk so she couldn't pretend to ignore me and type while every other girlie has her ears pinned to listen. I'm in charge of the office Christmas party, I tell her, and if she volunteers to help decorate, I can get her the afternoon off to go shopping for tinsel with me. I had noticed the sense of style in the hats she wore and the rings on her fingers so I figured she was the girl for the job and she must have turned a hundred colors but sure, she says, she'll go. Why wouldn't she, for crying out loud? An afternoon off is an afternoon off and she figured I was some up and comer to be able to finagle that for her.

"Well, Adam, we never stopped laughing the whole afternoon. I don't even remember why anymore. Don't forget, this is fifty years ago, I'm talking. We bought tinsel and crepe paper and grab bag gifts for everyone. That was her idea. I spent money like water. It was all from petty cash, but she was impressed by the way that I did it.

"By the time I took her home, I knew two things for certain. Number one: she was laughing so hard, I could do anything I wanted and, number two, I was in love, so I'd better watch my step!"

* * *

My father was teaching Adam to drive, and I was nervously alone. Nervous because my father was blind in one eye and had lost his driver's license and I was sure he would crash and kill them both. Nervous because I remembered him barking, "Turn right! Turn right!" when I turned left and nearly barreled into a tree.

Nervous because it was so quiet, I found myself talking aloud like he does, recreating arguments, first taking her side, then his, about how crazy it was to live here and what use was that pile of shoes without tongues? Nervous because I sneaked into his room to look around and one wall was covered with moldy cartons containing his old legal files but there was a new one filled with his present obsessions. He was still fighting the phone company over the bill that caused them to disconnect. He was threatening to take the revocation of his driver's license to the Supreme Court. He was suing to collect workmen's compensation benefits, claiming my mother died of a work-related injury while employed as his secretary.

She died of a heart attack. She had never worked as his secretary. The case had been turned down twice and he had to drive, unlicensed, to Albany for another hearing.

The papers were neatly filed but each letter was crazier than the last, misspelled, incoherent, coffee stained. A complaint to the oil company exploded with rage. A Playboy calendar hung over his bed. Cereal box toys littered the dresser.

* * *

"I've got one more, funny story to tell. Then I'm going to sleep. This is about the first time I brought your grandma home to meet my family in back of our lousy candy store. They didn't know it was lousy, I suppose. They only knew my pop was dead, I was the fair-haired son, and this strange girl was coming to steal me away. My mother was tight-lipped, and I worried she would say something mean, on top of worrying how Dot would react when she had to sit on a seltzer crate.

"And I warned them in advance that she came from the Bronx, where they had real kitchen chairs, and I must have laid it on too thick about her being short and delicate. So, in I walk with Dot and my mother stares and my baby sister, Celia, finally pipes up to break the ice. 'She ain't so short,' she says.

My father laughed hard, choking on his cigar, stomping his foot to stop himself. Trailing smoke, he headed for bed, pausing to pee off the porch, chuckling, "She ain't so short!" over and over. Adam and I were left in our usual discomfort. Only this time, he did not turn to his guitar.

"It's time," he said.

"Time for what?"

"Time to ask for the money." He seemed awfully sure of himself. "What are you afraid of?"

I was afraid my father would say no, and Adam would be

crushed. I was afraid my father would say yes, and I would look like a fool for being afraid. Or he might say yes, and I would sign all the papers and, at the last moment, he would leave me holding the bag.

"I'm not afraid. What makes you say that?"

"Don't you realize the point of that story? About her not being short? He's apologizing to you for yelling. Remember, that's what the argument was about. It's time to ask and go home."

"Adam, not yet."

"He didn't mean all those things he said. He's only teasing when he calls you names. When your novel is published, he'll be proud."

"Adam, please. He'll only make another scene."

"If you don't ask, I will."

"Adam, please...."

FIVE

I had not expected Mademoiselle Marlowe to be so pretty. Mimi had prepared me for her youth; not more than twenty-three, just out of Barnard and a year at the Sorbonne. Every time she used a French phrase – and her conversation was littered with *"Mon cher, Adam,"* and *"comprenez-vous?"*- her exquisite mouth sucked on the sound as if it were made of hard candy.

She had fragile skin and soft hair and sky-blue eyes that stretched wide. I could picture her bouncing through Paris, writing home breathless praise, on the brink of a hot affair, carefully eyeing every guy on the street to make sure she picked *la crème de la crème!*

The classroom walls were covered with Air France posters and ads for French movies and one large montage, cutely lettered, *"Mademoiselle De Paris"* in a rainbow of magic markers. There were snapshots of Mademoiselle at the Eiffel Tower and the Arc de Triomphe and flirting with whatever you call a French cop. She caught my glance and explained how Junior High French was more than grammar and vocabulary. She wanted her students to learn about *la cinema francais* and *tout le monde francais.*

Adam was standing awkwardly beside me and I could feel his body trembling through the floor. All the way to school, he had been doing his tough guy number but, in the classroom, the transformation was alarming. His body shriveled. His complexion paled. His head fell forward so heavily it looked like it would tumble off his neck. Both shoelaces had come undone and they dangled from his sneakers as if I had never taught him to tie them.

Mademoiselle signaled with a shrug that this was what he was like all the time, hostile, resistant, tormented, and I said I agreed with her educational philosophy and confessed I had been a lousy French student myself. But, in college, "had fallen in love with Proust and had studied until I mastered the language."

"You hear, *mon cher Adam?* Papa is right. It may not make sense now. It may be boring and difficult. But one day, the glories of French will enrich your entire life!"

"It's like learning to play the piano," I added. "You practice those scales and, *voila,* you're playing Debussy!"

"Well, I play the guitar," Adam hissed through clenched teeth.

"You don't play anything, as far as I know. You doodle. That's not playing. I never heard you play a tune from start to finish."

"That's exactly as far as you know."

"He doesn't apply himself with discipline to anything," I confided to Mademoiselle. "Which is exactly what we are saying. He doesn't study music. He can't read notes. He never practices!"

"How can you say that?" Adam gasped. "I practice all the time! That's what I'm doing when you think I'm doodling."

"I'm a writer, Mademoiselle. And every artist worth his salt knows that you haven't crawled until you have mastered Proust."

Adam turned from us and paced the room, scraping his heels against the floor, running a finger close to the wall so he threatened to ruin Mademoiselle's montage. How could I have explained to someone as innocent and charming as Mademoiselle that I had brought a kid into the world and, joking and flirting and battling to survive, I had done so much damage he was cracking up?

"I didn't know you were an artist, *Monsieur.*" She tried to help me out. "Why didn't you tell me Papa was an artist, Adam?"

He sprawled into a chair at the other end of the room, his mouth curled in that infuriating whistle. No one could get through to such a kid; no teacher, no parent, no analyst. A blanket of hostility engulfed him.

"Might I have read something of yours, *Monsieur?*"

"Oh, the publishing scene is so corrupt I decided years ago not to publish at all. Lots of us, a whole school of writers, are choosing that private path these days."

"How absolutely fascinating."

She was going to flirt through this session and so, I figured, was I. Let Adam see his loser of a father, also a failure as a writer and a lover and a son, can turn on the charm when required.

"All my friends feel that way. We support each other in our isolation from the mainstream."

"I'd really like to hear more about that."

"Maybe some night you'll join us. We often bring guests who are *sympathetique.*"

I winked at Adam, but the kid was not impressed.

* * *

Adam was getting up early each morning, thinking up projects, obviously getting ready to ask. They fixed the bathroom floorboards, sorting through a pile of half-rotten lumber planks to replace the thoroughly rotten. Afterward, they went for the daily driving lesson. According to my father, the kid had a natural talent. Not like me.

I could never relax behind the wheel. Never learned to bend my elbows, never steered with one hand, like Pop did. Still can't turn the ignition key without a sense of helplessness and bubbling rage. Tension in the shoulder blades makes me drive too quickly, with parched lips and heartbeat palpitating in my ears and eyes aching in their sockets.

* * *

He invited Adam out to see the full moon on the snow and I trudged along behind them. The property ended at a cliff from which you could see the surrounding countryside, sheathed in white satin.

"What do I need the Hayden Planetarium, where they charge you a buck and a quarter and you can't even pee in the snow? Right now, I own the world and that's something you'll never feel in the Hayden Planetarium. I own all those roads and houses and even the stars and the moon and the sky and nobody can take that away. You'll learn, Adam, as you get older, everything that means anything, life is going to take away. But damn it, this view of the stars, just let them try and I'll show them who's boss around here."

"Pow! Right in the eyeball. Right, Grandpa?"

He threw an arm around Adam's shoulder to launch into a lecture about the patterns in nature and how one star connects to another and the poor dope of a city kid oohed and aahed. and his body leaned close to my father's.

It made me jealous, I admit and, when my father turned away to pee, I whispered, "Adam, please don't ask for the money. He'll only kick you in the teeth."

"Why do you say such things about him?"

"He never gave my mother a thing. He's always sneered at me."

"No! He's proud of you. He can't wait to read your novel. He knows you're a true creative artist. In his own way, he loves you." To my amazement, the kid was near tears. He shook his head to push them away.

"Adam, please don't," I mumbled.

* * *

I was not working so well after a while, sitting at the table, pretending to write as deadlines flew by. I listened to Adam and my father howling and tried to laugh at their stupid gags, but the sound would not come. I was afraid I would never finish another assignment or crack another joke.

Every now and then, Adam asked how the novel was going. The question always came after a lull in the conversation and I could see from his blush how much effort it took. My father always perked up when he asked, awed that the kid should tread on such sacred turf.

I was usually taken aback so I said something absurd like, "Oh, you know how it is, Adam. I spend the whole morning changing a few phrases and then I decide I don't like the changes and change them back again."

Should I have confessed I am like every other factory hand, hauling the stuff onto the conveyor belt or I start to sink? Still when the system breaks down and I get hit with a string of bounces, well, I get through the bad times, too. And I do it all without grandiose claims about being an artist, having all the answers, skiing down for supplies in a snowstorm.

I survive, God damn it, and that's an art, too. But when I listened to my father finagle about connecting stars so my son leaned toward him, I remembered loving Mimi and then losing her and failing everyone and everything and, all of a sudden, Adam is on the brink of tears and I cannot figure out why.

Well, enough is enough. Nobody wins everything. Norman Mailer had his bombs. I resolved to ask the loony for tuition and take the kid home before the three of us got stuck here forever, hammering together to the skies.

This happened after a visit to my mother when she was recovering from her heart attack. For the first week, she had been in Intensive Care, always sleeping, barely breathing, and my father and I had been allowed in for five minutes each hour to stare helplessly at her ghostly face.

But time passed and the worst was over, they had informed us. She moved to a semi-private and was sitting up and eating by herself and even started squabbling with my father. She wanted some cosmetics and a book she had been reading and an emery board for her ringed fingers. My father grumbled that he would not know an emery board if he fell on one, so I offered to get it and drove to their apartment with him.

He looked worse outside than he had in the hospital room. I was afraid he would fall asleep at the wheel and offered to drive but, of course, he would not hear of it.

I said she certainly must be getting well if she needed a cockamamie emery board but he did not laugh at the joke nor at my effort to reassure him it did not make me smarter because I knew what an emery board was and he didn't.

He managed to park once we reached their building but stumbled as he left the car. I dared not try to help him. He would have been so shocked by my touch he would have swung out against me, as at a mugger. I allowed him to totter along, supporting himself on the fenders of cars, dragging his heels, mouth hanging open, and I kept up a line of chatter about how they should go to Florida when she was released. Why spend the winters in New York City? Travel around the world. Spend your money, Pop. There's plenty of dough and then some.

In the apartment, he fell onto the bed, fully clothed and shod, and I gathered her things and left him to sleep. I shouted goodbye from the door and said he should take it easy but, when I hit the street, I realized the one thing I had forgotten, after all that joking, was the emery board. I could have picked one up at a drug store but was sure she had a special kind and he would make a fuss about my not doing anything right.

I turned back, muttering all the way about this crazy family and their constant demands and how it was not enough I had to fulfill them but, even then, somebody would find something to complain about.

I had a key to the apartment because I was coming and going often to get her things and stock the shelves and make coffee and I used it on my return so as not to wake him. I heard the strange noises as soon as I opened the door, like animal whinnies more than anything, accompanied by loud clomps. At first, I supposed a parade of policemen on horseback was passing on the street. But how could the sound travel so clearly and when was the last time I had seen such a parade? I tiptoed to the bedroom door to see if a window shade was flapping.

He was on his hands and knees on the bed, banging his head against the headboard. He turned to see who had entered the room and I could not miss the fact that he was crying. I had never seen him cry before. My mother cried over anything, soaking up hanky after hanky, but my father's tears were like globs of oil. Each slowly descended his face, in and out of wrinkles like a creek crisscrossing a mountainside, taking forever to drip from his chin. He must have been weeping from the moment I left because his shirtfront was soaked through.

And those awful sounds. An enormous moan started in his gut and snowballed into his chest, only to be strangled in his throat and the horse whinny that emerged was merely the tip of his grief.

I remember the details because I was frozen in the doorway. He did not seem to recognize me, nor did he seem to care. And I, who had been afraid to touch him in the parking lot, certainly dared not approach him then.

"Pa," I muttered, "please. Everything is going to be all right."

"How can you say that?" he gasped. He did not look me in the eye. He did not seem shocked to hear my voice. "Everything won't be all right."

"It will be. It will. All the doctors say so."

"It won't be. It won't. The woman had a heart attack. The woman nearly died on me. How can it ever be all right?"

"People recover. She'll be good as new."

"The woman nearly died. How can you recover from that?"

"You can. You'll see. Everything will be all right."

"It won't be. It won't. Everything won't be all right."

"It will."

I should have touched him. I should have come closer. I should have, at least, moved from the doorway. But the two of us remained in the same positions, me saying she will and him saying she won't until, finally, his knees gave way. His head plopped onto the mattress and, in a second, he was sleeping.

I watched him for a while before leaving with the emery board and neither of us has mentioned the incident since.

* * *

Mademoiselle glanced at her watch. Then she scraped her chair back; an imperious signal the meeting was over.

"But we haven't discussed the suspension," I gasped. "Aren't you going to forgive poor Adam and let him back in class?"

"Time is up, *Monsieur.*"

I had not scored any of the points Mimi had drilled into me about how emotionally scarred the kid would be, how he might drop out of school and develop the screaming meemies if she failed him, how I would visit regularly to tutor him back to mental health if only she gave him another chance.

"Just a few minutes more, *Mademoiselle.*"

"I must prepare for my next class, *Monsieur.*"

"We're discussing life and death issues here!"

"I have a responsibility to my good students, too."

Oh, this Madame Curie was a bitch, to be sure, just out of Barnard, a year at the Sorbonne, major in French, minor in Castration. I flashed a look to let Adam know but the poor kid was slumped in his seat like a psycho. I had seen enough nut house movies to know.

He had his arms crossed tightly over his chest; the white coats would not have needed a straitjacket to cart him away. His right hand was resting on his left shoulder and he had twisted his head around to nibble on his thumb. His eyes were pressed shut as if he were trying to lock out the image of his failure of a father and who could blame him?

Instead of coming through for my troubled son, I had tap danced make-out routines which had been frayed before the kid was born and Madame de Stael had been laughing up her sleeve all the time. She cocked a brow to signal she had seen the nut house movies too and had spotted this pair of suckers at once. Just give the father enough rope, she had figured, and he would hang himself while the loony-tune son checked into never-never land for good.

She had curled me around her pinkie so, if I tried to explain, my tongue would turn left when it meant to turn right. All the arguments I had prepared got tangled in my brain and I did not remember what Mimi said I should say and what I shouldn't.

"Perhaps we could talk after your class, *Mademoiselle*. I came all the way from Manhattan to see you. Mrs. Dash and I are divorced, you know. I don't live in Rego Park. Can you imagine an artist living in *Bourgeoise* Heaven? I'd go bananas in a week. I am so impressed that you can stand it, a bright young woman, just out of Barnard, a year at the Sorbonne."

"There is nothing to talk about. Is there? It is not me who is unhappy with Adam. *Mais non.* It is Adam who is unhappy with me. Perhaps, with time, you can help Adam define his unhappiness and then I'd be enchanted to correct my faults and have him return to class."

Smug little psychoanalyzing Collette, she had no faults. That was obvious. Adam had faults. Anyone looking at his twisted body could see. I had faults. Who else had produced such a psycho? For all my father's faults, his son, at least, had managed to stay sane.

"Tie your shoelaces!" I screamed. "You look like a loony!"

"Oh, *Monsieur. Ce n'est pas necessaire!*"

She approached him bravely. I would not have dared, for fear he would attack in manic fury. But Miss *Parlez Vous Francaise* was about to show me up for the lousy parent I was.

"We are very fond of Adam here. We all are, even the principal. Adam knows that. Such a sensitive boy, and talented like his Papa."

But the poor kid was turning purple in terror as she came behind him, placed her hands on his shoulders, massaged his neck, whispering to me as if he could not hear.

"We all want him to do well and pass French and go on to high school and college, or maybe even Juilliard. Adam knows how fond of him we are."

The corners of his lips quivered, and tears welled in his eye. Mademoiselle was trying to help but, one touch of her buttery skin and every defense against his desire collapsed. No one knew better than I how secret need for a woman could cause such unbearable pain. It tugged at every knot in your system. Every damp spot filled to the brim, until you wanted to cry and come at once.

"In the beginning of the term, Adam was my favorite pupil, well behaved and interested. Sensitive and attentive. Charming and full of *joie de vivre.* But lately he seems intent on turning the classroom into a circus, hiding in the coat closet, passing dirty notes, so out of control that we know his behavior is due to trouble at home. But, *mais non,* we cannot have chaos. And when I try to reason, he turns sulky and silent like now! Tell Papa, Adam darling, that this is the truth. We know something is wrong, *mon cher,* but we cannot help if you will not talk."

She was cooing into his ear so that her breath must have tingled along his neck and the warmth of her body would be giving him chills; her flowery aroma tickling his nostrils. The little boy was in love with her and he did not even know it. And if he did, what good would it do him? She was as untouchable as she was desirable and, now that she was curling her fingers through his hair, he wanted to throw himself on his knees, bury his head in her lap, plunge into her softness.

"I beg your pardon, *Mademoiselle,*" I said.

And this would be the start of what Mimi has labeled my "psychotic episode." Yet I had never felt more lucid. A lifetime of rage bolted up from my groin, but the words did not taste red hot on my tongue, rather silvery cool like lemon sherbet.

"Yes, *Monsieur?*"

"I don't mean to be rude, *Mademoiselle,* but do you make it a practice to fondle all the little boys this way?"

Adam's face blanched with shock. Hers tightened into a fist. I knew I had hit a bullseye because she pulled away and straightened into military attention and pursed her lips and tried to look smug, but her hands kept flapping at her sides.

"I am sure you know more about child psychology than I do, *Madmemoiselle,* but I wonder if it is wise to fondle a pubescent boy..."

"I wasn't fondling! How dare you say such a thing?"

Her voice quivered, an octave too high.

"I think we should stay calm, *Mademoiselle.*"

"I think you should leave, *Monsieur.*"

She moved to the desk to give her hands something to do but I remained in perfect control, even smiling sympathetically because the poor dear was so embarrassed.

"You do realize that an adolescent boy could get upset and behave unreasonably if he is being regularly pressed to his teacher's breast?"

"I want you to go, *Monsieur.*"

She slammed a palm down on the desk. A little ivory pussycat tumbled off. Adam knelt to retrieve it. Mademoiselle's eyes locked with mine. Neither of us moved but I kept smiling and talking, of course.

"My ex-wife has been in therapy for years and, although I haven't felt the need, I've picked up a lot of information about Oedipal complexes and sexual conflicts. *Comprenez-vous?* You probably think you are helping the child. I'm not accusing you, *Mademoiselle.* There is no reason to get upset."

Now it was her turn to tremble. Even better, her glance ricocheted from blackboard to coat closet. I had recovered my tongue and could tease her with it for hours until she agreed to take Adam back, graduate him with honors, recommend him to the Sorbonne.

"I gather this is your first teaching job. Or maybe your first *dans l'Amerique* and in *La Belle France* they do things differently than they do in *Bourgeoise* Heaven. I'm not saying they do things better and I'm not saying they do things worse but, with our long standing Puritan tradition, we do not encourage older women to caress little boys because we are aware of the conflictual dilemmas created..."

"SHUT UP! SHUT UP! SHUT UP!"

For a second, I thought it was her but, no, it was Adam and a flurry of pencils and the little ivory pussycat came flying toward my head. It crashed into pieces behind me as Mademoiselle broke into tears along with it and I was silenced in astonishment. I had been so intent on pinning her to the wall with my dagger-like words I had forgotten Adam was in the room.

"SHUT UP! SHUT UP! SHUT UP! CAN'T YOU EVER SHUT UP?!"

There was no denying his existence nor his misery as, fists flailing, shoelaces flapping, he screeched out of the classroom, along the hallway, down the stairs, out of the building and no one knew better than I how pain could keep him screeching for years.

SIX

. . .

Adam came rushing into the house with astonishing news. He and my father had been working outside on a clogged septic tank and Pop's comments had kept the kid in stitches all morning.

He shouted at me incomprehensibly, his skin glowing from cold air. His eyes burned more brightly than the flame in the fireplace.

"Adam, calm down! I don't understand."

And I really did not though he had me in giggles at once.

"Grandpa says okay!"

"Okay what?"

"Okay what are we here for?"

He hopped around the room, too excited to stop for a second. He perched on the arm of the sofa, then rolled face down onto the pillows, then slid off onto the floor. But my laughter stopped.

"What do you mean?"

"Okay he'll pay for private school!"

That was what I had begun to fear although Adam was right; that was what we were here for.

"You asked him?"

"Who do you think asked him? You? Why are you so dense? I asked him and he said okay! 'Roger and over, I'll pay!' It was simple as one-two-three!"

He was stretched out on the floor, panting for breath, beaming at me, arms and legs stretched wide. He seemed to have grown a foot since we had arrived.

"I was getting ready to ask him, myself."

"Are you kidding? If I waited for you, we'd be here forever."

"Does this mean we can go home?"

"He said we should stay till New Year's Day. Then I can go back to the Big Apple, he says, pick any school my heart desires, step right up and sign in, Mister. Send the bill to Grandpa!"

"Wait a minute..."

"Wait a minute, balls! You know what this means? Good-bye, Mademoiselle Marlowe. Goodbye, grief from Mom. Good-bye, being the class dunce. Goodbye, fucking French! I'm going to start all over at a brand-new school. I'm going to work my ass off and graduate with honors! That's what I promised Grandpa."

He was squatting, his bony arms twined around his knees, perched on his haunches.

"Adam..."

"I'm going to stand up in my cap and gown and say, 'Ladies and Gents, I owe all this to my grandpa, the only one who had faith in me!'"

"How do you know he means it?"

"I'm telling you what he said. That's an exact quote. 'Step right up and sign in, Mister. Send the bill to Grandpa!'"

"I know what he said. I can hear the bullshit tone in his voice."

And he was up and striding again, making the walls tremble.

"Oh no. Here comes Mr. Put Everybody Down. Mr. Nobody Knows Better Than Me. Mr. Writer who..."

"That's enough," I shouted, aware that the discussion was not going the way it should. "What did you tell him? Did you mention Mademoiselle Marlowe? Did you talk about failing French?"

"Of course not, Jerk-off. He asked how I was doing in school. He brought it up, not me. While we were fixing the septic tank. But you wouldn't know anything about how to fix a septic tank. Mr. Lily White Typewriter Hands."

"Stick to the topic, God damn it!"

"So I figured, it's now or never, Ace. This is not the time to retreat since he brought up the topic. 'Well, Grandpa,' I answer, 'if you want the bareass truth, I'm not doing too good....'"

"Not doing too well..."

"I'm not doing too good in this sucker of a public school. I'd do much better in private school but Mr. Writer Who Never Earned A Dime can't afford the tuition. 'Hey Grandpa,' I says, as if the idea came out of the blue, 'if I got accepted into private school and promised to study hard and get all A's so my father looked like a horse's ass for not graduating college, would you pay tuition, huh?'"

"What did he say?"

"He says, 'Pal, you stay here till New Year's Day. Then go back to the Big Apple. Pick any school your heart desires. Step right up and sign in, Mister. Send the bill to Grandpa. Roger and over! You read me?'"

"Just like that?"

"Just like that! And you know why? Because I'm a winner who kept his eye on the ball."

"Adam, wait a minute..."

"Now you wait a minute, Buster. I'm on to your tricks. Don't pick the deal apart because you didn't finagle it."

"You don't understand."

"I understand plenty. You come on like Superman. Then you screw up everything."

"I'm sorry you feel that way."

"Mom feels that way, too."

"I'm sorry she feels that way."

"You certainly screwed up with Mademoiselle Marlowe. Everybody agrees on that. She went to the principal. Now it's for sure I'll get expelled."

"I'm sorry about that, also."

"You're just jealous because I had the balls to do what you couldn't."

"That's not it."

"What is it, then?"

"I don't want you to be disappointed."

"Do me a favor. Stop worrying about me."

"I love you, Adam."

"What has that got to do with anything? All of a sudden, you love me!"

"It's not all of a sudden."

"Oh yeah? How come you never thought of telling me before? But when somebody actually demonstrates he gives a damn, then you announce that you love me. You never gave me a thing and now, all of a sudden, you love me. Well, you're a one hundred per cent failure in my book and I don't need your love anymore!"

The kid has inherited the family talents; an ability to store up grievances until they will do the most harm, and the ability to toss them off with nonchalance so they explode in the face of the enemy. He strode to the door and opened it wide.

"Hey Grandpa! I love you for this. I really do and I'm going to make you proud, wait and see. I'll graduate with honors and win a scholarship to Yale!"

"Roger and over!" came by father's reply.

"What you don't understand is that your Grandpa will promise anything to make an impression and completely forget in a second," I mumbled.

"Maybe I'll give up music and become a lawyer," Adam hollered.

"Does he know how much money we are talking about? Does he realize we mean every year until you graduate?"

"Roger and over. He knows."

"I don't want you to be hurt. That's all."

"Roger and over. I won't be."

"Stop saying that!"

"What?"

"Never mind." The pain was coming from all sides. I could hardly catch my
breath. "I'm sorry I never said I love you before."

"What does that have to do with anything?"

"A minute ago, you seemed angry that I hadn't."

"Are you on the same Freudian trip as Miss Bleeding Gums? Stop psychoanalyzing me."

"I wish you had let me handle this with Grandpa, that's all. I wish you had let me straighten out the details."

There was silence.

"I hope he comes through for you," I sighed.

"He'll come through better than you ever did."

"I hope so, Adam. I really do."

* * *

It was so cold the snow froze as soon as it hit the ground. You expected it be soft and impressionable, but it was brittle and crackled underfoot. I snuck out while the others were sleeping to take a walk and think things out.

The blackness at night was all enveloping. The trees melted into the dark. Every memory was sketched across the sky and glowed for a moment before fading. Thoughts seemed to connect like the stars so that, image by image, even lies led to truth.

Though it was late, I called Mimi on my cell and promised to have the kid back on New Year's Day before lunch. I told her my father would pay tuition and even lied that it was me who had sealed the deal.

SEVEN

Maybe it had been a psychotic episode. I do remember I raced from the classroom after Adam as heads popped from doorways and questions followed like a swarm of mosquitoes. And once I hit the street, the impact of my brilliant insights, the echoes of my eloquence, all slid from my shoulders. It was possible that I had been – to use one of Mimi's fancy terms – "projecting." Let's say for a moment the kid had not been behaving like a catatonic, but like a normal boy with a confusing crush on his French teacher. Let's say Mademoiselle was sweet, inexperienced, maybe over affectionate but the sexual veil that had been tossed over the scene had been a result of my distortion. It would not have been the first time, and out on the street, I could easily see it, imagine the outrage of Mademoiselle, the mortification of Adam.

He was nowhere to be seen and I was terrified that he would do something crazy. Why would he hang around to hear his furious mother rip into his father because he had cracked up before his beautiful French teacher and, instead of saving the day as promised, hadn't known left from right?

"Oh God," I swore, scouring the neighborhood, "If Adam returns and is safe and forgives me, I'll never write another porn piece. I'll take a job so the kid can be proud, go to law school at night, finish a novel, pay Mimi the money I owe!"

I ended up at the Public Library, where I went when my father had humiliated me as a kid. But things have changed since those days. Only bag ladies hang around libraries now, not sensitive would-be writers. Adam, of course, was not there. He was probably watching a dirty movie in Times Square, shooting up in the balcony. But I stayed because it was warm and quiet and, I'll be damned, "The Naked and The Dead" was still on the shelves.

* * *

I shivered as I waited on Mimi's front step. Usually, when I arrived to pick up Adam, anger had added a glow to her cheeks. Her back arched, her jaw locked, her eyes ignited and there was still a glimmer of the defiant girl I had married.

I had called her at the office and warned her. Mimi dragged her spreading hips from the Toyota and wrapped her coat around her. She squinted to find me and, once she had, closed her eyes and kept them shut even after she had started to speak.

"What happened?"

"Come inside."

"What happened, God damn it! Where is he?"

I started to cry. Other writers concerned themselves with life and death issues, nuclear holocausts, human rights. I attend a parent-teacher meeting and the world crumbles about me. Mimi started to cry also, leaning against the tiny car our three fragile chassis quivered together in the fading, wintry light.

"Please, Mimi. Don't."

"Don't tell me, 'don't.'"

"The neighbors will hear."

"Screw the neighbors."

"You're absolutely right," I sobbed.

"All of a sudden, Norman Mailer is worried about the neighbors? His son is

wandering the streets for reasons he refuses to say and all he worries about is the neighbors!"

"I'm not the one who moved to *Bourgeoise* Heaven where you'd better worry!"

"I moved here to get away from hysterics like you!"

"I am not hysterical. You are!"

"I want my kid to grow up normal. Is that such a sin? I don't want him ripped from his *bourgeoise* roots by the King of Porn."

"I may be the King of Porn but at least I write. You don't paint any more."

"My goals have changed. All I want now is to go to his graduation in a string of pearls and a hat!"

"And that's why you smoke so much and your teeth wiggle in your mouth."

"Smoking has nothing to do with my problem. My problem is caused by tension. Tension creates a poison in my saliva. It's already eaten away at the gum. Now, it is gnawing into the bone."

"You twist yourself into a pretzel to be something you're not."

"One thing I asked of you. Only one. Take the kid to school and talk to his teacher so he doesn't drop out altogether."

"If you lived in Manhattan where it doesn't take me an hour and a half on the subway, maybe I would have come sooner."

"Is that what you want him to do? Drop out of school and screw up his life like we did?"

"Mimi, don't say that."

"You're still spouting stories about skiing down for supplies in a snowstorm as if everything turned out the way that we planned it."

"It still can."

"No, it can't."

Carefully, so that nothing broke, she allowed her pocketbook to slide down her body. I kneeled to retrieve it and rested for a moment at her feet.

"We screwed up our lives. Don't say we haven't. And if we screw up this kid on top of everything else, we're not worth a damn."

"Calm down. You're losing bone."

"I'm worried about him, Jeffrey."

"I'll take care of things, Mimi. I'll get a job. I'll write a novel. You can go back to painting."

"Two kids playing roles in 'La Boheme.' And Adam is making the same mistakes."

She bent low for a tissue from her bag, but I did not let go so that the contents spilled out before us. We both stared at the mess until she fell to her knees and I pressed her to me, clinging as much as embracing.

"Tell me what happened before I have a heart attack!" She pulled away to blow her nose.

"He ran away."

"What do you mean he ran away? Where did he run to?"

"When a kid runs away, he doesn't tell you."

"Don't be a smart-ass. Did you look for him?"

"I looked all over."

"Where did he run from?"

"From the classroom."

"Why did he run?"

"Because I embarrassed him."

"What did you do, try to charm her with your hostility?"

"Yes," I answered.

As quickly as there had been tears, there was laughter. It had always been that way between us. This time, she started it. Or maybe I did. Or maybe we started simultaneously.

I was doubled over on the roadway, her body arched over mine, both of us grasping our stomachs in pain, trying to talk but helpless beneath waves of laughter. The awareness of how stupid I had been and how she had known at once shattered all efforts at self control. I had failed her, that was true. But it did not mean that I had never loved her.

Then out of the blue, my brilliant plan appeared. I would take the kid to my father's for Christmas to finagle tuition money out of the bastard and, meanwhile she could take a break and, one by one, I would solve all our problems.

Making the same mistake she always had, Mimi believed me.

* * *

On our honeymoon, Mimi and I rocked the bed with such passion vibrations trembled in every corner. Dishes in the sink smacked together and cracked. She would weep as my sobs jiggled inside her, throwing us into unheard of positions, leading me into secret corners of her body where I found the comfort I needed. She called me a Greek God in bed and, afterwards, I felt like one. When the sensation waned, I blamed her for the loss.

EIGHT

On New Year's Eve, my father celebrated by turning on Adam. He began drinking at noon and criticized me for nagging the kid to get his things packed, then picked on Adam for doing it wrong. Each time I asked what was going on, he shouted that everything was hunky-dory!

"Roger and over! Some peace, at last. Soon as you two lemons leave, I can hammer those traffic signs to the roof. What do you think, I'm on permanent vacation like Mr. Writer and Mr. Guitar?"

I sat through dinner, waiting for the clouds to pass but they never did. The storm exploded while I washed the dishes and the kid was alone with him in the living room. I overheard the shouting but, at first, couldn't make out the words.

"You think you are putting one over on me, making a deal by promising A's and afterwards saying you are failing French!

Is this the time to break such news? The night before you leave and who knows when I'll see you again? I thought you were some big shot honor student and now I hear you're a loser like your father."

"I didn't say I was failing, Grandpa. I said I was suspended."

"I went to public school, not private, where they belted you black and blue if you failed so you shoved your homework up your ass. You pissed it out on tests and that's the way you passed!"

I hurried from the kitchen. My father was drunk, and Adam was stupefied by the sudden attack.

"Haven't you heard of hard work? You can't even play the guitar."

"What's going on here?"

"If you want the money, you've got to prove you're worth the investment. Before not after. Business is business!"

"Pop, calm down. Adam, what is he saying?"

"Don't calm down me, Mr. Writer Who Never Earned A Dime. You never graduated college, so this is one thing I know better than you."

"What is? What are you two fighting about?"

"I let you get away with murder, whining every time you did a little work. Don't think I'm proud of the mess you've made of your life!"

I turned to Adam.

"What is this all about?"

But the boy was frightened and slow on the uptake; my father answered before he could.

"When a husband can't satisfy a wife and a marriage breaks up and the kid fails French, that's a sure sign he doesn't know shit from shinola!"

"I think you'd better shut up," I said but there was no stopping him scatter-shooting curses into the air.

"I was married forty years and my wife adored me till the day she died!"

"We've heard this sad song before."

"Either the kid can pass a fag course like French, even if he has to cheat on the final, or I wash my hands of him as of now! I never asked nobody for nothing, and I never failed anything in my life."

"I didn't fail! I didn't fail! I said I got suspended!"

"Adam, go to bed. You're making things worse."

"He promised, Dad. He promised to pay tuition. Make him stick to his promise."

I rushed to the kitchen for instant coffee to sober him up and Adam followed, my father flinging curses after us both. "A promise doesn't count if you change the deal. You spread lies about getting A's and now I discover you are failing in French. First, you pass. Then, I pay!"

"What did you tell him that started this?" I asked as we waited for the water to boil.

"I didn't say anything bad. I told him about Mademoiselle and how glad I was to be free of her."

"What did you tell him that for?"

Tears welled in his eyes and I wanted to take him in my arms, but the teapot whistled. My father kept shouting from the other room.

"Don't try to finagle me, hatching up plots in there! All my life, I've known enough to get the deal straight before I reach for the dough."

"He's been depressed all day. Haven't you noticed?" said Adam. "I wanted to cheer him up. He's always had funny stories to cheer me up, I wanted to tell him one of mine."

"You told me you were getting all A's. You told me you

would graduate with honors! I dare you to deny you told me that!"

"He'll be lonely when we're gone. It made me feel awful."

"A deal is a deal! If you change your side, I can change mine."

I poured water for the coffee; black for me, light for my father. A glass of milk for Adam.

"I bought some doughnuts for a farewell celebration," I explained. "First you pass! Then, I pay!" came the voice from the living room.

"What exactly did you say?"

"I told him that he was the nicest grandpa in the world, and I couldn't wait to start a new school. I told him the truth. I couldn't go back to public school because I had been suspended and was in trouble with my French teacher, so I was especially grateful. What's wrong with that? I was trying to make him feel like a hero. I was trying to make him feel good so he wouldn't be lonely. What's he going to do tomorrow without us around, wander through the house, talking to himself? Aren't you worried about him?"

I brought in the coffee on a tray and, of course, my father spotted my trembling hands and intensified his attack.

"You crawl back to that public school and pass that French course, or I am through with you, as of now! You come back with a report card that says all A's and then we'll negotiate tuition."

"You want a doughnut, Pop? I bought some."

"If you're turning into a failure this early in the game, I wash my hands of you, which I should have done with your lousy father, but your grandma nagged me to throw good money after bad."

"Pop, if you don't want to pay, just say so. No need to call him every name in the book. You're saying things you'll regret."

"Don't tell me what I am going to do. I know what I am going to do. Roll up my sleeves and get to work. Fix this place up like a hunting lodge, add a ski lift, make myself another million."

"Listen to me, Pop. Don't blame the kid. He only wanted you to know the truth. He was trying to say that he loves you."

"What are you doing?" Adam screeched. "Who says I love him?"

"You shut up!" my father responded, both shouting at once. "No-good snot nose son of a bitch!"

"How do you know what I was trying to say? I never said I loved him!"

"Don't curse him, Pop. I'm begging you."

"What do I care if he curses me? Long as he coughs up tuition."

"Pop, did you hear me?"

"I don't throw good money after bad." Then, he faked falling asleep to win the

point.

"Please don't, Pop. Make it up before you doze off. You'll wake in the morning

and we'll be gone, and you'll feel awful."

Adam mumbled; the old man responded with phony snores. "Let him sleep. Who gives a fuck? I'll drop out of school. Play on street corners until I've raised the ante. You think I'm a loser? I'll show you both. Play with one hand, peddle dope with the other."

"Who cares if you leave?" my father hissed, eyes shut. "I was happy before you came. I'll be happy when you go."

"I'll be happy too," Adam hissed back. "And you can choke on your fucking money!"

Finally, they both ran out of gas; each poised for battle, waiting for the other to counter-attack.

"I'll bring in the doughnuts," I said.

"You stay here and straighten things out!" Adam demanded. "I'll get the goddam doughnuts!"

Adam headed for the kitchen and my father howled after him, "You can go and never come back!"

"He doesn't know what he is saying," I whispered to my father. "He's just angry and hurt. Leave him be for a minute."

No such luck.

"You think it's such an original idea?" he called after Adam. "Your father tried to leave and look what happened! Your grandma always hated this place and you think it makes her smart that she's six feet under instead of here with me? Well, I hope she hears me from the grave. Nobody can tell me what to do!"

Finally, his words dribbled off and he fell asleep, sitting up. At least, it seemed like sleep for a snore or two. Then his mouth popped open.

"I'm king here and anybody wants to argue gonna gets his ass blown off!"

"Pop please," I sighed. "You can yell from now till tomorrow, but you made a promise and now you're backing out. You did it to me. You did it to Mom. And now you're doing it to Adam, that's all."

"Of, for crying out loud, Jeffey." His voice was suddenly small. "I don't have the money..."

Another lie, I thought. "Come on, Pop. Tell the truth. Nothing stashed under the floorboards?"

"Me, with my piddling practice of bookies and whores, most of 'em never paid me a dime! Where am I supposed to dig up four years tuition?"

"But Pop, you were always such a big shot!"

"I've been bullshitting my entire life..."

I did not know whether it was true or not. The starving

artist, I knew, had not been able to pay his bill. About the rest, I wasn't sure. But he believed what he believed.

"Now, I don't have a pot to piss in."

"If you say so..."

"Whatever happens, don't make the same mistakes I did! Go ahead and write your novel. Make it a best seller!"

"I'm not so sure I can anymore."

"Don't end up a failure like me."

"You're not a failure, Pop."

"Not enough money to come through for the kid. It's too late for me but not for you! Go for the home run! I want you to promise."

"I promise, Pop. I promise to try."

"I know you can do it! But do me a favor. Don't tell the kid about the money."

"Pop, we've got to stop with the lies."

"Make up something! You're the writer!"

"There's no more making up I can do."

"Then put it in your book and maybe someday he'll read it. Now just go! No goodbyes!"

He had fallen asleep, for real, as Adam returned with the doughnuts.

"What did he say?"

"He's not coming up with the money, Adam. There are reasons but they are too complicated. It's not that he doesn't love you."

"Yeah, sure."

"He's an angry old man, Adam. Sometimes he explodes and whoever is nearest gets hit. He says things he doesn't mean. You've heard him say them to me."

"You deserve them. I don't."

"I didn't deserve them when I was your age either. When he wakes up, he'll be sorry. But forget about the money. It's too much to ask of an old man. I should have known. I'm sorry I dragged you into it."

We sipped on coffee, mine black. He drank my father's.

"What are we going to do, Dad?"

"I wish I knew."

"I don't really want to go on the road. I want to graduate. I'm sorry if that's *bourgeoise*."

"Why don't we talk to Mademoiselle? You'll promise to behave. I'll apologize. After all, it was me who screwed up. Not you."

"Not exactly. I screwed up, too."

"What did you do that I don't know about?"

He slipped a hand into his pocket.

"I stole some pictures," he answered. "I ruined the *Mademoiselle de Paris* montage. She was so proud. She'll never forgive me."

He passed the photos to me.

"When did you do this?"

"While you were hitting her with the isolation from the mainstream number. I had a gut feeling that I was never going to see her again, so I ripped them off the board. She'll think I did it out of spite."

They were the snapshots of Mademoiselle in front of the Eiffel Tower, Mademoiselle with the French cop, ragged pieces of construction paper still glued to their backs. I could tell that what had been left on the board was a mess. Adam was right. How would he ever convince her he had done it out of love?

"She sure is pretty," I sighed.

"The prettiest woman I ever saw," he answered glumly.

"Love can make you crazy, Adam. I wish I could explain but I'm still figuring it out myself. One thing I'm sure of. It's best if you go back and face her."

"What am I going to say, for crying out loud? When she sees I spoiled her montage, she'll flip."

"You could say, 'I'm sorry I took the pictures, *Mademoiselle*. My father is a jerk. My grandpa is, too. But the truth is I am in love with you and it makes me crazy.'"

"What will she say to that?"

"It might be wise to switch to Spanish."

There was no getting a laugh out of him, so we sat up beside my father all night, sleeping fitfully, staring out the windows at the trees, frozen in position in the landscape. We left some doughnuts as a farewell gift.

NINE

We drove back in silence, Adam curled in the corner by the window, me rigid at the steering wheel. All the miles, all the talk, all the time hadn't changed a thing. All week, he babbled a string of complaints when I wanted quiet, now he clammed up when I needed him to talk.

"I'm sorry, Adam."

"Stop saying that."

More silence. We had left my father sleeping in the chair to wake alone and find us gone.

I searched for something to say. No cars on the road. No noise in the air. Even the sky was cloudless. New Year's morning, seven a.m. Everyone else was dreaming or drunk.

"I'm sorry I ever took you there, but it was the only way I could think of to get the money..."

"What's the use of being sorry? It's too fucking cold. I've told Mom a dozen times 'If the car is going to be an iceberg, at least get a radio so I can listen to music while I freeze my balls off!'"

"She must have been delighted to hear that."

"Who cares?"

"What the hell. The motor is running. We're not stalled at the side of the road. We're on our way home. Maybe that's a sign of good things to come."

"Save it for your novel."

There was my opening. I knew what needed to be said. I rehearsed all through the sleepless night.

"Adam, I have something to tell you."

"Roger and over!"

"I'm not being funny."

"You never are."

"I want you to know what I do for a living. I want you to know the truth."

"I've heard this sad song before."

"Well, the truth is..."

"What is this, foreshadowing?"

"I write...how do I put this?"

"Sock it to me, Norman Mailer! What? What is it that you write?"

"Shall we say ....titillating stories for men's magazines?"

"Oh my God!"

"I've been at it for years."

"What the hell are you talking about?"

"I churn out dirty books every month and peddle shlock stories to flakes."

"I am so sick and tired of your bullshit!"

"I'm damned good at it too but it will never pay enough to cover tuition."

"First, you're a great writer, scribbling a novel on your pad and now I'm supposed to believe this!"

"I am not a great writer. I never managed to finish a novel. I peddle my stuff to magazines."

"What kind of magazines?"

"Juggs! Dude!"

I was beginning to yell, not what I had planned. And the car was weaving from lane to lane.

"You'd better cool down. We're going to crash."

"If we do, it's your fault."

We fell silent. I kept my eyes on the road.

"Dude?" he asked after a while.

"You read Dude?"

"I'm asking the questions!"

"All right. What's the question? I'll answer."

"How come I never saw your name?"

"I use pen names. I have a dozen."

"Why?"

"Because I knew...eventually you'd read those...those magazines...and I didn't want you to be...ashamed." His silence was driving me nuts. I kept talking. An ancient habit. It always got me in trouble. "What I want to say, Adam, is you shouldn't imitate your old man so much. He's nothing but a hack."

More silence. More ice. More stillness. More steam from my lips. I was staring so hard at the road that the white lines began to wiggle. There was no radio gossip to hide behind. No other drivers to curse. Exits kept passing by. The city drew closer. And the echoes of the truth were still rat-a-tatting on the windshield.

"Are you surprised?

"Not so much. I always knew something wasn't kosher."

He did not say anything more and, I suppose, there was nothing to say. But he remained stock still. His eyes didn't blink. Perhaps he was fighting tears. Perhaps not. Perhaps I only thought so because my eyes were fogging so badly I had to drive onto the shoulder and park.

"Let's pull over a minute. I need a break."

I lowered my head to the wheel, breathing as deeply as Adam was. At least, our rhythms were in synch.

"Jeez, I didn't mean..." he mumbled.

"It's okay...I'm okay..."

Maybe for the first time in my life, I ran out of words. It was his turn to speak and I waited until, finally, he broke the silence.

"I love you, Dad," he whispered.

Now, how was I supposed to respond to that? I could not crack a joke. I could not hug him. The stick shift was in the way. Damned seat belts. Nothing ever works like it does in the movies.

I white-knuckled the wheel to stay in control and allowed the silence to comfort us. Suddenly, I had a brilliant idea. At least, it seemed so at the time and was all I could think of. "Hey Adam," I sighed, and we shared a tentative glance. Then a smile, as he read my mind. "How's about you take over the wheel for a while?"

He beamed in response: flattered, intrigued, no doubt relieved.

"You really are bananas."

"Come on. There's isn't a car on the road. Grandpa says you have a natural talent."

"What I don't have is a license."

"Go slow and who's to know? Come on."

"It's not that I couldn't. Believe me."

"It would give me such a kick."

"Really?"

"And, later on, I'll write Grandpa. Imagine how he'll howl!"

"If he ever gets the letter!"

We giggled and knew that what had been said could not be dismissed. More would follow. But, for now, Adam nodded, and we switched places. He slid behind the wheel and I sat by the window, watching in awe as he glided the car back onto the road, elbows bent like my father's.

END

GAUGUIN & DEGAS

BY STEVEN FORSBERG

"**D**o you remember that morning when we took the kayaks from Manasquan, out past the jetty, and we were going to paddle off shore and then up to Monmouth Beach? Do you remember that day? I wanted to go to that beach place, the one that takes down all the walls to let the breeze in . . . right on the sand. What's it called?"

"Um . . ." I cast about for it. Unlike the Lafayette Mill, the beachside place in Monmouth didn't mind if we showed up in shorts and flip flops. "It's the . . . wait . . . the Tin Soldier. Right? The seafood bar with all the license plates on the ceiling and the Springsteen scribble on the bathroom wall? They've got it covered over with plexiglass, like holy writ."

She jabs me in the shoulder with a painted fingernail. "That's the one! Do you remember that day?"

"Of course. Why?"

"I made it about two-hundred yards off shore. I was still hearing the goddamned music from *Jaws* in my imagination, watching for Richard Dreyfuss, but I was excited. I'd never done anything like that, thirty miles, or whatever, in a kayak."

"And?"

"And we weren't five minutes out from the jetty, when a big wave splashed over the front of my boat –"

"The bow," I interrupt.

"Yes, whatever. Don't be that guy."

"Sorry. Go on."

Kate fidgets with her bracelet, a polished tourmaline she picked up on a hike near Bar Harbor the previous summer. I'd purloined it from her backpack while she was peeing behind a birch tree, had it set in white gold for Christmas. "Where was I? Oh, right . . . that wave splashed over the *bow* and drenched me, not five goddamned minutes out from the jetty. We had three hours of kayaking ahead on the north frigging Atlantic. Sure, it wasn't cold out, but that water was cold. My shorts, my wallet, my cell phone, my godfustikating underwear . . . all of it, wet, damp, *moist*, and uncomfortable all day."

"What's your point?" I ask. "It's kayaking. You're gonna get wet."

"I know, but not that wet and not that soon after leaving the frigging pier. The goddamned interior lights in my car hadn't even gone off yet. Don't you see? That's my life. That's me. That's what the universe does every time it gets a chance. I'm the one who manages my husband, my kids, my job, my secret stash of cash. I get everyone settled someplace safe, where they're happy and content and busy and not thinking of me at all. I make arrangements to do a little boating with the love of my life, and boom . . ."

"Boom?"

"Boom. The universe looks down on me and says, *There you go, Katherine. Enjoy the day. No, really. Have a lovely time, but try doing it with a wet ass, wet money, wet phone, wet underwear, and just enough discomfort to . . . you know . . . mitigate the experience.*"

"I'm sorry." I apologize and mean it. I take her hand, run a thumb over the pale green stone. "I didn't, you know . . . know all that."

"Oh," she dismisses me, and the chilly phantoms of a half dozen ex-boyfriends pass through my chest. "Thank you, love. But it doesn't have anything to do with you. Trust me. It's just me and the universe. I'm the one who saves money for two years to take my kids to Disney World. I plan and arrange and organize and set up a hundred-and-six details to make everything perfect for them. We stand in line for the attraction . . . pirates, mice, ghosts, spacemen, Peter Pan, whatever . . . and just as we get strapped in, my daughter barfs on me. It's a gorgeous day. I've spent two years planning, thousands of dollars, and there I am – splashed with cold ocean water or warm baby puke. That's me. Welcome to me and my life and my story. It's blood and mud spattered and often marked by damp underpants. I just can't land 100% on my feet. It's always just a little less, just a bit off center. Life's a malfunctioning seatbelt that yanks uncomfortably at my neck as I drive through Paris at night for the first time."

"Do you think it's because you feel too much?"

"Is it possible to feel too much?"

"I suppose it . . . well, I guess . . . sure."

"Love, no," she's patient with me. "I promise, it is not possible to feel too much. This is all between the universe and me."

"Nature?"

"Sure, her, too," Kate explains. "Periodically, she reminds me that I'm not allowed to have everything . . . wait, no, to *feel* everything."

"What's the difference?"

"Because then it becomes mine. Granted, I might not remember it all, but I can recall the beauty, the aromas, and sensations whenever I need them."

"So . . ."

"So sometimes, the universe decides to upset a variable or two in my delicate equation, light the frigging thing on fire, truth be told."

I nod. "Like wet underwear all day."

"Or baby puke in Florida heat. Exactly." Now she holds my hand while I shift.

"It's vindictive? Like it has a score to settle?"

She considers this. "No. Nature just keeps the playing field level. Every time I think I can squeeze a couple of extra drops out of life, you know, just half a glass of happiness to push me through another five loads of laundry on a Sunday afternoon, nature blows a whistle and throws a yellow flag on my lawn. I swear; my life needs a built-in bucket and mop."

"I get it." We turn into the parking lot, my windshield wipers keeping metronomic time with Elton John, something about sad songs. "But I don't see how that's not feeling too much."

"I'll explain it for you, Dr. Fastidious."

"Paris at night for the first time . . . it's a life changer."

She extends her seatbelt, punctuating the metaphor. "Imagine it with a seatbelt that half chokes you the whole time. That's me."

"Well, you should let me buy you lunch. Make it up to you."

She unbuckles, gathers up her handbag and my small umbrella, built for one. "I think that's a lovely idea."

Rain rinses the parking lot clean of regrets as we hurry inside.

I follow Kate; she follows a host, hostess, wait staffer, whatever we call customer service people these days, an older woman – maybe sixty – with graying hair loose over her shoulders. She's pretty, even in the banal black pants, white blouse, and conservative jewelry uniform of the Lafayette Mill & Wine Bar. Pretty Gray, she must be new here. I don't remember her, but I like her right away, might have had her for tenth grade English thirty years ago with Guy Montag and Juror Number 8.

Our lunch escape. Two years running. Long enough; it doesn't feel like cheating – *adultery*, lovely term. Rather, it feels normal. Natural.

Watching Kate walk remains one of life's simple pleasures. She played college soccer twenty-three years ago, still carries herself like an athlete. It's not that I objectify her physically from time to time; it's just that I . . . well, objectify her physically from time to time. In the best possible way, I promise.

Her walk is purposeful; that's sexy. She's always got something to do, someplace to go. She doesn't sway or saunter, sidle or some other S word. Rather, she walks deliberately and allows all the best bits of her to work their everyday influential magic on me.

Sashay. She doesn't do that either.

Kate is a woman I would watch walk from the fridge to the microwave, from the car to the mailbox, from the cereal aisle to the produce section with a plastic basket over one arm, and I'd be content for the afternoon. Is that objectification? If so, then yeah, judge me. I think it must be rare for someone like me to be in love with a woman who goes through life as if her hair was on fire and her underwear had been dipped in the north Atlantic.

Unfinished bits of poetry, God awful stuff I've heard or read online, try to complete themselves while I bear witness to her crossing the room. I do my best, flail at it. But I'm no poet. None of it comes together. Forty-five years, a Ph.D., three healthy kids, twenty-three years of marriage, and seventeen, tenure-securing publications later, I take my girlfriend (friend, lover, soulmate, whatever she is) to lunch. We sneak, still, two years later, and all I want is to be able to write poetry about her. She walks; I watch and write, scribbling brief lines, snippets of something articulate and persuasive on the walls of my mind. Exactly none of it sounds like Edna Millay or anything Springsteen might have scrawled on a bathroom stall.

If time tests us,
Sends us on errands apart,
We'll have these memories alphabetized.

Buried treasures:
Amiable breezes,
Incoherent, in-close conversations,
Aromas, textures, flavors,
Sensations unprecedented,
Indelible at our fingertips.
Even time can't frighten us.

Okay, I'm no Wislawa Szymborska, but I am a slave to my moments.

Moments both rule and ruin me. Watching Kate walk; that's one of my moments.

She's worn a cocktail dress to lunch on a Thursday, a sleek number, aerodynamic and confidently petulant.

I'm in an off-the-rack blazer, something I might wear to lecture.

She's dressed up, unnecessarily so.

Following her to our table, I notice – for the thousandth time – minute, discolored blemishes on her back and shoulder blades. They're imperfections. Kate couldn't care less.

I don't believe she has any idea what that means to a man who grew up in the late 1900s. We watched MTV and believed that women were supposed to be sculpted from smooth clay or gaudy, Italian marble. A woman with a clutch of freckles across her back – even a lean, athletic woman – was damaged goods.

Jesus, we were palsied idiots, the lot of us.

Tall, pretty, with energetic boobs, an athlete's ass, and strong legs . . . that woman was one of the untouchables as she writhed on the hood of some heroin addict, guitar player's Corvette.

Who does that on purpose?

Growing older, we learned that she might have a mole on her back, unsightly freckles across her breastbone, knee and elbow scars, handfuls of soft flesh, especially after childbirth and breast feeding. And some of us gave up; the dumb ones decided those women were throw aways. They'd never live up to the quintessential beauties in the Van Halen videos or the *Victoria's Secret* catalogue.

Why Mikhail Gorbachev didn't nuke us all to raspberry Jell-O is a Christian miracle.

Later on, others realized that those blemishes, marks, and scars only helped to make her different, special, and most importantly: accessible. Yeah, that. We were shallow. We'd grown up in the shallowest decade of the twentieth century. But we could be taught. Thank Christ, a few of us learned despite the pickled morons in our ranks.

Following Kate, I notice that her dress shows off a splash of blemishes across her shoulder blades, one clearly in the shape of a capital H, which I assume stands for *Hello Jackass*. She has a scatter of freckles below her neck that might be a connect-the-dots map of Ivy League colleges and universities, assuming Dartmouth moves east into Maine, and Cornell relocates to Buffalo. Vertigo threatens to dump me summarily on my ass as I follow, transfixed and stupid. She isn't bothered that I've seen, touched, tasted, or rubbed up against her imperfections. Only I am bonehead enough to make a big deal out of them.

Clearly, I don't deserve this woman.

I don't deserve the woman waiting for me at home either.

But I'll try harder. I promise.

Pretty Gray – I forget her name five seconds after she says it – shows us to our table. We think of it as ours, tucked into a recessed alcove beneath the outstretched arms of the mill's post-and-beam skeleton, three-hundred years old. It's dark, shadowy. Colors don't do good work here, one of the prices we pay. Immersed in ambiguous time, we give up colors. The spectrum shines unabashed outside the window, but in here, it's centuries-dried bones of a Revolutionary War-era grist mill, modernized, post-industrialized, polished, packed full of pretentious wines, and propped up as a rich asshole's Sunday brunch venue with two-for-one cocktails Tuesday and Thursday for anyone with a campus ID.

And good French fries, if you order a burger. Confession: I want the fries. Working class kids always want the fries, no matter how old, wise, or educated we get.

From above, Brandenburg concerti ride piggy-back with cuts from the Stones' *Hot Rocks*, depending on whether you're in the dining room or the wine bar.

Downstairs, a venerable system of cogs, wheels, and braces turns unendingly. The periodic squeal and rub of damp wood on damp wood reaches us in the dining room. This place is steeped in memories: colonial farmers, scores of millers, a two-ton millstone, Revolutionary War skirmishes in fields across the river, and all of it wrapped in the inevitable splash and roll of the waterwheel, the rumble and turn of the mill's innards. They're reminders from the basement: We're ephemeral. Live with it. You want true love? You willing to pay? Fine. Grasp at it with both hands and lie to yourselves. We'll grill the shrimp while the immutable guts of this place remind you that the clock is ticking.

There's a metaphor in here somewhere, but we don't give a shit. Good wine and succulent smells distract us.

I order Portobello mushrooms, grilled with a Dijon braise and asparagus tips in hollandaise.

Kate wants ribs, a full rack, dunked generously in BBQ sauce with potatoes and garlic mushrooms.

I eat with a knife and fork, dabbing at myself with a linen napkin.

She tears ribs from the rack with her fingers, leaves sloppy prints on her wine glass like a kid playing in mud. In twenty minutes, her napkin is an atrocity.

I ask for more; Pretty Gray forgets.

Kate doesn't notice.

Two drinks later, we're relaxed, reminiscing. Someone smarter than I am, perhaps involved with pharmaceuticals or deep space exploration needs to bottle this, sell it at CVS: Reminiscing Adult Contentment.

I'd pay anything for it, $200 an ounce. Anything.

We met at a visiting professor's spring semester lecture. Soft-money grants require visiting faculty to present ninety minutes on something so pointlessly esoteric that only other Ph.Ds. and brown-nosing students would even consider showing up. That April, Dr. Noone remembered queuing up power point slides and tiresome commentary on: *Paul Gauguin, the Antidote to Impressionism*. My kind of lecture. I loved it. Two paintings of blue dogs, orange virgins, and periwinkle Tahitian sunsets and Gauguin had my undivided attention.

Get deeper. Go full throttle. Momentary impressions are for chickenshits. I loved the idea. Not that I could live my life that way. In naked honesty, sure, I'm addicted to moments. I love and live for and create powerful moments whenever I can. I let them swaddle me, wash over me, transport me, whatever metaphor makes sense that day, but not a half hour afterward, I'm back to being me.

I'm going to say that again, because that part feels important. I'm back to being me, essentially-unchanged me. I'm not an alcoholic, a drug addict, a sex addict, an obese food junkie, none of those things. But I am a man who can only let go – really strip naked and dive into life – for a moment or two at a time.

Not Kate.

She's different. She's Paul Gauguin.

That afternoon, she sat nearby, politely chatted me up during the cookies and juice reception in the library. And I don't know if she had my number that very day or if it took her a week or two. But it wasn't long before she understood me better than anyone I'd ever known and did it effortlessly.

I'm still trying to understand her.

"It's a field of play," I try convincing her. "There are clear parameters. You just have to decide to embrace them with me, and things will . . . maybe make more sense." I form a makeshift pitch with my hands, wonder if it might actually be Ameslan for *soccer field*.

She half draws a rectangle on the tabletop with her fork. "It's a prison, a nice prison but still a prison with a truckload of razor wire, locked doors, guards, and steel reinforced bars on the windows."

"Do they have nice prisons?"

"They don't. We do." The restaurant's polite domesticity leans on her. Kate pushes back against it, ever defiant. "I imagine us meeting on the fifty-yard line, holding hands whenever we can. You have your half of the field, and I have mine. Sometimes life pulls us away from one another – often, if we're being honest – and one of us has to stand there, midfield, waiting, while the other goes off for whatever reason." She feels the allegory losing strength beneath her fingers. But she won't let it go. "Yeah, that's it: Our field of play. We're trapped out here, and sometimes we have to wait a long time, can't go to the sidelines, can't go up in the stands. You know?"

"Meh, you're merging on a mixed metaphor, but I get it. Sure."

"The corners are the worst," she says. "They define the whole thing, this . . . *place* we've created. I mean, I understand why we're trapped, but I don't enjoy being trapped, my love."

"We constructed it."

"We did," she concedes.

Three days after the lecture, we fucked on her kitchen counter, without hesitation the most influential emotional experience of my life, thanks to Paul Gauguin and his profound abhorrence of Impressionism.

What's curiously coincidental is that I'd never liked Gauguin. I thought him a coward for leaving his wife and children, fleeing for the South Pacific where no one could criticize his irrational, lunatic painting. He just packed up and sailed away. I'd judged him for decades, even read *The Moon and Sixpence* twice and couldn't wrap my head around Gauguin as a genius.

Yet after hearing Dr. Nooneremembers brandish his bullshit excuses for Gauguin's selfishness, I found myself neck deep in tawdry sex with Kate, a modern foreign languages professor from Ohio. Her kitchen counter might as well have been a Tahitian beach awash in sunset. I'd not looked at my wife or children the same since that moment.

Moments. See? Twenty-five months. Three weeks. Four days. They stack up after a while.

My family fell into shadow, that colossal, undeniable

shadow Kate casts across everything around me. Gauguin an asshole? Sure. But I only needed three days to fall as far as he fell sailing all the way to the South Pacific.

And I never left town.

Pretty Gray brings bread on a miniature cutting board.

I slice a section for myself, spoon a helping of butter onto my bread dish.

Kate tears off a handful. "You ever been to Italy?"

"No. Why?"

She tears another ragged morsel, chases it with Médoc. "Italians don't cut bread, Dr. Fastidious."

"They tear it?"

"They tear it."

I hold the loaf for her inspection. "But this is French bread."

"Meh," she chews with her mouth open, teasing me. "Multiculturalism."

"Tell me something I don't know about you." Kate pours a third glass of wine, *Cuvée du Château Someplace Nice*. It tumbles into her glass, an absurd restaurant chalice that might hold half a bottle. There's no doubt we're going to be drunk before much sand spills through the hourglass.

I notice her wrists, wiry and strong, her loose-fitting watch, that tourmaline. I key in to so many details, even now. She pours with unchecked enthusiasm for a forty-three-year-old on a Thursday afternoon. The mill's politely musty dining room, the absence of light, the exposed beam skeleton, something about the place fills her with not-so-quiet confidence. Nothing bad can happen to her here.

I, on the other hand, might be entirely screwed. My life's jury remains out on that question.

"C'mon, spill it," she encourages, pouring for me.

"You know everything," I spear an asparagus sprig, bite the end off. "There's nothing you don't know."

"Tell me . . ." She turns this over a moment, "your favorite 1980s video game."

I finish the sprig. It's sloppy with hollandaise. I try hard not to recall that it's a fancy word for undercooked egg yolk. "My favorite 1980s video game –"

"That's the one."

"How can you not know that?" I ask, not-so rhetorically. "No woman has ever inspected or interrogated me so thoroughly, literally."

"Not even –"

"No," I interrupt, regret it. "Not even her."

"So?" She sips from her glass. Her lipstick smudges the crystal rim; I want eagerly to drink from exactly that spot.

"Tempest."

"Never heard of it."

"Of course you haven't," I say. "Because you love competitive games, Space Invaders and Pac Man, I'm sure."

"That's true!" She rouses at the wellspring of memories. "You know me so well."

"They're competitive. That's you."

"Frogger, best goddam video game ever. I was a master. I bet I can still wipe the floor with you."

"I'm sure," I slice another sprig slopping up egg yolk. "Tempest was a great game, but not one you'd play against friends."

"I could beat you. No doubt in my mind."

"Sure there is. Give yourself a minute."

Frown lines wrinkle glassy skin above her nose, their first appearance today. "What's that supposed to mean?"

"You're the most competitive person I know, have known in years. Division-I soccer will do that, I guess."

"But . . ."

"But you're also the only competitor I know who tallies all of your own shortcomings without tallying anyone else's. I have no idea why you do that. You decide before you begin that your weaknesses are going to cause you to lose, but you never take into account your opponents' weaknesses."

She doesn't argue. Ripping a rib free in an act of senseless violence, she pulls off a stretch of meat with her teeth. "Why do you think that is? Ignoring the fact that you might just be the William Shakespeare of absolute bullshit."

"Dunno," I offer. "First born, daughter, overachiever. Never good enough for driven parents, a community that expected too much from you. Meh, it's Monday-morning psychology, but add it all up and you get a woman who's abundantly aware of her weaknesses living in a world where she should be a senator, a CEO, a leader in every sense of the word."

"With great tits?"

"You have no idea."

"But I do keep score unfairly."

"Just *your* score. Yes."

Kate sucks smoky BBQ sauce from the bone, licks it clean in such an unsexy manner that I feel myself harden beneath the linen napkin in my lap. Gesturing with the naked bone, she adds, "I could beat you in Pac Man."

"You could," I change the subject, steer us clear of discomfort for now. "But not Ms. Pac Man."

"It's the same game, love."

"Nah, I'd own you."

"How do you figure?"

"I'm a feminist."

"*I'm* a feminist," she says, as if the role is reserved solely for middle-aged mothers.

"I'm better at it than you are."

She lifts her arm, mimes with the rib bone. "Which one do you think it was?"

"The rib that started it all?" I ask. "I'm pretty sure that was a metaphor."

"A bad one." She drops the bone to her plate, drinks more wine. "Frogger. I'd kick your ass."

Kate searches for lipstick. I don't know why; we're barely through the first course.

"Don't," I say, then reconsider. "Please. You don't need –"

"Okay." She tosses it back, stashes her handbag beneath the table.

"Are we selfish?" I ask without thinking

"We invented selfish, darling. You can't tell me this is the first time you've bumped up against that question."

"No."

"Of course not." Then digging for the bag, Kate finds the lipstick and applies it with practiced dexterity to the wine label, scribbling *SELFISHLY* in blood-red capital letters. "There," she admires her work. "I've always goddamned hated lipstick, anyway."

Pretty Gray, clearly not an ostentatious lipstick user, watches amused from the prep station.

Kate leans in, elbows on the table, ignoring whatever convention or manners that might've adhered after her escape from middle America. I'm a little tipsy; so I hold my breath while trying to capture her in a mad Impressionist's glimpse of staggering perfection.

Edgar Degas, my favorite.

How all of them didn't hang themselves in some Parisian garret seems an artistic feat. Imagine seeing wonder and beauty for a fraction of a second, then requiring weeks to paint it, all the while ignoring acres of second-class beauty so as not to mar the image frozen on your mind's canvas. Unexpected encounters with utter beauty – in the form of one so profoundly committed, so entirely given over – those moments were reason enough for all of Paris to fall into a wine bottle in 1874. Who wouldn't?

Silver pendant, silver chain, tan porcelain face framed with fallen hair, twin freckles along a jawline half in shadow, lipstick kiss about a crystal glass, candle flicker, stained napkin a handful of well-traveled road . . . *yes, please, I'll need two months with this moment alone.*

She breaks the spell. "You want to talk about the future?"

"I do, the field of play, especially."

"You sure? Because I sometimes worry –"

"About me?" I consider the ropy-veined backs of my sandpaper hands. They look nothing like hers.

"About you," Kate reaches for me regardless.

"I'm ready."

She leans farther forward, that silver pendant nearly dipping into a shallow puddle of garlic mushrooms. I expect her to whisper. She doesn't. "I need you to convince me."

"Why?"

"Because I'm not going anywhere near the future without you."

And again, I realize that Paul Gauguin was right: Impressions, the immutable ones that deserve immortality in oil or acrylic, can only leave one starving. Bugger all useless Impressionism. All of my moments – so neat, so controlled – will only lead to me losing this woman forever. I need a measure of rented courage to get through the afternoon.

"So what's the first corner?" She mocks my Ameslan soccer field with sticky fingers.

"On our field of play?"

"Yup." She dismembers another rib, has maybe six left, licks her fingertips and rubs the vestiges on her napkin. It's only a square foot of white cloth, but it already looks to have been used as a bandage in a triage tent.

"The first corner," I fork mushroom into my mouth but continue anyway. "The first corner is revulsion. We share that. Yes?"

"Which revulsion? I think we might have stockpiled a few flavors of that vintage."

I swallow, fork up another portion, then leave it on my plate. "The revulsion I feel when I think of you with your husband, with Henry. That revulsion. You're not supposed to be with him. You're supposed to be with me, even though I know . . . well, I know better."

She waits, just a beat, giving me time to finish my thought, then, clearly having considered this in quiet moments, says, "Yes, that. I know it well. And I agree: You're not supposed to be with her, physically, ever again, especially when you two go away together like pretend married people."

"We are married."

"I'm aware of that, Dr. Obvious."

"I know it's selfish, but –"

"We're not talking about what's selfish," she cocks an eyebrow. "We're talking about what's real, the real parameters of your . . . *our* . . . field of play. I hate that term."

"Field of play?"

"Hate it. I don't know why."

I give her a second, then go on. "Anyway, yes: revulsion. Physical sickness. I don't . . . I don't ever want you with him again, especially not in your bedroom, or, well, in a hotel room, certainly not a hotel room."

"I understand. No, really, I do." She pushes her hair over her ears, and I realize that the Earth could crash brashly into the Sun and I would never be cured of this woman. "That's the first corner."

"Degas."

"Degas? C'mon, Renoir at the very least."

"You're drunk."

"Getting there. Yes, Renoir."

"What about Manet? You have a Manet print in your office."

"Are you forgetting Maine last summer?"

"You rely too heavily on the loose chronology clanking around inside your head. Just because I demonstrated momentary appreciation for Renoir when I was drunk, I'll remind you, does not mean that he merits my vote today. So I say again: Edgar Degas."

"Reckless. You're reckless. I swear to God you need a library card to check out a working brain. This shifting allegiance of yours is off-putting, unsettling. I think you should have sex with me later."

"Will that fix things?"

"Yes, it will."

"All right then. Degas."

"Fine, Degas it is."

. . .

In the corner, Pretty Gray delivers a bacon cheeseburger with the same quiet consistency with which she might serve braised venison tips. She pays attention to details, even seemingly unimportant ones, giving them consequence. I appreciate that.

After dropping off the burger, she makes eye contact with me, just for a second, but in that glance communicates something I'm already too drunk to catch. I try grabbing for it as it passes, but I miss. I'll worry about it later.

Kate and I fuck on the periphery of a timothy patch as the sun rises over Monmouth battlefield. An indifferent cedar tree shields us from the worn bicycle path as felonious squirrels chatter and wrestle in the underbrush. She rolls to all fours so we can watch dawn color the sky as we come together.

We fuck on the area rug beside her fireplace as her children watch Harry Potter films upstairs. Natural gas flames and Christmas tree lights flicker and flash, washing her favorite Renoir print in garish red, green, and gold. She hums a lunatic's vowel song as she rises to me, playing the silent game so as not to wake the dog.

We fuck in her basement, the last safe haven for the wicked. Here she straddles me, touches herself, lifts her breasts before sliding up, creeping forward to kneel unannounced astride my face. She comes into my mouth; errant patches of whisker stubble remind me that she shaves in a hurry, not sexy, just getting the job done before helping her kids with math homework. Her narrow thighs color the basement in heady, unchecked lust.

We fuck beneath the great elm behind the research library at four in the morning when sodium arc lights near the biology building color the quad eerie silver.

We fuck on a hotel balcony, fourteen stoplights coloring the street rhythmic red, amber, and green.

We fuck in all the colors, painting together – she like Gauguin, me like Degas.

They will be our undoing, my moments and her experiences.

I recall a hike together the previous October, an aggressive, rutted trail above the Delaware in the shadows of the Water Gap. Autumn had draped Pennsylvania with the reassuring, muted hues of fall. I reveled in the idea that I'd need a fleece to keep warm. New Jersey summers are akin to a season in the steamier districts of Hell. So an autumn hike requiring a fleece and maybe a pair of wool socks was a rare and special delight. Kate's legs are longer than mine, so I often scramble a step or two keeping up, my malfunctioning clockworks stuttering beside her Division-I grace.

"Tell me a Gauguin story," I asked, not quite winded, but struggling.

"You know them all."

"Yes, but you're better at telling them, and from the looks of that hill, I'm going to be sucking wind like an industrial furnace in about five minutes."

"You're in fine shape, love. I don't believe you."

"You don't have to keep up with you."

"Fine," she thumbed through a file folder of memories. "Did you know that Gauguin didn't start painting until he was thirty-five? And he did it to help ward off the stress of being a stock broker."

"Everyone self-medicates," I said. "It's not surprising. He probably also drank gallons of wine and screwed half the women in his neighborhood."

Kate tossed her head. "Meh, you're probably right. He had five children with his wife and then managed to fire off five more after jetting down to French Polynesia."

"Good lord, five more? And him not making much money painting."

"Oh," she agreed, "almost nothing, like on the verge of starving for years. No one gave a pinch of poop for his paintings until 1906, when a Parisian gallery displayed over two hundred of them."

"Well, that's not bad," I tightened the straps in my pack, started up the muddy incline.

"Dr. Fastidious," Kate corrected. "Gauguin died in 1903. He had no clue that he'd been leading the most important visual artistic movement of his generation."

"Damn."

"Damn is right," she said. "He just wanted to paint . . . needed to, I guess, if you go in for all of that romantic artist bullshit."

"You do."

"Oh, honey, I do. You don't."

"Yeah, not so much," I said. "But you've got to respect the guy a little. I mean, he had it made in Paris – stockbroker, wife, family, nice place to live for the turn of the century."

"Nah," Kate had pulled ahead a step, now slowed for me. "I get it. He needed more. He was gonna grow old as a largely discontent cog in a largely uninteresting financial wheel. Who wants that?"

"Oh, I dunno," I said. "Maybe just me and about a hundred million of my closest friends."

"You don't understand contentment."

"What?" I asked, out of breath now and happy I could keep her talking with just one word.

"You grew up as a Gen-X kid. I did, too. We were the first

generation to fall victim to the American marketing machine: color TV, magazines, product placement in shows and films, and all of it funneling the single, prevailing message that left or right, black or white, tall or short, male or female, everyone, frigging every single one of us was force fed for the entirety of our lives."

"What's that?" Still panting, I let her run with the ball.

"That you are just one purchase away from happiness."

"Wait . . . what? Wait." The notion took root. "You know . . . you're right."

"I know I'm right, love. I don't need you to confirm it for me."

"God, you're sexy," I said. "If I had an ounce of stamina in my body, I'd toss you into those bushes right now and have my way with you."

"Yeah, promises, promises." She passed me a water bottle. "When you think about it, it's creepy. There's almost no commercials, no ads, no magazine pages, newspaper blurbs, nothing that any marketing executive anywhere pays for that attempts to sell us more than one thing at a time. We have been brainwashed: Happiness – not contentment, actually, just *happiness* – is one purchase away."

"Your next purchase."

"Exactly."

"So what's this then?" I indicated the river, the colorful hardwoods, and the path, winding off in the direction of Thoreau's back yard. "Isn't this happiness? What doing?"

"Nope," she took a long drink, capped the bottle, and stuffed it in my pack. "This is contentment, much harder to earn, and nearly impossible to hang on to for very long."

"Wait," I said. "So if you're right, our choices are to buy happiness one purchase at a time or to struggle for real contentment by finding or creating opportunities to come out here and hike this trail?"

She winked. "Spot on, Dr. Sexy. Or to run a marathon, swim the English Channel, write a great poem, raise decent children, teach students to appreciate Victor Hugo . . . you get the idea."

"We can't purchase contentment," I said, uselessly. She was already there, waiting for me, two steps ahead again.

Kate leaned in for a kiss – *he can be taught!* – then pulled back suddenly when a black bear as big as a Volkswagen ambled up from the riverbank. "Holy shit!" She backpedaled, then grabbed for my pack strap and yanked me along. "Holy shit, do you see that thing?"

I spun, expecting a machete-wielding sociopath in a hockey mask. "Jesus! Look at him. He's gotta be four-hundred pounds!" The bear rose onto his hind legs and swatted the air between us with a paw the size of a frying pan.

Then two cubs, fuzzy and rolling along like hyperactive basketballs, tumbled from the underbrush. One tripped over his brother, skidded to a clumsy stop, then stumbled to his feet with a delighted bark. All the while their mother watched us, never threatening, but making certain we understood that her to-do list included getting these two watered, fed, washed, and back up to the den in time for afternoon naps.

"Shit, it's a *her*," I corrected myself. "It's a mother bear. We're dead. Should we run? I don't think we're supposed to run. What should we do? Lie down? Are we really gonna do that? Lie down and play dead?" Useless, that's me.

"It's okay," Kate whispered as if we'd come across a stray puppy. Still backing away, she said, "It's fine, Mama. You have a good morning. We're just gonna make our way back down here and never bother you and your kiddos again. Everything is . . . just . . . fine."

Mama Bear offered her own yelpy growl, warning us off; I nearly shat myself. "Jesus fuck!"

"Don't," Kate squeezed my forearm. "Don't scare her."

"Scare her?" I whispered. "You think she's scared of me? Have you lost your mind? She's literally standing over there right now wondering which of us would taste better all slathered in honey."

Kate giggled. "Well, darling, clearly that's me."

Too shocked, neither of us managed to get our cameras turned on in time to snap a photo before Mama Bear dropped to all fours and trudged off behind her twin knuckleheads, still wrestling in the leaves. Kate and I stood for a long time without speaking, periodically hearing her bark incoherent instructions at the hellions. Eventually we lost track of them as they crested the hill.

"And *that*," Kate said. "Is exactly what I mean. How many suburbanites can say they had that experience this morning?"

"The ones queuing up for McGriddles and hash browns at McDonald's, their hangovers causing their eyes to bleed and their rectums to leak? Not many."

We backtracked to the car, pretty confident that Mama Bear and the kids were long gone, but not wanting to risk getting an arm ripped off then having to explain it to our spouses' divorce attorneys. All the way, I watched from my spot, about one step behind Kate, as she nearly floated down the path, her spirit as light as the chilly breeze brushing the river valley with autumn serenity.

Now she drags the flat of her palm beneath one breast. "Don't you wish my boobs were bigger?"

"Appeal to negativity, sort of." I answer. "And no, not even once."

"I do."

"You're an athlete. What're you going to do with bigger boobs?"

"Just a healthy C cup. That's all." Kate presses upward on both breasts now, displaying them prominently beneath that diabolical dress. She understands how it pushes my buttons, knowing that despite the view from the balcony, she has plenty of boob tucked in there.

I prop my chin on steepled fingers. "You know what my favorite thing about your boobs is?"

She releases them; they settle back into middle-aged obscurity. "I want to know what your five favorite things about my boobs are."

"Five?" I feign disbelief.

"Five, Dr. Fastidious."

"Oh, dear . . . I could list a hundred things."

"We don't have that kind of time. I'll take the top five." She slips fingers inside her narrow shoulder strap and unapologetically bares her right breast in the candlelight. Reminiscent of its eighteen-year-old self, it's remained shapely, defying gravity twenty-five years later. And I confess I adore the pale, untanned, pinkish triangle of skin about her coppery nipple. She never tans topless like so many women from her neighborhood. Those isosceles triangles of demure white flesh, those are mine.

"Good lord," again, I offer up my best shocked-and-offended look. "Put that thing away. You'll change the weather."

"Five things, hero. Ready, set, go."

I pour us equal measures of Médoc therapy, empty the bottle, and mime to Pretty Gray for another. "Number Five: I love that you have stayed in shape through pregnancies, breast feeding, and middle age. Your boobs are small enough that time has little effect on them. They remind me of college women I dated back in the fourteenth century."

"But . . ."

"But better. Much."

"Good. That's correct." She twirls two fingers like my grandfather used to do, urging me on.

"Number Four: I love that your right boob has to try so hard to be as perfect as your left, but it's an ongoing struggle you don't notice, because you're so busy being such a tireless mother, sister, friend, professor, support system, and colleague for so many people."

We both notice that I didn't say *wife* and tacitly agree to let it pass.

"That's a good one." She takes hold of her lacy bodice, considers flashing me her left breast, but Pretty Gray returns with our wine. We wait for the older woman to uncork the bottle. Kate samples a mouthful in a fresh glass and nods for her to pour out. Pretty Gray does, then notices Kate's lipstick hand-iwork about the empty: *SELFISHLY*. She leaves it with us.

With two glasses before her, Kate uses a corner of table-cloth to polish a dab of BBQ sauce from her tourmaline. "You were saying."

"Number Three: I love that your left is the only utterly perfect breast in the world. It's a boob often imagined by the likes of Mailer, Hefner, Botticelli, Klimt, even Spielberg and Gloria Steinem but never captured in film, print, theater, visual arts, or conversation."

"Now, let's not get carried away." She tilts her head adorably to one side, tugs open her bodice, and peeks beneath her bra. Candlelight flits playfully from her necklace and earrings. I'd watch her all day without blinking. "Yeah, okay . . . it is better than the other one. How can you –"

"I pay attention to details. I am Dr. Fastidious, after all."

"Yeah, you are." She takes a last look. "Continue."

"Number Two: I love that you want to believe you're a true B cup –"

"Almost a C!"

"Barely a B," I waggle a finger. "Better . . . A-and-a-half."

"A-and-a-half?" Again, she lifts both breasts. "Have you been to the eye doctor recently, darling? Look again; these babies are almost a C!"

"A-and-a-half, much sexier for any guy with an imagination."

Outrage wrestles amusement for control of her face. "Are you suggesting that I lack imagination? I'll remind you, *Doctor*, that I have a Ph.D. in eighteenth-century French literature."

"And you speak four languages. I don't need a reminder, love."

"B."

"Fine. B." I grant the victory. "Still sexy."

"I'm glad you think so." Yet she doesn't bask in the win long. "So . . ."

"Oh, yes, right. Number One." I pause.

"And?"

"Sorry, I'm just . . ."

"Told you! I told you!" Her competitive nature takes hold again. She tears another rib free. "I knew you didn't have five."

"Number One." I settle back, content to watch. I've known no one who hears honest confessions with quite her level of delight. "Number One: The thing I love most about your boobs is that they're attached to you. And that's enough."

She sits for a breath or two, just staring at me, one sparerib still clutched in messy fingers. "You . . ."

"Yes?"

"Did you go to school or something? The College of Saying the Right Things?"

"It's just the truth," I offer.

"Oh, dear . . . you are so getting laid later."

"I am? I love that idea."

"Brace yourself." She considers the rib as if finding it there unexpectedly, then murmurs. "Because they're attached to you."

"Yes, that."

"Gauguin was a prisoner, too," she says. The wine has colored her teeth and lips disconsolate purple. "Have you ever thought of that? Tahiti was just a lush, tropical prison."

"He risked everything for creativity and love."

Kate nods, "and got trapped by it. Absolutely."

"Poor bugger."

"Confession."

"From me? Or for me?"

"Both," she says. "Confession: I took my top off at a Panama City bar, spring break when I was twenty-one and drunk with my friends."

"That's a confession? I thought all women did that. Isn't that why they invented Panama City, so fraternity rapists could choose light meat or dark meat and then have Daddy's attorney get them off with just a misdemeanor pinch? I think it's on the city letterhead, not kidding."

"Good point," she presses her breasts inward this time, just slightly. "It was a wet t-shirt contest. I strutted and danced and made a complete fool of myself. I've never told Henry about it; he wouldn't forgive me, even though it was two years before I met him."

"Was it fun?"

"At the time, sure. But if my daughter ever did it, I'd break her legs. Come to think on it, I'd break her legs if she even considered *going* to Panama City, friends or no friends. And that's unfair."

I take her hand. "You were a college kid, shitfaced and naive, not a mother who's spent the past twenty years reading about botched rape convictions in the newspaper. You can't make the comparison. That's holding yourself to an unreasonable moral standard."

"Heh, yup, that's me."

"Confession."

She smiles, forgives herself. "For me? Or from me?"

"For you," I say. "I had sex in a Dunkin' Donuts bathroom near Fenway Park in Boston."

"Holy shit!" she cries, then waves an apology to Pretty Gray. "Holy shit," she whispers. "With whom?"

"I dunno, some woman I met at a game."

"Christ, yeah, okay. Thanks for that one. That puts my 34Bs into reasonable perspective. How old were you?"

"Forty-one."

She nearly spits wine into her mushrooms. "C'mon."

"I dunno. Twenty-two, twenty-three, young and stupid."

"Well I'm pleased to hear that, because knowing you these days, you wouldn't even pee in a Dunkin' Donuts bathroom."

"Not without an ampule of Doxycycline."

She laughs. "Exactly!"

I grope for a tidy wrap up. "When you think about it, baring your tits for drunk strangers at twenty-one might honestly help you avoid stupid decisions at thirty-five."

Kate picks up my line of reasoning as if she'd been waiting for it. "You're spot on again, Doc. Every thirty-five-year-old woman wants her body coveted. I don't care who she is. Those of us who climbed up on the bar a time or two when we were in

college understand that it really isn't such a meaningful forma-
tive experience."

"But you get it out of your blood stream," I add. "Especially
you, Madame Gauguin, as you crash face-first through life."

"Yeah," she agrees. "Yet I'm still here now."

"You are. But I hope that's for other reasons."

"True, that's another story," she warns, "for another time."

"Another day?"

"No, later today. I've had enough wine to bare a boob, but
not quite enough for that conversation, not yet."

I toast her with my glass. "I'll be here, Tits Mahoney."

"Sure thing, Dick Donut."

When we made love that first afternoon, it was with such
youthful abandon that I forgot I was staring down the barrel of
late middle age, what morning news programs refer to as
"approaching retirement." Their limp-wristed emasculation of
"getting old" makes me want to vomit.

But when Kate and I find one another, I forget that I have a
softening paunch above my belt, that my hair is thinning, my
muscles atrophying, and my knees creaking.

I forget that I have as many years behind me as I do ahead,
perhaps more.

And I forget that when grading boring exams at my desk, I
am only a professor with essentially no money, no sex, and no
prospects for career advancement, who has been doing the
same thing for nearly twenty-five years.

What will happen when I reach thirty years, or forty, doing
the same thing? Will Grace and I communicate at all? Will I
still find Kate? Will we screw on her basement floor like
teenagers sneaking a quickie? Or will I have blown my brains

out by then? Or drank myself numb and senseless? That's the coward's way. I'll probably choose that one.

Downstairs, adjacent to the wine cellar, the Lafayette Mill's original heart pumps with metronomic reliability. Wood on wood, creak and groan, the massive, inexorable grist stone, we feel as much as hear three-hundred-year-old resonance through scuffed planks. The clock ticks for both of us.

"Your dick is enormous," she teases, flitting a finger through the candle flame.

"It's average," I remind her. "Nothing special. I'm just pleased the old man can still rouse himself when you beckon."

She peels rivulets of hardening wax, tosses one at me. "You should slide over and let me be the judge of how large – sorry, *enormous* – you are."

"Here?"

"I'm beckoning." She makes brief eye contact, then returns to the candle; the ghost of a smile suggests that she's as serious as she is tipsy.

"Fine," I take a quick glance around and shift to her side of our booth. Pretty Gray is occupied elsewhere. "What the hell."

I stand at an antiseptic smelling urinal, pissing $75 wine. The men's facilities, similar to the dining room and wine cellar, retain as much of the mill's personality and attitude as its renovators could salvage. The walls are wide tongue-and-groove slats, perhaps torn from an abandoned barn, sanded and varnished so customers never have to give up the fantasy that they're visiting an eighteenth-century grist mill, even while taking an expensive leak.

I run my fingertips along the unlikely juxtaposition of smoothly-sanded boards and bright, chilly porcelain and reminisce about where Kate and I have been together: theaters, cafes, restaurants (not all of them as assiduously disguised as the Lafayette Mill), art museums, poetry readings, faculty research presentations, student lunchtime recitals, campus classrooms, bike paths through the university, walking paths about the arboretum, hotel rooms in three states as we visited professional conferences, my living room, her guest bedroom, basement, the back seat of my car, the front seat of hers, the woods behind the fieldhouse, and even her kitchen countertops in our mad, desperate attempt to feel twenty-three again, albeit temporarily.

So many times I've asked why.

She has as well.

What addicts us, keeps us traveling together along this road to perdition? (I'm amused at the melodrama inherent in that question. Conveniently, it distracts me from the fact that I don't have an answer.)

Neither of us has ever had an answer. But part of me thinks the very reason we continue toward inevitable ruin is because we're traveling together.

Together is the only variable in our seemingly-perfect algorithm that neither of us can explain or abandon. Yet, I am convinced – and across the hall in the women's room, Kate agrees: *Together* is what transforms us, makes us nearly invisible in those cafes, restaurants, walking paths, and visiting faculty lectures. *Together* keeps friends and family from wandering into the university pool when we're swimming laps, side by side, four mornings a week, when we run neighborhood 1ok races, crossing the finish line within a half second of one another, or when we split club sandwiches in the student union with 200 kids milling about, ignoring us as if we move through life beneath a protective cloak. It is our *together* that will ruin us, but it is also our *together* that makes this field of play metaphor impossible to escape.

I wash my hands, consider myself in the mirror above the sink. Without my glasses and with my share of wine, I appear blurry, indistinct, as if I might reach through the glass and erase myself, efface my lies and leave the mirror empty, having forgotten I was here at all.

I'll wake tomorrow, return without guilt or hesitation to my old life. My wife and kids will welcome me back with only a breath of uncertainty: "Dad? Where were you? Down the hall? In the basement?"

And I'll have fixed everything.

I dry my hands and wish again that I might erase the man looking back at me. I rub vigorously for a few seconds with a handful of paper towels; no one's in here. No one sees.

It doesn't work.

"Make me laugh," she says later. "I need to laugh today."

"The wine and ribs not satisfying enough?"

Her eyes plead. I assume her visit to the rest room unfolded similarly to mine, that the women's mirror is equally as honest as the men's. "The ribs are lovely. But I need a good laugh."

My mind pings; I land on what I consider an oldie but a goodie. "Did I ever tell you that my penis was in the *Guinness Book of World Records*?"

"Love, I said *enormous*. I didn't say *record breaking*."

"Yeah," I nod. "Well, it was only in there until the librarian made me take it out."

Now she does laugh. It isn't musical or magical. It doesn't

lilt, bring rain to the desert or cause a respite in global conflict. But goddamn, that laugh transforms me, coats me in Teflon, and I feel the weight of guilt and anguish slide away in a mercurial cleanse. I owe her one, tally it, and silently promise to pay her back later, when she needs it.

Without trying Kate's rescued the afternoon. Granted, my tendency to self-loathe on these outings might return; it is a resilient demon, after all. But for now, that one joke and her blustery splash of genuine laughter have liberated me. Hoping to get a rope around the moment, I ask, "Am I the love of your life?"

"What's that?"

"Earlier, in the car, you said I was the love of your life, when you were talking about our kayak trip last summer and your wet cell phone. Am I?"

Kate motions for me to meet her half way across our table. "Darling," she whispers, "I've done nothing for the past two years and two months, nothing at all when I wasn't thinking about you. Somehow you manage it, getting into my head. I can't buy broccoli without hearing you joke about your childhood. I can't run on a treadmill without wishing you were there. I can't order a pizza without hearing you say *mushrooms and green olives, please.* And while I'm amused by the phrase and the quaint, silly way Cameron Diaz throws it around in movies, if there's such a thing as a *love of my life,* you're him."

It's my turn. All the interlocking tumblers in the solar system just clicked into place. Some physics equation I didn't pay attention to might actually tear a hole in the universe if I don't say the words aloud.

But I don't.

Rather, I go for a half-assed admission, half blanketed beneath a half-assed joke. "Well, my deep blue love, if that's how you really feel, then I should probably buy dessert."

She presses her lips in a mocking smirk. Kate knows me, forgives me. Thank Christ.

If I had a gun, I'd blow my brains out.

But it doesn't matter. She's found a festive mood, even tosses me another blustery laugh before draining her glass and pouring more wine. "One of these days you're going to learn that life is more than just deep blue moments."

"I like deep blue moments. Most people don't appreciate them."

"Like Degas."

"Of course."

"But Degas never plowed madly through life with barf on his shirt and wet underpants distracting him from a nicely cooked pork chop." She connects the dots for me.

"Like Gauguin."

"See? You really can be taught!"

My phone buzzes. I ignore it.

It buzzes again, so I change the setting to *SILENT*.

"Tell me a story." I shift on the padded bench, settling in for the afternoon. "Any story."

"Any story? You can't mean that."

"A story about you, something that gives shape and substance to your . . . well, life, for lack of a better term." Around us, a handful of people futz with their phones, chat, eat, and wander off to pee or visit the millstones downstairs. But nothing reaches our booth entirely in focus. A protective bubble has formed. I swear that our spouses could take a seat at the bar and never know we were here. This condition, this illusion of safe anonymity has nearly been the ruin of us multiple times, however. We run into friends and colleagues, students out and about, always unexpectedly and always a bright, breathtaking shock when we realize that yes, in fact, others can see us, recognize us, even question what we're doing out together . . . walking, drinking wine, eating breakfast, swimming, shopping, whatever.

But not today. Somehow, today that resilient bubble will shield us. "Yeah, tell me a story about you."

She pointlessly folds her napkin, sucks gravy off her teeth, says, "I like this idea . . . this game. Let's make it a game."

"So you can win?"

"Of course so I can win."

"Fine," I agree. "It's a game, the storytelling game."

Pretty Gray approaches; I barely notice. Kate pushes her plate to one side. "No, thank you, I'm still working on this."

"Yes, ma'am," she fills both glasses then slips beyond our invisible curtain.

Kate watches, then begins. "To tell you a story about me, I have to tell you a story about my mother."

"Alright."

"It'll make sense when we're done," she fumbles for a place to start. "You see, I think that women my age have more regrets than our mothers."

"How do you –"

"Wait," she raises a finger. "Lemme have another go at that. I mean . . . I think that women my age have our own regrets, but I'm often convinced, quite often, that we inherit our mother's regrets. I know they're a different generation and all that, but I don't believe you can find me a forty-year-old woman who doesn't haul around some of her mother's regrets."

"Okay," I loosen my tie. "Is that the story?"

"Silly man," she drinks. "I have a doctorate in French literature, the greatest stories in human history."

I chuckle. "Now, I wouldn't go that –"

"Hep!" Again with the finger. "Just relax over there, Mr. Deep Blue Love. I've got a story for you . . .

The intangible weight of self-loathing had become unbearable overnight. Nothing happens all of a sudden; she understood that. But this did. Misery, hanging from her like a rain-soaked parka, was all at once unmanageable.

"What the hell?"

"Hush," she waves me off. "You want a story or don't you?"

"The intangible weight of self-loathing?"

"Just sit there for five frigging minutes. Alright? I will wholesale beat your ass, skinny."

I skewer another asparagus sprig. "Carry on."

She combed through memories of seventh grade science for the weight of water.

Couldn't get it. Shit like that never sticks, frigging capital of Vermont. Who knows?

Anyway, the horizon whitened somewhere near Ireland. Uninvited cloud cover ruined her view as God left for work. She'd wished for orange-yellow, the color of contentment and . . . I dunno . . . island vacations, not this swath of disappointing gunmetal. November's a bad boyfriend; I swear to Christ.

Regardless, her feet left impressions in damp sand. The tide would erase them later. She considered briefly if anyone might wonder who'd been here. Perhaps an early dog walker would pass with a stick chasing Labrador, shaking off the Atlantic as only a wet Labrador can.

The weight of water: about eight pounds per gallon, more for seawater. Right? It's like eight-point-something.

You ever notice that nothing sounds quite like a Labrador shaking dry after a dunk in the ocean? Sorry, I'm wandering a bit, too much grape juice.

"You're doing fine," I say. "Keep at it."

"Thanks."

"It's Montpelier, by the way."

"Hmmm, the French," Kate perks up. "I do love the French. They have the best capital city names. Doncha think?"

So anyway, her dog, Rufus, had romped with Muriel through lawn sprinklers then shaken like that. He'd eaten an entire bag of ice pops she sneaked to the backyard while her mother folded laundry. This had to have been in 1968, give or take. Muriel hoped to share them with Jodi, Gretchen, and the black girl with no friends, the one who played guitar and sang like an angel greeting a new day.

What the hell was her name? She showed them how to play an E chord, an A chord, and almost a B7.

Clare Anne! That's the one, God damn it. Clare Anne, the guitar player.

"You see; you can play all the Beatles songs with those three," she explained while fitting awkward fingertips over silver frets. Black girls like the Beatles.

Muriel hadn't known, had been thrilled to discover it like a buried Spanish coin. And Clare Anne sang "Blackbird," while Rufus rolled in wet grass, just a couple of mismatched angels greeting a new day in 1968.

Shitty year, 1968. But . . . well, you knew that.

. . .

"I did."

Now Muriel strode gracelessly toward the frothing waves, ignored the horizon, all scribbled over by bloated clouds. Down here, the beach smelled of organic decay. A dog turd floated past her feet. She'd worn the sundress Mitchell bought for her in Boston. He'd said over and over, even to his friends that night in the Union Oyster House, how it made her look like . . .

I can't remember, God fuck it all.

"It's okay." I'm transfixed, can't wait for what comes next.
"You're too forgiving."
"Baton Rouge, another good one."
"French."

Her hips, ass, even the twin swells of rib flesh that rolled into human braille when she wrestled on an old bra tugged that exhausted sundress into something stretched thinly, too little jelly over so much bread.

Muriel wore it anyway.

You see, she wanted it to dance in the breeze, a Meg Ryan sundress. But the tide was falling, so winds brushed down the beach, yanked the loose skirty bits all up between her ass cheeks and above her thighs, a goddamned mess, not at all how she'd imagined it.

Sundresses. You guys don't know anything about sundresses. One minute, they're a flowy, sexy, feminine state- ment, and the next (generally after like two beers) they're just a clumsy floral pennant, your Aunt Ethel's curtains all wonky and bulging in the wrong places. Kill me.

"Well, I promise I will never wear one."

"You're not helping, love. You're . . . in the way."

I purse my lips. "In the way?"

"Yeah, just . . . just sit there for a second. I'm almost done."

"You're gonna need toilet paper," her mother scolded when the girls had gone. "Rufus is gonna be shitting out chewed pieces of plastic for weeks. You're gonna need paper. Just carry some around, Muriel. Because you're gonna wanna grab at the end of those bits and give them a yank. Rufus won't be able to poop them on his own, honey."

She'd cried, as much at the mortifying possibility of having to pull ghastly pieces of plastic from her dog's asshole as at the notion that her mother was disappointed in Muriel for wanting to share ice pops with popular girls from school.

They never came to that cheap fibro house again, Jodi and Gretchen. She'd tanked her one audition.

Clare Anne did.

She visited until she made new friends in middle school, but Muriel never told anyone. The friendless girl strummed that guitar and sang "Blackbird" a thousand times better than Paul McCartney.

Now with her ankles disappearing into chilly mud, Muriel felt herself sink. The weight of this discount, plastic denouement pressed her feet farther down. The sodden parka about her shoulders seemed bulkier here. Seawater spilled across the tops of her feet, squeezed from spongy sand. Cold inevitability trickled from her ankles to her toes.

Nothing happens all of a sudden, not sunrises, sundresses, Beatles songs, and certainly not handfuls of Flurazepam. Eleven Flurazepam – all that were left in the bottle – they don't happen all of a sudden. Right? Christ, that takes some commitment.

But if that's the case, then why can't you get your memories straight, dumbass? At this moment in this place, you're supposed to be swaddled in memories, the very best memories, the comforting ones, the love, happiness, and peace memories. The magical stuff. You're supposed to wear a dress that flows in an onshore breeze tousling your hair like Meg Ryan, so you can face the weight of the deepest water.

Eight-point-frigging-something pounds per gallon in the ocean.

You're supposed to be in a dress that rises gently like linen curtains, not a twenty-year-old rayon sack that clings and bunches with buttons threatening to burst at the sheer size of your puckered ass. You're supposed to find yourself awash in golden sunrise, God's final gift, just for you, two minutes of utter perfection, just two fucking minutes.

Not you. You're stuck with those bitches who abandoned you for inviting a black girl over to play, or extricating plastic from a suffering dog's rectum, failing to recall seventh grade science, or mining your literary lexicon for a simile to capture the sound of a long dead Labrador shaking off sprinkler water.

It's supposed to be deliberate memories, dumbass; not this bullshit.

You see, she'd messed up again, even something this simple, the simplest of simple things: walking into the ocean. Walking! Who fucks up walking?

I interrupt, hate myself for it. "So what happened? What'd she decide to do?"

Kate steals asparagus from my plate. "Getting there, big guy. Almost home."

Standing there all stupid and clumsy, Muriel decided to give it back, return everything, erasing each item from her imagined blackboard. Then she'd be through.

Eleven Flurazepam, one size-8 sundress wrestled over a size-12 ass, three-hundred-and-six paces from the boardwalk, three-hundred-and-four empty footprints, temporary reminders of a permanent decision, one dog turd rolling on wet sand, and a hundred-billion gallons of icy, forgiving cleanse, just waiting.

She stepped into the bubbling, froth, felt the stab of bone deep chill, and the weight of failure again. Muriel vomited up wheat toast and Flurazepam, then turned and fled.

The ocean, now all grayish white in the gathering dawn, effaced her puke . . . yeah, effaced; that's right . . . then her footprints. She didn't return again until summer.

And that's my story," Kate says, retrieving her plate for another rib.

"Holy Christ," I can't drum up anything useful. "Holy Christ, you're good at this game."

"Shit! I told it before I knew the rules. How will I know if I've won?"

"You won," I say, "whatever the rules are."

"A mother's regrets," she gnaws resilient flesh from the bone. "Young women don't realize they're inheriting their mother's regrets until they're older . . . too old to do anything about it. I think it's like matter or energy or whatever it is that scientists always say."

"Matter cannot be created or destroyed," I fill in the gap.

"That's the one," she wipes her hands clean. "Middle age women learn that lesson hard: Your mother's regrets cannot be destroyed. Someone has to carry those bricks around."

"So . . . nature or the universe or something out there didn't want her yet? Wasn't done with her? Is that the takeaway message?"

"And I've been carrying her ever since," she drops the rib bone. "Not that I mind, but I hadn't expected it, hadn't expected to have my relationship with my mother shift from mother-daughter to . . . whatever we've had for the past fifteen years."

"But she's you, love," I venture onto thin ice, pray it holds me. "You realize that? Or are you just projecting yourself onto that morning to make it more picturesque in your mind?" I don't push the issue, hope I haven't buggered our day.

"No," she offers me a gentle shake of her head. Her earrings dance. "You may be right. I want that morning to have a neat story arc; she deserves at least that much from me. The dog turd and the easterly wind do the trick."

"But you also want the wet underwear and the baby barf. Right? There has to be a broken Parisian seatbelt clotting up her view of the sunrise?"

"Is this about me or my mom?"

"Oh, this is entirely about you," I risk another step across the pond. "I don't believe most suicide attempts play out like a Ron Howard film."

Her face clouds over. "So, wait, are you suggesting that I *want* the wet underwear? The broken seatbelt? Because I don't."

"No," I raise my palms in surrender. "I'm just saying that maybe nature doesn't need you to feel absolutely everything."

And that quickly, it passes. She smiles and I'm reminded again why I fell in love with her. "Silly man," she toasts me this time. "How much you have left to learn about life, Monsieur Degas."

"Life? I don't know about life?"

"Nope," she replies. "*The Bugs Bunny Guide to Middle Age Survival.*"

"What's that?"

"You remember all those times when Bugs Bunny smashed through walls and left Bugs Bunny shapes, like perfect, in the side of the house? He'd lose his shit and just crash headlong through the sheetrock like a naked, raving lunatic?"

"Of course," I say. "He did it all the time, whenever things weren't working out the way he had them planned."

"Exactly, darling. Exactly."

"Like Paul Gauguin."

She winks. "And entirely unlike Edgar Degas. Just in case you're keeping score."

Outside the window, amiable afternoon light stretches itself in an effort to preserve the day. Bright yellow and vibrant green have lost their tug-of-war with less youthful, pretentious hues, shades spread thin, like . . . what had she said? . . . too little jelly over toast. Soon, we'll have to leave.

"Let's go outside." Without preamble, Kate stands, collects her glass, our bottle, and her handbag. "I need a little air."

"Where're we going? Isn't it raining?"

"Nah," she gestures toward the window. "Bright as a genius's SAT scores. "C'mon, just to the patio. We'll have a drink."

I wave to Pretty Gray who nods. And again, I follow Kate along a narrow corridor. Heat from the fireplace on our right and the kitchen on our left make the little gauntlet humid and uncomfortable. With only pin lights over the rest room doors to guide us, Kate makes a sharp left. Now sunlight from the mill's patio floods the hallway. "Here it is," she pushes open the door and a chill breath dries the budding sweat above my hairline. "C'mon, it's nice out here."

Afternoon light reflects off wet grass, leaves, and the mill pond, momentarily blinding me. I shield my eyes until they adjust to discover eight small tables around a faux-colonial wet bar. Most are empty. Only two couples brave the uncertain weather. A pair of middle-aged women shares white wine, while two kids, early twenties, have opted for burgers and beer. I blink the world into focus then join Kate at the railing. She's balanced the bottle up there as she gazes downriver.

"Over here," she says. "Isn't this nice? Just a little fresh air to clear my head."

I prop my glass beside the bottle. My eyes hurt and the glare is brutal, but she's right: cool breeze and the waterwheel's steady *andante* slap some sense into me. "Yeah, next time maybe, let's just sit out here. I could get used to this view."

"Can't see much today," she also shields her eyes. "This glare is a cheap whore."

"I've been thinking; if we decided, maybe next spring, to go down to —"

"Kate!" This from behind me.

"Fuck," I whisper. "Make some excuse. I'll be inside. I won't turn around."

"Katherine Hedges!" A woman's voice, three or four Chardonnays into the afternoon, interrupts again. "Is that you, Kate? Come over. We're just having a drink!"

Kate turns slowly on her heel. Barely audible, she says, "Neighborhood Bitch Squad. Go back in. I'll tell her it's a department thing, a college thing."

"In *that* dress? Are you high?"

"Just go. I'll take care of this. Take the bottle."

"Should I stay? Play it out with you?"

She doesn't hesitate. "No. Her husband is good friends with Henry. If he gets wind of you, we're really screwed."

"Shit."

"I'll be back," she raises her glass, just another shitfaced, discontent suburbanite.

I cross weathered planks with my head down, hear Kate: *Oh, hi Naomi! What brings you out here?*

Then the back-and-forth hyperbolically-extended vowel pleasantries of women who barely tolerate one another:

Just a quick wine with Margaret, you know, from Kyle's baseball team . . . looking at a condo.

Yeah, yes, oh hi . . .

Your friend want a drink? He can stay . . .

No. No, just a department thing, but I've got a minute.

The motherfucking door is locked. I yank on it twice for good measure. "Jesus Christ," I knock, press my face to the glass, hope to see someone in the corridor, maybe Pretty Gray or a stranger taking a leak.

Nothing.

Overhead, the wind picks up. Scudding clouds are white-caps on a bay. On any other day, I'd stop to enjoy them.

"Sir, I'm sorry, sir, but that's the wrong door. If you come over here, I can let you back into the dining room." The bartender beckons from the opposite end of the deck. "Just over here, sir."

I force a smile. "Sorry, yeah, great." I have to run the gauntlet. My options dwindle from three (Break the window. Meet Kate's drunk neighbor. Kill myself on the spot.) to two (Meet Kate's drunk neighbor. Kill myself.) to one. "Thanks! On my way." I gulp wine and make it three steps toward the bar before

Kate's bad-dye-jobbed, leopard-printed, obnoxious-jewelryed, blue-eye-shadowed, bicycle-pump-breasted, white-wine-drinking, real-estate-agent neighbor stands, and in smeary elongated vowels that could only have been invented in pretentious American suburbs, feigns enthusiasm to meet me. If I listen to her for another ten minutes, I'll be in a diabetic coma. "Why hello, Professor . . . please, come, take a minute to join us for a drink, just a quick one."

Ten years evaporate from my life in that moment. I open my mouth to reply but what emerges sounds like the last gasps of a drowning house cat.

Kate tries to rescue me. "We've kind of gotta get back."

"Oh, nonsense," Naomi shakes my hand in both of hers. To lunch, she's worn more jewelry than I've owned or purchased in my lifetime. "You university types are all the same. Your department party can hold off for five minutes." Her breath smells like a wintergreen Altoid someone has plucked from the floor of a fraternity basement.

I look to Kate.

She shrugs: *We're fucked. No sense going down sober.*

Finally, I brandish my favorite, cocktail party grin. "Thanks a lot. I'd be delighted." And for only about the second or third time in the past two years and two months, I seriously estimate the cost of a divorce attorney. I am still distracted by obscene calculations when Kate, our bottle empty, ushers me back into the dining room.

"Well, that was fun." Safe at our table, we don't argue or blame one another. Brief encounters with people we know have become an inevitable reality of our relationship. Today, however, was worse. Despite collaborating to find silver linings, we only manage to nail one to the church door.

"She was drunk," Kate says. "That helps."

"Yeah, hopefully she gets plenty drunk, falling down drunk, maybe forgets the whole thing."

"I don't know." She drinks water for the first time all afternoon. "Her kids will be getting off the bus in a couple of hours. She's not one to be shithoused on a weekday."

"You're in that dress. It's too much for a department lunch."

"I know." She pulls a little sweater over her shoulders, also for the first time all day.

"We're both clearly drunk." My bench seat has grown uncomfortable. I'd rather be standing.

"I know."

"There's obviously no department luncheon here on a Thursday afternoon. Half the staff is teaching right now." Panic tightens my stomach into knots, if anything in there can get itself knotted up.

"I know."

"And we're not in the same department."

"I know." Her frustration spills in nearly tangible waves across the table. "Kenny, her husband, is gonna know by dinnertime tonight."

"What does that mean?" I try to control myself. "You know, with regards to Henry?"

She brushes hair behind both ears simultaneously. When she does one at a time, it's sexy. Both together means our protective bubble is deflating around us. "I dunno. I dunno . . .I'll, well, I'll watch how long or how often he's on his phone, I guess."

"Christ."

She laughs, just a wet splutter, nothing endearing this time. "You keep summoning him, love. He can't help us today."

· · ·

Three minutes later, Kate's made up her mind. "I'm going to get drunk, darling. I suggest you join me."

"You want another bottle?"

"I want you to suck my nipples, press them between your tongue and the roof of your mouth until I beg you to let go. Can you do that? And then maybe the same, with my . . . you know . . ."

"So we've had enough?" I look around for Pretty Gray, figuring we'll get the check.

"No. More wine. Definitely." She toys with her napkin, as if it might yank itself into something modern and gregarious. "Maybe some cheesecake."

"What are you gearing up for? Some important event I don't know about?"

"Yes," she replies simply. Palms pressed flat against the table, she inhales afternoon, candle smoke, French wine, BBQ spare ribs, and her own dose of self-loathing. "Yes. Surviving this."

"Okay. More wine." I find Pretty Gray, understanding that I am going to wear this hangover like a wet fur coat.

Before our third bottle arrives, Kate draws her lipstick like a gunslinger and scrawls *FIERCELY* across label #2 in crooked graffiti. Uncertain what it all means, Pretty Gray pretends that nothing's happened and leaves both empties on the table.

Many of the films and TV shows we watched for decades tried to convince us that it was right to covet the thin (but not too thin; she's gotta have some shape), blonde, ponytailed cheerleader with an IQ in the low-average range of the Wechsler scale. Sure, she would play hard-to-get but then put out at a keg party for a guy, bigger, prettier, shallower, stronger, with better hair. They would orgasm together on a bed of rose petals and live happily ever after in a well-appointed, suburban home with above-average children in matching travel soccer uniforms and matching *A*+s in honors geometry.

Or these women made outrageous salaries as important corporate attorneys or literary agents, living in downtown condos and attending swanky dinners, dancing at clubs until 4:00 a.m. and screwing passionately on the hood of an imported sports car as the sun rose over the East River.

We were told to covet this woman – thirty years ago her name was Heather – to protect her, fight for her, go to war for her, if necessary. But no one taught us how to talk with her.

So we married Heather's friend, her wingman, Plain Jane, and lived happily, wondering what ever happened to the budding supermodel from high school. Later, we discovered, thanks to Facebook, that she taught fourth grade, gained seventy-five pounds of hips and ass birthing three kids, one of whom had already been diagnosed with Autism, and lived essentially as boring an existence as any of us. There's no such thing as 4:00 a.m. orgasms. 4:00 a.m., as we suspected, remained reserved for wet diapers, puking babies, and labradoodles needing to go out to urinate over our failing snapdragons.

Yet we often wondered if deep down, she (Heather, if you're keeping score) could still fulfill all those thirty-year-old dreams, dusty now on a memory shelf behind dental plans, 401ks, and vacation rental properties in Orlando. Could she be the woman we imagined at seventeen?

Probably not. But we still wanted to know and wondered, if given a chance, she might covet the opportunity to prove it to herself. Or to us.

But none of this was about real love. Rather, it was all about nostalgia, settling, and imagining (pestilentially) *what if?* So when Kate found me that April afternoon, with amiable springtime draped over us, I thought: *Yes, pick me. I want to know. Don't you?*

And here we were, two years later, connected by a thousand, multi-colored, triple-knotted strands with no hope of escape. We risked everything, and neither of us had the first inkling how to protect all that we'd bet. It scared us, but not enough for either Kate or me to retreat to the sidelines of our soccer pitch.

No way.

I'd done it: I'd found a surviving "Heather" and discovered that she was an ambitious, creative sex partner, and she was a brisk conversationalist, and she was a terrific athlete, cook, swimming companion, and lunch date.

Yet, in her own home, at her own desk, and reading her own student exams, she was like me: no money, no sex, no prospects for significant career advancement with only the promise of twenty more years doing what she'd been doing for the last twenty.

Who could possibly blame us for triple knotting all those bits of connective twine?

(That's rhetorical, by the way. We both knew who.)

"I wanna be a poet," I say. "Because of you."

"You can't be a poet, dear." She spears a section of red bliss potato wet with melted butter. "Poets are honest. You're not honest."

"I know," I say. "But it should matter that you make me want to be a poet."

"It does." Another potato.

"I'd write about you and your . . . beauty. It's perfect, your beauty. Did you know that?"

"You'd be a terrible poet, love. I mean . . . I love you. I do. But no."

I try not to feel offended. "Why?"

"Because I'm not honest either. I'm not. There's no beauty here."

"Just us."

A third bit of potato, this one dragged through her puddle of gravy. "Just us."

"You know, I don't tell you this enough, but I'm just drunk enough to say things I might regret tomorrow –"

Kate interrupts, her mouth still full. "I often question my own behavior." A dribble of gravy slips across her chin. She collects it with a fingertip, serves it to me.

I want absolutely every meal I eat for the rest of my life delivered in exactly this manner. "Thank you, delicious, but you're not listening. Most days, I wish I had the confidence and self-assurance to tell you."

"What?"

"That I want you to break free, just to burst into a hundred-thousand brilliant colors and be wildly, stupidly happy."

Her brow furrows. "I am wildly, stupidly *content*, silly man, right here. I don't need more than this. And I know you have grand imaginings . . ." she gestures with both hands, ". . . about my potential and creativity. Whatever. But I'm not going anywhere."

"You're in love with the wrong man, Madame Gauguin."

"You're drunk, Monsieur Degas," she says. "Besides, I have the nicest handcuffs in the jewelry store."

I reach over and steal a piece of potato. "I don't know where I'd be if I didn't have you to tell me when I'm wrong, cousin."

"I know: you'd be miles and miles behind where you are right now."

. . .

"How is it possible that I can love you and you can despise yourself?" I ask this, hoping for a simple and direct answer (X=9) that I can cling to when dread and uncertainty wake me at 3:00 in the morning.

She only pauses a moment, as if she's practiced this response in the mirror. "Because you don't see all of me."

"I do," I argue. "I've studied every inch of you, have reflected on everything you've ever said."

"No, you're too forgiving. You don't see me, the real me."

"But I do. I know that you hold yourself to account for your dishonesty, for sneaking away just to be with me. I know those things about you."

"You think you do, love," she explains. "But you don't."

"What do you mean?"

"You detest the fact that you've become a liar. It keeps you up almost every night."

"What's that got to do with you?"

"But you don't hold me to the same standards," she says. "You accuse me of tallying my shortcomings without ever tallying anyone else's, but you never ask why you're awake at 3:00 a.m. hating yourself for being a liar and a shitty husband, while I'm sleeping soundly. How can you forgive me for that?"

"I . . . well, I don't really –"

"Exactly,' she continues. "I know precisely what level of no-good, fucking piece of shit I am. I don't forgive myself for one inch of it. You do. It's your weakness, not mine. My weakness is my ability to sleep."

"But you've said . . ."

"I have." She does the heavy lifting again. "I've said that I waited a long, long time for someone like you. So that erases a multitude of sins in my book. However, when it comes to sleeping soundly, we both ought to be looking in the mirror and hating what we see. You are. That makes you honest. I'm not;

so that makes me . . ." She gestures with her fork, conducting an invisible orchestra.

"Content?"

"Yeah, maybe," she admits. "Maybe I'm more content with this. Maybe I'm content with being a shitty wife."

"You got married at twenty-five."

"Yeah, that. The young-and-stupid excuse goes a long way."

"So how do you forgive yourself?"

"I don't," she says. "I just don't mix self-loathing with insomnia."

"You loathe yourself during the day?" I slice off another piece of French bread, smear it with butter.

"Why not? There's ample opportunity." She rips off a hunk for herself, two handed.

Kate pees again.

While I'm alone, Pretty Gray stops by. "Everything alright, Professor?"

I force a smile despite the tightening sensation about my throat. "Sorry, do I know you? I'm afraid I'm bad with faces."

"No, sir. Sorry. My sister, Sondra, works with your wife, Grace, at Owen, Hadley, and Bonacum. She's a paralegal there. I met your wife at the Christmas party last year. We're Facebook friends."

My heart grinds to a stop. "Oh, great. So . . . you're new here?"

"Yes, just a couple of months now."

"Oh," I smile again and imagine I look like a madman on his way to the gallows. "Well, it's a pleasure." I extend my hand, "I'm Andrew."

She shakes it firmly. "Nice to meet you, Andrew."

I'm left alone in our booth to wonder whether this is truly

the last afternoon I will ever enjoy. I silently promise not to say anything to Kate and regret that decision almost immediately.

But still I vow to keep my mouth shut as the Lafayette Mill walls creep a few inches closer.

"I would like to conduct an experiment," Kate works to control the slur creeping into her voice. "Before I slink home to the executioner with my tail between my legs."

"Sounds formal," I eat another mushroom. It's lost flavor as it's cooled. "What do I have to do?"

"Without being too obvious about it, have a look at the man at the bar." She peeks surreptitiously over my shoulder.

"Which man?" I ask before turning around.

"Oh, you'll know," she says. "Try – without embarrassing us – to get a decent look at the guy. I want to know what you see."

"I'm going to see something different from you?"

"Infer. I want to know what you *infer* about him, whether you're right or wrong about people and whether I'm right or wrong about you."

"Oooh," I play along. "Alright, yes. A fun experiment. Um . . . how about if I find some excuse to go to the bar?"

"Double Woodford Reserve on the rocks with brandy-soaked cherries."

"What?"

"You heard me, Doc."

"We're already over two bottles in, gonna end up in handcuffs and not the good kind."

Kate inspects our third wine bottle. "Over half left. We're okay."

"Double Woodford Reserve on the rocks with brandy-soaked cherries?"

"Yup, *extra* cherries. The executioner is probably checking his texts right now."

"Extra cherries?"

"Clearly you didn't grow up with an accountant for a father. But yes, brandy-soaked cherries, as many as he'll give you without DEA approval."

"I'm on it." I get up. My legs are wonky. "And I'm drawing inferences about the man at the bar while I'm up there."

"Yes."

"But you're not going to tell me who he is."

"Nope."

"Okay," I acquiesce. "I'll be back."

Kate's right: The stranger at the bar ranks among the most physically appealing people I've ever imagined, not encountered, *imagined*. He looks as if he's the love child of a weekend-long orgy featuring young Sean Connery, Harrison Ford, Rita Hayworth, and Halle Berry, all of them getting after it with enthusiasm. Sliding onto a stool, I imagine the four of them screwing willy nilly on some Lake Como balcony and then raising the child on grass-fed veal and Scandinavian salmon sperm.

Comfortably fifty-five in a bespoke suit, salt-and-pepper hair, and a watch that costs more than I make in a semester, he clearly approaches life with all the listless engagement of a bored billionaire out slumming on the Jersey coast. He's fit, not excessively muscular or hyperbolic, but trim with little fat, none of the droopy kind, expensive teeth, and no wedding ring. He chats amiably with the bartender between sips of Scotch and brief notes in a leather day planner. Even his pen looks like it might've run $500. He doesn't glance at his watch, and I can't see a cell phone. He might be waiting for someone, but he doesn't appear to give a shit if anyone shows up.

Yeah, alright, I understand Kate's desire to conduct this experiment, because in less than fifteen seconds, I loathe and lust for this man in exactly equal measures. If I want to sleep with him, Kate's thighs must be tingling.

I order her double bourbon loudly enough to guarantee that Indiana James Bond Solo hears me, then retreat, anxious to learn what comes next in our little science lab.

"So?"

"So . . ."

"What do you think?" She accepts the drink without comment.

I lie. Well, I don't exactly lie; I withhold a thimble of truth, so just a junior varsity lie. "I think he's a self-absorbed douche bag. He's obviously divorced, probably has a half-dozen kids somewhere. He buys them material shit to keep them happy while he jets off to see the northern lights in Bergen with some perky, twenty-seven-year-old intern who keeps him happy at least until the cash and the Viagra run dry. I imagine he's abandoned his wife, has run through dozens of girlfriends in the past . . . hmmm, twenty years, and makes pretend money working with multinationals and federal contracts or other useless consultants with nebulous job responsibilities they discuss at cocktail parties on airplanes but which no one truly understands. Everything on him, including his watch, his teeth, and his chemically-inflated penis are probably paid for with some corporate expense account he never sees, never even thinks about. And while he can probably trot along for a few miles on a treadmill, he doesn't exercise outdoors (except for golf, yachting, and polo, which aren't sports), and he hasn't eaten a slice of pizza or an honest bowl of ice cream since the Clinton administration when he was getting his MBA at the London School of

Economics on his maternal grandmother's dime – probably tobacco money from somewhere in Chesterfield County, Virginia. That guy," I wrap up with a flourish, "looks like someone who truly cares what style underwear you have on, probably calls them *panties*. Jesus Christ."

Amused, she trails a finger about the rim of her glass. "So you adore him even though he probably has the emotional range of cracked linoleum."

"I do!" I grin and steal a swallow of bourbon. "I love him and want him dead, all at once."

"Ha! I knew it."

"Then why did you send me over there?"

"Because while you're bullseye accurate about him – right down to the chemically-enlarged penis – and what a loathsome fellow he probably is, you must admit that every lust-worthy cell in your delicious loins wants a shot at him."

"As do yours, I assume."

"Of course," she doesn't hesitate. "I'd screw that boy within an inch of his life right here on this table. Well, after I finish these ribs. They're delightful."

"So what's the point, dear? I'm not sure where we're going in this rabbit warren you call a brain."

"Darling," she explains as if I'm eleven and feeble-minded. "I wouldn't enjoy it."

"Why?"

"Because he's not you."

"But . . ."

"And thank you for my drink," she sips. "I need one more nail for the coffin. Tap those heels, Dorothy! There's no place like Paris. There's no place like Paris!"

"So I'm supposed to believe that you prefer me over him? Ahead of *that* guy? He looks like Dorian Gray at his retirement dinner." I jerk a thumb over my shoulder. "C'mon, I'm convenient. Don't you think?"

"What do you mean, convenient?"

"I don't really have a social life. I don't have many friends. I'm never out drinking with the guys. I don't watch sports all weekend. Nothing takes my time away from you except my kids and my work. It's like I'm on a convenience store shelf any time you need me . . . or want me."

"And I'm –"

"Nope," I cut her off. "It's not the same. You're a wife and a mother and a professional in a world that doesn't wanna let you be those three things simultaneously. You have a healthy social life with lots of friends. Don't you think this relationship would have evolved differently if I had any kind of demanding social schedule at all?"

"Of course not," she starts, then gives it a second to percolate. "Actually, to be fair. I don't know. But I can tell you that in a world where all things are equal, I choose you over him every day of the week."

"But all things aren't equal, love. Some days they're downright unequal."

She frowns. "You're suggesting that if you were more self-absorbed, we wouldn't be here?"

I try ripping the bread; it's curiously satisfying. "I dunno. But I do wonder if what we're calling true love wasn't just a fantastically convenient recipe that happened to fit both of our lives like a nice pair of gloves."

"So?" She turns her palms to the ceiling. "Who cares? If it's true love today, who cares what got the rock rolling down the hill? We met and our lives fit together. I don't think that's points against us. I think that's serendipitous fortune that we happened across one another. Hollywood's bullshit recipe for love is exactly that, just bullshit. It's fantasy. Real people have to start somewhere."

"What would you think if I spent all afternoon watching college football and drinking beer with my friends rather than out hiking or swimming with you?"

She doesn't miss a beat. "I'd hope that you text me at half-time. And if it got to where I felt like you were ignoring me to be with them, I'd ask you about it."

"Because you'd feel ignored?"

"Because I'd want to confirm that you're the person I believe you are," she explains. "You're not giving yourself enough credit. I chose you for a reason, for a hundred reasons. I'm not an idiot. If I wanted a beer swilling, keg fly, I'd have trolled the local bars, not the Post-Impressionism lecture circuit."

"I don't wanna fight."

"We're not fighting, love. You're having a crisis of confidence, just a small one. But I'm not taking it personally." She catches a passing busboy, requests a dessert menu.

I try for a key change, just a modulation in pitch. "I'm largely uninteresting."

"I disagree," she accepts an elaborately printed card from the teenager. "Oh, Christ, they've got amaretto cheesecake with caramelized almonds. I just came in my pants."

"No one saw." I pretend to search for voyeurs. "Lemme have a look. I'll choose something, too. We can share."

She passes it over.

"Holy shit, they've got *Herrentorte*. It must be a new chef."

"What's . . ."

"It's Viennese, the working class's answer to *Sachertorte*, which is arguably the most irritatingly snobbish dessert in central Europe. Generations of oppressive Habsburgs gorged themselves on it for frigging centuries, while the Austrian people slaved on farms, eating gruel and, I dunno, dead squirrel or something."

She smirks and I want to bend her over the table and make love with her in that sinister cocktail dress.

"What?" I ask.

"You're uninteresting?"

"Largely, yes. I think so."

"*Herren* . . . whatever. Sure thing."

"Trust me," I'm already forgetting why I decided to be such a prick. "Have a slice. It'll change your life."

"It already has, you dumbass."

"Vienna," I say. "We should go."

"And you also know that I'm not wearing any underwear of any particular style, how disappointing for James Bond over there."

"Liar."

Beneath my feet, the mill's grist stones take another lap around the basement, amusing a new clutch of tourists visiting the Lafayette Mill for the first time. I sense the vibrations through my bench cushion. Outside the window, afternoon is losing a colorful skirmish with evening.

Kate's distracted. She's watching Pretty Gray stash a folded handful of bills, probably singles, into her apron. From here, it looks to be about $400. It's probably $50. I'm just waiting until she pulls out an iPhone to text Sondra or Sandra (whoever her sister is) to rat me out to Grace on Facebook and end life as I know it.

"Look at that; will you?" she says. "Forty years later and still living on tips."

I offer an unconvincing shrug. "Maybe she's a retired vascular surgeon, just a little supplemental cash, something to do besides baking cupcakes with the grandkids and inserting stents into bloated German businessmen."

Kate stares, doesn't look at me. "Like my mom. As much misery as she's lived through, she's still working, still pushing the rock up the hill. You know? Sixty-seven years old and zeroed in on the same target she chose at twenty-three. Who manages that?"

"Not us," I murmur into my glass.

"I spent thirty years criticizing that woman, and now I'd give anything to understand what keeps her upright. It's like I've aimed too high, should've been content with what I had: decent guy, good dad, Christian values, solid family life, no real emotion or connection. But what the hell, that's what novels and vibrators are for. Right?"

"C'mon, your parents weren't that happy. Just because they navigated forty years without shooting each other doesn't mean they'd do it all over again. Your mother, if she knew, might celebrate your decision to let yourself have this, us, me, all of this."

"She might," Kate admits. "That's true. I wish I knew."

"Ask her."

"No, now . . . well, I mean."

"Why not?"

"Because if she disapproves, there will be nowhere for me to hide from myself. That's become so important these past two years. Right now – with her and my dad, at least – you and I are Schrödinger's cat. As long as I keep my mouth shut, I have a fifty percent chance they'd crucify me and a fifty percent chance they'd cheer. That's gotta be good enough. No matter how broken and lost my mother managed to get, she didn't do this. Maybe she should have."

Kate's got a point, and it's clearly (sort of) working for her. So I don't push the issue.

She interrupts my thoughts. "But I do wish I knew what

they'd say. Even just a half smile and a brief nod, especially from Mom, would free my soul; I hate to admit it."

"Corner number two? Remember that conversation?" She prompts, plenty drunk now. "What's that one?"

"Really?" I try to divert us. "If you want, we can talk about next week's –"

"Corner number two . . . please." She's determined. That's fine.

"Well, corners number two and three kind of go together."

"Oh, great," she finishes her wine – the bourbon's long gone – and pours another. "One minute then. I don't wanna be entirely sober for this bit of chit chat. Alright with you?"

I reach for the bottle. "That's fine. I'll join you."

She swills another mouthful. "Right. I'm braced."

Another sloppy dollop of BBQ sauce has fallen onto the taut expanse of tan flesh beneath her left collar bone. I wipe it up with a fingertip, then taste it, hickory smoked pork.

"Yummy?" she teases.

"Wonderful. I should have ordered the ribs. Who eats Portobello mushrooms on purpose?"

"You do." She dabs at her breastbone with the battle-scarred napkin, makes it worse. I pass her mine. "You're the only man I've ever known who will consume fifteen-hundred calories of alcohol while avoiding five-hundred calories of meat and potatoes."

"You love me."

"I do," she admits, "but when it comes to watching your waistline, you're a bit of a bitch."

"I am an exceptional bitch," I confess. "But I'm avoiding your question."

"I can't imagine why, Dr. Fastidious."

"Right. I get it. Corner number two on our inevitable field of play –"

"Prison?"

"Resort."

"Resort prison," she experiments with this, decides it'll do. "Sure. Why not? Resort prison, a downright pleasant vacation from which there is no escape, like Gauguin's island." She motions around the mill's darkened interior. "Take this place with its bones all naked, candlelit frigging cave, no colors; even the restaurants we choose are prisons."

"I thought you liked it here." I'm a whining middle schooler.

"I do," she explains. "I love it, because it's ours. But I'll give you a hundred dollars if you can find something, anything in here that's brightly colored on purpose."

"I . . . I dunno what to say."

"Corners two and three . . ."

I wait as she helps herself to another swallow of fortifying grape juice. "Corner number two is the honest realization that forty years later, dishonesty has become a fundamental tenant of my life . . . our lives."

"That's a good one. You're insightful, Professor." Another rib, only two left. They've got to be cold by now.

"And corner number three, indelibly linked –"

"Wait!" She extends a palm like a traffic cop. "Lemme guess."

"Have at it."

Through a mouthful of pork, she says, "Corner number three on our Resort Prison Playing Field, Dr. Fastidious Love of My Life, is the troubling fact that . . ." She takes a second, brushes bread crumbs from the table. Her eyes widen with clarity. Tears try to well up but she blinks them away. She's tougher than I'll ever be. Kate says, "It's the troubling fact that I've begun to forget who . . . how . . . no, *who* I'm supposed to be. Yes?"

I nod. "Who? How? Why? Any of them work; just insert one into the keyhole and hope it doesn't fit."

"You're not making any sense, love." She's rallied. Dry eyed, she grins. "But you should get me out of here soon."

"We're almost done."

I try my hand at poetry again. Maybe shithoused, I'll hit one out of the park.

Kate's not in the mood, so I mumble a few lines to myself.

A love song,
One of the good ones
A romantic movie,
With that first kiss done well,
Good poetry,
Motivating,
Slow burning fire that flares without warning
Into something lucid and warm,
Impossible to capture
Or keep,
But deliriously lovely to witness.

She ignores me.

Later. She's crying.

A hundred-thousand brilliant colors. We're 500 miles from a hundred-thousand brilliant colors. Christ, shoot me. The wheels are off the wagon. "Hey," I say. "Insult me."

"Why?"

"C'mon, one of your good ones," I encourage. "Have at me. I need one, a cheap shot."

She finds tissues in her bag, blows her nose without embarrassment. "Well . . ."

"Yes?"

"If we could make wine from stupidity, you'd open a vineyard." She tosses crumpled, snotty tissues onto the table.

"See? Not bad."

"What's corner number four?"

"There's no need. We've been over it." My vision tunnels. The DUI fine is going to run me close to three-thousand dollars.

"There's every need, dumbass. If we're going to be here, chained to these fucking $75 bottles of Bordeaux, we ought to be able, at least, to finish what we start. Don't you agree?"

I tear off a confession-sized morsel of bread. "Yeah. All right. But this is a bad idea."

"Corner number four."

"Is –"

"Don't," she hides her face, buries it in both hands. She sucks clumsy breaths through wet sobs.

"Corner number four is –"

"My kids." She has to be the one to say it. It's muffled behind sniffles, coughs, and nearly silent weeping, but I hear.

"And mine," I add. We've narrowly avoided this issue all afternoon, not ripped the Band-Aid off until just this moment. "Every hour, all our stolen evenings, early mornings, weekends, every time we've manufactured some bullshit reason to be together, have pawned our kids off on Grace or Henry –"

This stings her. "Don't say his name."

"On our spouses, yes," again, I acquiesce. "The hundreds of days, thousands of hours we've finagled our lives to create time together. That's corner number four on this field of play."

"Yes," she reaches for her napkin, realizes the state it's in, then takes mine again. Wiping her face indecorously, she says,

"I'm a bad mother. I'm dishonest to the point where I live a lie, multiple lies, so many that I have to live them, not just tell them or believe them. They're too numerous to recall without a frigging Abacus. And I've given up, given away, thrown away –"

"Thrown away."

"Time with them."

"Yes."

"That's the one. That's the transgression I'll have to answer for when you and I finally arrive at the gates of Hell."

Pretty Gray, still just an older lady at work on a Thursday, watches from the servers' prep station. I have no idea whether she will be the lynchpin in our gallows, but real fear of this otherwise pleasant woman has been simmering in my soul for two hours. Regardless, I try another old joke, maybe lighten the mood and keep us from getting kicked out. "On the bright side, I figure if we do get to Hell there's no more wool sweaters. Right?"

Kate doesn't hear me or doesn't care to. At this juncture those two outcomes are essentially interchangeable. And somewhere across town Pretty Gray's sister and my wife chat agreeably over afternoon coffee.

I puke politely in the men's room when no one's around, wipe my mouth with sandpapery toilet tissue. Leopard-print, inflated-boob Naomi on the patio and Pretty Gray's visit to the Owen, Hadley, and Bonacum holiday party pushed me over the edge. Kate and I have dodged bullets before, but this feels different. For the sixth or seventh time this year, I promise to quit alcohol.

Quitting alcohol, I do it all the time. I'm an expert.

So I puke again, politely.

. . .

"Do you remember the bears?" Kate asks.

"Of course. I can't imagine I'll ever forget them."

"They're the reason."

"I don't understand."

"They're not the reason. They're . . . a good example."

"Of . . ."

"Of how a woman like me ends up in an affair with a man like you, well, what started as an affair, anyway. This isn't an affair anymore. But it's why we ended up together, way back at the beginning of the road or whatever."

"Bears?" Intrigued, I use Kate's double-finger twirl, encouraging her to continue.

She dives in without preface or context. "When I'm sixteen, they tell me I've got to be myself but to work at being smart, athletic, creative, an independent hard charger but also periodically to turn on sexy, demure, or playfully appealing for some moronic ritual, prom for pity's sake. *Wear makeup and low-cut tops. That's how you get boys.*

When I'm twenty, they tell me I've gotta be myself but only as long as myself consists of smart, athletic, creative, a hard charger, whatever, but sexy and appealing – can't forget sexy and appealing, because I've gotta get a man and convince him to get down on one knee before I'm thirty.

Eighteen to thirty. Can you believe it? Until we retire – and who really retires around here anymore? – but eighteen to thirty is the only real time we get, especially women. Those years, more and more, have become the tragic stretch that defines us. Twelve fucking years – the very time that Gauguin spent painting in Tahiti."

"You're right," I say, not wanting to interrupt but surprised at how accurate she is. "I've never thought of that before. From high school graduation to the neo-natal ward. Whaddya know?"

"See?"

"Yeah, but what does this have to do with bears?"

"Be patient," she goes on. "At twenty-five, they tell me I've gotta be myself and smart, athletic, blah, blah, blah. *Fix your makeup, Katie. Tug on that thong!* But now I'm supposed to get all aflutter and willywaggy when he does get down on one knee, even though he – at 5'10" and 170 pounds is gonna lasagna, French fry, and IPA himself to about 235 by the time he's thirty-three, overworked, stressed, exhausted, wildly horny for some twenty-four-year-old waitress he meets after a beer softball game with his friends and now able to bring me – the doting wife and mother of his two-point-five above-average children – immense sexual pleasure for about ninety-four seconds twice a week.

And at twenty-nine, they tell me that I've gotta be smart, athletic, sexy, creative, bullshit, bullshit, bullshit, but now I've also gotta balance being preggo on multiple occasions with being dazzling at whatever career I'm pursuing between ninety-four seconds of sexual pleasure, dirty diapers, spit up, spin classes to get a rope around my burgeoning ass (while Hubby's tubby belly swells) house cleaning, Harry Potter movies, appeasing my pushy mother, Hubby's psychopathic mother, and . . . wait for it, folks . . . the Neighborhood Bitch Squad, fucking cunts, the lot of them."

Amused, I ask, "Are all suburban, professional women this articulate when shitfaced?"

"Hell, no, Doctor. I'm much more articulate. Read the research. Self-absorbed, suburban women are the most potentially dangerous group of wrongly-empowered misfits since the NAZIs. They actually rule the world. Think about it."

"Leopard print out there on the deck? Naomi?"

"Na – frigging – omi, who, because she's high on Adderall, Percocet, Gray Goose vodka, and Chardonnay from Thursday to Sunday, insists from time to time that Hubby – *my* Hubby not her Hubby – slide his half erect penis into her mouth, again for about three minutes, when she's feeling lonely and unappreciated. And lather, rinse, repeat, lather, rinse, repeat, lather, rinse, repeat until you wake up one morning and you've turned forty-three with two teenagers living in your house, eating your food, and watching your TV while you fold their laundry."

"So what happens at forty-three?" I ask, a bit winded. "Why now?"

"Because, love, by now you've come to realize that all of it, the 80s, 90s, college, feminism, grad school, marriage, professional aspirations, marriage, parenting, home ownership, marriage (in case you missed it), 401ks, and dental plans . . . it was all a bright and perfect lie – well, no, not exactly a lie – rather, a fantasy. J. R. R. Tolkien couldn't have crafted it better."

"No one can do it," I say uselessly.

"No one can do it. And you know what's most heartbreaking? It's that the things we learned as kids, the stuff I did as a strong, smart, independent young woman, those things don't work anymore. The rock is just too big and the motherfusticking hill is just too goddamned steep."

"Like what? What doesn't work?" I pour her the very last of our wine.

"Do you remember the bears, that day by the river?"

"You asked me that already."

"I'm drunk, shithead. Gimme some slack." Kate's eyes flash in the candlelight. "The old canal path by the river . . . I remember that mother bear. She was willing to rip our heads off to protect her kids but just really wanted to get home and turn on Disney Plus or maybe take a nap and then empty the dishwasher."

"Of course, I remember her," I blush at the vivid memory of my terror.

"We'd been talking about contentment."

"Right, and most people's tendency to try and purchase happiness one credit card swipe at a time."

"Ex – fucking – actly! You see, those of us who grew up doing it right, working hard at contentment rather than just loading Disneyfied happiness onto our Mastercard, we're the ones who are utterly screwed at thirty-nine, forty, forty-three, when we finally realize that everything we did for thirty years to actualize contentment, none of it remains effective."

"The hill and the rock?"

"Bubbelah, look at my life."

"Yeah," I laugh. "Okay, so . . ."

And Kate responds simply, soberly; all hyperbole and mania evaporate. "I end up in a love affair with you. And because you're you and not Indiana James Bond Solo over there – who is a mistake; he's just marking time until he becomes another middle-aged wife or mother's mistake – but because you're you, I end up in a love affair. Then I end up in love, and then I end up here: entirely imprisoned in my favorite . . ." she gestures to the Lafayette Mill's post-and-beam skeleton, "albeit colorless, prison, where I don't really care to escape from, because you're here. But if you weren't here, I'd surely shoot myself. I'd cut off my ear and mail it to you or move to French Polynesia and have five children."

I nod stupidly, with nothing of any merit to offer. "Real contentment gets too expensive."

She finishes the wine. "And real cynicism is on sale, 75% off! The stuff from eighteen to thirty doesn't make a dent these days. My young woman's salad bar of contentment strategies, none of them can even nudge that rock."

"What are they?" I ask, hoping to move the conversation someplace safe. "In any order, your top ten."

Kate sits back, grins. I would follow her, head first, into a live volcano. "In no particular order?"

"Your top ten."

"My top ten young woman's contentment strategies, alternatives to purchasing happiness at Sephora for $275."

"Yes, please," I say. "But you can't go with *hanging out with my kids*. We know that one."

She hesitates again, takes it seriously. "Okay, in no particular order . . ."

"Take your time."

Kate corrals the last empty wine bottle, roots in her handbag for lipstick, and writes *IRRETRIEVABLY* in clumsy letters. This one, however, she hugs close like a recovered artifact, staining my favorite cocktail dress with the letters *VAB* above her left breast. "Alright," she begins, "One: Running a 5k. I used to do this as a kid. If I run for stress now, it's a half marathon or a marathon, too much. No one has that kind of time or those knees anymore. So I'm gonna go with running to start. No, not just running – exercise.

Two: Gustav Mahler, Symphony number 6, the *Andante Moderato*, third movement. Trust me. You'll never hear a better piece of music, and while I still listen to it and love it, that fifteen minutes of magic doesn't entrance or move me like it did twenty years ago."

"Mahler? I didn't see that one coming."

"Check it out later, love. Trust me."

"Okay! Go on, please."

"Three: Now don't laugh at me, but I'm going with the Harry Potter books. I love them, escape into them. Well, I used to, and it breaks my heart that her storytelling and those characters can't transport me any longer. But when I turn sixty and give up, I'm going to rediscover them, relive it all."

"Alright," I shrug. "I wasn't expecting that one, either, but that might be the saddest thing I've heard all semester."

"And you claim to have been paying attention." She tsks me playfully, points a drunk finger at my chest, asks, "Where was I?"

"Um . . . four."

"Four: Cooking. *Bobó de camarão*, German chicken with Fontina cheese and sundried tomatoes, grilled salmon with goat cheese, it used to bring me such joy to cook. I'd spend all day in the kitchen, preparing ingredients and listening to Debussy. But now, I dump healthy food into my crock pot at 5 a.m. and scoop it sloppy onto plates at 5 p.m. while sucking Chardonnay through a Mickey Mouse straw.

Um . . . what's next? Five. Yeah, I guess. Five: Being with Henry. I used to love spending the day with him. All I coveted, every day, was time alone with him, in his arms. Jesus, he's so strong. But now it's an effort, being together. It's sad, not tragic or heartbreaking, but sad, because when we sit awkwardly at some expensive bistro for some occasion no one really wants to celebrate, the ghosts of both of us at twenty-six waft around the table, whispering, *Really? You two are a big, frigging disappointment. We had grand dreams, and now all you have to discuss is the mushroom gravy and the London broil?* We literally strain for every word we say." Kate exhales slowly. "Sorry, that one gets me when I admit it out loud."

"We can stop," I say. "You don't need to –"

"No, this is good. It's . . . good. Six: Parties with my friends. These are now just recycled conversations about twenty-year-old Europe trips, processed cheddar cheese, weight loss, and complaints about our kids' Algebra teachers. I come home from parties with my friends these days and feel like I have to peel off sticky layers of tedious bullshit we all endure every time we get together. Getting hammered is the only antidote, and if I'm going to get hammered anywhere, I'd just as soon it be with you, not them." She presses on. "We're cooking with gas now. Alright! Seven: Christmas. I spent thirty-five years excited about Christmas. From the moment we put away the last Thanksgiving dish to the morning Dad and I would take the tree out to the landfill and watch it roll sort-of forlornly down the embankment, I was all about giving, cooking, wrapping, baking, decorating, caroling, sharing, and all of it under the most brash array of colorful blinking lights and vacuum-clogging tinsel you can imagine."

"And now?"

"Well, you know . . . I still love getting things for my kids, but the rest of it – except for the lights; I do love the lights – the rest has gotten pretty shallow; you know? Coated with one too many layers of cheap plastic."

"Yeah," I agree. "If I see one more Hallmark movie with the same vapid plot line, I might jump out of a flying sleigh myself. So what's next? Only a few more to go."

She checks her watch, frowns at it. "That was seven. Eight: My sister. But we don't have time for that conversation today. So let's just press on to number nine."

"Alright."

"Nine: Watching sports. I would follow players and teams religiously, especially premiere league soccer and NBA basketball. But now, they all seem like hyperbolic cartoon characters, entirely transfixed by their own press releases, their plan to win single-handedly, and their ridiculous bank accounts. No thanks. It actually makes me a little sad and a little sick to watch these days. All the hype and none of the excitement." She looks like she might editorialize on this longer, but I've gotten the point. So she moves on. "Ten, another quick one:

Going to the movies. Do you remember going to the movies when we were young? I would get so excited. I'd sometimes go on a Friday night with my roommates. We'd sneak in peach schnapps. Or I'd go on a rainy Sunday and see three films in a row. It was magical. I just let the directors and actors have me, and my soul would be transported. I'd gladly go on whatever journey they were leading."

Kate closes her eyes, reliving some sincere love scene or redemptive character transformation. "But now, it's a hundred dollars, twenty-two dollars for popcorn. Popcorn! It's the largest cash crop in the frigging hemisphere. We ship millions of tons of it to nations all over the goddamned world. Whenever we place an embargo on a hostile leader, we end up letting thousands of acres of it rot, because it isn't worth the cost to harvest. And they're gonna charge me twenty-two dollars? Are you kidding me? Then I get in there and I'm either sitting directly in front of two soccer moms from my neighborhood who won't shut the hell up through the entire film. They're such self-absorbed pussies, they forget what it means to be polite for five frigging minutes. Or I get to sit in front of the entire high school lacrosse team who burp, fart, jerk off, throw shit at one another, or get up and move around for two straight hours. No thanks. Nope. Used to be magic; now it's just another opportunity for irritating people to get under my skin."

"Jesus," I say. "That's quite a list, my dear. I didn't know that you –"

"Eleven."

"Eleven?"

"I'm an overachiever. Fire me."

Again, I twirl two fingers.

"Eleven: Going home to see my parents."

"Oh, yeah," I agree. "Hadn't thought of that one."

Kate's words limp over to me. She's emotional about this

one. "Things shifted. I don't remember feeling it happen. But the comfort of tradition, the predictable, reliable, steady nature of everything about that house . . . it's only there as a shadowy reflection of what it was twenty years ago. And I can't figure out why, except that I'm getting older and doing more and more of my shopping at those 75% off sales for middle-aged cynicism."

"That's probably it."

She closes her eyes again, and another flood of nostalgia irons the wrinkles from her face. "I'd fall onto the carpet, stay there for three days. Dad would bring me light beer in cans while we watched Ohio State trounce Penn State or old movies, *North by Northwest* or his favorites, Abbott and Costello. It was a place I knew I could return to whenever I needed renewal, a battery charge, a kick in the ass, whatever. And now I'm just another adult in their kitchen, drinking wine from grown up glasses and eating too much cheese. Just once, I want my father to make me a double Manhattan in a Flintstones jelly jar, while Mom's simmering meat sauce fills the house with the most warm and comforting aroma I've ever known."

I decide to end it. We're headed rapidly for a bad end to an otherwise lovely afternoon. "And all of this leads to me?"

She shakes her head. "To us. Here. The *here* part is important, well beyond anything anyone would justly refer to as an affair."

"That's just how this started."

"Yeah, a big rock and a steep motherscratching hill, too steep for parents, parties, friends, 5ks, or even Gustav Mahler."

"So you find me."

"I do, yes."

"Others don't."

"Others find *him*," she tilts her head toward the bar and Indiana Solo. "But he can't get them here. No way."

"Imprisoned."

"Exactly," she says. "Perfectly, contentedly imprisoned. How often does life paint you into a corner where your best, most delicious option is to fall in love with a man who will willingly give you his heart and willingly take yours? And I mean hold on to it forever. Imagine that. We're trapped here, you with my heart in your hands, and me with yours. I'm not putting it down, giving it back, ignoring it, dropping it, or whatever metaphor captures this best."

"No," I say. "Neither am I."

As drunk as Kate has managed to get, I believe her. Her vision sharpens and, clearly pissed, she takes a final swat at post-modern bullshit values, not unlike a mama bear warding off suburbanite hikers. "We, as a culture, not just you and me, but we've gotta stop blaming and ostracizing middle-aged women for falling in love with men like you. It isn't the last unfair, dishonest, double cross women get served cold on a tastefully conservative platter from Bed, Bath, and Beyond, but it's certainly one of the deliberately shitty ones. And what's our option? Live with regret? Welcome misery when it shows up unannounced on Sunday afternoons while my husband and I have nothing to talk about?"

"Well," I don't know what to say. "That certainly answers my question, love."

She winks, and I hope she understands that it's about time for us to go. We've ridden this horse about as far as she'll carry us.

Charcoal twilight creeps across the aged plank floor. It wanders out the west-facing window, headed home.

Kate says, "Gauguin died at fifty-four. Can you believe it? He chased passion halfway round the globe, then only got to dunk in it for eleven years."

"Doesn't seem fair, especially when you consider the role he played introducing the world to a new century."

"Fifty-four," she repeats. "What am I gonna do by fifty-four? It's coming up fast."

I fill the space between us with nothing comforting. "Tenure, teaching, writing your articles. You'll finish your book."

"Yeah, I suppose," she looks away, catches the last of the light. "I read somewhere that not one of his paintings remains in French Polynesia. They've all been gobbled up by museums and collectors here and in Europe."

I chuckle. "That'd be you, love. You'd fly twenty hours to Tahiti to see the Gauguin collection only to find all of them moved to the Louvre."

"Yeah," she says, and I get my last genuine smile of the day. I'll keep that one as a drift off tonight before bed. "Talk about wet underwear and broken seatbelts."

"So what's going to happen?" She meticulously folds and refolds the soiled napkin, then drapes it over her clutter of bare rib bones like a funeral shroud.

"What do you mean?" I pass $400 in cash to Pretty Gray who, in the failing light, looks even more like a hovering schoolmarm. We never use credit cards.

"I mean: What's going to happen? What bad is going to happen? What's coming for us? When . . . I dunno . . . when will we be ruined by all of this?"

Not one inebriate bone in my body wants to answer. But I realize, knowing her, that we'll sit here until the next ice age if she doesn't get a reply, my best guess at least. She's as smart as I am, as worldly as I am, as educated and experienced as I am, and every bit as capable at just about everything we've ever tried together. Yet, she won't be able to get herself upright if she doesn't hear me take a stab at a rhetorical question for which we both know there is no productive response. "So?"

"What's gonna happen to us?"

"Yeah." She slides two empty wine bottles to the edge of our table. If I wait much longer, she'll begin sacrificing them, first SELFISHLY then FIERCELY. Kate still holds IRRE-TRIEVABLY tightly against her chest. "I wanna know."

Empty wine bottles, I should've known. "Nothing, love," I finally lie. "Nothing bad is going to happen to us."

She seems comforted, and the spell breaks. "Sure, yeah. Well, that's good. Right?" She wipes both eyes, first right then left with uncertain fingers. "Henry texted earlier. The kids want me to pick up sushi, and I gotta drop my car off at the garage. I hit a nail, need a tire plugged. I'll . . . I guess I'll have him pick me up there."

"Yeah," I wipe my hands on the tablecloth, finish my water. "I'll head home, too."

"Text me later?" Kate pulls her sweater closed, gathers up my umbrella. We've made misery manifest; she might as well carry an umbrella.

I say, "Sure, of course. I'll check in with Grace and –"

She cuts me off. "I want you to say, *Let's run away right now.*"

"I want to . . . I want to ask you every day. I never miss a day."

"Good then. Right?"

"Yeah," I nod. "Good." And I follow Kate into the burnt amber vestiges of twilight as the Lafayette Mill & Wine Bar's millstones grind away another evening in the basement.

MEXICO BEACH

BY D. E. LEE

1994

The second time I saw Jonah Rae was twenty years later. He was sitting alone riffing on an unplugged Gibson Les Paul on the low platform stage of the Breakwater in Mexico Beach, Florida. A hazy shroud of pale white light backlit his presence. His gaze was fixed on a spot on the wooden floor, but this appeared to be a hollow, secondary source of attention. So intent was his focus on the sound from the guitar that had the building collapsed around us, he would have been the last to notice. He certainly did not see me.

I'd passed in front of him and sat at a table out of the sunlight and the scurrying path of the servers setting up for the day and attempted to reconcile what I was seeing with what could not possibly be. In the twenty years since I'd last seen him, he was unchanged in appearance, manner, and style. At first, I doubted it. But, his intricate fretwork, like a fingerprint, convinced me otherwise. The only thing missing was the glass bottle on his left pinky, his trademark slide. Even without it, his playing, faint as it was, enthralled me.

It also set loose memories from when I was in high school, clear images of scattered four-by-fours on white sandy beaches, the warm salty air of the Gulf of Mexico sticky against the skin, and the cool taste of canned beer on the tongue. In those innocent days, we met up in locales known as White Point, Turkey Neck, or The Circle, places spoken of and agreed upon during the week, though no one knew exactly how. By Friday night after the Saudad High football game there'd be a slow, inevitable congregation of cheerleaders and jocks, skaters and heads, geeks and freaks. Someone would throw open the doors of a pickup, punch a tape deck, and the sound of Southern rock would sear the night. Abiding in our bayou town menagerie, we'd move about in our respective tribes, the classification being easy and never quite real. The barriers were fluid, or, in retrospect, they had been fluid, but as we'd grown up were now solidifying into what we would become: classes of people who would rarely interact with each other after graduation.

Jonah Rae was big in the Panhandle in those days, as I recall, and toured the roadhouse circuit with the band Shoestring Slater; they released a demo we all treasured, now lost to history. The sound was rough denim Southern rock laced with the creamy cool silk of Rae's blues sound. A single song might last half the night once he'd slipped into a mesmerizing groove, the way he did twenty years ago at the Breakwater on Mexico Beach, the night he disappeared.

About an hour later, a man sat next to me. He introduced himself as Sawyer Burnett, the owner of the club. I was on assignment, I told him, for *Pickin & Grits,* writing a piece on the resurgence of Southern rock and had just come from Tallahassee, taking the backroads to Panama City, my next destination. I'd been here before, I said, so for old times' sake pulled in and what do you think the odds are that on my first visit I had seen Jonah Rae's last performance and here today he's back on the stage?

That ain't Jonah Rae, Sawyer Burnett said. You saw the sign outside, didn't you? That's Boggy Boy Blaster out of Valparaiso.

Burnett was a young man, too young to have known the Breakwater in the mid-70s. He told me his father was the owner back then, but his father had passed on.

Had he heard of Jonah Rae?

Everybody around here's heard of Jonah Rae, he said. They don't talk about it as much as they used to but get someone on it and half your night's gone. It was so long it's now been reduced to one or another theory. They's one bunch'll tell you he hung himself during the break and they's another says he was killed off by the cartel. Shoestring, you mighta know'd, got involved in some sort of distribution scheme that went bad is the way I hear tell.

I never heard he was killed, one way or the other, I said. You sure we're talking about the same person?

Burnett sat silently a moment. We watched Jonah Rae packing up his guitar on the stage.

Either way, Burnett said, we ain't talking about that fella. That there's Cody Yarbles. A kinda quiet boy, since you look like you wanna go ask him.

I intended to. But for the moment I was considering the accuracy of my memory. Was I so sure that I was willing to disregard evidence, such as the fact that the man putting away his guitar had not aged, if he were, in fact, Jonah Rae? I needed another witness, somebody willing to confirm that what I was seeing was no lie.

You might try the diner, Burnett said. Old timers hang out there quite a bit. Or, I tell you what, I'll see if my mother'll talk to you. She was around back then but she's been keeping to herself a long time now, so don't get up your hopes.

Boggy Boy Blaster was playing three nights, and I had to get over to Panama City for another show. I'll come back tomorrow, I told Burnett.

Jonah? I went toward him. Jonah Rae?

He was heading for the door and looked at me without reaction.

Ever hear of Jonah Rae, I asked.

Anybody knows the music knows him, he said.

He went out the door without another word.

Our memories seem to behave very much like the waters of the Gulf of Mexico, particularly those along the Florida Panhandle. Its emerald transparency stretches for miles off-shore but one additional step may send you down an unexpected drop; or an unseen riptide may tug you under, and your survival, swimming parallel to the shore, thwarts the common sense that's telling you to get back in as soon as possible. I'd never met Jonah Rae and had hardly thought of him during the intervening twenty years, yet I recalled the intoxicating peal of his slide, a bit of hair in the tone, like detail work on the gritty rhythms of Slater's music. And with crisp clarity, I also recalled the one time I had seen him on the stage in Mexico Beach and now found myself in the unworkable but nonetheless rapt study of the possibility that Cody Yarbles and Jonah Rae were one and the same person.

Today, a light breeze flowed from the south. I was standing barefoot in the wash of the Gulf. Before I'd left yesterday, I'd set myself up in a motel. That was a rather impulsive move. I traveled to Panama City, saw the band I was covering, and did some quick interviews. My itinerary called for a stay over to cover another band the next night and then to head to Mobile, but instead I returned to Mexico Beach, arriving around 4 a.m.

Now, to story this change of plan to Tom T. Hetrick, my editor.

A few months ago, Hetrick, a man who envisioned, with utter dread, deadlines as passing trains, told me he'd read my work in *Thirst*, an Atlanta-based underground mag back in the day and thought it was solid. He was running *Pickin & Grits*, a largely Southern journal of guitars and Southern rock bands and wanted me to canvas a several-state region in a rental and write a series of stories about the resurgence of Southern rock. I'd been doing stories on what would later be called the Seattle Sound since the mid-1980s and hadn't been aware of a resurgence. You're going to create it, he told me.

The Southern sound had been a spur for personal nostalgia, and the thought of messing it up with musical analysis or purple prose made me hesitate for fear of shattering that part of my past from which I regularly harvested good feeling in times of despair. But in the end, a weekly stipend of $475 and a chance to hear some cool-ass Southern rock and blues brought me in.

Hetrick had mapped it out: Nashville, Knoxville, Charleston, Macon, Jacksonville, Muscle Shoals, Gillsburg, Black Oak, and points around and between. At times, I stood on sidewalks staring at vacant, dilapidated buildings. Or empty lots. Once down a lonesome country road to see a swamp. But Hetrick had the notion that my sense of place would be heightened by these excursions to the landmarks of the South, so I went dutifully to absorb it all. Other times, whether in dives or halls, I caught up with the putative resurgence: Gov't Mule, Sons of Gator, O.R.G. Widespread Panic, Old '97s, Virgil Kane, The Other Band, or Arc Angels. Fascinating, all of it, but I'd touched upon something compelling here in Mexico Beach that I could not easily get away from.

Stepping out of the wash, I drew up the remnants of my memories of this seaside town, pierced through its heart by Highway 98, a coastal road originally built in the 1930s to connect Pensacola and Apalachicola, to find a convincing reason to linger. What I knew was scant and useless: Hurricane Kate, a category 2 storm, struck Mexico Beach on November 21, 1985. Its westerly path was diverted by a cold front out of the Mississippi Valley, and she chugged northeast, damaging oyster beds as she passed over Crooked Island before churning onward through several southern states and weakened over the Atlantic Ocean. Even less usable was the German U-boat activity in the Gulf waters during World War II. A history teacher who'd spent his summers assisting with archaeological surveys imported his experience into our classroom, fodder for imaginative thirteen-year-olds to bring that war to life and to our backyards.

The moment I had Hetrick on the phone, however, I hesitated, feeling at once a duty to preserve Jonah Rae's anonymity. In spite of Burnett's twin theories that Rae had hung himself or had been killed by a drug cartel, such events would have made the news, and so I dismissed them as causes for his disappearance. That meant he'd vanished of his own accord and had not asked to be sought out, whatever his reasons, and did I have the right to expose him?

Hetrick was grousing at someone offline. When I told him I was in Mexico Beach, he assumed that I'd gone south of the border, and when he learned I'd taken a side trip, he emphatically told me to get my ass over to Panama City and on to Mobile, as scheduled. He'd never heard of Jonah Rae, for one, and two, he was paying me.

Let me tell you a little about Jonah Rae, I said, and why it's important.

Hetrick was fuming at the other end; his therapist, I'd learned, had prescribed a series of breathing exercises to help him manage his temper. While he went through the motions, I pressed on, inventing parts I didn't know.

I started by putting Shoestring Slater on the map, the deep south, the Panhandle, on the same latitude as Dickey Betts, Duane Allman, and Ronnie Van Zant. Unknown, but rising, I said, and all of them, whether the mainstream understood it or not, were, in their music, doing something politically and culturally progressive. The Civil Rights era had irreversibly altered the South, I said, the very definition of what it meant to be a Southerner. Consider the significance of the studio sessions in 1968 in Muscle Shoals during which Skydog, a white man, and Wilson Pickett, a black man, lay down tracks for "Hey Jude," a British tune. In that moment, I said, as much as in any other, the roots of progress were extended into the cultural forms of the current Southern sound's resurgence. This is the angle, I said, the socially segregationist past homogenizing itself into the musically miscegenetic present, and it should be plain as daylight that Jonah Rae's contribution must not be overlooked or forgotten.

Hetrick was quiet on the other end. He'd set the phone down and was marking copy, or I'd piqued his interest, and he was working it out.

Rae, I said, was one of the best, up there with Allman, Hlubek, Trucks, and Caldwell. I saw him play, man. Then one night, in 1974, between sets, right here in Mexico Beach, he vanishes. The band continues without him, but it's a lousy show without his guitar. Shoestring Slater breaks up shortly afterward. Rae had an influence, I said. He fits in here. Let me find out how.

On the other end, I heard pages being shuffled.

You got one day, he said, and don't miss the Panama City gig.

I need three days.

You got two.

Sawyer Burnett offered me a beer. It was nine a.m. The sunlight was pale, coming at a slant from the left side of the wide waterfront window of the Breakwater club. East to west, there was no rising or setting sun on the Gulf of Mexico for the inhabitants of the Panhandle. They observed its passing the way one views the panoramic march of memories before one's eyes.

A woman who was cutting oranges at the counter brought round coffee in a white ceramic cup. I drink it black, I told her, and she left with a handful of unused creamers and packets of sugar.

Meanwhile, Sawyer Burnett was watching the news on a corner television. A drunken police officer had shot seven people dead in Falun, Sweden. Burnett was providing his own sorry-state-of-the-world commentary and while he spoke, needing nothing from me, I realized he was the sort of man meant to run a club because his prolixity could make most anyone feel welcome. For my purposes, this thin, nearly nonexistent barrier between the private and public broadcasts of his mind made it easy to turn his attention to my gaining an interview with his mother, someone he'd said would have known Jonah Rae.

Ever since my father, her husband, passed away, Burnett said, she's not been the same, and that's going on seven years now. She hangs on, so you can't say she's lost her will to live, but I don't know what keeps her going. She used to own a shop down the road a piece. She carved driftwood, made pelicans and lighthouses and such. She was good, too. But then one thing can mess you up. That's all it takes. For her, it was the death of my father. She was drained the moment it happened. Heart attack on the beach. Someone saw him out there, a tourist, and thought he was sunning himself, the way he was spread out in the sand.

Burnett drained his mug and looked a little as if he didn't know how he'd arrived from his assessment of the tragedies of the world to a discussion of his father's death.

I'd like to speak with her, I said, after a moment.

You see, this here's the thing, he said. She used to be this free spirit, you know. A bit odd in ways I never understood, but she's my mother, so it was not really for me to understand, if you get my meaning. Hated shoes. Hated clothes, in fact. We'd go off to secluded stretches of beach, and she was beautiful to look at. Her skin as dark as a pecan shell. But her eyes were such a contrast you'd think they was an angel inside her. They were blue, set like fine-cut gems inside those dark round sockets. You've seen people happy, haven't you? She was like that before he died.

He was clinging to the mug, and I was worried he'd be drunk before noon.

Listen, I said. She knew about Jonah Rae, didn't she?

You see, this here's the thing, he said. I told her who you were and what you wanted. She looked at me a long time after that and I thought something disturbed her, but I also saw a glimmer in her eyes, like a darting firefly off in the woods at night.

When you said I wanted to ask about Jonah Rae?

It crossed my mind, too, he said, but not until later. It all happened so fast that I couldn't quite remember. It was a simple question, but you got the sense, or I did, standing there, that several years of a lost life got broke free in her mind. That's what I saw, that jolt of recognition. And then she was boarding it all up faster than a glass factory slaps 'em up before a hurricane.

She didn't ask about it?

Not directly. You'd know if a person was even a little bit curious. No, I'd say the way she moved off it was more of a fright, or how she'd be if she got a cramp, she didn't want you to know about.

Did you ask? Clearly, you touched something in her.

It's like I told you, he said. Things are different with her now. That beach girl of old done long and gone, and she's downright Biblical in her plain attire, nearly sackcloth and ashes, and all she cares about is her knots.

He picked up his mug as if considering a third beer but decided against it.

About a year after my father died, he said, my mother started tying knots. I used to kid her a little, like all those years of going barefoot made her forget how. But she got herself a purpose, one she's not sharing. Now, I'd say she's put up any number of simple displays like shoelace knots, granny knots, and overhand knots. She sets them all up in picture frames or decoratively round some box or perfumed bag or something. I even seen her string them along like they were bells hanging on the wall.

Is this a hobby, I asked.

Obsession's what I call it, he said. She been at it for years now. Got collections of barrel hitches, basket weaves, Garda hitches, trident loops, and something called a Turk's head knot, which, she will tell you is very similar to the monkey fist knot. I don't know the half of them and there might be hundreds.

People cope in different ways, I offered.

He seemed to think about this a while and said, There's a fella that lives around here named Mollie and he's been digging a hole ever since he got shot in the eye. I ain't gonna compare him with her but I get your meaning.

I always liked your mother, the woman from the counter said. She wiped her hands on a cloth and came around. Sorry to intrude, she said, but we're low on triple sec and I'm out to get some.

After the woman left, we sat silently and watched an announcement on television about the Boeing 777's inaugural flight from Everett, Washington.

Slow news day, Burnett said.

He spoke with a kind of somnolent tone that often disguises something tumultuous below.

Drawing him back, I reminded him of my interest in speaking with his mother, adding that, given what he'd told me, I'd be considerate of her feelings.

He siphoned himself into a sigh, looking a little like a child being shamed into admitting some truth he'd just as soon stay hidden.

I thought I just explained it to you, he said.

I looked at him, hoping he'd read bewilderment on my face and go on. But he returned the look with a density that was both stubborn and petty.

You see, this here's the thing, he said. She don't want to talk to you. Or see you, for that matter.

The dispatcher at the police station offered coffee in a container with a lid. I accepted and sat on one of five identical black plastic chairs that were fixed by bolts to the floor.

Five minutes passed before the dispatcher looked over the counter and said, with embarrassment, I'm sorry, I shoulda told you, but I forgot. Chief ain't coming in today. She out of town. Maybe Officer Pipes can help.

Officer Pipes admired himself in his uniform. His hand fell upon the shine of his buttons and leather and asked what I needed and found time to fondle his brass while I told him.

You're looking for the old Chief, he said. That's who you want to talk to. His name's Strickland Yates and you'll find him in the Bayshore Nursing Home over in Saudad. He ain't likely to tell you much, though. His mind been gone these many years with that di-mentia. They say he's clear sometimes, so you might get lucky.

What about police reports from that time?

Nineteen seventy-four? Whew, that's a ways back.

He turned to the dispatcher. Hey, Mags, where they keep those old case files these days?

He need to go talk to Miss Palmer is what he need to do.

That you do, Officer Pipes said. Go see Nellie Palmer. She was the dispatcher the night Jonah Rae went missing. Now, that's a story for you.

I believe her, Mags said.

You and nobody else, Officer Pipes said.

What happened?

Oh, it's crazy what that ol' woman says.

It ain't crazy, Harold, Mags said. You just get all spooked too easy.

You got that right, Mags.

It dawned on me that I was fueling a workplace romance between these two, so I moved away from Mags toward the door and, as I'd hoped, Officer Pipes followed me; he wanted to tell this story.

Now, you understand this is what my daddy told me, he said, and he wouldn't make up something like this. Miss Palmer was at the station alone but that wasn't unusual or anything since nothing ever happens around here anyway. But she gets this one call, she says, the night that ol' boy disappeared, and it's a woman's voice saying something's got him, and the line goes dead.

Who was it?

No one knows.

What got him?

Don't laugh. Miss Palmer's sincere. The woman told her it was some sort of ghost or something.

You believe it?

What do you think?

Officer Pipes looked at me with a half-grin and seemed to notice something awry on his polished silver badge and dusted it with a piece of flannel.

Miss Palmer lost most of her hearing, just so you know, Officer Pipes called, as I went down the steps of the station to the wide white sidewalk.

Nellie Palmer lived down a narrow broken-shell lane that gave my black shoes a white dusting. Her house was peach and cream in the crackerbox style with a screen door facing south. Peering through it, I saw it had high ceilings, spinning fans, and a dog trot to keep it cool. She did not respond to my knocking. Mags had told me she was often behind the house in her garden.

As I went around back, I considered the significance of the dog trot. Some believe this breezeway allows ghosts to pass through a house without taking notice of its inhabitants. Officer Pipes had said the woman on the phone had spoken to Nellie Palmer of a ghost, so might it not be possible that Nellie Palmer's imagination had gotten the best of her?

I saw her long before she saw me. She was sitting on a garden stool shaded by lush pole beans. Wire cages containing tomatoes were on one side and the floppy leaves of yellow squash were on the other. She did not respond to her name being called, so I went right up to her.

Nobody's asked about that in a long time, she said, loudly, from under her straw hat. I was sort of hoping it'd all been forgotten by now.

She dropped a handful of dollarweed in a plastic bucket at her bare feet, which rested brown as a couple of pan-seared steaks on a pair of pink flip-flops.

I was all alone when the call come, she said, and they was something in that voice that shook me bad. They all thought I was crazy, so I stopped talking about it. And here you come dragging it back into the light. What for?

I told her, all but yelling so she could hear, that Jonah Rae was a part of something larger, and he had vanished, and I thought it was important to find out why.

He was born here, that rascal, and a lot of us called him Johnny. What happened that night, I'm not sure I believe anymore, what with everybody saying I'd lost it and my hearing getting worse all the time, maybe it's like they say. We got so many calls that night about him going missing that maybe that one voice was just something I made up.

Was it?

Like I said, it was a long time ago.

I'd still like to hear about it.

She scooted her stool deeper into the shade of the bean pole. I squatted next to her, lifting my clothing, wet with perspiration, away from my skin. We swatted dizzy insects from our faces.

Especially back then, she said, it was always quiet of an evening. If anything, you could hear the music from the Breakwater as far off as the edge of town. The Brasher boys might get rowdy down at Jay's Bottleneck but that was to be expected. No, there never was much happening here. On that particular night, a southerly breeze come off the Gulf slow and broiling like a wind over a campfire. All the same, they was something oddly calm about the night, sort of like the murmured way things get in the days before a hurricane strikes. Then this call comes in. It's a woman's voice, hushed and slow, like she's disguising it, and she says that he told her that she come from the sea.

She came from the sea?

Not her. She meant somebody else.

She said another woman came from the sea.

That's what he told her.

Who told her that?

She didn't say. After that, my phone blew up with calls reporting Johnny had gone missing. A couple of hours later, when I got to thinking about it, I realized the woman had been talking about Johnny. He was the one who told her that she come from the sea, whatever that meant.

That could have been a coincidence.

That's what Strickland said when I told him what I'd figured out.

Chief Yates?

Yeah. I thought it was important. But Strickland said, Johnny's an adult and if he wants to go off a-wandering like that, well, that's up to him. Ain't nobody suspecting foul play, he said, so it ain't none of our business.

When Strickland made up his mind, she said, that was the end of it.

But you didn't drop it?

How could I? I know'd Johnny since he was born and that call was strange coming like it did after he'd walked off the stage, which also struck me as very peculiar, given how much that boy loved to play music. No, it didn't sit well with me. So, I mentioned it to the sergeant and a few of the officers. That's when they started saying I was batty. As the years pass, I'm convinced Strickland musta said something to them. He could be like that.

What made you certain?

You get a feel for things. I was the ear of the office and come to know the voices of the town. Just hearing the tone, I could tell in an instant if the call was about kids stealing from the store, one of the Brashers taking pot shots, a heart attack out on the beach, or a kitten stuck up a tree. That voice come to haunt me over the following weeks and before long it come to me that it was Lucindy Jean Crowe making that call.

The sun overhead had dissolved the shade of the pole beans. When we stood to go to the porch, I saw that she was half my size, petite like a child.

She was Johnny's girlfriend, Nellie Palmer said. The cutest little thing. Don't you find it strange that she never called to report he was missing? Had she done it, maybe Strickland would've investigated. No, they was nothing special about her. It was my mind playing tricks again, if you ask anybody. But it always bothered me. That girl, she was something else. You know she had a twin? It's the funniest thing. Can't nobody tell them apart.

Light as a sheet of tissue paper, her hand draped itself across my forearm. She winked at me, indicating that she anticipated my next question.

I guess they coulda run away together, she said. Young lovers'll give up most anything to be with each other.

She gazed silently over her garden as if momentarily taken up with her own memories of first love.

She tapped my arm and withdrew her hand.

But I don't expect that's what happened. No. I don't.

They were standing in a loose circle at the end of the counter. Three old men in shorts, T-shirts, and flip-flops. Growls and laughter marked their presence.

A woman wearing a three-pocket apron set a glass filled with chipped ice and Coca-Cola on the counter in front of me.

You want some lunch, she asked, though her expression told me it didn't matter one way or the other to her.

A sip was all I needed to shake the heat.

The men studied me a moment.

You're that reporter everybody's been talking about.

Mostly, I'm curious, I told them. Just asking what folks remember.

A man don't just up and disappear, one of them said. That's what everybody'd like you to think. It puts a spin of mystery on something simple and clear.

You don't think he vanished?

Into thin air? No, hell, no. They had this manager. That boy was a tyrant and stupid.

He sure was.

That's the truth.

They was playing their hearts out and this manager—what was that ol' boy's name?

Done forgot.

Can't think of it.

Anyway, them boys was solid. Had 'em a good sound and they shoulda been going places. They was watching Skynyrd and all them others making a good living, and them boys was getting down on themselves going from one roadhouse to the next, going nowhere.

It was that manager.

It sure was.

He didn't do right by them.

No, he didn't.

He had something else going on and was just using them to keep whatever it was going on.

Wait, I said, you're saying the band was a cover for the manager.

That's right. He didn't have no interest in them boys. He was out for himself, doing some dealing—

Distribution—

That's the word. And they figured it out and Johnny, that boy was pure gold.

He sure was.

That's the truth.

He didn't want no part of what was going on, so one night, the night you're talking about, he just ups and walks away from it, plain and simple, just like that.

All that talent, I said, and he just walks away?

That's what he done.

Mm-hm.

Sure as I'm sitting here.

You ain't sittin, Mitch. You're standing.

You know what the hell I mean.

O.K., I said, so, where'd he go, where is he?

We were interrupted by a faint, high-piercing, oscillating whine.

Bobby, Mitch said, fix that earpiece of yours.

He adjusted the skin-colored device behind his ear and turned his head as if testing its precision and this seemed to jar a memory.

All he said ain't quite accurate. He done left out the part about the Colombians.

He sure did.

They was Mexicans.

It don't matter. You left it out. It was a big part of what happened that night.

It sure was.

Long before them Hollywoods was snorting it cocaine was making an inroad down here. The cartel had runners out in the Gulf, and they was dropping it along the beaches here and there. And they had pickups who'd go out and get it.

That's where the manager come in.

He was no good, for sure.

Johnny and the rest of them had to know about it and they mighta got themselves somehow involved in all that.

That they might.

No doubt about it.

And they'd've seen this was slowing them down. Musically, I mean. You fellas remember a couple of weeks before Shoestring Slater come back to town them two strangers showed up.

Their boat run aground.

I figured them for agents.

No, they wasn't. They run aground but what they was doing was searching for bales of cocaine they had to dump when the Coast Guard come after them.

Things was getting hot.

They sure was.

I told them that dispatcher had gotten a call that night. It was someone saying, She come from the sea.

She's talking about that ol' cocaine.

That Miss Palmer, she's a hoot.

Ain't she though?

Tell you what, she's a sweet old lady, that Miss Palmer, but you can't believe a word she says.

No, you can't.

Not a word.

She got a reputation of making shit up. She never could get her a man, and I expect that's what done it, plus she got the hearing problem.

Like you're the one to talk, Bobby.

Oh, hell, I don't need this thing. It's my wife what makes me wear it.

So, cocaine was washing ashore, I said.

That's what I'm getting to. The manager was seen with these two fellas just before dark.

Like they was old buddies.

Friendly as pie.

Now, I'm doing a little speculating here, but what I heard was Johnny was fixin' to narc on 'em and during the break he got capped.

They was after the whole band is what I heard.

He shoulda never walked off that stage.

No, sir, he never shoulda of.

And they was that young fella sitting there talking up Johnny's girlfriend.

They sure was.

And the other girl, too.

She come with him

She sure did.

They was two of 'em with that young fella.

One was the girlfriend.

The other come with the fella.

He wasn't known around here.

No, he wasn't.

He'd be the one to find.

Mm-hm. Find him and you find out everything.

You got that right.

They opened their wallets and left tips on the counter, but Listen, I said, how well did you know Jonah Rae?

The one who was not Mitch or Bobby said, Everybody around here knows him. He had this girlfriend, Lucindy Jean Crowe—

Nellie Palmer told me they were living together.

She got it wrong. It wasn't her. It was her sister that rented him a room was all.

She said, Lucindy Jean Crowe.

They laughed for several minutes then the one who wasn't Mitch or Bobby said, Their father's a real country boy and lives over near Tate's Hell, the state forest. He's a bit off, that ol' boy. When he had them twins, he musta wanted to play a joke on everybody and up and named them both Lucindy Jean.

He sure did.

Can't tell 'em apart.

Not without the social.

Or the fingerprint.

They got the same one, you know.

No, they don't.

Sure, they do.

The chipped ice in my Cola had melted, merged with the caramel coloring, into a pale, weaker version of the drink that'd been poured for me an hour ago, much like the tale these three men had spun.

The vendor handed me a sno-cone through the window of the roadside stand, and almost immediately it began to drip through its paper container. I slurped at it while crouching in the shade of a nearby palm tree that appeared to have been planted merely to remind tourists that this was Florida.

Saudad lay west beyond Panama City. Time permitted the trip over to visit Chief Yates and to catch the gig on my way back tonight. But if he was the sundowning type, it'd be better to see him in the morning when clarity of memory is best. I didn't want to go to Panama City, anyway. I knew enough about the band playing there: They were unknowns, eking out a living and looking for breaks. What I didn't know I could make up to satisfy Hetrick.

I found myself back at Nellie Palmer's. She was on the

porch and invited me to sit a-spell. My good ear's on the right side, she told me. I spoke in a raised volume to that ear, reminding her who I was and what I was doing. Then we sat quietly for a long time. Occasionally, she hummed to herself. The gulf breeze like the day's activity fell into a flat soft rhythm and for a moment I felt lulled, as if I'd been transported backward a hundred years to a time before condos and cars.

She asked if I wanted to stay to supper.

We ate in the kitchen at a table with a green-marbled laminate top with a silver edge. She stepped on a stool to bring things down from cabinets. As we spoke, I noticed that her story had changed from earlier this morning. She added details or omitted them. I never sensed that she was being evasive; she appeared to be experiencing shifts of memory, perhaps evoked by food preparation or the texture of flatware or my presence in her kitchen. Things not available earlier were now calling forth different memories, and I thought of the men in the diner, how their own stories were influenced and perhaps altered by the opportunity my questions offered.

One detail in particular struck me. Earlier Nellie Palmer had said she hadn't seen Lucindy Jean Crowe in ages, but now she let slip that she'd seen her in the past couple of days.

Did she know of her whereabouts?

She runs a little bed-and-breakfast up in Wewahitchka. Why she'd do that is anybody's guess. Wewa is too far north for the tourists who want to go to the beach and it's a too far west for anybody wantin' to see the state capital. Why it's out in the middle of nowhere, it sure is. But you know they say she's a little touched in the head.

I recalled that the men in the diner had said her father was a bit off.

Which was it, Jonah Rae's girlfriend or her sister?

Nellie Palmer didn't rightly know. You couldn't tell them

apart, she said, and they was always playing that for a laugh, but you know what one thinks is a joke another might see it as low-down mean. They was once this fella name of Charlie Brasher, a smart boy but he had a growing problem. He never got any taller than what he was in the third grade and that of course bought him more than his share of teasing. But come along prom time and one of them girls gets all friendly with him and lures him into inviting her, and she heartily accepts. Well, you can see where it's going, can't you? Here come Charlie looking right proper in his daddy's car. He knocks on the door, but it's the other sister, the one that's got no clue what's going on, that opens it up. Well, after the one that been tricked got over being mad, they had themselves a good laugh at poor Charlie's expense, didn't they? But I said it was hurtful then, and I still do.

The sun was clinging red and gold to the jagged tops of pines when we sat again on the porch. A mockingbird made a racket in a nearby juniper.

That sound reminds me a night long ago, she said. I'll never forget it. Strickland and I were lovers once, but if you go and ask him, he'll say it weren't so. He had his wife to think of. Even after she'd been dead ten years, he'd tell me, Let's keep this between ourselves, and so we did. But I expect everybody knew, even his wife.

Why would he want to keep it quiet?

Things was different in those days. Times was changing all around, but down here they wasn't. He mighta been doing it for my sake as much as anything else.

How so?

We all liked the man, but we also knew what he was about. They was a man name of J. Davis Brasher. Everybody called him J. Davis, or sometimes Old Man Brasher because he had five or six younguns running around all the time—

Charlie Brasher?

Yeah, he's one of 'em. But they was something between Strickland and J. Davis that went back as far anybody can remember, and neither of them's saying what. Some'll tell you Strickland's got evidence that J. Davis ruined his own daughter. But I know Old Man Brasher and that don't seem right to me. Not at all.

Strickland, being the law around these parts, eventually got the upper hand, and they was times Strickland would drag in Brasher's wife and put her in the back cell for questioning, but between you and me, they weren't no questioning going on. Nobody would say a thing. Lord, I used to stare down at my hands a-trembling when he'd walk her out to the lobby and send her on her way.

And Davis, he never reported it, never went to the county or the state?

It ain't as simple as all that. Strickland had something on J. Davis and in public he was like a whupped dog. But that Brasher clan was gunning for Chief Yates amongst themselves. They had to do it like they wasn't doing it. One night, they run him off the road. Another time they took off a bit of his ear with a sniper shot. That was the worst of it. Most times, they was just this deadly tension every time them two come together.

Strickland's atop of things, mind you. As many notes as you're taking on him you can be sure he's taking just as many on you, and he don't forget a thing. He got lots of friends here. And they protect that man. He knew about give-and-take, and he was on the give side most of the time, so when he calls for it, it up and gets done.

A cool, quick breeze shot across the porch.

A spell of rain's coming, she said, turning her hand in the wind like it was tap water.

After a while, she said, Where you staying?

On the way back to the motel, I watched heat lightning over the Gulf. Its silent illumination was reminiscent of the flashes of information that were filling my notebook, faint and mirage-like, and without a coherent pattern. What next came to mind was even more haphazard, having no discernable connection to anything that had come before; yet it was haunting to have it materialize so suddenly in my ears: The tune she was humming earlier was "Wayfaring Stranger."

Nowadays, I regret passing up the chance to purchase the Shoestring Slater demo. It'd been going around at five dollars a cassette one night at Turkey Neck, a little slip of land jutting out into Tom's Bayou. At the time, it was cool to own music, but you think about what might be useful to hang on to only later.

I had a little time to sift through my notes before heading over to the Breakwater. The walls of the motel were no barrier to the sound of the waves outside, and I was reminded of what the dispatcher had said about the sound of live bands being heard at the edge of town.

Boggy Boy Blaster's first set would start in about an hour. While traveling the circuit, you'd often hear rumors of incredible shows, gritty singers, powerful bassists, kick-ass drummers; you'd hear about the bad ones, too. Acts that were rising, and those on the slide. Sometimes you never heard a thing. Boggy Boy Blaster fell into that last category.

From snatches of overheard conversation from those who'd seen the performance last night, I'd harvested opinions that the band was crazy, fantastic, awesome, and great, but these plaudits did nothing for me, apart from offering a sense of their direction as registered by the collective sensibility of tourists and partiers.

No one had mentioned Cody Yarbles by name. But I wasn't

surprised. If Yarbles and Jonah Rae were somehow the same person, his playing would have gone unnoticed on a conscious level. Rae's notes blended into the rhythm like a finely stitched thread that only after many listens could you detect. But once you'd discovered it, you'd follow it like an addict after the next fix.

On white legal pads, I traced chronological lines from the roots of Southern music to its present state, a task that shortly proved futile. At best they were porous containers: gospel, blues, rockabilly, jazz, country, rock, soul, Western swing; it was all there seeping up like the bones of the first creatures that walked the earth.

I made a list of names of those whose style or sound seemed influential:

Robert Johnson
Elmore James
Elvis
Jackie Wilson
The Rolling Stones
Merle Haggard
B. B. King
Free
Bob Dylan
Hank Williams, Sr.
Bob Willis
James Brown

The list had grown to two pages before I stopped.

I was certain of only three things:

1. The era of Southern rock began with the Allman Brothers and ended with the plane crash that killed members of Lynyrd Skynyrd.

2. The catalyst was the Civil Rights Movement and the assassination of Martin Luther King, Jr.

3. Young white males were rebelling against the conventional images of the South, the confederacy, the ignorant hick status, and ideas of racism. Southern rock music gave them a way to embrace their Southern pride without embracing the stereotypes. As a result, they became the long-haired hippies from the South.

Marketing ensured that rebel flags and the redneck country boy image remained intact, but these were images of the South that, in fact, had been eroding with each passing year.

After I'd written all that, I made large Xs on every page, crumpled them up, and shot the balled pages into the wastebasket one at a time. I'd stayed on in Mexico Beach because I wanted to find out what had happened to Jonah Rae, not embark on a study of Southern culture.

Jonah Rae had never been pivotal to these events because he'd never gotten out of the roadhouse circuit. Musically, he stood with the best of them, but without an audience talent does not exist. His walking away, I imagined, was the very statement he wished to make about talent, but I was stubbornly convinced that he'd meant to express another idea, one that as yet had not been clear to me and whether or not he would have approved of my exposing his talent to the light he surely meant for someone to grasp and promote this idea, whatever it was.

For thirty minutes, I sat still and listened to the sound of the gulf murmuring through the walls. Before long, a pure tone surfaced from the noise and let me know that I'd been given a chance to set something right, and it felt sacred, this sense of purpose. No matter what the outcome, I promised myself, I would quietly step aside once I understood what his disappearance meant.

In the meantime, I was satisfied that I would know one thing before the night was over. The frisson of that upcoming moment was intense. Very shortly, I'd hear Cody Yarbles on stage, and I'd know instantly whether or not he was, in fact, Jonah Rae.

She ordered a couple of cans of Old Milwaukee, one for me, one for herself. She was the Chief of Police and had heard I'd been poking about town.

Had there been a complaint?

The beer arrived. She popped the tab on my can and slid it toward me. She fiddled with her own tab, moving it back and forth until it came off.

You'da know'd if they was, she said. They's some good people hereabouts, some settled in their ways, and some as likely to shoot first, and me being peacekeeper and all, I'd just as soon nobody got upset.

Her name was Irina Dooney, laid back in jeans and cotton pullover. She didn't know much about Rae's disappearance, or seem to care.

Before my time, she said. That thing's like an ol' ghost story now, more mysterious with each passing year.

Still, I said, you must have some theory.

Sure. It's a waste of time.

Not even curious?

She looked at me a moment, then turned toward the performance on stage, where bursts of red, orange, and yellow light seemed to melt the band. The bassist was in shorts and jackboots. The drummer, a torn top, white sneakers. Cody Yarbles, barefoot, was in long jeans; his hair covered his face. He was like a matchstick exploding through the blur of the noisy bubbin crowd. We didn't say anything else until the band took a break.

I asked what she thought.

Her critical analysis of Boggy Boy Blaster was summed up

in a word: loud.

She agreed to wait until I returned.

A door through a dark passage led to two more doors. One, I knew, went to the beach from the side. The other to an area enclosed by a tall wooden fence. A picnic table supported a tub of ice and whatever beverage the band wanted floated in the slush. Boggy Boy's few groupies hung around on the other side of the fence; they were trying to get them to look over. The lead singer, Frankie Briggs, spoke of working hard, encouraging fans to follow, and swapping venues with other bands.

We've been promoting a band from Gainesville to a guy we know in Tallahassee, and if it works out, we got a gig in Gator land in exchange for Seminole territory, he said. College towns are the best, always a crowd. If we ain't playin, we're checking out the other guy. He's the competition, and you never know who he's gonna be opening for one day, and that's a way in.

Meanwhile, the drummer, Gordon Kroll, was teasing the groupies over the fence, tossing them bottled drinks and sliding his drumstick through a knothole in one of the boards.

Briggs said he'd met the bassist, Jay Jay Yocum, at Okaloosa-Walton Junior College in a philosophy class taught by this surfer dude professor—

Larsman, Yocum said.

Yeah, we were always talking in the back of class and he called us up one day—

He told us to shut up, Yocum said.

Kroll was a friend from high school, Briggs said, and we enlisted him, and one day Jay Jay hears of this dude that's genius and we road trip out to Mexico Beach—

Dude was insane, Yocum said.

And there's Cody sitting outside a bait-and-tackle shop with a mini-amp cranked and he's using this butter knife for a slide—

Love at first sight, Yocum said.

And we start talking, and he says he got the idea of slidin' with the knife from Sylvester Weaver, an old blues guitarist. We jam a while, and we all know it before we say it—

A pearl of a sound, Yocum said.

Remember that fuss his mama put up when we said we were taking him with us?

She liked to come unglued, Yocum said.

I glanced at Cody. He was sitting off by himself, sipping water, gazing as if he weren't aware of the other two talking about him.

Speaking to Cody, but looking at Briggs and Yocum, I wondered if it'd be possible to talk to his parents, if they were still in town, to get another perspective on the band's formation.

His mama's long dead, Briggs said.

And he ain't got no daddy, Yocum said.

His daddy was a guitar, Briggs said.

They broke out laughing, like they'd played me. Even Cody seemed to smile at this.

Meanwhile, Kroll had climbed up the fence and was making out with a blonde from the other side.

Back in the club, Irina Dooney was chatting with Sawyer Burnett at the table. I took the remaining empty seat and thanked him for the access. I asked how his mother was doing.

She all right, he said. But that ain't getting you through the door if that's why you're asking.

I was just asking. No harm meant.

Got you a reluctant witness, Chief Dooney said. She turned to Burnett. He need to talk to Mollie, don't he?

He might learn something, Burnett said. Or he might just get himself shot. Either way, I expect it to do him some good.

They pointed out a man named Mattie Faris, who was

leaning back against the bar near the main door. He sported an eye-patch and had two fingers wrapped around a can of beer.

He was always accident-prone, Burnett said. He got clubbed with a baseball bat and started slurring his words. Mattie became Mollie and out sympathy, I guess, everybody just took to it, so my daddy says. He's been helping with the load-ins, long as I can remember. That was before he got himself shot in the head and went a little nuts.

Was he the man who was talking with Rae's girlfriend the night he disappeared?

Burnett looked over at Chief Dooney.

You heard that one, too, she said. It weren't Mollie, I can tell you that. They also tell you they was another girl with them, and ain't nobody seen her before, either?

That's how I heard it.

They ain't nothin' to it, Burnett said. This here's the thing. The longer that story hangs around here the more characters it takes on.

That it do, Chief Dooney said.

Thick stretches of pine forest occluded my view of the Gulf on my way westward along 98 toward Saudad. Had I been blindly plopped down on this highway, I would never have guessed that a vast body of water lay just beyond.

My fascination with what lay hidden beyond appearance began when I was an adolescent browsing the Saudad library, as often peeking at naked women in art books as searching for an unread volume of the Hardy Boys. I still recall the chastising eye of Mr. Mullett, the librarian, warning me off my pornographic endeavors.

One day, he called me over to his desk. We were the only two in the place and perhaps he was bored because he told me his ancestors had founded Saudad, and did I ever wonder about the name? Like the majority of the town's population, I never had.

His forebear was Bartolomeu Cabral, a Portuguese who spoke fluent Spanish. He rose in the ranks of those under the command of Tristán de Luna y Arellano in the middle of the 16th century. The Viceroy of New Spain commissioned Luna to establish a colony in Ochuse Bay, what is now Pensacola Bay. More than a thousand soldiers and settlers arrived in eleven ships in August 1559. A month later, a hurricane destroyed all but three of the ships, including the entirety of the food stores, which had been left on the ships until suitable shelter could be built on shore. The next two years were spent trying to stay alive. One group traveled north to the Indian town of Nanipacana on the Alabama River, while another headed up to Coosa, a town in Northwest Georgia, known to exist because of de Soto's expedition in the earlier part of the century. These inland excursions saved many of the newcomer's lives.

Cabral, however, slipped ranks, and went east to explore the Florida Panhandle. I like to think, Mr. Mullet said, that he was like Ponce de León, searching for the Fountain of Youth.

Was his wife with him, I'd asked. Today, this seemed like a stupid question, but I was barely twelve at the time.

Mr. Mullett took his time considering how to answer. He said that Cabral was unmarried but likely made deals with either the Chatot or Apalachee Indians, and probably both, but however it happened, he prospered and founded a town he named *Suadade*, a Portuguese word that describes a feeling of both melancholia and nostalgia for things that may never happen or for things that may never happen again. The *e* was dropped somewhere over the centuries. There are conflicting stories about why Cabral chose this particular name, said Mr.

Mullett, but I like to think it was no more than that he simply missed his home.

Now, every time I drive past the Welcome to Saudad sign at the edge of town, as I did this morning, I think I understand the feeling Cabral must have felt; I often missed my home town, too.

I found Strickland Yates in the common area of the Bayshore Nursing Home off Partin Drive. I'd come early, it was just before nine o'clock, hoping to catch him in a lucid moment.

He wore a plaid shirt and a brown sweater. A bit of crumble cake had fallen in his lap, which I took the liberty to clean. I spoke a while about his time in Mexico Beach, about the police department, and about the night Jonah Rae disappeared, but apart from occasionally licking his lips, he did nothing other than stare past me as if I were not there. I tossed out familiar names: Fanny Yates, his wife; Nellie Palmer, his lover; J. Davis Brasher, his enemy. Nothing registered.

As I struggled to find a way to draw his memories out, it occurred to me that memories are not locked inside us. They are not like water from a well requiring only an adequate bucket to draw them out. They are a kind of behavior that ebbs and flows under conditions that make them more or less likely to appear. I was reminded of the morning I stood on the beach. The shades of blue and green depended on sunlight for their existence; the waves needed the wind to make them appear. Whatever part of the brain made memories possible was for Strickland Yates no longer working properly.

Then on a lark I said, She came from the sea.

His eyes fixed upon mine. His voice came out in a low growl.

You can't trust that Lucindy Jean Crowe, he said. She was drunk and delirious and out for the dime.

He said no more, and I left him to his solitude.

Ahead lay a charcoal sky, the rain Nellie Palmer had forecasted with her turning hand the previous night. East on 20, south on 77, and east again on 22 brought me to Wewahitchka. My interview with Yates had left me with three possibilities, which I'd pondered on the two-hour trip:

1. The dime meant Lucindy Jean Crowe was after someone's money.

2. The dime meant Lucindy Jean Crowe was after someone's cocaine.

3. Chief Yates was talking nonsense.

I held tightly to the first two possibilities.

The bed-and-breakfast wasn't hard to find. It was a white two-story home on Florida 71 between Old Dairy Farm Road and Alabaster Lane. The residence itself was several hundred feet from the highway. A white sign with black lettering at the entrance read

L. J. C.
B. & B.

What appeared to be dogwood flowers had been painted in the corners of the sign; they were now faded.

A dusty shell road led to the house. An occasional drop of rain hit the hood of my car with a hard tap, as I drove up.

Who I'd hoped was Lucindy Jean Crowe, the former girlfriend of Jonah Rae, answered the door. She looked past me as if she were expecting someone else. Dark and brooding, not unlovely in manner, she was clearly uninterested in what I had to say. Her laconic speech made me feel anxious, and once she learned I was not wanting a room, an invitation to the interior of her home was not extended.

Yet, she did not close the door and retreat within.

You were seeing him back then, I said. A woman phoned

the police that night. She seemed to know something about his disappearance. Don't you care what happened, or do you already know?

The sky rumbled in the distance. A droplet of rain smacked my shoulder.

I haven't thought of those days in many years, she said, her tone off-hand. He was never interested in me. You've confused me with my sister.

I was told—

You were told wrong.

She did not react when I mentioned Cody Yarbles's name or become piqued when I told her that he greatly resembled Jonah Rae.

I heard Yarbles play last night, I said, and it was the same brilliance.

What you are suggesting, she said, isn't possible.

Did she have a child?

My sister? Never.

Maybe one you didn't know about.

The light was gray and blue. A cool wind rushed past, followed by a deep rumble.

You are looking for something that doesn't exist, she said. After a moment, she continued. People know your business whether you want them to or not, and don't you think I'd know if my sister had had a child?

Where can I find her?

Mexico Beach is the last I saw of her. We had a falling out a few years ago, and I don't keep up, not since I moved out here.

Asking what they'd fought about seemed out of bounds, and I let it go. I was about to leave when I heard movement inside the house.

Is someone there?

No, she said, without turning. Unless it's Jack, a man who does a little work for me in the yard.

I drove through a blinding downpour back to Mexico Beach. Lucindy Jean Crowe, I was certain, was withholding something, but what gnawed at my gut was the impression she'd left me of being someone who'd lost a sense of who she was.

She helped herself to club soda as if she were at home instead of at the Breakwater. I stood dripping, having just dashed inside from my car. A flash of lightning briefly tinted the room blue; it was followed by a succinct crack of thunder. Sawyer Burnett's back was to me. He was going through receipts at a table.

She offered me a short fat bottle.

I suppose I should call you Chief Dooney, now that you're all done up in your blues, I said.

We sat at the counter. I twisted the cap off.

I'm no Officer Pipes, she said, but I clean up pretty nice when I have to.

She was in a reminiscing mood and said she'd never known anything but the sun and sand growing up. I was your standard-issue beach girl, she said. My hair was long and blonde, and shoes never touched my feet unless I was in school, and I majored in skipping, so you could say almost never.

But shortly after graduation, she wanted to see what else was out in the world and left Mexico Beach in the early 1980s to study criminal justice at F.S.U. A year later, she dropped out. Wanting work, she passed the State Officer Certification Exam and landed a job in Pensacola.

For me, it was city life, she said. Took a while to adjust to the one-ways around Palafox and Spring, but I managed. One of the first crimes I'd been called to was just off Cervantes, a little ways down H Street. Past a decrepit chain-link fence, over a broken cement walkway, we found signs of struggle inside the house and the bludgeoned body of Timothy Grange; his wife, Angela Grange, was missing. Now, it wasn't my duty to investigate, I was patrol, but this being my first homicide, I'd check in with this sergeant detective, name of Sheely, to see how it was progressing, and one week he'd tell me it was the wife who'd done it and the next week it wasn't. They never did find her or evidence sufficient enough to incriminate her. I give Sheely a call now and again. He's long retired and that case, last he told me, is as cold as a can of beer in Siberia.

Speaking of which, she said, capping her empty bottle. How's yours coming along?

You were telling me Mattie Faris was someone to talk to, I said. Whereabouts is his trailer?

Best way is west on 98, hang a right on 19th, and then go left on Nannook. All the way to the end you'll find a sandy road slithering off into the woods. Take that, and you'll find him.

Now mind you don't get shot, Sawyer Burnett called from across the room.

He's playing, right?

No, he ain't, Chief Dooney said. See Mollie got himself shot back in 1982, a drug deal gone wrong—

Cocaine, Burnett said.

—and he ain't been the same since. They say he's moody, one day to the next, and can't tell yesterday from today or tomorrow; it really messes with him.

You're telling me he's unreliable, is that it?

I'm telling you don't get your ass shot off.

. . .

Mattie Faris was standing waist deep in a hole behind his trailer. He'd been digging since morning but had to quit once the hole started filling with water from the storm, which had now abated, leaving a sky of pale gold in the west and a horde of shrill mosquitoes about our heads.

I thought it was a septic tank problem, but he informed me, without flinching or jest, as he climbed out, that, no, he was digging his way to China.

Once, I'd embarked on a similar quest, so I didn't question his motive. But I was four at the time, not forty.

Inside, he sat across from me on a brown pleather sofa. Atop the coffee table between us was a revolver, a scattering of bullets, and a bottle of Jim Beam, which he poured into paper cups, offering me one. He settled back, placing his muddy boot on the edge of the table.

The patch is for the public, he said, but it itches, so I leave it off here.

Pink skin as smooth as plastic at its center resided in the space where his right eye had been. His beard was full and settled against his throat. He stroked the curly hairs downward to a point, pulling them slightly to the left. His face looked like a possum hanging from a limb.

You want to know about Jonah Rae, he said. I guess you're gonna write it up for one them big magazines and get you a hefty sum for it.

I didn't care for his insinuation or his angle and down-played it.

He seemed unconvinced and proceeded with a hint of expectation in his tone, as if we were in on it together.

Before I left high school, he said, I was already doing load-ins and -outs at the Breakwater. Jackson Burnett was running things then. He was a fine man; he looked after me. His son's the same way, but his son's a mama's boy through and through.

Bands would swing down from Atlanta, and you'd hear all about the people they met and who they played with. It was a fine time to be alive, around all that excitement.

A good band expected you to have electricity, and that was about it, he said. They dug the venue, just a little waystation, where the jam was good and the patrons appreciating all of it. But a lousy band, well, they walk in like they was Elvis or something, expecting you to feed 'em and house 'em and keep the grass coming. They'd gripe about the crowd or lack thereof it. Well, the locals'll come, but, man, you gotta bring your own following. Nobody's gonna do it for you. Them jackasses just didn't get it.

Shoestring Slater was a kick-ass band. Good as they come. We already knew about them because of Johnny. About every six months, they'd come back and play a while, and it was S.R.O. all the way out to 98.

They was working all over and didn't need to come back. But they did. And that's what I mean about your following. You gotta feed the people.

Now that boy Johnny, he could play like a plugged-in nightingale, a real lightning bolt of energy, and smooth—let me tell you. Smooth, like spreading sweet butter on soft bread. You could taste that sound of his.

They was working the coast of the Panhandle the last time they swung by, the night you want to know about, and it was different, just plumb different, you could tell. They'd gotten themselves into something awful.

Faris crumpled the paper cups and tossed them to one side. He set up two fresh ones and tipped the bottle into each.

What they was into was cocaine distribution. That manager sure as hell was. I can't say for certain about the boys. Oh, they knew about it, all right, and it made them just as liable for what happened next.

Now, get this. Somehow or other that manager passes off his brick to a woman who, it turns out, was not the intended buyer, and she's gone, and he done lost both the marching powder and the cod. Now he ain't got nothing for the seller, and what's he thinking while he's standing there in that deep deep dog shit? He's thinking, blame it on the band. And that's what he done, and before you can spit your juice, he's hopped the next train to Portmandoo.

I asked Faris to let me go over my notes to make sure I'd got it right, but I found my gaze settling on his missing eye. Had he lost it the same night from a cartel bullet? Irina Dooney had said it'd been shot out in the early 80s, and the disappearance had happened before that. Yet, his detail suggested intimate knowledge of what went down. On the other hand, how much credence do you give a man who's digging a hole to China?

The night Jonah Rae disappeared, I said, you were there?

I was.

Tell me about it.

Faris lurched forward. He turned his head to look me straight on.

How about we do a few lines first.

We settled on getting high. He broke out a pouch and rolled a few numbers.

On that particular night, he said, the moon was big and fat like someone had just sliced open a huge yellow watermelon up there. And they was this warm breeze from the south, you know just coming in low, and all abouts it was quiet and still except for an occasional breaker shoring itself up on the beach. It was a night for loving if they ever was one.

Well, the boys was nervous from the first, like I was telling you. They was on high, watch-yo-ass alert, and they got to talking amongst each other saying that if they just stayed up there on the platform and kept going through the night that maybe they'd be all right. But Johnny, he just can't take no more. He says he's going out. He gotta take care of something, he says.

There weren't no talking that boy down, and I tell you every bit them tried to stop him, but no, he says, he's going, and he never come back. The band was messed up after that.

Where'd he go? I asked. You said he had to do something. What?

For a long time, Mollie Faris sat sunk in the brown pleather chair with his eye closed. My head was starting to feel light and easy. He seemed to say something aloud that I couldn't quite catch, but it wasn't meant for me, as far I could tell. I thought he'd dropped off to sleep. Then a smile broke across his face.

I don't know if you're ready yet for this next part, he said.

The bud was pinched between my fingers, and I looked at him, and I guess this was enough to convince him.

So, it's a few years later, he said, and I'm at this party and Lucindy Jean Crowe is there—

Which one?

He shrugged.

Anyway, she's wasted like the party girl you always dreamed of, and I ain't gonna lie to you and tell you I was all too noble to take advantage of that, and I set about to corner her market. I'm sure I made a few implausible gestures and fished up some downright lies, but it wasn't long afore I had her out on the beach strolling, or you might say I was holding her up, and at one point she just plops right down like a wore out kitten, and so I'm sitting in that cool, white sand with her, and she starts getting all soggy sad on me. It's a mixture of anger and jealousy, and she's weeping, and now it's starting to freak me out, man, like this is one crazy bitch and she's gonna yank out a gun and start shootin' or something.

But, no, through all them tears she starts mumbling. That

woman. That's what she says. That woman come from the sea. Over and over she says it, like it couldn't possibly be true, and she's gotta convince herself. And me, being the sympathy type, I sort of encourage her to tell it a little and get it off her mind, so we can get cozy and enjoy ourselves.

Did she say who it was?

She didn't say.

Now, mind you, he said, this is all the God's honest truth what I'm relating here. That woman come right out of the Gulf of Mexico, Lucindy Jean Crowe says to me, and she come to live with her and Johnny at their place. She says the two of 'em holed up there in the mother-in-law house and never come out for nothing.

Well, one night, she tells me, she's lying in bed fuming with jealousy and hears this woman moaning, hears it somehow way across the yard and through them walls, and she goes out and can see a light through a hole in the blind and puts her eye up to it and liked to fall out seeing what she's seeing. That woman that she says come from the sea is making love to Johnny's guitar. I swear it's the truth. And ol' Johnny, she says to me, he ain't nowhere to be found. She was blind with rage at first, but unable to move. Now how long did she stand there? Half an hour, an hour? Maybe all the night long. She didn't know. This rage, she said, turned itself into fascination and then enslavement, as if a spell'd been cast upon her. She recalled only that she woked up in the grass, her body wet with dew, and she never said another word of it until that night she told me on the beach.

I'd lost track of time and realized we'd switched places. I was now sunk in the brown pleather chair where Mollie had been, and he was spread out on the gray tufted sofa where I had been. He was talking, or he had been talking for quite some time, and I was now once more aware of it, but the topic had drifted far away.

Blackouts were mandatory in those days, he said, but folks in Mexico Beach probably didn't get word, or they thought it wasn't meant for them, but you know they was German U-boats prowling the Gulf waters during the war, and one night a merchant ship, the *Jenny Coombs*, is heading east out of New Orleans and all of a sudden finds herself lit up by the lights of Mexico Beach. A U-166 punches a hole in her, and she goes to the bottom.

Anyone survive?

Not a soul.

But mark this, he said. Most don't think of the Gulf of Mexico as an enchanted sea, but the old folks can tell you they's spirits coming ashore all the time. You and me, he said, we know too much. And once you get to knowing too much and can explain every little thing, you done lost it.

He sat up, his tone on the cranky side.

You go poking your nose around and you gonna hear a lot of shit, he said. They'll say she's mad. She ain't. They'll say she got her a twin. She ain't. It's been two decades now and all them stories got jumbled and nobody knows shit about it. They'll even tell you they seen her walking around pregnant—

You saw her?

Not me.

Who then?

Tell you what, man, you wanna chase it down, then you go on and ask Sawyer Burnett's mama about that. Oh, and one other thing, young fella: When you grab holt of that chunk of payroll don't you forget where you heard it first.

And he wouldn't say another word.

It was 3 a.m.

Before he let me out the door, Faris gave me a cassette.

I turned it over in my hand.

That there's the demo tape, he said.

Shoestring?

That's right. Not many of them left.

Outside, I felt a ragged head coming on that was going to pester me the rest of the night and probably far into the morning. I kept my fingers on the cassette in my pocket and went back to the motel. I thought about the revolver on Faris's coffee table and wondered if he'd intended shoot somebody or if it was there to remind him that only one shot really mattered.

The windshield had collected a light diaphanous layer of salt. I had driven the rental a hundred feet away to face the Gulf in a wayside parking area with an entrance sign telling me it was closed after dark.

I'd found a couple of unopened Myer's minis in the trunk while I was looking for a cassette player that might have been stolen a few weeks earlier in Valdosta. All I could recall of that night was that I was on Bemiss and North Oak, or thereabouts. The dark rum came into my possession and the cassette player left it.

I pushed the tape into the rental's deck and wrote down the song titles as best I could recall them on a 3x5 index card with a golf pencil.

1. *Angel of Mercy* - 3:05
2. *The End of the World* - 6:12
3. *East River* - 9:09

An image of isolation, the grim fuzzy slide of Rae's guitar merges with distant toms and a rising, menacing bassline. Something awful happened out on the East River and you're going to find out what it is. *Heart of Darkness* set to music.

4. *Lemon Pie* - 3:14

5. *Lincoln Continental* - 5:01

6. *Wirebound* - 8:27

7. *Waterlights* - 6:47

Pure fusion of gospel blues and jazz. The lead singer's vocal comes across like an afterburner until about four minutes in. Then the intensity of Rae's notes up and down the neck obliterates the rasping sound of the voice, dissolving them together into a silence that leaves only the echo of the sound.

I paused the tape. At the end of this song, the band is bantering with the mics on. One voice is grainy and faint, and it says, This is why I have a chainsaw. I played it again until I was able to recognize the voice. It belonged to Cody Yarbles.

8. *I'll Be On My Way* - 4:18

Rockabilly fun. The protagonist is dedicated but his fidelity wavers the closer he gets to her.

9. *Apple Doos* - 4:38

10. *Air* - 12:40

A brooding piece about the Rosewood massacre in Levy County in 1923. A waystation on the Seaboard Air Line Railway, every building was burned to the ground after a black man was lynched over accusations that he beat and raped a white woman. This song alone could have done it for Shoestring Slater. The lyrics are spare, as if applied with fearful tenderness, and Rae roams freely along the fretboard, his notes laconic with an ironic nostalgia; he is a man lost in thought, contemplating his remorse among the ruins.

11. *Come To My Room* - 7:46

The final track is the only pure love song on the tape. Cary Boucher had stolen my heart in high school, but for months I couldn't acknowledge it, and she seemed oblivious to what she'd done. Then one night at a party down at the trestle on the Shikoba River we looked at each other, and in that moment it all seemed to make sense, and we slipped into the back of an empty van. Neither of us had done it before. I recalled the music under my skin, her unsnapped jeans, the heat of a yielding nipple, and the hot juicy peach between her legs. We didn't speak before or after. We were simply and momentarily released from some awful pang of desire. For the remainder of the school year, we rarely saw each other, and until tonight Cary Boucher had not once crossed my mind.

If the music had not restored my memory of that night, I might have forever questioned the existence of Cary Boucher, and the facts of my own life.

Saying I needed it, Chief Dooney handed me a hot cup of coffee. My couple of hours of sleep, the shave and shower, did not deceive her perceptive eye. We sat in her office, the window offering a glaring view of the Gulf across 98. I told her what Mollie had said.

I'm not surprised. That rumor floated long ago.

But what if it's true?

Mattie Faris don't know the truth. Didn't you believe me?

Anyway, Burnett's mother won't talk to me.

Guess she's been asked one too many times.

Who else would be asking? And why her?

Dooney adjusted the blind, making the sunlight puddle on the floor. The dust rose like steam from a bubbling cauldron.

I wasn't there, she said, and all that happened a long time ago. But from what I've heard, it galled her into isolation. You wouldn't be the first to come poking around, you know. They was the curious always about, some persistent reporters, and somebody, maybe a family member, hired a P.I. to check it out. Folks around here got tired of it all pretty quick. They just wanted to get on with their lives, and I suspect they were willing to accept the most likely answer.

Which is?

He was killed by the cartel.

So, where's the body?

The library clerk gave me spools of microfilm and pointed at the readers in a nearby carrel.

The labels are faded, I told her.

They old, all right, she said. Nobody never come here looking for them, so I scooped up what I thought you might want. If you don't want 'em—

No. It's all right.

The enclosed room was sweltering. I spooled the first strip and rotated the knob. Whoever had written these documents to the stock had been distracted by drink or fatigue. Birth certificates were snug against land plats, which were cozy with adjacent obituaries, and city council clippings alongside box scores. This arrangement proved to be highly inconvenient, but about an hour into my search I ran across a folo story that proved to be something I believed would be vitally important to my investigation. The machine had print capabilities and I zipped off a copy, plus one more.

I'd exhausted my reels just before noon.

The clerk looked up from her desk where I'd set the spools.

Find what you wanted?

Are there any more?

That's all we got, she said. You might try on up to Wewa. The overflow gets up there.

Each printed document cost me a nickel. I gave the clerk a dollar. She returned me ninety cents. The exchange was fair, yet I felt the loose jingle of encumbrance in my right pocket as I turned to go.

Outside, it was as hot as it was in the reading room. My

hands dripped with sweat and dampened the pages. I'd hoped to see more clearly in the bright sunlight the blurred image of Lucindy Jean Crowe's birth certificate. Its typeface I recognized as Courier 10, the brusque and austere style of government documents of that time. The hasty signature at the bottom looked like an ink sketch of a mountain range; it was illegible but suggestive of the name *Hocks*—Dr. Hocks or perhaps Dan Hocks. Holding the fact of her birth in my hand baffled more than clarified an already mystifying event. As if the back of the document might contain the testimony I sought, I hurriedly flipped the page over. But there was no record of a twin, just as Mattie Faris had claimed.

Officer Pipes opened the door before I reached it. As I went through, he polished the knob and said I'd have to wait a little. He stood nearby and told me about running coon dogs up on 386 near Bear Swamp Road. Mags looked up from time to time to give me a squint that told me she thought Officer Pipes was quite the man.

Hell, it's probably lost, Chief Dooney said, hearing about my morning's snipe hunt. Or it's possible the clerk was confused about what you wanted. You mighta noticed she ain't all there.

If I didn't know any better, I'd think you were all a part of some big cover up.

Well, ain't we the ones? Us Southern hicks? Steeped and suspicious in our conspiracy theories?

She was perched on the edge of her desk, chuckling at that idea.

Truth is, she said, you'd find a better accounting of the townsfolk if you was to check the inside covers of their Bibles.

They do a census and the hospital sends its records, but there's ways of things happening that never come to light.

She opened the door for me and said, Now, I got some chiefing things to do, so.

I turned at the door, not quite ready to leave.

You said her old man was out near Tate's Hell. I think I'd like to pay him a visit and see if I can clear this up.

If you're set on it, maybe I best accompany you. Might do to have a familiar face.

You mean it might be safer.

That, too.

She couldn't go until tomorrow morning. This meant I had to come up with something good to tell Tom T. Hetrick. I needed another night, and that's all there was to it. I'd wire him a piece to give him something to edit, appease him a little, but I could picture his discomfort already. He'd be grunting like a doodlebug rolling a big ball of shit over this one.

I was half into a tuna fish sandwich when Mitch sat opposite me at my table at the diner.

Where's your buddies, I asked.

Bobby's getting roto-rootered, and the other's done took his wife shopping, if you can believe that.

Mitch seemed genuinely cut up about it.

Well, since you're here, I said, tell me what you know about Tate's Hell.

Unless you got a mind to go hiking, he said, what you're really wanting to know about is ol' Percival Crowe, ain't it?

You saw right through me.

I got that kinda mind, he said.

Well, you and the fellas the other day were saying he was touched in the head, if I recall it right.

Did we say that?

It's right here in my notebook.

It mighta been better if we said he had his ways.

He looked over his shoulder and leaned in.

I expect he buried more than few of his own out in them woods. People you knew existed, but then they didn't, like they never been born, and, tell the truth, might off being better if they never did.

I thought I might go see him.

You might wanna consider backing away from that one.

Why's that?

Hell, boy, it's like an unbreakable code out there. That family, they ain't letting nobody in on it.

Like a cult?

More like survival.

What do you mean?

Look. You and I know what they's doing is a dead end for the gene pool, but you aim to head out there and tell 'em that? No, you ain't. They'll scatter the moment they see your dust coming up the road. They been at this a lot longer than you or me. Yes, sir, they gone tribal out there and best you leave 'em be.

Far off in the shadows, I saw a man smoking a cigarette by the

L. J. C.
B. & B.

as I drove slowly past. She'd said she had a man working for her, and I had no reason to doubt it.

The Wewahitchka branch library had the singular advantage over the Mexico Beach public records office of being organized.

I spread the newspaper clipping I'd printed from the reader flat on a table. A body had washed ashore eleven years after Jonah Rae's disappearance. Decomposition was such that identification was impossible. The erosion had left a match with dental records inconclusive. The only definite characteristic was that the body had a bullet hole in the back of its skull.

This kind of brutal story, though, should linger, but as I discovered while surveying the archives of the time, the account vanished from public interest quicker than you could wrap up a pound and a half of mullet.

I skimmed the news for the years surrounding the discovery of the body. The name Dewey Brasher appeared often and this drew my curiosity to his activity in the tale, and I followed it as far as I could. One of J. Davis Brasher's sons, he had lodged complaints against Police Chief Strickland Yates in the years leading up to the discovery of the body on the beach. Broadening my search, I found that whenever a Brasher name appeared it was usually on the police blotter for drunkenness and disorderly conduct. Even Charlie Brasher, the kid Nellie Palmer had told me was tricked by one of the Crowe sisters, was there, June 19, battery against a police officer. The only name that didn't show up in the blotter was that of Dewey Brasher, and this led me to believe that he had got himself an education, and with it, a different approach to bringing down their nemesis.

There'd been a state probe into allegations of misconduct. The stories ran for nearly two years, and the timbre of the reporting suggested that Yates's time was up. However, an omission in the coverage struck me as both peculiar and significant: (1) the omission itself and (2) the fact that the news had failed to observe it.

A little over a year after the state's investigation began, Dewey Brasher dropped out of sight and was never mentioned again. The probe found no wrongdoing, and Yates remained in office.

Six years later, a body washed ashore.

The inference seemed clear-cut: Yates's men had assassinated Dewey Brasher.

Yet, a letter to the editor disabused me of drawing a tight conclusion. The letter appears a week after the body had been found. The writer is anonymous, the tone confessional, and the style provincial. The writer claims access to intimate knowledge of evidence tampering and when it all comes to light, the writer avers, everyone will know that the body on the beach belonged to Jonah Rae.

In a light rain, I stood at a pay phone listening to Hetrick spit into the mouthpiece at his end. He wasn't buying the blown gasket story I'd rigged for my reason for staying another night.

I assured him I'd be in Mobile by tomorrow evening, or he could dock my pay.

He was going to do that anyway, he said, but ultimately what could he do but relent?

And so, I had my extra day under his threat to leave me stranded, high and dry, a-way down south in Dixie.

. . .

Irina Dooney was waiting at the station the next morning. We rumbled north in her jeep on 386 toward Dalkeith. I told her what I'd found in the archives.

Before my time, she said, the sun just glinting off her orange-tinted sunglasses.

Are you saying you weren't aware of it, or you don't think this might be important?

I'm saying when you hear hoofbeats, think *horse*, not *zebra*.

She allowed more time than necessary for this trite expression to sink in before continuing.

Back in '84, she said, a fire took out most of a block along the main strip, including half the police station and the entire dental office. No telling how many records was lost.

We said little else until we arrived at Tate's Hell.

The road narrowed, changed to white sand, and opened up onto a clearing in the middle of which leaned an old cracker home with gray, faded siding, a misshapen red tin roof, and a long porch going around on the southern side, which faced, a little farther on, a long trailer perched upon and barely clinging to dirty gray columns of cement block. Beyond that, a field of sugarcane bent around a thick, shaggy growth of pine and oak. We stepped around the chickens roaming freely in the yard. A gang of slobbering, snarling dogs descended upon us and challenged our entry into their territory.

Ambling down the porch came Percival Crowe in an open khaki dress shirt and olive-green pants. The insignia on his cap proclaimed his occupation as a Fish and Wildlife Conservation employee.

Dooney spoke to Crowe about his sugarcane crop, the seasonal migration patterns of tourists at the beach, and the recent storm before she introduced me, saying that I had a few questions, if he wouldn't mind.

Ain't got nothing to say, unless you compelling me.

She wasn't, she assured him.

As I awaited the outcome of this little pre-interview negotiation, I furiously swatted at strafing yellow flies and my attention was drawn to the distinct patter of feet coming from inside the house. Small fingers separated a blind and a pasty hand drew a curtain aside. Muted, occult voices mumbled in the dusty blue recess of the house.

Satisfied he was not required to talk, Crowe reasserted he had nothing to say.

There's no record of a twin of Lucindy Jean Crowe, I said, injecting myself into their circle.

Dooney shook her head and squared around on me, her face pulsing faintly with the threat of bodily harm.

Let's go, she said and her hand tenured my forearm.

As we rolled out of the clearing, a woman came out of the trailer and descended the short, metal steps. She wore a house-dress, circa 1940, barefoot, hair unkempt. I pointed her out to Dooney.

That's her, I said. That's the woman who runs the B. & B. That's Lucindy Jean Crowe.

Dooney didn't look. She drove quickly and stoically out of the clearing.

More'n likely, she said, once we'd found the main road, you're seeing what you wanna see. These are private folks, and I best not hear of you snooping on back, pretending you're the county water authority or something like that just so you can get your story. Percy lets me know what I need to know, and I do the same, and that's how we make it work. And if I don't know something, it's because he got a damn good reason to keep it from me.

What annoyed me on the long drive back was not that Dooney had questioned what I'd seen but that I was also questioning the evidence of my own eyes. I found myself staring through the open door of the jeep at the pines rushing past. They were identical, in some sense, in their tallish shapes and greenish coloration, and yet they were also distinct. Their fleeting presence registered in my mind, but for all their division, they remained, essentially, one thing, a pine tree, and I was not mistaken about this or what I had seen.

I imagined a situation in which Irina Dooney had phoned Percival Crowe, who in turn had arranged for Lucindy Jean Crowe to come down from Wewahitchka and appear on the steps as we were leaving, but for what purpose? What was Chief Dooney keeping from me, and why?

The jeep rounded a long curve, the wheels thugging repetitively like breakers on the beach, setting me into a doze. I closed my eyes and through that half-light of the noonday sun I steadied myself with facts: I had looked into the face of Lucindy Jean Crowe in Wewahitchka. The woman coming down the steps from the trailer was also Lucindy Jean Crowe, drastically altered. The same, yet different. Did no one else see this?

Soon, I felt myself become entangled. The very memories of what I'd felt certain I'd seen were washing away in a tide of alteration brought about by converging perspectives, none of which, the more I considered it, governed the truth.

I clung to my notebook, taking what solace I could from the jottings inside, as if they were the physical sign of everything I knew.

As a teenager, Sawyer Burnett said, I worked in the kitchen, and we had us a competition every day to see which of us barbacks could make the best chili. I used to slap a label on my big silver kettle that read *El Primo*.

He moved a basket of Saltines within my reach on the table and sat across from me, expectant. After one bite, I acknowledged his talent for making chili.

You know I have to ask, I said.

Figured as much, he said. You see, this here's the thing I have to admire about you, and about her. You're about as persistent as she is private. They just ain't no getting through when them two goats come head to head.

He left to take a phone call. When he returned, he said, I was wondering about this story of yours and if you had in mind of covering the venues, not that I'm asking.

It's mostly about the bands but, sure, if it's worth it.

You see, this here's the thing, he said. Folks'll come to hear the bands, all right, but many as come because they curious about the strange origins of the Breakwater.

A ghost story?

It's always a ghost story when you get one that's believing and another that ain't, he said. And this one starts out with a tear-away shack back in the early 1930s, during the tail-end of prohibition. They weren't no roads as such but if you know'd how to get here or know'd somebody that know'd how to get here, so it's said, you'd find you some nice corn whisky or a mug of rum a-waitin'. That fella up at Tate's Hell you was wanting to see—

Percival Crowe—

His forebears was running rum along the coast, across to Tallahassee and up to Atlanta and over to Birmingham. They had a nice little thing going. And of course, they was keeping us happy down here, too, and they wasn't asking much, except a little help keeping a lookout for the feds.

Now, also about this time, we'd get us some wandering

musicians and give 'em a steady gig for a night or two and not long after, about 1938, a more formal structure was put up right here where we sitting. And it was also when them U-boats started appearing, and one night, we hear it done sunk a ship right off our coast. The ship was the *Jenny Coombs* and the captain's got his daughter aboard, a young woman of about twenty-three years, so it's said, and when the ship gets herself sunk, nobody knows about it until it don't arrive where it's headed.

Well, on this exact same night, this ol' boy over from Texas way, a fella name of Smoker Caldwell, is playing in the shack in exchange for some good booze and a night's rest from the road. Now, he's a talk-singing bluesman, erratic as all hell, a bit of irony in every lick of the instrument, and if you was paying close attention to the lyrical progression, you'd think you were going one way only to find yourself somewhere else. I'll tell you one thing, though: That boy sure could tear it up on "Jesus is a Dying Bed Maker," so it's said.

He paused. You got you a funny look right then, he said.

I'd been wondering how a black man came to play for a white audience or why he would.

I done some thinking on that, myself, he said. What you gotta know to keep a successful business going is people. It's what my daddy taught me, and we had us many a talk, and one night he was telling me they's always a line and a mood to balance. Cross the line and hell's to pay. Fail to conjure the mood and they's coming out the dance hall faster'n a bell clapper in a goose's ass. My daddy says people kept slavery in they minds and come out to see the black musician because he was cast in the role of the slave, there merely for the profit of his white master.

Is that what you believe?

I believe one group is always looking to ride horse over

another. It's shapes and forms that change. Right now, we in a sinking phase. It ain't fashionable to publicize your hatred, so it sits there under the surface like a suck-mud bottom awaiting a foot to step in it.

The woman who'd been cutting oranges the day before came in. She greeted us and went to work.

You see, this here's the thing, Burnett said. It's like you fall for the one woman you can't ever have for whatever reason—she's married, she don't like you, she don't even know you, like you seen her in a picture one time or something. Well, you just can't erase that feeling, tell it to run off and bother somebody else, now can you? So, what you do is go about acting like you ain't in love and that feeling goes to sinking and when it sinks so far down you can't see it no more, you stop believing it ever happened. And that's the best that's ever gonna come of it.

After a moment, he chuckled.

You know I was saying earlier that you was a goat but you more like a mule dragging me far afield of what I was saying. So on that particular night, getting back to it, the moon's sitting way up high and round and a light breeze is slipping over every-thing, and that ship's out there sinking, and nobody's mattering because they all happy with the music, the whisky, and the good times.

And then all of a sudden this woman come walking up out of the water onto the beach, and them that saw it says it was like she was there but she wasn't, like you could catch a glimpse of her out the corner of your eye, but once you turned to look her straight on, you couldn't see her; or they was afraid to look her square up for reasons they could never quite bring to words. Some say she was a shimmering thing, pale green like a shade of the emerald waters on a sunny day and some say it was some-thing else entirely, like maybe they was all seeing what they wanted to see. But on one fact, they all agreed: She come right up into the gathering and take ol' Smoker Caldwell's hand and lead him off. He ain't never been seen nor heard of since.

He paused and I looked at him for a while.

Is that what you believe?

You see, this here's the thing, he said. Folks keep wanting to hear about it, so I keep talking about it. Believing ain't even a question for me.

I'd been sitting at a corner table in the diner eating an egg and cheese sandwich and scuffling with my resistance to a compulsion to carry out a reckless idea. Mattie Faris had said I needed to talk with her if I wanted to get to the bottom of this thing. Sawyer Burnett made it clear she would not see me. This left only the option of dupery, and my plan, from at least one angle, appeared honest enough that I could get past any ethical dilemma. People do meet by accident, I contrived, and most will capitulate to fate if it strikes them unexpectedly. My vague and unlikely idea was to tail her to a public place and casually bump into her, thereby avoiding a scene and striking up a conversation.

A handful of Burnetts were in the white pages, but the only one without a clearly masculine name was that of L. J. Burnett. An hour later, I'd found a spot off the road not far from her house, which was one of several broad ranch-style homes that were widely separated by large plots of conifer and live oak, sagely bearded with Spanish moss, and served as fences between the respective dwellings.

The plan had its difficulties, foremost among them, she might not leave her house. Then, too, I felt like a creep once I took up my station in the shade, fearing that anyone spying from a window might feel apprehensive about my presence. Compounding it was that the more inconspicuous I tried to make myself, the more menacing I felt I'd become, and it was all over something I had not yet done nor intended to do. I had to admit that my behavior, seen from a distance, might appear to be that of a stalker, although I myself was not a stalker. In spite of these misgivings I hunkered down, knowing there'd be no other way to meet her.

To alleviate my anxiety, I listened to the Shoestring Slater cassette. On track No. 5, Slater launches, seemingly out of nowhere, into a revved-up Ventures sound with clashing guitars on "Lincoln Continental." It's a catchy tune that's fast arriving and storms off with a pounding bass. The later punk era might have been proud to own this one. The singer laments in a strained vocal what he can take in the relationship and what he can't and concocts for himself a sure getaway: It takes a Lincoln Continental to leave that girl behind.

Half an hour later, she walked out of the house snapping her purse, and shut my mouth if she wasn't Lucindy Jean Crowe. What was going on here? Were there three of them? Or was it some trick being played on me, like the one played on Charlie Brasher decades ago?

I had no time to work it out. She backed out of the drive and headed east. A few turns later, she parked in the slotted space of a grocery lot.

I strode at an angle so I might first appear in the corner of her eye and make her vaguely aware of my presence and this would make our convergence, from her perspective, seem like pure coincidence.

My opening line was ready. I'd counted on a quick look of false recognition, then a casual statement offered with an easy, inviting smile to soften any resistance.

Her heels clicked like sonar beacons to my ears, the sound accelerating as I approached. Then I sensed that she'd picked up speed, our paths no longer on a course of intersection, but it was little enough to hasten my step to realign to the point at which we would meet.

But I did not expect for her to stop abruptly and turn to face me.

I was stunned by what she then said. As soon as she'd said it, she turned heel and went into the grocery, leaving me alone on the sidewalk.

How dare you come back here.

Even today, I cannot shake the vicious sensation of her cold, hard look, the acrimonious tone, or the disgust and hatred aimed at me. The lance that pierced me hurt all the more because I could not defend my innocence, for clearly, she had mistaken me for someone else.

Later, you think of the right thing to say.

Only once had I ever been to Mexico Beach, and that was twenty years earlier. It was unlikely we had ever met, but even if we had, it was impossible that she could have remembered my face from so many others over the years.

Nonetheless, her spiteful tone left me standing there dazed on the sidewalk, as if she'd impaled my head on a tall spike and set it out for public display.

For days after, the words still rang in my ears, and have never quite left me.

How dare you come back here.

An afternoon rainstorm kept me indoors at Jay's Bottleneck, the sort of grimy bar that exists within a smog of cigarette smoke and subtle challenges to fights with fists. There were four of us. The woman behind the counter looked full and soft, like you'd pick her if you needed a shoulder to cry on. Two men in damp open shirts and ball caps sat talking quietly at one end of the counter, while I sat alone at the other. The anemic house speakers lent the guitar strut of "Honky Tonk Dancer" a fuzzy quality, as if the instrument were being cranked out through a transistor radio.

Lightning cracked close by and the door opened and a man no higher than the bar stools walked in. He sat next to me. The other two men turned.

What do you say, Charlie, said one of the men.

The other lifted his beer.

Hank. Henry, Charlie said. You boys behaving?

No, they ain't, the woman behind the bar said, bringing Charlie a Schlitz.

Charlie lit a cigarette and looked at me. I was certain he was none other than Charlie Brasher, the one who got fooled on prom night by the Crowe sisters.

How's that investigation coming along, Charlie asked.

I guess everyone knows what I'm doing here, I said.

Some'd say you got a lot of balls. Or a death wish if you was to listen to others. It's probably smart you hooked up with Dooney. She's one that moves through the strata and gets away with it.

Strata?

Town folk, country folk. Each got a way of seeing things.

And where do you fall in?

Country, for sure. Unlike my brother, though, I know what ain't right and also when to keep my mouth shut and work it from the inside.

You're talking about Dewey, I said.

That'd be him.

I ran across some news clippings of Chief Yates being investigated. Dewey's there for a while and then he's not.

Yeah, we ain't seen him in a decade now. You musta heard of the body washing ashore. We figure it's him, but ain't no evidence for it.

Some say it's Jonah Rae.

Well, now, there's a conundrum for you, ain't it? You got two missing persons and one body. I expect who it is depends on what you wanna believe. A lot done happened over them years. You hear the one about the stranger who was chatting up Johnny's girlfriend the night he vanished? Everybody that takes an interest hears it eventually. I don't believe it myself. But if you find that man, you'll know everything you wanna know, so they say.

At first, I believed they were all speaking of someone who had been invented to further the mystification of the events of 1974. But each new mention of this man's existence made me consider the possibility that he was somehow integral to the disappearance of Jonah Rae.

How about this one, Charlie said. Some say ol' Chief Yates is my daddy. You heard that one?

I had not.

Was a time, for who knows why, Yates'd round up my father and my older brothers and haul 'em out to the jail and he'd come pay a visit to my mother.

You're serious.

He looked at me and lit a cigarette.

I recalled that Nellie Palmer had said that Yates brought Brasher's wife to the jail, not that he went to her house.

That ol' Miss Palmer, Charlie said. She's sweet all right, but they's something a little odd about her.

Why your mother?

She was a nice-looking woman, and everybody knows Yates and Daddy been at each other since who knows when, and I expect it had something to do with all that, but the truth is nobody's saying.

What makes you think Yates is your daddy then?

Somebody musta made mention of it. Maybe it was Dewey.

He was friendly with one of Yate's officers, and we all know a good night of drinking'll unzip a tongue faster'n a whore can unzip a zipper.

Half a pack of cigarettes lay smoked and crushed in the ashtray.

Outside, the rain had stopped, and a humid white steam rose from the asphalt. I felt it swirling about me as I walked, coldly dampening my fingers, which uselessly attempted to close around something of substance.

On my way to the dispatcher's home, I crossed the vacant wet asphalt of a Baptist Church parking lot. To the northeast, the sky was black over Tate's Hell, where the storm had gone. It radiated with blue light from time to time but was too far away for the sound of thunder to reach me.

Nellie Palmer poured glasses of sweet tea and we sat on her porch and swatted mosquitoes. I told her I'd run into Charlie Brasher, who seemed to think his father was Strickland Yates and had she heard of this?

She had not, or she could not remember.

What were those two so mad about, I asked.

She looked off into the western, salmon-colored sky. Her face, in profile, held a resigned smile.

We all grew up together, she said. Nothing in the least unusual about our lives. They was a little school over yonder where the grocery is now, and at that time we didn't know a thing about stations in life, affluence, or society; we were just kids a-funnin' and a-learnin'. But, of course, it was always there. It existed in the lives of our parents who was rearing us to be just like them. Strickland and J. Davis were often inseparable. But they'd also get to tussling on the playground at times and who beat who depended on who'd had a recent growth spurt.

But they was also a difference between them two boys that mattered more than anything else. Strickland's daddy was the police chief, just as Strickland would later be, and a meaner cuss you never did find. He used to whup Strickland with a switchcane right out on the street and leave him bawling and shamefaced right where he beat him. That's what done it to him, made him hard and impenetrable. And so, it went on like that until we get ourselves into high school.

We all rode a bus up to Wewa and they was coming in from other places as well. This one little girl name of Esther June Dixon, well, she come from Wetappo, and don't you just know them two boys fell hard for her. Or, more like, J. Davis fell, and Strickland was wanting to beat him at it, so he fell too. Esther June, for her part, likely coulda had anybody at the school, but she pegged herself to J. Davis almost right from the start.

She later became his wife, I said.

That's correct, Nellie Palmer said. I often felt sorry for her. Like all of us, during that time in school, we just didn't have much sense of the ways and wiles of romance, or we was just starting to see it in the picture shows, and took it for what it was, and we was fooled for the most part, trying to swap what we know'd was life with what we dreamed it was.

Esther June loved the attention and encouraged it, not for any particular reason; she was in her own way only doing something natural and innocent, and that's probably why people took to her. But especially those two because I guess whether she knew it or not, she was throttling their engines something fierce. She just ain't had no vision of how it might all turn out.

Now, for their part, them two boys, Strickland and J. Davis, they was like a couple of spark plugs, firing off with every turn of the engine. But it wasn't like grammar school where you could go off and rassle at the insult of a skunk eye. Here you had to impress with brain in the classroom and brawn on the field. Only when the anger or frustration was too big to hold in did you ever go off to pound the other fella.

It happened sometime after the corn was all plowed under that Esther June musta tired of all this business about her, and she outright spurned Strickland Yates. The injury on his face was like it was back when his daddy was beating him on the streets. I'll never forget that look.

J. Davis, by this time, was faster, taller, and stronger, and, if I don't say so myself, quite the handsome young man. More so'n Strickland, so it weren't about that anymore. Strickland, however, didn't quite see it that way, and not accepting her word he went after J. Davis, who flattened Yates with one punch with everybody standing around in the lunchroom. You could feel it come over him, this intense fire of shame. It was war between them two after that.

Now, this would be long about December, just as basketball's getting underway, and everywhere you see Esther June, she's wearing J. Davis's jacket.

Nellie Palmer sat quietly smoothing the hem of her housedress over her knees. For some reason, I smelled honeysuckle, though I saw no vines and couldn't be certain they were in season; yet the fragrance, which had not been here when I arrived, was now offering itself up for my pleasure.

He was beat all right, she said. But he had learned a thing or two from his daddy about how to muscle or to motivate the bigger or better man. So, one night Strickland and a few of his boys had it out with J. Davis in the locker room after the game against Port St. Joe.

Had it out?

All them that knows what went on in there is all dead, except Strickland, and he's as good as dead now. But that night marked a shift in balance to the favor of Strickland Yates. Not just that time, but for the rest of their lives.

J. Davis, he weren't never the same. The funny thing is, Strickland musta thought he'd get an easy time with Esther June after that, but it had the opposite effect on her. Right after graduation, she up and married J. Davis Brasher, and they had 'em a baby before the turnips got pulled.

In the years to follow, Strickland ran rough on J. Davis and his family. He crushed them is what he did; he did that to a lot of people. And J. Davis just let him do it. Whatever it was they had between them, it musta been some kind of unbearable for J. Davis to carry it for very long, and that boy just plain out buckled.

Strickland took, but he never got, she said. He's sitting over there in that nursing home all alone right now. All his life, I bet it never did occur to him that his own cruelty was the reason Fanny Yates took her own life.

Inside, on the way to the bathroom, I lingered at a long narrow display table in the hallway. It was adorned with an oblong doily, a black, leather Bible, assorted candles, and a silver-framed photo of a young Nellie Palmer, who looks as if she is gazing at a field of flowers. Next to her in the photo is Strickland Yates, who looks as if he's playing bad cop in a police interrogation. He has his arm around her shoulder. Her cheek is flush against his chest and her arms embrace him across the middle. I was struck by her expression of happiness.

When she'd said he had crushed a lot of people, I wondered, had she been talking of herself?

Hetrick phoned as I was zipping my packed bag. He informed me the scene was shifting and wanted me in the East Village tomorrow evening to check things out at the SideWalk Cafe. A woman named Cortez would pick me up at the airport.

Officer Pipes was waiting in the lobby. Chief wants to see you, he said.

We rode in the patrol car to the station. Chief Dooney and I walked over to the diner for a cup of coffee.

Get what you come for, she asked.

Boggy Boy Blaster had moved on. I never did have a chance to speak with Cody Yarbles, except in rushed exchanges of information I could have gotten from his fans. The resemblance between Yarbles and Rae was uncanny, but in the end, I could not, nor ever did account for it.

I considered Chief Dooney's question and it made me smile.

I found out more than I wanted to know, I said, about things I wanted to know nothing about, but nothing about the things I wanted to know.

I told her about the cassette Mollie Faris had given me.

All the songs taken together, I said, remind you of something that is simultaneously splashing in and yearning for those lost days of innocence. Yet, there's also a distant, heavy feeling, a sort of haunting presence, that's letting you know it can never happen again, and within that recognition lurks an unbearable sorrow.

I put the cassette in her hand.

She turned it over, slipping her index finger into one of the toothy sprocket holes.

I guess, she said, looking up at me, I'll like it if I can dance to it.

At last light, I stood on the shore of the Gulf. The water massaged my feet, the wind feathered my hair, and the setting sun warmed the side of my face. All that I'd encountered in my short stay in Mexico Beach, I realized, lay as far beyond my grasp as the teeming salt life out there beneath the surface of the water.

. . .

Hank and Henry were at the counter perched precisely as they had been earlier in the day but now, they were wearing checkered shirts. They moved very little, not even to face each other, and I could not tell if they were talking to or staring at the woman behind the bar.

I had been unable to sleep, so I went for a walk, crossing 98 to the north to Nutmeg Street and looked at the short decorative palms and the concrete-block houses with flat roofs behind chain-link fences. Constructed in the 1950s, these homes were sold on the promise of being able to withstand the blast from an atomic bomb. I turned west on Argonaut Lane, a road too narrow for the passage of more than one car at a time. Wooden power poles were set close to the asphalt like a tree-lined avenue. At the end of the road was Jay's Bottleneck, and I thought a beer might help. I sat where I had been sitting earlier in the day and the woman behind the bar asked if I wanted the same. I nodded, and she placed a beer in front of me.

Soon, my eyes adjusted, and I saw in the far corner of the room a woman sitting at a table that had three opened bottles on it. Her hand languidly lifted a wine glass to her lips. When it was apparent that no one would be returning, say, from the restroom, to join her, I sat next to her without introduction or permission.

She was drunk. I refilled her glass with malbec and not knowing if she were the woman who ran the Bed & Breakfast in Wewahitchka or the woman who came out of the trailer in such an awful state at Tate's Hell or the woman who chastised me on the sidewalk in front of the grocer's, I began speaking to her as if we had been good friends all along.

She regarded me a moment, as if her memory of me would snap to at any second. Apparently, it did not. The wine recaptured her attention and after sipping she dabbed her lips with a napkin and looked at the entrance door. She said she was waiting for someone she had been expecting for some time. He appears to have stood me up, she said.

Sensing that the arrival of this person might solve the mystery should he ever show up, I purchased two more bottles, a Miller High Life for myself and a demi-bottle of malbec for her; my intent was to keep her right where she was. I poured the wine and probed gently, enticing the veiled past, reminding her of the charming days of summer yore, and leading her to recall the night that Jonah Rae had disappeared.

Perhaps overcome, she latched onto my arm, shaking it to stop me from talking.

That never happened, she said. Never, never. That never did. Don't I tell you that how many times? Never.

I weighed my next sentence carefully. She was aware that she was speaking to me and denying that Jonah Rae had disappeared; or, in her inebriated state, she confused me for someone else, someone who'd suspected her of having done something, and was defending her innocence. Or was it a warning of some kind?

My role felt paternal, and I decided to play it out and said, She came from the sea.

She tightened her grip and looked at me.

Ain't I in love with him?

I nodded

You are, I said, but I want you to tell me.

I am in love with him, she said, and she come from the sea and took him. We was together, the two of us. Oh, they said we was living in sin, and I'd die before my daddy found us out. We was to be married and woulda been all right then. But she come from the sea and took him. He snuck her out back, where he had his studio, and he forbid me to see her. Their shadows moved against the blinds. I never saw how she done it, I never did, because I was in love, and I didn't see that she'd enslaved him. He made me promise not to tell it, and I never did. They was out in the cottage where no one would know.

And then it come a time I just can't stand it no longer, and we fight, and I tell him it's her or it's me. There come over him a look of pain, like I was tearing at his skin. He up and tells me somebody's after her, and we can't just turn her out. It wouldn't be right, he says. So, I love him, so I believe him. He's got his reasons, ain't he, to spend all that time out there? He's practicing that guitar and recording them demos and such, ain't he?

I lit the cigarette she'd barely managed to produce from her purse. She could not take her eyes off the door. It struck me as out-of-place, or ironic, that "Blue Sky" came through the frail house speakers and the sound seemed to settle on us.

While she pinched out a flake of tobacco sticking to her tongue, I divined where she was going: the jealous lover, the other woman, the disaster that would follow when it all collided. After I'd lost hope of ever finding out what had really happened, it was a reprieve to now find myself mere moments away from having the mystery that had kept me in Mexico Beach finally being brought to light. Already, I was convinced that it was Jonah Rae's body that had washed ashore ten years ago. In a matter of minutes, I'd learn how she'd done it.

I woke up one night, she said. It was an ungodly noise that shuddered me awake. It was just past midnight and storming. The walls was flashing blue and the rain was pounding something awful on the roof. Johnny wasn't in the bed. He wasn't in the house. I went about calling his name. From the kitchen, I saw the light in the cottage was on, and I was afraid something had happened, so I took the handgun that Johnny kept under the bed and went out to see.

About halfway across, I stopped. My feet was in a puddle, I

was aware of that, and my hand was holding the gun tight. Other than that, other than a general sense of getting soaked, I felt nothing. And that's when I thought it. Right then, like it was cutting through me like a flash of lightning. Was I gonna shoot 'em both dead?

The light in the cottage drew me on, stripping me of all sensation, and my eye found a chink in the blind and went right up to it. The entire room was laid bare to my vision. Johnny was sitting awkward in a chair, like he was sleeping, but in a dreadful way; he could not have been comfortable like that. On the other side of Johnny, the woman was standing there naked. Imagine my shock when I saw that she looked just like me, as if I was there inside and not out on my knees spying through the blind. She was looking at me and acting like she ain't seen me. I was froze in my place. I knew, somehow, she was wanting me to see what she was gonna do.

For the next couple of hours, she lay writhing with Johnny's guitar between her legs. I could not take my eyes away from it. All the while, she kept looking at me, like she was seeing me deep inside, and it made me drop the gun and lift the hem of my nightgown. After that, I don't know what happened. I woke up half-naked and soaking wet on the grass. I scrambled up and went into the cottage. Johnny and the woman was gone.

She nearly knocked over her wine glass reaching for it. I wrapped my hand around hers, steadying it, helping her to sip and to bring the stemware back down to the table.

Everybody thought I was mad of grief, she said. They all know'd what Johnny was to me. But it weren't that. No, it was the image of her loving that guitar that made me that way. I can't, to this day, make it stop.

To keep her going, I ordered two more bottles. She watched the door, her head sagging, as if she might fall into a stupor.

A little while later, she said, I was visiting a friend at the maternity ward over to Port St. Joe and as I was passing through one hallway to the next a door come open and through it I saw her with a baby at her breast. At first, I wouldn't believe my eyes, so I kept going, but a compulsion come and struck me, and I wheeled around and run on back. I never know'd how long a hallway might be or how confusing. I went about this way and that until some ol' nurse took holt of me, and I was telling her that I had to find her, and she was telling me to hush. Hush, now, hush, she kept saying. They was a number of them all about me and they was keepin' me from gittin' after her. They wasn't understandin' me. They wasn't listenin'. Don't you see? If I could find her, I could find him.

She looked up. You understand me, don't you?

A warm draft of air flowed through.

She saw the bar door open before I did. A long, jacketed arm made a motion. *Come along*, it said. She was up and across the room, moving with an agility and haste I would not have guessed she could have managed in her drunken state. At the threshold, they turned, and I saw in vague outline the figure of a man. His arm went around her shoulder and the door closed.

It had happened so quickly, I hadn't thought to rise with her. A moment later, like an afterimage, I recognized the outline as that of Jonah Rae, the way I'd remembered him, or the way I'd wanted to see him. I bolted for the door and ran around the corner of the building to the parking lot. I arrived just in time to see their taillights vanish in the darkness of the night.

I stood for some minutes in the damp air coming off the Gulf and stared in the direction they had gone. I stretched my hand out as if, by an act of will, I could somehow recall them from their destination or from my memory and once and for all close around something solid, but only the salty mist of the night collected there.

.   .   .

2009

The first time I saw Jonah Rae he walked off the stage during a performance at the Breakwater in Mexico Beach, Florida. He never returned. It was 1974. For a time, we talked about it, and then we didn't. It vanished from our conversation and our memory.

I'd written about the resurgence of Southern Rock in 1994, but the part about Jonah Rae was cut. Tom T. Hetrick, then my editor, said it was insignificant. Adding citations and a different slant, I later found a place for it in *The Journal of Southern History* out of Rice University. Then I was off to cover the anti-folk scene in New York City. I didn't think I'd ever return to Mexico Beach, but here I was, in 2008, checking into a motel for a reunion.

In those days, 1974, my friends were Kai Bogna and Roberto Zabien. A year or two out of high school, Kai inexplicably got married, and sensing our shift into adulthood and our eventual separation from each other, we set out on a road trip to Atlanta. At the time, we didn't think of it as a farewell-to-youth tour but in retrospect, that's what it amounted to. We'd heard that Shoestring Slater would be at the Breakwater and we'd been listening to their music throughout our final years of school. Everyone talked about how you just had to see Jonah Rae to believe he was real. That was to be our first stop.

We'd traveled all afternoon without air-conditioning in Kai's dark blue Camaro, which he'd got cheap from a friend of a friend of a friend. Its hood stripes were patterned with outlines of bird guano. Blue smoke plumed from the exhaust, and the chance of our really making it to Atlanta was joke du jour.

Seeing Jonah Rae and Shoestring Slater was, truth be told, merely a passage to our real intent: meeting girls. Kai's marriage, now six months old, was a looming presence that was never mentioned. Kai, the rambler, reveled in his freedom.

Pooling our cash, we took a single room in a cinderblock motel whose lobby had a dank smell, as if a roaming dog had come by recently lifting its leg against one of the potted plants near the front desk. As soon as we opened the motel room door, our fantasy of opportunity collided with the reality of our austere room. One bed, one chair. Limited make-out space. First dibs, we decided, would rule. All others would settle for beachfront trysts; or if the girl had her own place, all the better.

We tossed down our bags and went to eat, full of hope and peelers out for the bare golden leg, the soft bikini bottom, and the round alluring eye.

I'm writing this two days after the inauguration of President Barack Obama. His speech, ushering in an "Era of Responsibility," has inspired me to pen my own effort at responsibility: a confession. I'm not certain that I had said all that I had wanted to say to Kai last year at the reunion. The reason I hesitate is that I fear that what I will say, what might have been lost while we were talking and drinking in Mexico Beach, will somehow hurt him. Of all my sins, hurting another person unnecessarily is a torment to my soul.

In June 2008, Roberto had sent an email proposing a reunion. I didn't know what to make of it. Unlike Roberto, Kai was consistent in not making contact with me for more than two decades.

Roberto, on the other hand, arrived into my life like the occasional summons for jury duty, always unexpected and usually inconvenient. I might be strolling through a Publix and my phone would ring with an unknown number. Later, there'd be a five-minute voicemail from Roberto, telling me about his latest doings. Or I'd answer the phone, and we'd talk a while, the conversation inevitably leading us to the past: *Remember that time when . . .* , it often began.

It might be three years before I'd once more hear from him. He'd say he was heading to Jacksonville and could he stop by? But the day came and went and he never arrived, and then two years later, as it really happened, I heard a persistent knock at the door and when I opened it I was standing before a chubby, round-faced, balding, and total stranger. Only after he spoke my name did he revert to the nineteen-year-old I'd known so long ago. Over a meal, I'd learn that he'd moved from Saudad to Savannah to Plano, had married a woman from a church he'd been attending, and they had three children. He was a teacher now. So was his wife. Over that same meal, he'd learn what I'd been up to all these years.

These eruptive jumps of information were like loose and shifting sediment we felt obligated to get through to reach, finally, the bedrock, the point at which, when we were nineteen, we had truly been friends. Therein lay the warm, intimate territory where we'd left off, and we'd spend the entire evening laughing ourselves silly, as if we were still unfettered young men, stuck in that era and not thirty years later. Apart from that time of our youth, we had nothing in common, no anchor to hold us in a present reality.

I had not heard from him in five years. Then arrived the email addressed to me and to Kai that read:

Come on, guys. Let's meet up before we cash in our Fritos.

Roberto loved the distorted phrase, and we loved him for it. Kai responded the same day. The only question for me was whether Roberto would actually show up.

. . .

The Gulf was shushing lazily onto the shore the night I arrived and stood on the balcony of the El Governor motel. Kai had already arrived. He was staying at the Driftwood Inn. We had a laugh over Roberto's fleeting presence in our lives; Kai's experience had been much the same as mine over the past couple of decades. We agreed to meet at the pool bar of my motel in an hour.

Kai wore a Hawaiian shirt and a straw hat. He was an older, paunchier version of his youthful self. His hair had not grayed. He'd had repaired the only blemish on his otherwise handsome features: a chipped front tooth.

As he said he would, as far back as high school, he had become a neurosurgeon, practicing out of Atlanta. He had a kid somewhere and any number of failed relationships. I seem to get hooked up with borderline women, he said. He was still driving a Camaro, one without oil leaks and nicely licked with hot flames over the hood.

By midnight, the bar had closed, and Roberto had yet to arrive.

At 3 a.m., Roberto phoned me. He'd traveled by car from Montgomery, where he was now living, and had forgotten at which town we were to hold the reunion and couldn't find it in his phone. I helped him navigate to the El Governor, where he settled into a room two floors below mine on the eastern end. I told him we were meeting at Sharon's Cafe at 9 and to get some sleep.

The next morning, we went into the cafe under the checkered sign inlaid with two yellow smiley faces and sat at a booth facing U.S. 98. Within two hours, we'd mapped out the surface of our lives over the past thirty years. Our historical information packed no emotional energy, but it served to link our existence from 1974 to the present.

A group of women in shorts and T-shirts came in. Kai

stared, aping a dropped jaw. Roberto and I chuckled at his unflagging zeal for the chase.

Well, he said, what about it? You up for it?

Roberto reminded him that he was married and had three children. Kai saw no impediment and reminded him that he had a few days off from the fam and urged him to go wild.

Kai wanted to get to the beach. He'd brought a gym bag filled with Frisbees, tanning lotion, and silicone spray. Was a time Kai and I would spend an entire day tossing Frisbees to each other or alone against the wind. We'd target locations on the beach where any number of slim bathing beauties like islands in a white sea were stretched on towels and set out to dazzle them (so we thought) with our flicks and hammers, our spinning catches, extended nail delays (which the silicone aided), grabs behind the back and between the legs, and anything else that might get them to look up at us. My chicken wing toss won a trophy for distance in Panama City one year.

Today, Kai hit the beach like a gung-ho soldier charging downhill with his sword drawn. Roberto camped on a wooden bench under a large umbrella. I hadn't thrown a Frisbee in twenty years. The first few tosses felt nice, and the groove returned, and I got one behind the back, whipped around, and hammered it back to Kai. He spun, caught, and flung it back. A wicked wind snagged the disc and sent it arcing high across the sky and I raced to the spot where I predicted it would land, stumbled, and fell on my butt. A spasm of intense pain shot through my back, and I sat there for several minutes trying not to cry.

A young blonde woman with gorgeous bronze legs stopped and said, Are you all right, sir?

Sir.

She meant: old man.

I told her I was fine, and I limped from the beach and sat

with Roberto who bought me a gin and tonic to help me heal. Kai stood at the edge of the water, his back toward us, and tossed the Frisbee out over the Gulf where an incoming wind caught it and returned it to him. He did this the better part of the morning, eventually meeting a few women who were impressed by his skill or his charm.

Under the cabana umbrella, Roberto told me about his career in teaching, his methods for gaining compliance in the classroom, and the difficulties of motivating the unmotivated, but this conversation soon dropped out, replaced by the starter phrases of the past: *Remember that time . . .*

Our tacit agreement was to swim in the charted waters of our mutual experience. Outside of that, we had little to say and the breeze from the Gulf and the jumbled conversation of others inhabited our thoughts until we could go a little deeper beneath the surface.

He aroused me from the hypnotic drone of the indolent breakers coming ashore.

He was the world to Peg, Roberto said. I saw it the day they married. I knew she would suffer.

A real shame they didn't make it, I said.

Kai was still tossing Frisbee to himself on the beach and we were talking about his marriage to Peg Coutee.

I never did hear what happened at end, Roberto said.

All I recall, I said, is that they married and moved over to Panama City.

You went over a few times, didn't you?

Yeah, a few times, but it's all vague now.

Seems like you ought to remember a few times.

I get confused, I said. Old age and all that.

You got that right. You looked pretty bad out there on the beach.

You look pretty scary yourself, I said, and you're just sitting here.

How'd he hang on to those good looks? He always had it, didn't he?

Yeah, he's like our own personal Bill Clinton out there, just chugging right along.

We watched Kai toss the Frisbee. He caught it like a little boy snagging a fly ball out in right field and turned to see if anyone else saw it, too.

He wasn't ready to settle down, Roberto said. I saw that right off.

Well, the girls, yes. He could never get enough. But he was seriously looking at schools at that time, too.

One night, Roberto said, he told me neurosurgery was all that really mattered to him.

Peg got him distracted, I said. Says a lot about her.

Do you know if he got her pregnant and maybe felt obligated?

No, I don't. He used to come back to Saudad on weekends all by himself and he'd call me and say let's go out, and we'd go, and you could tell he wished he weren't married.

Bet she was jealous.

Maybe, I said. Maybe not. She would have had a hard time of it if she were. But Peg was real innocent, that's what I remember, and I think that's why he had such a hard time himself. No one likes to destroy the innocent.

Yeah, I remember that, too. She was sweet, really sweet.

Roberto closed his eyes; his hands drooped like discarded gloves on his rotund belly. The distant shrill cry of seagulls played flute over the percussive beat of the breakers, regular as a heartbeat.

You ever meet Nixie Rayo, I asked.

Don't think so. Was I around?

Yeah, but you were tied up with school or something and didn't go out as often.

We ordered a couple of beers and a basket of fried clams.

Nixie was something special, I said. She was hot for Kai, and he had his own way of not quite looking at things straight on, if you know what I mean. So, he was married to Peg over in Panama, and he'd come over for the weekend to see Nixie every now and then.

We watched Kai on the shoreline finishing a conversation with two young women in bikinis. He was smiling and making subtle motions for us to come down there and get in on it. We laughed and waved. He was too much.

Nice as it sounds, I said, I guess I'm glad I never got into that sort of arrangement. We were already drifting apart by that time, anyway. The clubs weren't as much fun anymore.

The beer and clams arrived.

Any of those places still there, Roberto asked.

We drew up a list, of places, of things we recalled, as if we were trying to convince each other that it was not possible that time could pass or that the places of our youth could vanish:

Victors. Just off Perry and First. We were wallflowers.

Cash's. North of Santa Rosa Boulevard. That guy that pulled a knife on us, what did he want?

Hog's Breath. Also, Santa Rosa but back across the Miracle Strip. It felt open, breezy, and the slanting wooden floors had nails that snagged your sneakers.

The Green Frog. Right across the street from Hog's Breath. Later, it was a gay club. After that an Asian titty bar.

2001. Over in Destin, maybe around Sibert Avenue. Snobby people.

Joe & Eddie's.

That wasn't a club.

We used to eat there afterward.

I guess we'll count it.

Hightide. Down an access road off Santa Rosa, the water tower behind it rising like the bulb end of a thermometer from the flat roof.

Pelican's Roost. On the island, beachfront, gin and tonics on a hot day.

The Green Knight. Over in Destin, on Highway 98. The twenty-foot paladin out front painted in forest green, except for the yellow gloves that held a lance upright.

King's Den. Like a castle downtown on the Miracle Strip. A biker hangout.

The Little Bar. On the island, they had matchbooks inscribed, "We install and service hangovers."

Peddler's II. I don't recall that one. Neither do I.

Faux Pas. One night the big screen showed what was going on in a back room. Video was new then. Did you see it? I missed it. I imagined it. That was better, no doubt. Poor girl. It's always poor girl. It is.

Kai strode toward us. He wanted water.

You guys need to get out there, he said. The women are everywhere.

My hair was gray, and Roberto was corpulent. Somehow, in his enthusiasm, Kai failed to notice these Kryptonitic features sapping our power to tempt the opposite sex. Besides, a storm was building to the south and would soon be ashore.

After lunch, we retreated to Roberto's room in the El Governor. The rain was light now, and we lounged on the balcony with beer we'd purchased from a convenience store. Kai was restless, talking about what we were going to do that night. *Was* there anything to do, he wanted to know? He called our attention to a boat scooting along in the Gulf.

There's one lucky bastard, he said, getting caught in a storm like that and making it back in one piece.

He turned to me.

Remember that time near the East Pass in Destin?

Kai had purchased a nineteen-foot Midland from a friend of Nixie's brother. It burned as much oil as his Camaro, but he was undaunted. We'd gone fishing near the jetties, a series of large rocks set down on either side of the pass. The jetties extended hundreds of feet into the Gulf.

We were caught in a sudden rain, I told Roberto, though he'd heard this before.

Kai stood to act it out.

This squall comes along, he said, and we're out there without any navigational aids and this wall of water is falling on us.

Disorientation hell, I said. I've never been so turned around.

Kai starts laughing.

Yeah and he grabs up this little umbrella and pops it open, and the thing tears apart and goes flying out of the boat.

I was certain we were going to smash into the jetties, I said.

So did I. But then it just cleared. Bright as could be. Like it never happened.

We sat watching the rain shower and drinking beer and quickly filled our time with anecdotes that only we would ever understand or find amusing. The afternoon soon dried out like the episodes of our past and to break a weary silence Roberto asked Kai about Nixie Rayo.

It's been a long time since I thought about her, Kai said. He looked at me. Wasn't she something?

Yeah, she was.

I can't remember how we even met, it was so long ago, he said.

We were out riding one night, I told him. You know how we did, looking for girls in their cars, intending to follow them to the clubs.

That's right.

And one night you saw her—

She went right past me, and I just thought, oh, baby, *she* is so *fine*—

And she gets in the left-hand turn lane, I said, and you did that thing, pulling up fast and slamming on the brakes to get your tires to squeal, and she looks back out her window, and you say, Are you all right?

Yeah, I can't believe I used to do that. That was dangerous.

Usually, we were ignored.

Almost every time.

But Nixie Rayo got out of her car.

I thought she was gonna beat us up, he said.

And she motions for us to come over.

Oh, she was fine, he said.

It was three in the morning, I said, and the streets were empty, and we must have stood there fifteen minutes talking in the left-hand turn lane. And then she says she's got to go but before she leaves, she kisses you.

Now, *that* was a kiss, Kai said. My heart was beating like a couple of boots in the dryer.

And then, the best part, I said. She looks at me on the other side of the car and in a magnanimous gesture I will never forget she walks all the way around the car and kisses me. Just as long. And probably longer.

Kai chuckled. It wasn't that long, you dog.

Well, that's how I recall it.

Kai turned to Roberto. I thought we were going into a wild, wild night.

Me too, I said. But then she left.

Roberto was grinning the whole time.

You two, he finally said. And where was I?

I think you had school the next morning and didn't go out, I said.

And look where it got you, Kai said.

Roberto sighed.

He was in love with the story, the idea of it, wanting it as much as we did to continue to exist in memory, the only place it now resided.

In the wet, winter days following Obama's speech, I spent my time reconstructing the events of the reunion at Mexico Beach the previous summer. What I've lost track of is what I said and what I wanted to say, and the intervening time has twined my memory into something I can no longer easily unravel. It seems to have its beginnings on the night we met Nixie Rayo.

Kai told me he'd been invited to visit Nixie at her parents' home. Why did he want me to come with him, or did I somehow insert myself into his plan? To this day, I cannot recall precisely.

We arrived around ten o'clock that night. She lived with her younger brother, who had just turned eighteen. Her parents were touring Switzerland.

She fixed drinks from bottles in disarray on the kitchen counter and chatted easily about nothing in particular. She turned on the television. *The Candidate* with Robert Redford was playing. She snuggled between us on the couch. Right around the part where Melvyn Douglas tells Redford he's a politician now, Nixie went upstairs to use the restroom and while she was gone Kai and I looked at each other. Without saying so directly—and how could he?—he wanted me to leave. But he didn't want me to leave. And that's what confused me.

Shortly, Nixie came halfway down the stairs and called, Will you come get this for me?

We both stood. Nixie's invitation up the stairs had been purposely ambiguous, I now realize. She was after the head dog, and while I swayed in the disorientation of my own velleity, Kai bounded up the stairs. Some moments of inaction stay with you forever.

One early evening, a few days later, I stopped by Nixie's house on my own. She wore white cutoffs and a peach tank top. We sat on stools around the kitchen counter and drank soda in tall glasses with ice. She was a hair stylist, she said, and asked what Kai did and was he always so funny? Yeah, he is, I told her, and asked if her parents were enjoying their trip. She said they were and wanted to know if Kai was really going to be a neurosurgeon. He's been saying that for years, I told her. He's off to college after our trip.

A droplet of water fell from her cup to her bare thigh. She spooked, making more of it than was called for, and laughing, wiped it away with a napkin.

Where to, she asked. Atlanta, two weekends from now; we're stopping first at Mexico Beach to hear Shoestring Slater. Ever hear of them? Oh, yeah, she said; they're great. What club, she wanted to know. You mean in Mexico Beach? Yeah. The Breakwater; it's the only one there, right on the beach. Is he a huge fan? That's me, I said, but Kai and Roberto, the other guy going, are all pumped for it. I bet, she said. Is he seeing anyone?

It took me a moment to recall that not only was Kai seeing someone, he was in fact married to the woman he was seeing.

No one, I said.

She smiled, and I had no idea what the smile was meant to convey.

I don't know, Kai said.

What? Are you afraid to tell her?

I just don't think she'd like it.

Oh, come on, man. It's just a road trip with your friends.

That's exactly what she wouldn't like.

We were walking along Clay Avenue near 13th Street where Kai and Peg had an apartment in Panama City.

She sniffs my crotch when I get home from work, Kai said. Is that weird or what?

Sounds like it'd be all right.

The first couple of weeks, yeah, it was kinda funny, he said. But you see what I'm saying, right?

Roberto's all set but his car's blown a gasket, and all I've got is my parents' Vega, and they're not gonna let me take it, so we were kinda counting on the Camaro.

You know more oil goes through that engine than the Alaskan pipeline.

We'll pitch in. So, what do you say?

We rounded the corner beneath a streetlamp. Insects orbited the bulb like electrons around the nucleus of an atom.

I'm not sure how to tell her, he said.

Peg and I get along pretty well, I said. I'll talk to her.

He winced. He preferred the middle state, one foot deep in the desire to take off with us, the other keeping a toehold on peace with the wife.

Don't say anything, he said.

O.K., relax, I said. I won't.

The next morning, I told her.

Kai had gone to work. Peg, her back to me, fixed eggs on the stove. Her bare feet were narrow, her heels round and flaky like the skin of a brown onion. She wore a long, pinstriped dress shirt that belonged to Kai. During a different visit, she'd told me that she liked to keep Kai near her body and accomplished this by donning his apparel; she liked the loose feel of his briefs under her clothes.

She was used to telling me things like this. I'd known her as long as Kai had, all the way back to elementary school. She'd always been this stringy, delicate kid. During sophomore year, I developed a crush on her. She was going with a guy named Ted Greenway, a junior with an after-school job and facial hair. It was naïve, but at the time, I thought I could draw Peg away by taking on a chummy role with her. We began to call each other brother and sister. The result of my auto-emasculation was that I was no longer a competitor and, thus, no longer a threat, and trust was instantly bestowed upon me. I took her hand when-ever I liked, put my arm around her shoulder, hugged her close, and she in turn shared her secrets and reciprocated my encroachment into her territory, and the only thing that ever bothered me was the rising desire for her that I had to quell for the sake of appearance.

Time and my adolescent yearning passed; I got over her and have thought of her as a sister ever since. During all those years, it never once dawned on me, until many years later, that by thinking of her in this way I had killed any chance I'd ever have with her.

Even back then I was someone to go to when you had trou-ble. I listened, I suppose, and people often opened up to me, so when Peg and Kai argued, she came to me for advice. I relished my role as her confidant, but sometimes she told me things that I had no business hearing. One night during the last few months of high school, we were sitting in my mother's car waiting for Kai to finish his night job janitoring at a Southern

Bell switching center. She wanted to know if anal sex was normal and did it mean she was bad? In her Trinitarian upbringing doing something like that had never occurred to her.

Kai told me it was all right, she said. He's gentle. He's loving. So why do I feel dirty and so wicked?

The right side of her face was lit from a streetlamp, a dark shadow obscured the left. I watched her silently a few minutes before speaking. I could hardly picture her sullied like that, and yet I found myself aroused, desiring it for myself, and this reaction mortified me, for I saw that it was spawned from envy and made me question my own motives. Over the years, I've considered how I might have turned that to my advantage but, in the end, my allegiance was to Kai, so I pushed all other consideration to the side.

Do you love him?

She nodded.

Then it's all right, I said.

This morning, her bottom lightly dented the pinstriped shirt and made a ballet of the round deft activity beneath. I hadn't thought about it since senior year, and my fascination, I discovered, had not diminished. She turned, a nice affable smile brightening her face, and sat across from me while I ate. She said she'd been thinking about something Kai had told her before he left that morning.

What'd he say?

He kissed my ear, and said I tasted like sugar-coated corn flakes.

It was like Kai to come up with something silly like that.

He knows his cereal, I told her.

After a bit, at what felt like the right moment, I told her that Roberto and I wanted Kai to come with us. It wouldn't be the same without him, I said. To alleviate her worries, I told her where we planned to stop, and I'd make sure he called every day.

I'd miss him too much, she said. A whole week?

Tell you what, I said. Why don't you come over when we get to Mexico Beach?

Are you sure? I don't want him to get mad at me.

It won't be a problem, I said. He'll like seeing you there.

You really think so?

Absolutely.

I said that to appease her and, honestly, because I didn't think she'd really do it.

I returned to the home of Nixie Rayo some twenty years after the night she had kissed me and Kai, one after the other, in the left-hand turn lane. The house was on Gardner Avenue just before the intersection with Cherokee Road. All the homes through here were two-storied colonials with an occasional Georgian revival interspersed. Close to a bayou, the residences were hidden by sprawling oaks dripping with Spanish moss. I drove slowly—but only now does it occur to me that I harbored an impossible fantasy that she might show up, a sedate woman in her forties, walk out of her home, and tell me why she had gone to Mexico Beach that night.

The Breakwater was congested with blue-jean clad locals and wild-eyed groupies. Moving about in a game of musical chairs we eventually grabbed an available table, whose only strategic flaw was that it backed the entrance. To scope out the incoming babes we had to lurch around and make our intent obvious, and this cost us in cool points and subterfuge. But perhaps I was the only one thinking along these lines. Roberto sat like a child looking at holiday lights. Kai was popping up and down with excitement, and, Check 'em out, he said, and he bit his knuckle to demonstrate the intensity of his carnal enthusiasm.

They came in swaying to a primitive beat, three young women in triplicate, stamped from the same mold, and wearing jeans that both invited and denied the imagined caress, a fantasy adventure for the fingers over the seams, the loops, and the buttons; and crop tops that divided the ensnared eye to the sun-licked skin above, where their breasts hung like the Tablets of God, holy and untouchable; or below, to the frilly hemlines falling just at the ribs, where a tongue would become parched on the plains of their supple skin. Even now, how awful, how terrible, how wonderful it all was.

Give me the look, Kai said. Come on, baby, give me the look.

One of them turned, and Kai was smiling all over and up from his seat. He said he'd be back, and he was gone.

Roberto squeezed through the crowd to the bar for a pitcher of beer. The jukebox supplied the house music. "Lord, Mr. Ford" made everyone feel snappy, and the surge of chattering exuberance squeezed the house into an intoxicated frenzy when Shoestring Slater jacked into their first number.

Across the room, Kai was charming a young woman; the motion of his hands suggested he was telling her something about the lighting or the music, things he knew nothing about, but that was beside the point. Not long after, he caught my eye. That naughty boy face of his was telling me he'd wind up with the room tonight.

Roberto, taking nearly half an hour, returned with the beer. He'd run into a woman, Nancy Loering, who had been in his accounting class at the college. He drank a quick cup with me and was off to see the woman's apartment. I didn't hear from him again for five months.

She had this gorgeous aquarium, he said, in November, over the phone, and we watched it.

All night?

Yeah, he said, pretty much.

His voice was distant, perhaps in a daze, as if he weren't really sure what had happened, if he could only remember.

Shoestring Slater were lighting a fuse to "Chicken Shack Boogie," stretching it out and slicing it with the bone knife of Rae's extended slide solos. A nice-looking woman sat next to me in the chair Roberto had abandoned not five minutes earlier. She stared at the band, her fingers wrapped around the stem of a wine glass, and I assumed she was a groupie. By taking her perspective, I saw that it was Rae she had her eye on. In profile, her lips moved as if Rae's fingers were gently playing on them, and it made me smile to watch her.

Then I felt a hand rest on my shoulder. It belonged to Nixie Rayo. She slipped the plastic cup from my fingers, leaned against my shoulder, and sipped the beer.

I thought about what you said.

What, what did I say?

A beach getaway with Kai, the way you said the morning sun would look over the Gulf.

I never said that.

Whatever you said sounded like that.

She shifted.

There he is.

Her hand slid around my neck; her hip launched away from me.

She snuck up on Kai, and he deserted the woman who'd been interested in his assessment of sound systems. Their arms playfully around each other, Kai and Nixie seemed lost in their own little world. I found my attention drifting back to the band and to the woman sitting next to me. She was enthralled, and I turned my chair, as much as to watch her as to enjoy Shoestring Slater, who had completed a few of their own songs and were now working through a surreal version of "Hey Joe."

I had started a conversation with the woman, and all was going well until Peg appeared in the corner of my eye. She wore a white skirt; it was like a flag calling out to me, and I went to her and brought her back to the table. The band was unstrapping, about to break between sets.

Where's Kai, she wanted to know.

He'll be back in a minute, I said.

I never thought I'd make it. I was afraid once I got into town, I'd never find it.

Only place here, I said, didn't I tell you?

Yes, you were right. And you're sure he'll be glad to see me?

Absolutely.

But, no, I said to myself, he will be agitated and look to me to get him out of the situation he'd put himself into. So, I was busy trying to figure out how to get Peg out of the Breakwater.

The band were walking off the stage.

Peg straightened up suddenly. There's Kai, she said, and, rising, Who's that with him?

I placed my hand on her back to postpone her ascent and watched them disappearing around the corner. The woman sitting with us at the table was also watching them.

Kai and Nixie had followed the band, or had appeared to merge with them in a narrowing movement of people down a dark corridor, but it was unclear because of the distance, the bustle, the light, the smoke, and the conviction in my voice when I told Peg she was mistaken; she had not seen Kai but Jonah Rae—the only name that came to mind on short notice— going off with that woman. Peg looked at me incredulously. She couldn't believe that I'd asked her to doubt what she had just seen.

The wine glass fell over and cracked loudly. Like a pool of blood, the spilled wine ran across the table and dripped from the edge. The woman stood and clutched the back of her chair. She seemed oblivious to the mess she'd made. Then a prolonged sound like a seagull came out of her and she ran off in the direction of where Kai and Nixie had gone, leaving Peg and me staring at her rudeness.

Listen, Peg—

No.

She wouldn't hear it.

Walk me back to my room, she said.

As we were going out, "Hey Joe" was playing on the juke-box. In the parking lot, the beams of passing cars flickered over her eyes like distant search lights. She stared straight ahead. I took her hand, and it was trembling.

Several months after the reunion, in November 2008, a weak tropical depression settled over Jacksonville, where I was living. It seemed determined not to leave. The downpour lasted six days. Many streets were flooded and impassible. Roofs leaked. On the afternoon of the fifth day, I started a partial list of overflowing waterways:

Craig's Creek at Hendricks Avenue Park
Miramar Creek
McCoy's in Hollybrook Park
Hogan's in Confederate Park
Big Pottsburg Creek at Hogan Road
Cedar River at San Juan Avenue
Trout River

I stopped writing. Roberto phoned to ask if I had spoken with Kai since the reunion. I said I had not, but there was nothing unusual about that. Where were you, I asked. We were supposed to take him to the airport together.

I overslept, he said. I have a hard time in the mornings.

He slept with a machine to help him breathe.

Anyway, I called Kai this past week, Roberto said, and he asked me something that was odd, and at the time I didn't take it very seriously. You know how he'd say things, and you'd just want to laugh because he was always so funny. But later, today in fact, it struck me that he was in earnest.

What'd he say?

He wanted to know if I'd ever gone out with Peg.

What'd you tell him?

I said no. But why would he ask, thirty years later? Did he ever ask you?

No, I said. He never did.

After we hung up, I sat in a club chair angled so that it faced a western window and watched the rain batter the glass, and it reminded me of the rain that battered the windows of the lobby of the El Governor the last morning of the reunion. Kai and I sat across from each other. I'd never told him what had happened at the Breakwater, Peg showing up unexpectedly, and, though it was now decades later, I finally disclosed the events of that night.

You're a pal, he said, saving me like that.

Obviously, you and Nixie needed to get away without Peg knowing it, I said, so what else could I do? But wasn't it six months later that you and Peg split up anyway? Saving you, it turned out, was term-limited.

My gratitude, he said, is for that night alone. Who could know what would happen after? You know what's funny? When we finally did break up, I wanted her more than ever. I tried to tell her that, but it made her cry, and I couldn't take it. You can't make a woman understand what you really need.

After you and Nixie left the Breakwater, I said, Peg asked me to walk her to her room. I dallied, telling her I wanted to see the rest of Shoestring Slater, but Jonah Rae didn't return after the break, and it pretty much sucked after that, so Peg and I started walking down 98. Outside, she no longer wanted to go back to her room. She wanted to walk on the beach. We removed our shoes and went down where the water was slate black and sort of humming itself gently onto the shore. I sensed that she was vulnerable, ready to shatter like a crystal wine glass, and being delicate with her preoccupied my mind. We sat awhile on the beach talking, and at some point, she said you were probably back at the motel and wouldn't it be nice to surprise you? No, I told her, it wasn't likely; you were out with Roberto. But you *were* in the room, weren't you? There with Nixie instead of your wife. To be honest, I suspect that she somehow guessed that this was why I was forestalling her from going there.

Did you tell her?

No. Not about Nixie. She just seemed convinced that you were with someone else.

Why would she think that?

I don't know. A jealous mind, perhaps.

What'd you tell her?

I told her you were with Roberto.

Did she believe you?

I can't say. She went off on a tangent, telling me that her parents were very strict, very religious, and you'd done something to get them to let her go at seventeen, and she'd abandoned everything for you.

I told her not to do that.

She said that. But she wanted to, so that you would know how much it meant to her, and she started saying things I really didn't want to hear.

Like. Personal things?

Yeah, things like that.

The rain beat hard against the panes. We looked up at the gusts that shook the windows.

At some point she leaned against me, and I thought it was natural to put my arm around her, a friendly gesture, and it was getting late, and I told her I'd walk her back to her motel. But she didn't want to go back to the motel.

Where did she want to go?

It'd taken me thirty years to tell Kai what had happened that night. In a half second, his reaction told me that Peg had never spoken of it.

As we sat there quietly in the motel lobby, he kept looking at me as if I were going to spring the joke on him, like he was ready for it and wanted a good laugh. The joke never arrived, and the flicker of thought that then crossed his face he kept to himself, but I imagined he was justifying my action for the sake of a lifetime friendship he trusted more than a woman who in a moment of anguish had wandered farther down the beach than he thought she would.

His features relaxed, and he said, Do you think Roberto's gonna make it down?

He didn't, and I drove Kai to the airport in Panama City to catch his plane for Atlanta.

Roberto had left by the time I returned to Mexico Beach. In November, over the phone, he told me that when he'd figured out that we'd already gone, he decided to catch up with us later, another reunion, maybe next year, and drove back to Montgomery.

The rain had ceased by the time I returned to the El Governor and had loaded my bags. I strolled out to the beach.

The waves were gray and crashing fast and hard on top of each other and just beyond them was a rocking motion in the water that felt hypnotic and brought to mind the last time I was here, in 1994. My eye drifted to a woman wearing a blue windbreaker, yellow pedal pushers, and a floppy hat. She was strolling barefoot through the thick swash. For some reason, I imagined that she was the woman who had come from the sea and was now coming for me. I was so far removed from that strange tale that I hardly believed I had heard so many speak of her and attach such importance to her existence. At that moment, however, I was ready to believe anything, but it would be sentimental to suggest that a ghostly hand had touched my face, or the wind, as it were.

The beachcombing woman raised her arm swiftly and caught her blowing hat with one hand to keep it on her head. She glanced at me, smiled briefly with a touch of melancholy upon her lips, and passed by without a word. Without meaning to, she had left me with a pang of loss that reminded me of an event that took place on the morning of July 12, 1972.

Roberto, Kai, and I were eating breakfast at Joe & Eddie's off the Miracle Strip just before dawn. Our night on the town had been, as they often were, a luckless adventure. But we felt relaxed and there was nothing left to do but to eat, go home, and sleep. Around us, women in party dresses and men in collared shirts, like us, were talking in the easy drone of the weary.

We'd finished eating and were talking about the night and Roberto, during a lull, produced three slips of paper and a pen. Uncharacteristically, he'd remembered that we had agreed to fill these out together—as if for good luck or to create a sacred bond of friendship—and had brought them along, since they were due very soon. When we'd finished completing the draft registration forms, he sealed them in a stamped envelope and slipped it into his pocket.

We sat in silence, heavy as a moment of reckoning. The moment was unsullied, its truth already vanishing into memory, our imaginations ripe with adventures to come. We piled into the car. It was Sunday morning. The Miracle Strip was straight and uncluttered all the way home.

BIOS

Aron M. Woldeslassie has been living, writing, and performing in the Twin Cities for over a decade. His writing has been featured in *The Almanac, Mpls. Saint Paul Magazine, The Nordly,* and mnplaylist. His comedy has been seen in a variety of venues including *Minnesota Tonight, Rinky Dink, Vector 9, Smash Bang Sketch Comedy,* and *Uproar.* When he isn't actively writing, Aron works as a director for *Morning Edition* with Cathy Wurzer at *Minnesota Public Radio.*

Sara Hosey is the author of the novel *Iphigenia Murphy* (Blackstone 2020) and the academic study *Home is Where the Hurt Is: Media Depictions of Wives and Mothers* (McFarland 2019). Her writing has appeared in publications including *Casino Literary Magazine, Feminist Formations,* and the *Journal of Literary and Cultural Disability Studies.*

Edward M. Cohen's novel, "$250,000," was published by Putnam; his nonfiction books by Prima, Prentice-Hall, Lime-light Editions, SUNY Press. His story, "Peroxide Blonde," won the 2020 Key West Tennessee Williams Prize. His collection, "Before Stonewall," won the 2019 Awst Press Book Award and will be published next year. This novella was originally published online by Eclectica.

Steven Forsberg is a retired English teacher living on the Maine coast where he pretends to know more about catching lobsters, navigating a sailing vessel, and differentiating between IPAs than the other grumpy old men in his neighborhood. He's never quite recovered from "Of Mice and Men," chapter 4 but believes that Markus Zusak might just save his soul some unexpected Thursday afternoon. In his spare time, he examines Gauguin and Degas prints with a magnifying glass, wishing he'd been born 100 years earlier. Stop by to insult him at stevenforsberg68@gmail.com.

D. E. Lee's novel, The Sky After Rain, won the Brighthorse Books 2015 novel contest and is available in paperback. Awards include Pushcart Prize nominee, finalist in Prairie Schooner's 2018 Book Prize, Honorable Mention in the Cincinnati Review's Robert and Adelle Shiff 2018 award, Nimrod's 2011 Katherine Ann Porter Prize, and the 2014 Nelson Algren Award. His short fiction appears or is forthcoming in South Dakota Review, Palooka, Little Patuxent Review, Quiddity, Lunch Ticket, Alligator Juniper, The Lindenwood Review, The Write Launch, Broad River Review, and others.

OTHER TITLES BY RUNNING WILD

PAST TITLES

Running Wild Stories Anthology, Volume 1
Running Wild Anthology of Novellas, Volume 1
Jersey Diner by Lisa Diane Kastner
Magic Forgotten by Jack Hillman
The Kidnapped by Dwight L. Wilson
Running Wild Stories Anthology, Volume 2
Running Wild Novella Anthology, Volume 2, Part 1
Running Wild Novella Anthology, Volume 2, Part 2
Running Wild Stories Anthology, Volume 3
Running Wild's Best of 2017, AWP Special Edition
Running Wild's Best of 2018
Build Your Music Career From Scratch, Second Edition by
Andrae Alexander
Writers Resist: Anthology 2018 with featured editors Sara
Marchant and Kit-Bacon Gressitt
Magic Forbidden by Jack Hillman

Frontal Matter: Glue Gone Wild by Suzanne Samples
Mickey: The Giveaway Boy by Robert M. Shafer
Dark Corners by Reuben "Tihi" Hayslett
The Resistors by Dwight L. Wilson
Open My Eyes by Tommy Hahn
Legendary by Amelia Kibbie
Christine, Released by E. Burke
Tough Love at Mystic Bay by Elizabeth Sowden
The Faith Machine by Tone Milazzo
The Self Made Girl's Guide by Aliza Dube
Running Wild Stories Anthology, Volume 4
Running Wild Novella Anthology, Volume 4
Magpie's Return by Curtis Smith
Gaijin by Sarah Sleeper
The Recon: Trilogy Plus 1 by Ben White
Sodom & Gomorrah on a Saturday Night by Christa Miller

UPCOMING TITLES

Running Wild Stories Anthology, Volume 5
Running Wild Novella Anthology, Volume 5
American Cycle, by Larry Beckett
Mickey: Surviving Salvation by Robert Shafer
The Re-remembered by Dwight L. Wilson
Something Is Better than Nothing by Alicia Barksdale
Antlers of Bone by Taylor Sowden
Take Me with You by Vanessa Carlisle
Blue Woman/Burning Woman by Lale Davidson
Stargazing in Solitude by Suzanne Samples

ABOUT RUNNING WILD PRESS

Running Wild Press publishes stories that cross genres with great stories and writing. Our team consists of:

Lisa Diane Kastner, Founder and Executive Editor
Andrea J. Johnson, Acquisitions Editor, RIZE
Barbara Lockwood, Editor
Peter A. Wright, Editor
Rebecca Dimyan, Editor
Benjamin White, Editor
Andrew DiPrinzio, Editor
Lisa Montagne, Public Relations Director

Learn more about us and our stories at www.runningwild-press.com

Loved this story and want more? Follow us at www.running-wildpress.com, www.facebook/runningwildpress, on Twitter @lisadkastner @RunWildBooks